LARK *and* TERMITE

LARK *and*
TERMITE

Jayne Anne Phillips

ALFRED A. KNOPF

NEW YORK

THIS IS A BORZOI BOOK
PUBLISHED BY ALFRED A. KNOPF

for Elie (1974–2005),
for Audrey (Boulder, 1975),
and for Cho,
infant boy born and died
in the tunnel at No Gun Ri,
July 1950

GI's corrupted the native term *han'guk saram,* which means Korean, into the derisive slang "gook," which was indelicately applied to all Asians, even in later undeclared wars.

—ROBERT J. DVORCHAK,
Battle for Korea

Because no battle is ever won he said. They are not even fought. The field only reveals to man his own folly and despair, and victory is an illusion of philosophers and fools.

—WILLIAM FAULKNER,
The Sound and the Fury

Is your mouth a little weak
When you open it to speak, are you smart?

—LORENZ HART AND RICHARD RODGERS,
"My Funny Valentine," from *Babes in Arms,* 1936

Contents

July 31

July 26

North Chungchong Province, South Korea

Corporal Robert Leavitt
24th Infantry Division

He'd shipped out to Occupied Japan in December '49; whatever baby was a tucked seed inside Lola's sex, a nub the size of a tailbone. *You want to marry me? You going to tell your mother who you're marrying?* His mother wouldn't care, he told her, his mother was dead, he wanted a woman who'd been around, he wanted her, he'd got her and he wasn't leaving her, he never would, not really, was she hearing him? *I hear you, I'm hearing you.* Mother may I, mother me. *Left you too soon, didn't she. Left you to me.* But he's gone from Lola now, gone for months; the baby is inside her, cushioned and pure, isolate. Winter at the base in Tokyo was like clocking a job in uniform, all of Occupied Japan an American colony with its own clubs and bars. Tokyo felt fake, soft, a movie set. When Colonel MacDowell invited select soldiers to learn Korean in a pet project he called Language Immersion Seoul, Leavitt said yes to minimal advancement and a change of duty. He was in Korea by April, one of sixty LIS army enlisted men installed at KMAG. Korean Military Advisory Group was a remnant: a few hundred army brass and their support staff of minions and enlisted men. They'd nothing to do but stay put, a supposed symbol of preparedness overseeing largely symbolic Republic of Korea troops. Leavitt imagined his baby moving in a fluid, muscular nest he couldn't touch or feel while the American military flexed its own small fist in divided territory, but KMAG's isolated outpost disappeared the June morning North Korea invaded. Four weeks of near-constant combat since are a continuous day and night bled into Leavitt's brain. Battle and the mayhem of retreat have changed the taste of his saliva and the smell of his sweat, but late July is Lola's time. Any hour, any moment. If the baby was already born, an armed forces telegram might follow Leavitt for weeks across the rutted fields and dirt roads of this bloody rout. He tells himself he won't need any telegram. Lola's voice drifts close unbidden and it's like she's standing in the war next to him. No matter how loud the ordnance or artillery, how loud his own heart hammers, he hears her. Words she said when he could touch her. *You found your mother because she wanted you to. All those years, her asthma pulled the air from that little store while your father stood in the doorway. She wanted you out of there.*

He keeps moving. Near noon of this infernally hot day, Lola's voice moves him forward. Two or three emptied villages in the immediate area constitute Leavitt's detail: "evacuation" of refugees whose unrecorded exodus proceeds apace with the American retreat. These double train tracks running west to Hwanggan are a godsend, boundary and direction for what is otherwise panicked flight and chaos. Replacements under Leavitt's command are soft recruits from Occupation forces in Japan, rushed in by boat and train to reinforce besieged American troops. Most have never seen combat or heard artillery fire. They're raw troops moved out at first light into countryside mired in another century. Rifle fire punctuates the darkness before and behind them; they've heard the terms "circular front" and "infiltrator's war"; they're sleepless and jumpy and they're right to be scared. Many of them will die before Leavitt can teach them a thing. He has nothing to teach the Koreans in his charge, but the urgent crowd of two or three hundred thins and lengthens to a moving column once Leavitt signals the platoon to direct them off the road, onto the tracks. Easier here, a semblance of control, but there's no evacuation possible, certainly none directed by Americans. No numbered Hangul signatures in someone's logbook. No logbook. Everything in South

Korea is clogged or broken. Equipment shipped quickly from American bases in Japan is constantly displaced; troop movement maddeningly slowed by refugees streaming away from the fighting. The South Korean inhabitants of numberless rural villages flee behind whatever resistance American troops can offer, their mud-wattle houses left empty, outdoor cooking fires still warm. There are conflicting accounts: Chinese Yaks or American F-80s strafed the area last night in advance of troop movement. Thatch roofs, saturated by weeks of rain, burn wet and smoky once they're set afire. Smoke veils the air like souls in drifting suspension, declining the war's insistence everyone move on.

The heat is dense, thick, and the rice fields at dawn are bright green emanations, alive with the sick fragrance they call night soil. Piled waste from countless country latrines, shoveled into pails and buckets and leaky ox carts, fertilizes the earth to yield and yield until the fields themselves are night. The spongy ground sinks underfoot, ripened and dark as any fermented secret. The ground breathes. Decay held still too long, Leavitt thinks. He keeps moving. Lola talks to him. *Nothing is wasted, nothing is waste. You think you didn't need to know exactly what you know? How many boys your age blow a horn like you can and then enlist in peacetime? You wanted out of Philly mighty bad.* Philly is gone. Villages here are encampments sunk in a time before radios or jeeps, before horns or jazz or English words. Skinny, wary dogs wolf any shred of slaughtered chicken, duck, fish gut dropped to the ground while women tend outdoor fires and infants slung in cloth *podaegi* ride the backs of girls. Older babies stagger across the patches of ground reserved each habitation and squat when they like, teaching themselves, their trousers cut out so the cheeks of their asses plump like cleft fruit. Now those babies are gathered up, quiet in the heat. Lola says lines from the beginning, like they can start all over. *You know me now, don't you. Say you do. Whisper.* She's his own phantom, a smoke drifting close to him. The war makes ghosts of them all. Fifty years, a hundred years, they'll still be here: vestige mist moving along a double rail bed near a wobble of a stream, the South Koreans in their white clothes, the GIs in mud-crusted khaki.

Since Osan, Leavitt doesn't think beyond the war. Osan was July 5; Leavitt knows it was a Wednesday—he wrote the date and day on a letter to Lola the morning of the attack. Forty-eight hours later, one of three survivors in his group, Leavitt moved to another platoon. He moved to another, then another, moving up incrementally in rank as his superiors were killed and not replaced. He commands a platoon now and he sees that war never ends; it's all one war despite players or location, war that sleeps dormant for years or months, then erupts and lifts its flaming head to find regimes changed, topography altered, weaponry recast. The Red Chinese and the NKPA are only the latest aggressors to pour across Korea like a death tide. Leavitt imagines thousands of war dead, disbelieving their own deaths, continuing to die and die on the same swaths of contested land. The American troops press on through heavy air, discounting their apprehensions as vague scent, cloud scrim, their own shot nerves, but Leavitt senses the dead furling like smoke from the vented earth, wandering the same ground as the living. Any American who stood at Osan and Chochiwon, at Kum River, should be dead. The majority are dead. Korea is choked with phantoms who will never get home. The Koreans themselves are phantoms, moving with their bundles and baskets, their children, their old people.

Even the villagers' footfalls sound ghostly. Diverted onto the railroad tracks, they keep a dull time, their sandals slap-thudding the muddy ties. At least they're off the road, or what passes for a road. The Americans traverse dirt trails they've broadened, rutted, bled into with trucks and bodies. All roads lead here, to these double tracks, to Lola and away from her.

Married, they'd stayed in her room for days before he left, taking longer and longer as time ran out. He shoved the bed against the wall and put the mattress flat on the floor. There they woke and slept on a stable continent whose silence never betrayed them, turning each other in circles like a clock whose two hands remained in circular, continuous alarm. Crying, Lola was nearly impassive, her face wet and still as though she couldn't or wouldn't give in to sobs. He'd never known a woman who cried like her, like she'd forgotten she was ever a child. Holding him with her silky hands, her face an inch from his, she breathed into his mouth through parted lips, and her eyes showed faint lines at the corners when she smiled. In five years, she told him, she'd begin to look her age. Good, he'd said, I'll be ready. They've been apart now longer than they were together and he feels he's more than made up the eight years between them. He can protect her now, even from herself, from him. *You found her, didn't you, on the floor. She kept vanishing for years and then she was finally gone. You're here, let her go.* Breathing, he keeps moving. He'd thought death leached air away in gasps, in the fishlike toneless labor of his mother's asthmatic wheezing. Death was small then, like the click of a light turned off, or a sigh of air escaping from a radiator. Not here. Death surges in the ground like a bass line, vast, implacable.

The past he remembers, Lola, his stateside time in the service, Japan, even Seoul before the invasion, seems to have occurred in an adjacent dimension not quite connected to him, and the mirage he lived as a kid in Philly is cut adrift. The tenements and storefronts, the glittery concrete and asphalt, the chain-link fences bordering throbbing neighborhoods miles from the Liberty Bell, are some dream he no longer believes. Barber's poles ran their spiraled colors in the morning smash and bang, and every deli and bodega pledged its loyalties to a numbers runner smoking cigarettes and drinking coffee at a back table. Dented trash cans stood sentinel by the curbs, agleam in the pinky bronze light of late-summer afternoons. Neon signs flashed hot-pink PIZZA and lime green BILLIARDS all night as smoke borne on jukebox phrases eased from the doors of bars. On Shabbat mornings he played stickball, marbles, basketball with the Italian kids, the envy of his Jewish friends because his parents weren't religious.

Noon on he worked in the grocery for his old man; they lived in the cramped apartment over the store. Every school day, three hours after classes, Leavitt worked for the old man. His mother cleared a shelf under the counter for his books, found a swivel stool with a back, told him to stay in it and do his homework if the old man wasn't there. As he often wasn't. Mostly, he lived elsewhere, and ranted and drank when he was around. She was the one who kept it going. Kept the radio going too, tuned low to Benny Goodman, Nelson Riddle. She was all for that dreamtime music, played in ballrooms and swank clubs she'd never see. Leavitt learned clarinet in the school band, then played a beat-up cornet until she traded some junkie musician groceries and ice cream for his trumpet. You practice, Bobby, she'd say. Sounds nice, she'd tell him. After she died, collapsed on the floor beside the old man's treasured refrigerator case, Leavitt refused to even enter the place. Sixteen years old, he used the separate apartment entrance and narrow stairs that bypassed the storefront until he moved out. The old man soon changed the locks, and Leavitt lived with friends or girls. Two years later, in '45, he graduated high school with no family in attendance. Days, for three years, he drove a delivery truck for a liquor wholesaler. Nights he played with one band or another in bars and clubs, had a run of nearly a year with a white jazz band that played downtown and wore suits. But he liked playing the black clubs, where he learned more and made less, and the pros called him Whitey with tacit affection. He was good enough to patch gigs together, but there was finally no reason to stay in Philly.

One cold November day in '48 he enlisted on impulse and the army bused him south three days later; he took to basic so hard the brass kept him on at Fort Knox for seven months, assisting drill instructors. Fort Knox billed itself as the "Home of Armor," but Leavitt found he had no interest in driving tanks. They were dark, heavy, close inside, the men clutched together in a mechanized hole, breathing one another's air. The tank crews loved the big guns and considered themselves invulnerable, but Leavitt wanted out, into infantry, where he could see and hear and move on his own. He'd come in fit but he trained compulsively, embraced army hierarchy and chain-of-command etiquette, pushed himself to attain firsts in every drill. He saw it all as protection, survival, his own invulnerability: if he attained perfect form, he increased his options while his mind-set remained his own, and the essential privacy he cultivated was assured. Nights he lay in an upper bunk, silently practicing fingerings, his trumpet fit to his mouth, tonguing the familiar mouthpiece while men snored around him.

The first weekend basic ended, he made his way to Onslow's Club in nearby Louisville. Onslow's offered booze, music, girls who lived upstairs and quietly sold their favors. Not Lola. She had three rooms on the top floor and didn't sell herself to anyone. Onslow played decent piano with a dependable no-frills drummer while Lola sang standards and blues. He was old enough to be Lola's father and then some, arthritic, "retired," with his cane and his bad knees, his once-powerful arms and barrel chest, and his hamlike hands coaxed an unbelievably fluid sound from the best-tuned Steinway grand in Louisville. The second night Leavitt took his horn and sat in. By the third set Onslow said they should make it a regular thing. He'd pay Leavitt in free drinks and food, girls if he wanted them. Leavitt didn't; he wanted Lola. When she finished he slipped unbidden up the stairs behind her, honed in on her, completely certain. The sounds of the club under them throbbed in the walls as she ascended above him through the narrow stairwell, hips and thighs a gauzy oval in her pale sheath skirt. Moving in near darkness like a slow, detached shape, she turned on the stairs as she paused to look down at him. Leavitt sees that shape now in his fragmented sleep or behind his eyes, glowing, asexual, like a flicker of light opening into himself. He can't shake the feeling that seeing her, wanting her, playing behind her in the club, making love to her days and nights in her rooms that became his rooms, were practice for staying alive. Then as now he moved in what he couldn't quite have, get to, reach, until her body gave it up to him like flames he sparked inside a darkness. She was luminous ground he worked and sowed, sweated for and lost. They found each other in blinding, convulsive instants that

seared him open. *You sure you want this? It's not me. It's you, find-*
ing me like I'm your last chance. He moves alongside the Koreans,
touches the service revolver strapped to his waist in its snug holster. He can't control his thoughts. Walking, he fantasizes being
with Lola one more time and shooting them both while he's still
inside her, ecstatic, desperate to stay with her, not to die here. He
imagines white explosive orgasmic nothingness before he thinks
about her body as it must look and feel now, swollen full, the baby
nearly born. *I'm carrying high and round, tight as a drum full of*
water. I know it's a boy—he turns like a fish and he sees and hears
for you, every sound, every thought I haven't written. He thinks of
the baby enclosed in her darkness and hurtles away from them,
sucked into a space behind his own eyes where his brain keeps
time and his blood beats in his ears.

Carefully, he moves on with his tribe. He's a refugee in his own
life, sans family or possessions. Like the Koreans, he owns what he
carries. He thinks of these farmers, old men, women and children,
moving across exposed ground with no weapons but his and those
of the boys he commands, and grips his rifle tighter. The flat green
rice fields are behind them now. Green and brown hills in the near
distance come together like a landscape of loins and thighs,
smooth from far off, mud ruddled and steep underfoot. The
NKPA had dressed in peasant garb to surround American forces
at Chonan, and command changed twice in one night. Leavitt cut
his way back alone through barren, rounded hills just like these:
tracks and worn trails crossed with runoff and scrub pine and
verge, nothing to hold on to, nowhere to hide. What was left of
his scattered company took four days to find their own lines,
straggling groups of three or four retreating piecemeal through
barrage and sniper fire and continuous NKPA incursion. The last
day, he'd met up with Tompkins.

"One minute test," Tompkins had repeated in Korean, "where
are the fucking ROK?" Taejon had fallen. Eighty thousand Republic of Korea soldiers had simply taken off their uniforms and
disappeared, dressed in white, and joined the southward flow of

refugees. Numerous American kids would have done the same if white clothes had offered any protection. Instead they fled while they could walk, leaving M1s and Browning automatics too heavy to carry. "Babies," Tompkins said. "White man's gotta have guns. Now command will hump them back here to pick up their god-damn rifles, and whoever isn't dead will get his ass creamed."

Just off the transport ship from the States, Leavitt had signed on to play swing at the Officers' Club in Tokyo. Dance music and standards, home away from home. The place was a cement-block rectangle called the Match Box, fitted out with ceiling fans and a central raised platform for the band. That first night, he and Tompkins replaced musicians who'd finished their rotations and shipped out. Tompkins was a drummer; he liked telling everyone straight off he was Seminole and did any jack man want to discuss it. He was a big guy with a hawklike nose, a nose that could pass for Jewish without the wide jaw, the heavy-lidded, nearly black eyes, the high, broad bones of the face. Leavitt misheard his name; at the end of the first set, he asked why the hell Tompkins' mother named him Irving if he was Seminole. "My mother was Semi-nole," Tompkins said, "and my father was a big dumb cracker named *Ervin*. That's Spec. 4 *Ervin* Tompkins, Belle Glade, Florida: inland, near Lake Okeechobee. Plenty of Seminoles with cracker names. What about you, Philly boy, your old man named Irving? He like his boy playing jazz?"

"His name is Meyer," Leavitt said, "and no, I've not seen him lately."

"That so," Tompkins answered. "Sounds like you might have scratched up a living here and there with that horn. You twenty-two, twenty-three? You got four or five years on most of these boys." Tompkins was nearly thirty, an old man; he'd missed World War II serving time in Kissimmee. Involuntary manslaughter, first offense. By the time he got out the musicians he'd played with in West Palm and Boca had died in Europe or moved on. The recruiter didn't seem to mind that Tompkins had gone to jail for hitting a drunken adversary too hard. Tompkins figured the peacetime army was a better meal ticket than digging ditches, and here he was, in an Occupation force of uniformed kids. "You and me are senior partners," he said. "Most of these boys are so snot-nosed and soft nobody'd take their money in Hialeah."

Florida, to hear Tompkins tell it, was full of towns that might have been named for women: Hialeah, Sanibel, Kissimmee, Belle Glade. Storybook names for storybook places. Korea was no storybook. After Chonan, he and Tompkins traveled by night and hid by day when the NKPA moved. They found the swarm of the retreat east of Taejon and were told to wait a day for replacements. What's left of the 24th moves now in broad daylight, visible as fleas on a pup's belly, flanks exposed, easy to surround on flat, low land. They're setting up perimeters in a sea of moving refugees, with nothing but bazookas and 4.2 mortars to lob against Chinese tanks.

MacDowell is dead, shot in the chest at the fall of Seoul, but the ROK 6th Division he advised had defended the approach to Chunchon through numerous guerrilla incursions. The 6th was combat ready and held for three days, until adjoining units on both flanks collapsed and fled, leaving them no choice but retreat. Leavitt supposes most commanding officers actually fighting this disastrous string of first stands are dead; who knew if MacDowell had prolonged their lives or doomed them by inventing Language Immersion Seoul? GHQ would have shipped the 24th over within days of the invasion anyway. Leavitt and Tompkins would have landed in Korea as disoriented, stupidly arrogant and panicked as all the rest.

Instead, relative veterans, they move in a hard scare more like anger than fear. Not so stupid. The first months with LIS were an extension of the illusion in which KMAG functioned: the illusion there was time. Time for a first group of sixty enlisted men to learn phonetic Korean while they "assisted agricultural projects"; time to minimally increase forces without alarming politicians happily demobilizing a successful American military that, after all, deserved a resumption of civilian life. Language Immersion

Seoul only deepened Leavitt's belief in language and sound as the
only tincture of reality, particularly in this place; all else in Korea
seemed hallucination, the immense unraveling of a completely
foreign history. Six ROK instructors drilled LIS six hours a day,
six days a week, ten men to a classroom; mimeographed texts on
Korean customs and history, tape recorders, timed recitations of
romanized Hangul phrase and response. Daily minute tests were
evaluated for tonal accuracy. They were granted weekend leave
based on twice-a-session minute test scores; the tests now seemed
particularly asinine and yet vitally important. The slight, finely
built ROK instructors were polite and consenting except during
drills and tests, when they betrayed an urgency and frustration
that were infectious. Leavitt heard the hatred and distrust, the
discomfort, the resentment in their voices, as warning and knowledge. They were angry and their country was defenseless; everyone would pay. Meaning didn't matter; the real content of the
words was in sound itself. Leavitt punched out answering phrases
in sliding nasal tones that were precise and nonverbal as musical
scales. At night he decoded innocuous phrases about spicy food or
the conversion of miles to kilometers, aware KMAG knew nothing. Or KMAG knew and could do nothing. They were minding
a volcano. The ROK instructors stood poised like bantams,
shouting. *Igot chungeso issuseyo?* Which of the following items do
you have? They communicated an instinctive, coiled tension
Leavitt now recognized as fear.

Officially the newly imported enlisted men were support staff;
afternoons they filed orders and requisitions, made supply runs
for the mess. Leavitt and Tompkins were partnered in their own
so-called agricultural project; they drove a supply truck to the
docks for fish, vegetables, freshly slaughtered meat, *maekju* beer,
and rice vodka called *soju* that could take your head off. Tompkins
was happy in Seoul. He used supply runs to scope out clubs, bars,
brothels; he liked the native food, sushi and barbecued *kalbi ccim*,
pungent *ccigae* stew. This food is healthy, he'd tell Leavitt. You
seen any fat Koreans? You notice how they turn seventy before

their skin wrinkles? You're no Korean, Leavitt told him, no matter how much kimchi you eat. But Tompkins insisted they drink *ssanghwa* tea in the barracks at night; he maintained the bitter herbs extended concentration. Their scores on minute tests were always highest; nights they were confined to quarters, they practiced scatting Korean phrases just as they'd improvised swing at the Match Box. In Tokyo they'd watched officers jitterbug with their perfectly coiffed Japanese dates. The women were child-sized girls in upswept hairdos and sheath-style kimonos. They side-fastened their dresses right up to their chins with a hundred hooks and eyes: a married officer on extended rotation might buy them a little house or apartment near the base. Tompkins scoffed at them: "Fuck the white man and the white man fuck you."

"Like you're not white," Leavitt remarked.

"White like you white, Philly Jew boy. No Florida cracker tell you I'm white, or you neither. We knew how to fight before we joined any army." Tompkins smiled. "These good ole boys got their asses on another powder keg in Korea."

"Yeah, well your Seminole ass is here as well."

"Ain't that the way," Tompkins said softly. "I need me a hell of a whaling."

Those weeks in Seoul before the war, Tompkins liked to pretend the Korean whores fucked him instead of the other way around. Every day around four or five, he'd say, "I feel like getting out. Wanna talk about it?"

Leavitt would repeat his stock response: "We can talk about it."

"You sweet bohunk," Tompkins would say. "What the hell, no Jew has hair like that." He'd grab Leavitt's tight blond curls and hold on.

The papa-san at the place Tompkins frequented always looked delighted to greet them. *"Chon bul, chon bul,"* he'd grin, payment in advance, no matter how stridently Tompkins insisted the girls *ssage haejuseyo*, make it cheaper. "You big *minam* Americans," he would tell them, gesturing with an extended forefinger, "you number one men."

Tompkins always demanded a full hour. Leavitt would follow him up the stairs and take the adjoining room. The walls were, literally, paper: floor-to-ceiling screens that turned one room into two cell-like cubicles, each with a bed, a sink, a chair, a kerosene lamp on a table. Shadows, seemingly those of a giant and his children, moved across the walls as Tompkins stood or turned or lay down, lifting one partner and then another an arm's length above him as though she were a pet or a baby. Leavitt closed his eyes, allowed an angel to kneel before him. He wouldn't put himself inside them: he adhered to this small fidelity like religion, like another charm, enjoying the control itself, the tension and the heat. The women laughed at him and blew him kisses, poised themselves naked over him to tempt him. It didn't matter which woman, which girl. In Korean, he'd tell her what to do, how to dance, moist in the little room, not dancing as she did in the bars but as she had in her village, slow ceremonial dance that was ritual and folklore. They'd all come from a village, years back or not so long ago, all the women and the girls. A girl who'd grown up in Seoul might protest she didn't know those dances, but he'd keep asking, say he knew her mother had taught her, back when she had a mother. She'd dance then, as they all did, slowly, a prayer beyond language, a shape moving in afternoon light or near darkness. The swanlike turn of the arms, the flex of the arched feet, were always the same. She would arch her back as the last sequence of movements ended, her torso very still. Sometimes she would cry and Leavitt would ask her to lie down, open toward him in his chair, touch herself until the crying stopped or turned to sighs and whispered gasps. The only sex they responded to was with themselves, and they seemed to think him so strange or nonthreatening they occasionally forgot he was there, or perhaps shared their privacy as a gift. Regardless, when the performance seemed genuine enough and time was nearly gone, he'd stop the girl and pull her to him, so aroused he was shaking. Finally she'd minister to him with her mouth, both of them listening as Tompkins rammed himself again and again into the youngest, most

petite girl he could find. Tompkins called her his lucky star. Leavitt could hear him call out, nearly crying with adoration, begging
her, stroking and praising her. Tompkins paid his favorite girl and
her pals with *sonmul* and *tambae*, gifts and cigarettes, separate
from the papa-san, and by the second week the two or three
youngest would be waiting. Some nights they all went with Tompkins; they seemed to demand this of the papa-san as their due if
business was slow.

Afterward, Tompkins would say he felt guilty, but the older
ones gave you the clap. "Tight and light is right," he'd say.

Tompkins is right about something; he's still alive and not a
scratch on him. Leavitt is unscathed as well; they're fucking
charmed, Tompkins says, *voodoo san*, but it was Tompkins' voodoo. Leavitt feels a bruised apprehension deep in his gut, like it's
only a matter of time before a soft core inside him betrays the
hard, fast reflexes he's honed to a pitch. Tompkins plays war like
it's filthy sport. I'm not really here, he liked to whisper, but
MacDowell had picked them both, let them in on secrets that
detonated.

Leavitt supposes MacDowell's idea wasn't wrong. If KMAG
had imported thousands of infantry two years ago, enrolled all of
them in MacDowell's LIS program instead of the sixty they'd
imported through Tokyo GHQ, the NKPA might not have
poured in so fast, driven their unresisted tank convoys down the
one paved road. The Imperial Road, Koreans called it, the old
royal highway from Pyongyang to Seoul, but it was peacetime and
the road was empty. GHQ allowed Colonel MacDowell his little
hobby. Now Leavitt wonders how many LIS guys aren't dead or
captured. The few left are all the more alien for their use of a borrowed language understood in scraps. Rumors are passed on and
revised in languages secret from one another. Nearly secret. Leavitt understands a portion of what he hears until he stops listening,
concentrates instead on getting the Koreans to a secure location.

Days of drenching rain have given way to ascendant heat; the
mud fairly steams, sucking whatever touches it. American troops

and matériel struggle north to the front as the front moves relent-
lessly south. The NKPA are pressing hard; an electricity of threat
swells the damp humidity. Leavitt and Tompkins command two
stretched-thin platoons assigned refugee management. They're to
assist and direct evacuation of villages in the way of the war, keep
the road clear of ox carts and fleeing farmers, but their more
important objective is to rendezvous with their own company by
nightfall, set up defensive positions, protect the retreat. Their
recently arrived force is strung out along a moving human border;
boys accustomed to soft Occupation life are dying merely to
engage and retreat. Leavitt can only keep them moving, reined in
where he can see them.

A streambed and culvert along the opposite side of the railroad
tracks run with trickling water; the Koreans seem to think it's
drinkable water, but Leavitt calls to them not to pause. *Gaesok
kaseyo!* Keep going. Sounds of artillery fire drift closer as he
squints into the tracks. The land deepens; ahead the tracks pass
levelly across broad, matching concrete bridges; identical tunnels
under the bridges span a stream and a dirt road. He'll halt the column there, let them drink and rest in the cool of the tunnels,
radio command. Tompkins has the radio. Typically they stay in
sight of one another, but the new troops are so raw that Leavitt
walks point and Tompkins brings up the rear, mom-and-pop
style, in case they're fired upon. The refugees move forward in
near silence; they walk steadily along the tracks through muddy,
saturated land. Far off the foothills steepen, forested and green,
against a broad horizon so impenetrable it looks painted against
the sky. The land is oppressive, ancient, dominant, cultivated in
small patches, borrowed for scant lifetimes of subsistence farming.
Lifetimes on the move now, blinks of an eye. Whole villages emptied out, moving, frightened populations, imported armies—
none of it matters. Generations of political animosity and serial
foreign occupation are passing weather, and the hulking mountains watch. NKPA controls those mountains, that sky. Leavitt
warned his men at dawn to stay close, stay tight. Now he pulls in

the straggling platoon with shrill, aptly timed whistles, accompanied in his head by Lola's words, private sounds soft with darkness. *Baby? You tired? Come here, baby.* He's past tired. There's no tired, just a tight-strung, alert exhaustion fueled by watchful fear and barely controlled rage. Pressed and pressed, falling back in panicked or slow retreat, they're outnumbered and little supported, fingers in the fucking dike. Fear and anger turn in his gut like a yin-yang eel, slippery and fishlike but dimly human in its blunt, circular probing, turning and turning, no rest. This alone, the exhaustion, and the mud, the heat—he shares with the Koreans on the tracks. *Changma* rains have pounded Korea the past two weeks. The runny mud has solidified to warm, pliable clay, and rumor has it tanks are circling in behind them. Infiltrators in peasant white have repeatedly moved behind American troops by joining crowds of refugees. No way to know.

Leavitt's shrill, pursed-lipped signals (*here's a kiss for you babe*) pierce the dull slip-timed sound of movement across the wooden ties of the railroad tracks. Easier than struggling through mud, but the necessity of measuring each step proves too much for the old people, some of the women struggling with infants and bundles. They've fallen out onto the gravel between the two lines of track, straggling on at a slower pace. Leavitt lets them; he can't afford men to police both sides of the column, can't guard against infiltrators on both flanks if in fact they exist. He wants all his men where he can see them in case of snipers or attack; he fears the new replacements are so green they'll fire on one another if they're spooked. He calls to the Koreans rhythmically, consistently, on the beat, partly to calm his own men: *Ppalli.* Hurry. *Kapshida.* Let's go. The refugees need no urging; it's their civil war, their homes and lands lost, he's merely a conductor. No savior here. The saving will come later, American command assures Leavitt, Tompkins, all the men who've survived the past month to lead boys barely out of basic. Leavitt's hoarsely tonal shouts of *Ttokparo! Ijjokuro!* serve as adjacent percussion to other pictures he remembers intensely, starkly, across a terrible gulf of time and dimension. In another world, on an American morning lost to him, Lola whispers phrases on clean sheets in their room above the club. *My beautiful blond Jew, my Pennsylvania boy.* She loved to tuck her forearms under him as though he were her child and hold his sex to her mouth, drinking him in, her lips and tongue everywhere. Teasing him with her teeth, biting a little, then harder. He uses her words that were sex and song a year ago to keep his feet moving, keep him tensed and angry enough to stay alive and ride his boys like the ruthless fast-promoted cannon fodder he's become.

This failing police action is UN in name only. The Americans, caught completely off guard when the North invaded in June, are scrambling, their asses hung out to dry. Ironically, the three months in Seoul with LIS before the invasion have made Leavitt one of the 24th's more acclimated platoon leaders. Language Immersion Seoul was a pilot program MacDowell had hoped to expand. Regardless of any affiliation with Intelligence, MacDowell told them, more military capable of "social interaction" would be useful as tensions seesawed and North Korea continued its Red Chinese–inspired posturing. That was probably bunk. As far as Leavitt could tell, there had never been American Intelligence in Korea. Intelligence stayed dry, ate better, dressed in street clothes, and failed.

Clearly, some of those involved in LIS were being considered, quietly interviewed. That first day in Seoul, they'd had a file on the desk: Leavitt's high school transcript, the citywide Latin prize he'd won, the community college scholarship he'd turned down to spite his old man, records from Fort Knox. They'd made inquiries.

"Musician," Colonel MacDowell had said, jerking his head in Leavitt's direction.

The four-month language-immersion course in Seoul was MacDowell's idea. He'd personally selected candidates from the Occupation force in Tokyo and presented each one to Colonel Wright the first day with a short declaration. MacDowell spoke pidgin Korean but had higher hopes for Leavitt and the others.

"Tonal familiarity," he explained over Wright's desk, "auditory sophistication."

Wright nodded, clipped, efficient. "Your instrument, soldier?"

"Trumpet, sir," Leavitt replied.

MacDowell slapped Leavitt on the shoulder like a jovial fan. "Heard this boy at the Match Box Officers' Club, in Tokyo. Been there a month and got himself into a band. I collared him, first night."

"So I hear," Colonel Wright replied, as though the sessions at the Match Box were famous. "At ease, son." He addressed Mac-Dowell. "You bring the whole group over, Mac?"

"Offered to. Leavitt here and one other soldier took me up on it. A drummer, I believe. Tompkins, wasn't it, Leavitt?"

"Tompkins, sir." Nothing tonal about Tompkins—as a musician, he was all instinct, strength, endurance—but Leavitt supposed Language Immersion Seoul was an experiment open to anyone MacDowell wanted to pull in. He'd also posted calls for those with aptitude in mathematics.

"You'll do well, both of you," MacDowell said, "and I wouldn't be surprised if you get yourself another band together here—a good many of the boys are musicians." He went on to explain that the South Korean instructors were already formulating a higher-level course for those who showed "exemplary aptitude."

Standing there in Wright's office at KMAG, Leavitt allowed himself to fantasize speaking Korean and playing jazz for the rest of his overseas rotation, but the North Koreans, as it turned out, weren't posturing. The invasion was well-planned extended ambush, dress-rehearsed at Kaesong. Now Leavitt holds a dull conviction that Korea is the beginning of an ending Hiroshima and Nagasaki only faked.

Along with her pen-and-ink sketches of him, of rooftops out their window, Lola had taped magazine pictures on the wall by her bureau. One was a *Life* magazine full-page color image of a mushroom cloud. *Look at it: the death flower. The biggest hottest flower anybody ever died inside.* Die inside you, he'd whisper, inside you. Many of her tacked-up drawings were façades of buildings or bridges in the West Virginia town she'd left and said she never wanted to see again. Surfaces. Shape of a scrubby island off a riverbank, stone arches of a bridge. Signs: a MURPHY'S FIVE AND TEN CENT STORE sign in letters curlicued and bold like a circus might use to spell its name. Walking beside railroad tracks in Chungchong Province, policing this hurried flight, he imagines the images he saw from Lola's bed. Her sketches were never in color. They were grainy no. 2 pencil, shades ranging almost black to silver, pressed deep into rag paper whose first layer was nearly scratched away. At certain points of contrast, the white left extant seemed to glow in the dark.

Trying to remember is a game he plays during the endless days and at night when he's not on watch and sleep is never sleep. If he can put the images in their places, find them on the walls, he might call back the room itself and lie down in it and wait for her.

He doesn't lie down, ever. Sleeping, he props himself upright, ready to jump to his feet. American forces have fallen back seventy miles in seventeen days, no Intelligence involved; they stand, hold, and fall back, ever more decimated. Korea has dropped its mask and filled Leavitt's head with pictures, sounds, words he's heard before and words he's never heard; signals whose crossed lines pass through him in phantom frequencies. *You're the best, babe, the only one—there, right there, babe? Baby? Baby?* Remembering Lola's voice, Leavitt tenses as he walks. He'd listen for *baby* or *Bobby* or *love* or *babe* or simply *yes*: one pulsing word rapidly repeated; her breathy, questioning intonations timed to each thrust were a signal she was nearly there. Sounds that were no longer words meant he could let go and stop thinking, pound in hard just where she'd put him inside her. No woman he'd ever been with responded so strongly, so unmistakably, the spasm of her muscles a deep interior rippling that touched off his own wrenching orgasm. Lying still afterward, completely drained, unable to lift his hips, his head, he could move his fingers inside her and play her sensation like a thing he actually controlled.

The week she told him about the baby, the week before he'd shipped out, they thought he'd be gone a year, doing his time in Occupied Japan. He'd come back to her, to the baby. He'd even hoped, after he arrived in Korea, that specialized status in LIS might help him secure a leave when the baby was born. Lola planned to convince the right people she was in such bad shape that a leave for her husband was advisable. She could be convincing, and old man Onslow had connections; one hand scratched the other in the Kentucky lowlands of Onslow County. Onslow was a fallen Louisville blue blood whose family name graced the county courthouse, and his club filled a definite need at nearby Fort Knox, a straight shot down Highway 31. Onslow knew people and was kin to half of city government; he depended on Lola to keep his girls clean and well advised while he ran sex for soldiers as a sideline business. He'd done numerous favors for the brass at the base, hushing up soldiers' messes, meeting their particularities with understanding. He shared his windfalls with Lola as though she were his blood or his business partner, or maybe just to buy her silence. Lola was unpredictable—she didn't live under anyone's thumb, including Onslow's. He seemed to approve of Lola's alliance, probably saw Leavitt as keeping her happy before conveniently disappearing overseas. He didn't know they had plans until they married, two weeks before Leavitt left. Even then he seemed to assume Leavitt might not reappear, might come to his senses far from Fort Knox and the complications of marriage to a woman like Lola. The baby was proof to the contrary; Leavitt was alive inside her. She'd already talked to a doc who frequented the club; he'd swear she was nearly dead after the birth. The army would ship Bobby back for an emergency leave; he'd do a few more months abroad, and then his rotation would be over; they'd decide together whether he stayed in the military or mustered out.

It's laughable now, their plans and schemes. No one is getting out of Korea, not for years. The "specialized" soldiers of Language Immersion Seoul are leading platoons and evacuating villages, shouting orders and instructions. Terrified South Koreans address

Leavitt in fast, complex streams of language he can't understand against a backdrop of artillery and flight. *Ihae mot haeyo*, he repeats, I don't understand. *Ijjokuro*: this way. Hurry. No: *naeil*. *Jigum*: now.

All month he's carried a snapshot of Lola in the breast pocket of his stinking fatigues, wrapped in a cellophane-encased cigarette pack against the rain: Lola in the hammock they'd strung on the third-floor porch off her room. Even in black and white, her dark red hair looks red, and her eyes look blue, the pretty lines at the corners a little deeper. She rests one hand on her rounded belly, her smile languid and sweet, like she's about to pour him a glass of that minted tea she spikes with a little rum. This morning when the platoon hurriedly pulled out, the new replacements stumbling and nervous, Leavitt missed the carefully flattened cigarette pack and Lola's picture. Losing it was bad luck. On the back she'd written *Seven months along*. He will be hearing any day. It could be happening. It might have started. She'd knocked off the juice, she said, and even the cigarettes, could he believe it? She still sang weekends, sitting primly draped behind the piano in the silk kimono he'd sent her from Tokyo. At the end of the set she'd slip it off and stand up in a dress cut simple as any Mrs. Brown's jumper, but black and sequined, clinging tight across her breasts and swollen front, and her shape inspired wild applause. That was Lola, never who you thought she was, inspiring hordes of boys to whom she was off-limits. Why had she let him upstairs that night, years after she said she'd stopped with men—she had her girls to love her and packed roomfuls of boys to fend off. Something about the quality of your attention, she told him, and the fact you're a solid musician. Two flights of narrow stairwell to her room, each dim landing a turn farther into silence, until they might have been stepping into space.

Louisville was hopping now, she said, full of green Fort Knox recruits and basic-hardened boys hot to knock hell out of this tiny little war. Enough, she wanted to leave as soon as he got back. Florida, she'd written him, Coral Gables. She'd picked the town based on the name alone and the fact it bordered the sea. They'd buy a cottage first, then something bigger. Run a little tourist home, she'd said in her letters, a guesthouse. There were always vacationers on budgets and big-city tourists tired of the cold. She was saving all she could. *I can be respectable, if I'm not run out of town for corrupting a minor.* He's no minor. He was twenty-one when they married; she was twenty-nine. Jesus, she was wild about him, with a hunger like a man's. He's glad about the baby; he's put his mark on her, held his territory until he can get back and claim her. He thinks about her with other men, in a past before he knew her, and blocks images out of his mind. He never asked how she smoothed arrangements with a character like Onslow. Lola has a past and a kid, a daughter who lives with her older sister in West Virginia. The sister manages a restaurant, pays a mortgage on her own house. Noreen was the strong one, Lola said, and nobody's fool. It was better. Leavitt imagines an ultra-respectable schoolmarm type, kindly enough to raise Lola's daughter while she disapproves of singers and bars and military towns, disapproves of Lola, no doubt. Lola sends money every month and keeps a picture tucked into her mirror: a school picture the size of a big postage stamp. Skinny kid, serious and pale, like Lola without the auburn hair and smatter of freckles across her cheekbones. Lola wouldn't say her daughter's name, even to him. *I gave her a bird's name. Maybe she'll grow up safe and fly away.* There were other small pictures clipped together in her drawer, one each year since the daughter was three and went to live with the aunt. Lola never showed him, never looked at them, only kept the newest one where she saw it every time she looked at herself.

When he asked about the kid's father, Lola was silent. But who the hell was he, had she loved him like this, like them, their room, their bed? God no. He was a sleepy sort, she'd had to walk him through it like a brother. Served his purpose and back where he came from, good riddance. "Ah, you mountain folk," Leavitt said and touched her, "fuck your brothers and nothing to it."

"Yeah, sure," she said, "and I've got one leg shorter than the other, and no one in West Virginia has ever stood on level ground or worn shoes."

"Nobody's your brother," he told her. He moved her under him, looked at her, licked her eyes, touched her hairline with his tongue. "Nobody, remember it."

"You're my brother," she'd answered, breathing. "You're the first and the last. After you, there's no one."

He believed her. He didn't ask if Coral Gables was a reunification fantasy, divided factions drawn together beside the sea. Coral Gables was a beach town near Miami, Tompkins said, near Hialeah, where the horses ran. If Leavitt can get out of Korea, a daughter is fine with him. In Florida, he'd know her name.

Rural hamlets here are derivations of one another, dirt track villages of shabby wooden buildings. Leavitt has scribbled the similar romanized names of the villages emptied today in his dirty, palm-sized notebook: *Chu Gok Ri, No Gun Ri, Im Ke Ri*. No plumbing, no electricity. What did the refugees carry in those bundles on their backs and heads, what did they gather up when the soldiers appeared, rousting them out before the North Koreans swept through? Intelligence warned some carried ordnance and mortars to North Korean units. If they did, Leavitt thought, they were North Korean infiltrators. He'd heard South Koreans speak among themselves and understood enough to know that most of them hated the North. Whole villages emptied at news the NKPA were closing in; they were considered bloodthirsty puppets of the Red Chinese, and their readiness to slaughter civilians was legendary. Remaining ROK units couldn't be trusted with the few North Korean prisoners they'd taken; they shot them outright. Still, both sides took advantage of the American inability to tell them apart unless they were uniformed. Leavitt takes off his helmet, wipes the sweat from his face without breaking stride. *Ijjokuro*, he calls to the Koreans, this way.

Leavitt turns to sight Tompkins far to the rear. They're reunited, Tompkins says, together in hell. Now Leavitt wonders if they're meant to die together. Or if Tompkins will survive and be the one to find him. He made Tompkins take Lola's address and a letter for her; Tompkins didn't reciprocate. There was no one but his mother, he said, and notification plans were bad luck. Death was dead, not a good way to get out. Getting out was good though; they needed to get out. "Keep your ass in my sights," Tompkins liked to tell him, "I'll get you out." He said he'd know Leavitt's ass anywhere, and he'd haul out whatever was left of it or die trying. Then he'd wink. "Feel like getting out?" he'd ask. Where were the girls from Tompkins' preferred brothel now? Dead or running. Running, Tompkins said, they'd got out. No doubt, the girls were way south, waiting for Tompkins to catch up. But he couldn't, not yet. "She whaled me good," he reminisced sadly of his favorite, "my lucky star."

This morning at dawn, Tompkins had been matter-of-fact. "Definitely," he intoned, "gonna get out today. Wanna talk about it?"

Leavitt deadpanned his stock response: "We can talk about it." Like a charm, a set dialogue.

"Ain't no talk," Tompkins insisted. "Out we go. Today's the day."

The double railroad overpass is closer now; Leavitt can see that the tunnels below are slightly curved and relatively deep; he can't see through them. The dirt road moves through one into dark shade, the stream through the other. They're stone or concrete, bunkerlike, arched, like two deep eyes angled slightly askance. He'll keep the Koreans on the tracks as long as possible, then direct them down the grassy incline to rest in the shade of the tunnels while Tompkins radios command. They'll advise the refugees to proceed south on their own, circle the men back to regroup, reduce chances the platoons will be stranded or cut off.

"*Towajuseyo!*" A girl stands full in front of Leavitt, blocking his path, burdened by the nearly grown child on her back. She fills his vision, shocking and sudden. "*Towajuseyo!*" she says again, and repeats, "*Towajuseyo!*" Help me. Please help me.

It's a demand, not a request. For a moment he wonders if he knows her, one of the girls from Seoul. Had she danced for him while he held himself apart, while he kept himself from her until she remembered who she was? But no, this one is a village girl, beautiful, petite like most of them, dressed in the usual white garments, a purely rural girl who has never been to Seoul. She's the incarnation of those ritual dances whores never forgot, and she is angry, unafraid. She seems as furious as Leavitt feels, as they should all feel, walking away like this, losing everything. Frantically, she gestures toward the tracks. An old woman has fallen or maybe just collapsed. *"Halmoni!"* she says, *"Halmoni!"* Not her mother; it's the word for grandmother or great-aunt. The girl runs back to stand over her, looks at Leavitt, pleads with him angrily as though it's his job to help only her. This girl has never left her village. She's forgotten nothing and is fiercely herself: she's the child's guardian, the old woman's protector, and she stands legs outspread, one arm flung out, planted to provide the old woman a barrier. The crowd in white—all of them, these farmers, wear white—parts around her, barely disturbed, moving on. She glares at Leavitt, enraged that she needs help, angry at herself. She can't carry the boy on her back and pick up the old woman, yet she won't put the boy down, not here, even for a moment.

Monitor, do not assist. Those are his orders, repeated to his men just hours ago as this venture started. Where is fucking Tompkins? He has the radio. Leavitt looks to his left to see Tompkins a hundred feet back. Leavitt's whistle rends the air, signaling the platoon to tighten along the perimeter of the refugee column; they are to stay to the left of the tracks where they can see one another. Keep everyone moving.

Leavitt looks at the old woman, at the girl. She stands, unbending, staring at him, waiting, holding the child. The boy tilts his head oddly. Too old to be carried, he's crippled, slow-witted, something. Leavitt nods at the girl, *yes*, and dread breaks over him. Something imminent approaches, something to hurt them all, carry them away. Is it her? Someone in the crowd? Unlikely an infiltrator would attack here unless the crowd was full of them. Infiltrators typically moved singly, regrouped in the foothills, circled in behind advancing American forces big enough to be worth the trouble. The girl looks at Leavitt, willing him closer. Her eyes burn into him, her perfectly oval face nearly opalescent. She could be the kid's mother or his sister, who could tell, the women here all look so young until they are suddenly ancient. Leavitt steps back to sight his men down the line, staggered shapes in fatigues, then he wades quickly into the crowd. As though on signal, the girl reaches out, shifts the burden of the child to him, and bends over the old woman. Stronger than she looks, she lifts the old lady to her feet and half supports her, moving on as though Leavitt will simply follow. He nearly does, but reaches out to touch her shoulder. *Kujjokuro*, he shouts; to the side, move to the side, out of the flow of the crowd. The kid's legs circle Leavitt's waist; he shifts his carbine to one shoulder and clasps the boy to his hip. *Bikyuh,* he says calmly, out.

The girl needs no further direction; she stays close and follows Leavitt, urging the old woman along. The boy weighs nothing. He must be eight, nine. The grip of his thin arms is firm, the aspect of his upper body wholly tense. He moves his head, listening, the curved shell of his ear turned up. Their faces are inches apart. Leavitt sees into the boy's stunning, nearly reflective eyes: the obsidian irises float a pale blue milk and his pupils are invisible behind blue splashes of cataract. He's blind. That's why the girl wouldn't put him down. The cloudiness in his eyes seems to subtly pulse or dilate; the boy *looks* with complete attention, seems to see past Leavitt or into him. He's not slow, or not exactly; he seems preternaturally alert. Leavitt has difficulty looking away but averts his eyes and quickens his pace through the crowd. He feels the girl's frantic hand on his lower back and slows just enough to accommodate her struggling progress with the old woman. "Follow me," he calls to her in Korean, "stay with me." Moving quickly, edging through, he feels the boy's small body go rigid, his apprehension heighten to a nearly audible pitch; Leavitt imagines the clear, high tone of a tuning fork struck in midair. It's that kind of focus, emotionless and pure, so sharply true that nothing else exists. Suddenly he understands, and he hears what the boy hears. Planes. Thrumming overhead, closing fast. There's no way out. The refugees move doggedly forward. Perfectly exposed, they're a white column seemingly moving in formation, and the strafing begins.

Winfield, West Virginia

JULY 26, 1959

Lark

I move his chair into the yard under the tree and then Nonie carries him out. The tree is getting all full of seeds and the pods hang down. Soon enough the seeds will fly through the air and Nonie will have hay fever and want all the windows shut to keep the white puffs out. Termite will want to be outside in the chair all the time then, and he'll go on and on at me if I try to keep him indoors so I can do the ironing or clean up the dishes. Sun or rain, he wants to be out, early mornings especially. "OK, you're out," Nonie will say, and he starts his sounds, quiet and satisfied, before she even puts him down. She has on her white uniform to go to work at Charlie's and she holds Termite out from her a ways, not to get her stockings run with his long toenails or her skirt stained with his fingers because he always has jam on them after breakfast.

"There's Termite." Nonie puts him in the chair with his legs under him like he always sits. Anybody else's legs would go to sleep, all day like that. "You keep an eye on him, Lark," Nonie tells me, "and give him some lemonade when it gets warmer. You can put the radio in the kitchen window. That way he can hear it from out here too." Nonie straightens Termite. "Get him one of those cleaner-bag ribbons from inside. I got to go, Charlie will have my ass."

A car horn blares in the alley. Termite blares too then, trying to sound like the horn. "Elise is here," Nonie says. "Don't forget to wash the dishes, and wipe off his hands." She's already walking off across the grass, but Termite is outside so he doesn't mind her going. Elise waves at me from inside her Ford. She's a little shape in the shine of glare on the window, then the gravel crunches and they're moving off fast, like they're going somewhere important.

"Termite," I say to him, and he says it back to me. He always gets the notes right, without saying the words. His sounds are like a one-toned song, and the day is still and flat. It's seven in the morning and here and there a little bit of air moves, in pieces, like a tease, like things are getting full so slow no one notices. On the kitchen wall we have one of those glass vials with blue water in it, and the water rises if it's going to storm. The water is all the way to the top and it's like a test now to wait and see if the thing works, or if it's so cheap it's already broken. "Termite," I tell him, "I'll fix the radio. Don't worry." He's got to have something to listen to. He moves his fingers the way he does, with his hands up and all his fingers pointing, then curving, each in a separate motion, fast or careful. He never looks at his fingers but I always think he hears or knows something through them, like he does it for some reason. Charlie says he's just spastic, that's a spastic motion; Nonie says he's fidgety, with whatever he has that he can't put to anything. His fingers never stop moving unless we give him something to hold, then he holds on so tight we have to pry whatever it is away from him. Nonie says that's just cussedness. I think when he holds something his fingers rest. He doesn't always want to keep hearing things.

My nightgown is so thin I shouldn't be standing out here, though it's not like it matters. Houses on both sides of the alley have seen about everything of one another from their second-floor windows. No one drives back here but the people who live here, who park their cars in the gravel driveways that run off the alley. We don't have a car, but the others do, and the Tuccis have three—two that run and one that doesn't. It's early summer and the alley has a berm of plush grass straight up the center. All us kids—Joey and Solly and Zeke and me—walked the grass barefoot in summer, back and forth to one another's houses. I pulled

Termite in the wagon and the wheels fit perfectly in the narrow tire tracks of the alley. Nick Tucci still calls his boys thugs, proud they're quick and tough. He credits Nonie with being the only mother his kids really remember, back when we were small.

Today is Sunday. Nick Tucci will run his push mower along the berm of the alley, to keep the weeds down. He does it after dusk, when he gets home from weekend overtime at the factory and he's had supper and beer, and the grass smells like one sharp green thread sliced open. I bring Termite out. He loves the sound of that mower and he listens for it, once all the way down, once back. He makes a low murmur like *r*'s strung together, and he has to listen hard over the sounds of other things, electric fans in windows, radio sounds, and he sits still and I give him my sandals to hold. He looks to the side like he does, his hands fit into my shoes. His eyes stay still, and he hears. If I stand behind his chair I can feel the blade of the mower too; I feel it roll and turn way down low in me, making a whirl and a cutting.

Sundays seem as long as a year. Sundays I don't walk up Kanawha Hill to Main Street to Barker Secretarial. I'm nearly through second semester, Typing and Basic Skills, but I'm First of Class and Miss Barker lets me sit in on Steno with the second-year girls. Miss Barker is not young. She's a never-married lady who lives in her dead father's house and took over the school for him when he died of a heart attack about ten years ago. The school is up above the Five & Ten, on the second floor of the long building with the long red sign that says in gold letters MURPHY'S FIVE AND TEN CENT STORE. It's a really old sign, Nonie says, it was there when she and my mother were growing up, but the store was both floors then. Now Barker Secretarial has filled the big upstairs room with lines of Formica-topped desks, each with a pullout shelf where we keep our typing books (*Look to the right, not to the keyboard, look to the right*—). We have to be on time because the drills are timed and we turn on our machines all at once; there's a ratchety click and a rumble, like the whole room surges, then it hums. The typewriters hum one note: it's a note Termite could do, but what would he do with the sound of us typing. We all work at one speed for practice drills. We're like a chorus and the clacking of the keys sounds measured, all together. Then at personal best we go for speed and all the rates are different. The machines explode with noise, running over themselves. Up near the big windows, for half the room, there's a lowered fake ceiling with long fluorescent lights. The tops of the windows disappear in that ceiling and I hate it and I sit in the back. Barker Secretarial stopped with the ceiling halfway when they realized they didn't have the money for air-conditioning, and they brought in big fans that roll on wheels like the wheels on Termite's chair. Miss Barker gets those fans going and we all have to wear scarves to keep our hair from flying around. With the noise and the motion I can think I'm high up, moving fast above the town and the trees and the river and the bridges, and as long as I'm typing I won't crash.

I tell Termite, "It's not going to rain yet. He'll still mow the alley. There's not going to be stars though. It's going to be hot and white, and the white sky will go gray. Then really late we might have that big storm they talk about."

Big storm they talk about, Termite says back to me, in sounds like my words.

"That's right," I tell him. "But you'll have to watch from the window. Don't think you're going to sit out here in the rain with lightning flashing all around you."

He doesn't say anything to that. He might be thinking how great it would be, wind and rain, real hard rain, not like the summer rain we let him sit out in sometimes. He likes motion. He likes things on his skin. He's alive all over that way. Nonie says I put thoughts in his head, he might not be thinking anything. Maybe he doesn't have to think, I tell her. Just don't you be thinking a lot of things about him that aren't true, she'll say.

But no one can tell what's true about him.

. . .

Termite was pretty when he was a baby. People would coo over him when we walked him in the big carriage. His forehead was real broad and he had blond curls and those blue eyes that move more than normal, like he's watching something we don't see. He was so small for his age that Nonie called him a mite, then Termite, because even then he moved his fingers, feeling the air. I think he's in himself like a termite's in a wall.

I remember when Termite came. Nonie is his guardian and his aunt, but I'm his sister. In a way he's more mine than anyone else's. He'll be mine for longer, is what Nonie says. Nonie isn't old but she always says to me about when she'll be gone. She looks so strong, like a block or a rectangle, strong in her shoulders and her back and her wide hips, even in her legs and their blue veins that she covers up with her stockings. Your mother didn't bring him, is what Nonie told me, someone brought him for her. Not his father. Nonie says Termite's father was only married to my mother for a year. He was a baby, Nonie says, twenty-one when my mother was nearly thirty, and those bastards left him over there in Korea. No one even got his body back and they had to have the service around a flag that was folded up. Nonie says it was wrong and it will never be right. But I don't know how Termite got here because Nonie sent me away that week to church camp. I was nine and had my birthday at camp, and when I came home Termite was here. He was nearly a year old but he couldn't sit up by himself, and Nonie had him a baby bed and clothes and a high chair with cushions and straps, and she had papers that were signed. She never got a birth certificate though, so we count the day he came his birthday, but I make him a birthday whenever it suits me.

"Today could be a birthday," I tell him. "One with a blue cake, yellow inside, and a lemon taste. You like that kind, with whipped cream in the center, to celebrate the storm coming, and Nick Tucci will get some with his ice tea tonight, and I'll help you put the candles in. You come inside with me while I mix it and you can hold the radio. You can turn the dials around, OK?"

Dials around OK. I can almost answer for him. But I don't. And he doesn't, because he doesn't want to come inside. I can feel him holding still; he wants to sit here. He puts his hand up to his face, to his forehead, as though he's holding one of the strips of blue plastic Nonie calls ribbons: that's what he wants. "There's no wind, Termite, no air at all," I tell him. He blows with his lips, short sighs.

So I move his chair back from the alley a bit and I go inside and get the ribbon, a strip of a blue plastic dry-cleaner bag about four inches wide and two feet long. It's too small to get tangled and anyway we watch him; I take it out to him and wrap it around his hand twice and he holds it with his fingers curled, up to his forehead. "I'll get dressed and clean up the kitchen," I tell him, "but when I make the cake you're going to have to come inside, OK?"

He casts his eyes sideways at me. That means he agrees, but he's thinking about the blue, that strip of space he can move.

"You ring the bell if you want anything," I say.

The bell on his chair was my idea; it's really a bell for a hotel desk, flat, and he can press the knob with his wrist. That bell was mounted on a piece of metal with holes, maybe so no one would steal it once upon a time, or so it wouldn't get misplaced. A lot of years ago, I sewed it to the arm of Termite's chair with thick linen cord. His bell has a high, nice sound, not a bad sound. He presses it twice if he has to go to the bathroom, or a lot if something is wrong, or sometimes just once, now and then in the quiet, like a thought.

"Termite," I tell him, "I'm going back in."

Back in, back in, back in. I hear him as I walk away, and now he'll be silent as a breather, quiet as long as I let him be.

I stand at the kitchen sink where I can see him, put the stopper in the sink, run the water as hot as it can get. The smell of the heat comes up at my face. The dishes sink into suds, and I watch Termite. His chair is turned a little to the side, and I can see him blowing on the ribbon, blowing and blowing it, not too fast. The little bit of air that stirs in the yard catches the length of that scrap and moves it. Termite likes the blue of the plastic and he likes to see through it. He blows it out from his face and he watches it move, and it barely touches him, and he blows it away. He'll do that for thirty minutes, for an hour, till you take it away from him. In my dreams he does it for days, for years, like he's keeping time, like he's a clock or a watch. I draw him that way, fast, with pencil in my notebook. Head up like he holds himself then, wrist raised, moving blue with his breath.

People who see him from their second-story windows see a boy in a chair across the alley. They know his name and who he is. They know Noreen and how she's worked at Charlie Fitzgibbon's all these years, running the restaurant with Charlie while Gladdy Fitzgibbon owns it all and parcels out the money. How Nonie is raising kids alone that aren't hers because Charlie has never told his mother to shove it, never walked off and made himself some other work and gone ahead and married a twice-divorced woman with a daughter and another kid who can't walk and doesn't talk.

Nonie is like my mother. When she introduces me, she says, "This is my daughter, Lark."

Nonie would be raising us anyway, whether Charlie ever did the right thing or not. And I don't know if she even wants him to, anymore. It's just Nonie should own part of that restaurant, hard as she works. Charlie does the cooking and runs the kitchen, and Nonie does everything else, always has, ever since she came back here when she left the second husband. She came back and there was Charlie right where she'd left him, living with his mother and going to Mass, and they fell right back into their old ways, and Gladdy fell into hers. Except the Fitzgibbons had just about nothing after the Depression. When Nonie came back, they'd barely held on to their house and the business. They would have lost the restaurant if Nonie hadn't saved it for them, doing the books and the buying and waiting tables herself.

Nonie can do about anything, but she says she doesn't do what makes money in this world.

Dish washing doesn't make money but I like it at home when

I'm alone. I'm so used to being with Termite, he feels like alone to me. He's like a hum that always hums so the edge of where I am is blunt and softened. And when I push the dishes under I don't even look at them; I keep my eyes on him, out the window. He moves that clear blue ribbon with his breath, ripples it slow in front of his eyes, lips pursed. Pulls air out of air in such still heat. Sees through blue, if he sees. Or just feels it touching him, then flying out. I can hear the air at his open lips. I hear the air conditioner down at the restaurant too. Nonie is taking orders in the breakfast rush and it's already crowded and hot, tables and stools at the counter filled, and the big box over the door is grinding its firm noise. Charlie calls it the system. Later, in the afternoon when most everyone has cleared out and Nonie is getting ready to come home, the system will be catching and pulling like it can't quite breathe, saying *sip, sip sip*. All wounded. Nonie leaves while it's sighing, when they're setting up for dinner. Charlie wanted me to take the dinner shift after I graduated, but Nonie said I wasn't graduating high school to be a seventeen-year-old waitress. Barely seventeen, she pointed out. I finished school early because she sent me early. No reason not to, she said, I could read, and school had to be as interesting as sitting at Charlie's all day on a lunch stool with a pile of Golden Books. She says I don't need a job. Termite's my job, and Barker Secretarial, when she can be home nights to stay with Termite. The point is to make things better, Nonie says, have a future. I'm looking at Termite and the alley past his chair, and it's funny how that piece of see-through blue he holds to his face looks how I think a future would, waving like that, moving start to finish, leading off into space.

I'll let him go on a few more minutes. Nonie says it's strange how I'm satisfied to let him be, and it's a damn good thing, because life is long.

Life feels big to me but I'm not sure it's long. I rub cereal off the hard curved lips of the breakfast bowls, and life feels broad and flat, like a sand beach rolling into desert, miles and miles. Like pictures of Australia I've seen, with a sapphire sky pressing down and water at one edge. That edge is where things change all at once. You might see the edge coming, but you can't tell how close or far away it is, how fast it might come up. I can feel it coming. Like a sound, like a wind, like a far-off train.

I used to be different. I don't know what I thought. Busy all the time, like I planned on being twelve forever. Already Termite's mother, one of them, best in school, cooking and cleaning at home like a housewife, doing my collections, like I was saving up for something. I collected seashells, not so easy since I haven't been to the ocean. And little novelty pitchers, doll sized, pitchers with faces or place-names or scenes painted on. I guess I started collecting them because Termite liked his so much—the tiny moon pitcher Nonie says was in his pocket the first time she ever held him. She says his pitcher was used as a perfume bottle and must have had a cork once, but the perfume is long gone. My biggest collection is color postcards of Main Streets, each a few cents at rummage sales, or dug out of the card box downtown at Topsy Turvy. I have two or three from every state, pasted up across a wall of my room. Nick Tucci built that wall so Termite could have a room of his own in half of mine. I wanted an archway between us, not a door, and Nick framed me the same size opening into the living room. Open arches on two of my walls, no doors. I can see and hear Termite all the time. The seashells I collected were for him. He likes it when I hold one to his ear.

Now I feel how all my collections are just sitting there. They're things I used to want, and I can't tell why I did.

I pull the stopper in the sink. The water circles the drain in a soapy funnel I wish I could stand inside, everything pulled round me, pulling tighter and tighter. That's how it feels when someone stares. People stare at you like you're food on a plate, and you can feel the power of how bad they want something. They stare at me one way, keep staring, but they stare at Termite and look away. Termite never stares. That's because he can't, Nonie would say, no mystery there. It's true his eyes move because his muscles are quiet and don't work, but I think he knows he can't want things, not hard, so hard, the way people do. He does things another way. He doesn't do anything, Nonie would say. I don't believe her.

He hurts her more than he hurts me. That's why she says what she does.

I wash out the sink and rinse my hands. It's time to get Termite. That alley cat is sitting in front of his chair again, watching the plastic move. That cat scares me. Really it just sits there, looking at him with its yellow eyes, and sometimes it gets down in a crouch. I see that cat at the rail yard when I take Termite to see the trains. I've seen it for years. The stray cats slink around by themselves and they're always alone. Low to the ground, afraid of the dog packs probably. I tell Termite the cats eat the rats and the dogs eat the cats, just like "Three Blind Mice." Then he'll do the first lines of the rhyme in sounds and I'll have trouble getting him to stop. He remembers cadences of songs and rhymes, like he recognizes sounds, not words. He doesn't need words. He needs his strip of blue, and the space under the rail bridge by the river. He needs to see the river while the train roars over top. He needs the rail yard.

He loves going there in the wagon when the sun glints on the rails. The tracks go off in every direction and the trains screech and hoot and begin to move, so slow we can keep pace just beside them. That close, the noise takes over, shakes in the ground. Termite sits up straighter and gets real still. He likes vibrations so big they get inside him. He's so pure he's filled up more than I could ever be, more than I am, running and pulling the wagon. Afterward, when I'm out of breath, on my knees and leaning back against the gritty wheels, I feel drenched, soaked, washed away, and the train is still blaring in a fade that streaks away from us, a fierce line hanging on. The yard is two blocks west so we hear the freight trains every morning, sounding at the crossing, and Termite makes sure I know how wrong it is he can't get what he wants. He doesn't say anything, only uses his elbows to sit up a little straighter and turn toward the sound, tilts his head, his ear like an open cup. There: the 6:52. I crank the window open a little wider to hear the fast bellow, the hush and hollow of it. Even from far away, it makes a quiet in the air it rips. It pours through.

I'll give him a moment. I'll give him one more moment.

Nonie hates the idea of blue cake, she says it looks like something old and spoiled, too old to eat, though it's light and delicate and flavored with anise. But Termite likes it, and he likes pink cake that tastes of almond, and mostly he likes me putting the batter in different bowls, holding them in the crook of his arm while I bend over him, stirring. I tell him how fast a few drops of color land dense as tinted black and turn the mix pastel. I make three thin layers, pale blue and pink and yellow, and I put three pans in to bake, shut the door of the oven fast to pretend I'm not making everything still hotter.

"Hot as Hades today," I tell Termite, and I move his chair so he gets the hint of breath from the window. The radio cord still reaches and he turns the knob with his wrist, slow or fast, like a safecracker, like there's some sense to the sounds, the static and the interrupted news.

"Don't try talking to me in radio," I tell him, but he does anyway. As long as he holds it, he'll be trying to make it talk. I take the radio out of his lap and put it back on the counter, and I hold a bowl of icing down low. I hold the little bottle of blue in Termite's hand, and we let just three drops fall. Divinity icing makes peaks and gets a sweet crust like meringue. Mine is like sugared air that disappears in your mouth. Nonie says I'm a fabulous cook. I could cook for a living, she says, but not at Charlie's, or anywhere like it. The egg whites can go bad fast in hot weather but I turn up the fridge to keep the icing cool on the lowest shelf. We'll eat the cake today, this birthday, and Nick Tucci will take some home to his kids. Nobody makes those boys cakes. Rat boys, Nonie calls Nick's kids, like she's disappointed in them. Delinquents like cake too, I tell her. You be sure cake is all you're making them, Nonie says. Then she'll say she wasn't born yesterday, like anyone ever bothers me. I tell her no one does. They only look.

It's true. It's like I've got a beam out my eyes that backs people off. Now that I'm older, I've got a clear space around me I didn't have before. I wonder if that's like a future, or a place where a future will be.

Pale blue divinity sounds like a dress or a planet. Blue icing does look strange, like Martian food, unless I trim it, save out some white for a lattice over the top, or garlands or flowers. A decorated cake looks like a toy, and people do want it. I'm putting the icings away to keep them cold and I've got my whole face in the fridge, near the steaming icebox at the top. The sweat across my upper lip dries in a sudden tingle and then I hear someone at the door. The bell rings in a way I can tell is new.

Good thing or bad thing, I think.

Termite gets quiet.

"Who can *that* be," I say out loud, like a charm. Like we're in a TV show about a charming mother and her kid. We don't have a TV. Termite doesn't like those sounds. Back then, all those summers, Joey always had the TV on at the Tuccis', and Termite wouldn't even go inside. He liked to be moving, or by the river, under the cool of the bridge. There are two bridges, opposite sides of town, both spanning the river; the spiny one for cars, all metal ribs and rattles, and the stone one for trains, wide enough for four lines of track. Once they used all the tracks, Nonie says. Now only two are kept repaired, but two arches of the railroad bridge stand up in the river just as wide, and two more angle onto the land. The tunnel below is still as long and shady and deep. There used to be a road inside but now the road is broken, smashed to dirt and weeds and moss. It's cool in summer, and the tracks run overhead on their uphill slope to the rail yard. Termite likes the tunnel best. The echoes.

The doorbell rings again, twice. Somebody won't give up.

I push Termite's chair out past the dinette into the living room. I leave him sitting by the piano and look through the window in the front door. I see somebody. Brown suit coat and trousers, in this heat. Tie and button-down shirt. Glasses. I open the door and there's a man standing there with his briefcase in his arms, like he's about to hand it over to me. Not an old man. Thick lenses in the glasses, so his eyes look magnified. Owl eyes. White blond hair parted to the side under his hat. Fedora, like a banker's.

"Hello there," he says. "Hope it's not too early to stop by. I was hoping I could speak to—" He looks down at the papers he's got on top of the briefcase.

"My mother's not here," I say.

"—your aunt. It says here your aunt. You must be Lark."

"You're from Social Services," I say.

He nods. "Actually I live two streets over, moved in a week ago. I was on my way to work, so I thought I'd stop." He smiles in a nervous way.

"I didn't think Social Services was open on Sundays."

He looks blank for a minute. "Oh," he says. "Well. I'm new, so there's a lot to catch up on. I come and go. That's a good thing about these small towns. It's more informal. And you can walk to work. Anyway, I can. I suppose you can walk to the high school."

"I'm not at the high school. I take a secretarial course." I've got my hand on the door and I push it shut just a little.

He steps up closer and looks over my shoulder at Termite in his chair. "This is your brother? Termite. A nickname, I'd guess. What's his real name?"

"Terence," I lie. I always seem to start lying to these people real quick. Even if I don't have to.

"By the way, my name is Robert Stamble." He sticks his hand out at me from under the briefcase.

Stumble, Stamble, I think. And from that time on he's stumble, stammer, tumble, someone tripping in my head. Right away, I think he'd better leave. He thinks he means well and he doesn't know anything. I can smell it on him like a hint, like the Old Spice smell of his aftershave. I hate that smell. Dads wear it in Dadville. I look at him closer and see that he doesn't even look old

enough to be much of a dad. He's pale pink as the rims of a rabbit's eyes, and blue eyed behind his thick glasses. Hiding in his
suit.

"Nonie's not here," I say, "and she says the check we get from
Social Services is not enough to be harangued or bothered about.
If you want to make a home visit, you should arrange it with her."

"You know," he says, "we're very much in favor of in-home care
whenever possible, and we want to support you. There may be
ways we can help. Physical therapy. Equipment. A wheelchair."

"I do physical therapy with him," I say, "a nurse at the clinic
taught me. And he's got a wheelchair, a big heavy one. We keep it
in the closet. He doesn't like it, but we use it for his medical
appointments."

Stamble fumbles around, opens the briefcase, shuffles papers.
"Oh, yes."

"It's one of the chairs Alderson passed on to the county," I tell
him.

Alderson is the state hospital that closed two years ago, one
town over. They shipped the craziest loonies somewhere else and
let go the ones that were only taking up space.

"Of course." Stamble looks up at me.

"Social Services sent it when they said he had to go to the special school."

Stamble keeps on. "Still, don't you find it easier than—"

I get it. He's seen me pull Termite in the wagon. I do most
every day. The wagon is deep and safe, with high wooden slats for
sides, and long enough I can stretch Termite's legs out. It's like the
old wagons they used to haul ice or coal. It was in the basement of
this house when Nonie moved in. She says it's probably older than
she is. "Termite doesn't like the wheelchair," I repeat.

Stamble nods. "He's a child. He should have a smaller chair,
one his size. Something portable would be easier for you."

"Portable?" I think about that. Coming into port, like on a
boat. Termite, bobbing on the waves. I'm watching him through a
round window small as a plate. A porthole. We're coming up on

a pretty little town by the sea, and Stamble blink, blink, blinks. For a minute I think he's fooling with me, or maybe he's nervous. Where did they get him?

He goes on at me. "Child-sized. Not as heavy. Some of them fold. Easier to take in and out of an automobile, whatever."

"We don't have an automobile," I tell Stamble. I step back. "Anyway, he doesn't like the chair he already has."

"Maybe he needs a chance to get used to it, gradually of course. Does he mind the medical appointments?"

"No, not really. I wouldn't say he minds."

"Because if he associates a wheelchair only with something he doesn't like, you might change that by taking him to do something he does like—in the wheelchair."

I shift my weight and stand so he can't see behind me. Termite stays real quiet. If he knows when to be quiet, I don't know how they can say he doesn't know anything. "Maybe so," I tell Stamble. "I've got to go now. I've got a cake baking." I'm easing the door closed.

"Hot day for baking," he says. "Someone's birthday?"

I nod and smile through the narrow space that's left. "You can call Noreen," I say. "If you want to talk to her." I shut the door. The knob turns in my hand and I hear the click.

"Very good to meet you," I hear Stamble say from outside. "Please let me know if you need anything. I'll see what I can do about a more suitable chair." Then I hear his footsteps going away.

Termite has his head turned, his ear tilted toward me, and he doesn't move. I walk across the room to turn his chair back toward the kitchen and then I smell the cake, a sugary, toasted smell with a brown edge. "Oh no," I say, and move him back just enough to get the oven open, grab the layer pans with the hot pads. The cakes are a little too brown on top, but not bad.

I show him one. "It's fine," I tell him, "a tiny bit burnt, not so you'd taste." *You'd taste,* Termite says, *you'd taste.*

"Don't you worry," I tell him.

Nonie

The Social Services people marched right into my living room, their hearts all righteous. He was three or four. Evaluation, they said, services. Maybe an operation so he can get out of that chair. That's an idea, I said. Then he can scuttle himself out to the street to get hit, or down to the rail yard to fall and cut himself up, or eat that poison they set out for the dog packs. Is that what I need to worry about? They going to give me somebody to watch him every minute? No. They going to take him down to the rail yard to see those trains he spends the day listening for? They going to keep him from walking straight into one? They going to keep those sandlot kids from chucking rocks at him if they find him out by himself? They going to explain to him why those kids are so mean, why they'd treat him worse than an animal? No. The doctors in Cleveland said no promises. That part I believed. An exploratory, they said, see the extent of the damage. Then they did tests, advised against "further trauma," told me to take him home. Minimally hydrocephalic, they said, and visually impaired. No telling what he would ever know or understand. And his spine hadn't closed right; he would never walk. The social worker was sorry. She said we could sign up for ADC support, though it wasn't much, or find an institution to take him if I couldn't manage. Aid to Dependent Children—what aid? There he sat in his chair the whole time she was talking, his pillows bigger than he was, straining to hold his head up. Eyes hard to the side, looking and looking like he does.

Lark will start in about how he doesn't like the special school, he doesn't like the bus, he wants to be here. Maybe you'd like me to quit my job, I tell her, so I can watch over him every minute.

Then so we're not out in the street over the mortgage and your school fees, maybe you'd like to take my place at Charlie's. Just go ahead and quit Barker's two years before you get your diploma, quit and bring in the money we've got to have. You for sure could do it as well as me with these ugly feet of mine, and we'd be in fine shape then. I try to tell her: Who takes care of him when I'm gone if you've got nothing but Charlie's?

She's got no way to better anything but get that diploma and a good secretarial job, same as I told her from years ago. That boy doesn't know where he is, but he sure would wonder if he was down in the rail yard getting beat with a stick, same as they beat those stray dogs they find out away from the pack. He's been happy enough in that chair ever since I put him there and he's not got any pain in those legs. I'm thankful the doctors let him alone. What would he think in a hospital with them doing things and making him hurt, when he's hardly been out of this house except to the river or up and down Main Street in the wagon? Who says he wants to walk around? Who says he's missing something? What's so great about walking around on this earth, I wish someone would tell me. Social Services going to fix that, make it someplace a boy like him can walk around?

Charlie can tell when I get to thinking about it. He's got his back to me, cleaning the grill, but he looks over at me. "You feeling all right, Noreen?"

The air seems hard to breathe, even in the restaurant. The heat presses right up against the big window, and the air conditioner over the door is gasping. "They might be right about that storm coming tomorrow," I tell him. "My joints are paining me."

"Supposed to drop by forty degrees, cool off and blow hard. Rain in sheets, two, three days, starting this evening. They say half the town will flood. If they're wrong, all that chili I made today will take up a lot of freezer space. Once the rain starts, we'll have the city rescue workers in here, and the state people if they call them in. Noreen, you want to leave early?"

"Think I will. The river is high. The alley will flood if it's a major storm. It's not like I haven't been through it before."

"It's what comes of living over there in the flood plain," Charlie comments. "Want me to drive you?"

"You're the only one here. I'll walk. I feel like a walk, unless Elise feels like a drive. Elise, you on break?"

She nods. "I am, and I'm not going back to that store for a full hour. That idiot girl of mine was late coming in and she owes me."

Charlie's in favor. "Fine. Why not bring everyone back here for dinner? I'll wait table, treat you like prize customers."

"Not tonight. I'll take some chili, and what's left of the buttermilk chicken. Despite your faults, Charlie, you're not a bad cook. Must be what keeps me around. I've got to be going."

Charlie reaches over, touches the face of the watch he gave me. It's a strong, delicate watch, just the width of his big forefinger. He moves the band on my wrist, pressing and caressing at once. He took me to a jeweler to have it fitted just right, so it moves but doesn't slide. "Right, it's Sunday. You'll be expecting Nick the gardener, coming by to fix things up. Mows on Sundays, doesn't he? He takes an interest, does Nick." Charlie shoots a glance at Elise, trolling for an ally, but Elise looks determinedly out the plate-glass window onto Main Street.

"Nick? I don't know what I would have done all these years without Nick, you being as occupied as you are. He's like my brother."

"I didn't say he takes an interest in you."

"Oh. You think he takes an interest in Lark? Well, Nick's not blind, but he's not stupid either. That's just you, Charlie, standing guard." Then I ask Elise, "How can I help being fond of him?"

She shrugs, like it's a real question.

Charlie keeps on. "I've said it before. They all take an interest in Lark. The Tucci boys, and Nick is one of them, have run through a portion of the available girls and women in Winfield.

Call it standing guard if you like. They're family and not family, and they're practically on top of you, all these years. That's shaky territory, with those boys the ages they are."

"It's all shaky territory. Show me territory anywhere around here that's not shaky."

At the counter, Elise clears her throat and nods toward the plate-glass window. Sure enough, here comes Gladdy, in her summer hat. She has the look of a sparrow wearing a plate on its head, bobbing along in a quick step. "Here we are," I tell Charlie. "I rest my case."

The door opens and the ring of the bell puts me in mind of Termite. One more sound that can't tell what it means.

"Afternoon, Gladdy," Elise says. "Hot enough out there for you?"

She waits a moment, to get her breath. Once in a while I surprise myself and understand why Charlie puts up with her, why we all put up with one another. But Gladdy, as always, can be relied on to scuttle sentiment.

"It's just fine," she says. "I prefer the heat. Open windows and a cross draft are all anyone needs. Not that expensive air-conditioning that is so loud and gives a person bronchitis."

Elise lights a cigarette. "You have bronchitis?"

Gladdy ignores her, but waves a hand in front of her face as though to shoo flies. She stands back and regards Charlie. "I noticed it again, Charlie. I can see the glass in that big plate window move when I walk past on the street. I keep telling you it needs tightening. One of these days it's going to crack straight across."

He smiles at her. "It's not the glass, Mother. It's you, moving the world."

"Very funny. But we don't have hundreds of dollars to replace that glass. Maybe a thousand dollars."

"She's right," I tell Charlie, standing under the wheeze of the air conditioner. "We don't have a thousand dollars."

"And there are reasons why," Gladdy shoots back.

Then I'm out the door and the heat is like a wave, even this late in the afternoon. I look back through the window and see Elise putting out her cigarette, getting up to follow me. Gladdy is trailing Charlie back into the kitchen, chirping away.

By the time I get to Elise's blue Ford, she's beside me, unlocking the passenger door, and we're cranking down the windows, hauling both heavy doors open.

"Wait," Elise says.

She's of the opinion cars have to be aired out in the heat, that various chemicals in the upholstery and floor mats and cushioned ceiling can harm a person when the air in a car is closed and hot. We stand here, leaning on the doors. Maybe Elise is right. I can feel hot air boiling out of the car like invisible foam.

"Well," I tell her, "at least we entertain you."

"That you do." She raises her penciled brows at me. "Gladdy was just saying how her leather watchband has been good enough for her all these years. Funny how there's never a need to worry about being hard on Charlie. Gladdy will always do it for you."

"True love," I say, "you can't beat it. You and I, now, we have to settle for life in general being hard on us."

"We can't complain," Elise says, and smiles. "You got the time, Noreen?"

"I do and I don't," I tell her. She's not really asking. It's a phrase she repeats in front of Gladdy, to remind her of a sore point. My watch belonged to Charlie's grandmother, his father's mother. She gave Charlie the watch when he was twelve, before she died—she adored him and had the sense never to like Gladdy. Gladdy can't abide the fact Charlie gave me a Fitzgibbon heirloom. He found a jeweler in Bellington to refurbish it with a flexible platinum band and says it was worth every penny. The emerald-cut diamonds beside the rectangular face are small but perfect. Guardians of our numbers, he calls them. I won't marry him until Gladdy dies, and I won't have him moving in with us either. Charlie says we're on my time, I'm in charge. He loves the watch and he loves me wearing it. The mother-of-pearl face glows in the dark just slightly, and he checks it, evenings in my bed, the nights Lark is at Barker Secretarial. He comes over and bathes Termite, puts him to bed, turns on the radio. Charlie keeps it tuned to a classical station, so Termite isn't agitated by words. Termite likes music without words, and he falls asleep surrounded. Then Charlie and I have time. The good hour, Charlie calls it. He closes his big hand around the watch and my wrist, firm and warm, like he's saved this for me, and he has. All these years. I'm standing here with Elise, and something quickens, flickers, at the memory of his hand in me. I've been married. It wasn't like this. We still want each other, we're practiced, it all works. Then he's up and gone before Lark gets home. We're not hiding anything, but it's our privacy, and it's how I want it.

Elise cuts me a glance. "I do believe I'm driving you straight to my place for a cold beer, Noreen. You seem to need one, and you won't get it at home. Seems to me you could relax your policy. How long is it now since you divorced the second husband, that high-flying alcoholic? Seventeen years?"

"Billy Onslow's drinking was almost the least of it," I tell her, "but I don't fault him. We were married seven months, but he stood in for me for a lot of years, watching over Lola." I rest the bag of food on the sidewalk. Elise will need to light herself another cigarette.

She chuckles and shakes her head. "Poor Lola, gone so long and still the elephant in the room. She got what she wanted, in a way. Well out of it and still pulling the strings."

"There aren't any strings," I tell Elise. "There's just what happened."

"There's Lark," Elise says, "and there's Termite."

She offers me a cigarette and I take it. We stand here smoking, adjusting to the heat.

. . .

Charlie will say how strange it is I lit out of here so fast without him, only to move back years later, after all that happened, even closer to the tracks and the river and the skinny houses of Polish Town. Well, a house on a grass alley two streets from the rail yard was what I could afford, and lucky to have it. Gladdy thought it was where I belonged, of course. When I was nineteen and Charlie's father died, she had a prime excuse for handing everything over to Charlie. The husband she'd driven to his grave was gone, and the son inherited all, including Gladdy. Your first responsibility is the business, she told him. Without your father, we could lose everything. You'll regret knowing such a girl. Don't make it a permanent mistake. Think of your religion, she kept saying. And you know, he did. He's Catholic to his bones, while it's all show with Gladdy. What if Noreen converted, he'd say, to watch his mother blanch. Charlie knew I wasn't about to take up Catholicism, but he didn't know I'd leave him.

I worked full-time at Murphy's Five & Ten the two years after high school, promoted to floor supervisor, learning bookkeeping. I'd saved money and I was going to marry Charlie or else. We need to wait, he said. How long? I asked. Gladdy will live forever. He called me unfeeling—his father had dropped dead a month before—but I was hell-bent. It was Gladdy or me; he had to choose. She's my mother, he kept saying, like that was sacred. Not to me. I'd pretty much raised myself and Lola. We'd done without mothering, and I thought it was time Charlie did. I knew a girl who had a cousin in Atlanta, so I packed two suitcases and rode out of town on the bus. Lola begged me not to go, and then she begged to come with me. I grew up here, I told her, you'll have to do the same. And don't even think of coming to find me until you've graduated high school.

I walked out on all of them. I rode buses three days and nights, washing my face in filthy restrooms, stepping over families asleep in the depots. It was 1936, hard times, but I felt free, almost grateful to Charlie. The cousin rented me a room and I got a job as a window dresser at Lowman's Department Store in Atlanta, then as a waitress in the store restaurant, a big place always busy with shoppers and businessmen. I got to know an insurance executive who took lunch and dinner at my station nearly every day. His wife had died the year before, and his two little boys a decade earlier, the same week, of diphtheria. It's not too late, I thought, I'll marry him and give him children. We'll live in his brick house with the floating staircase and have babies. But I couldn't. Doctors told me I never would. All Charlie's careful timing and confession and prayers had been needless: I laughed till I cried, and they were the last tears I shed over it, then to now. Barren, they called it in those days. Maybe so, but barren ground is strong, clear ground.

I left the husband after four years. He'd met a nice woman his own age and I gave them my blessing. Bad things had happened to him, and I didn't want to keep being one of them. He said I'd helped him through a difficult time and he paid a year's rent on my new apartment. The Depression was over. I left with my clothes and got my old job back at the restaurant. A lot of places folded, but Lowman's stayed open. War had started in Europe. The city seemed alive again, nervous and edgy; the restaurant was busy and hired more staff. Then Charlie showed up, with Lola outside in his car. She was out of control, he said. I was her sister. What were we going to do? He said it just like that—like we were family. And I knew we were.

Gladdy would have been happy if Charlie had married a nice Catholic girl and moved her in with them to do whatever Gladdy said. Just to spite her, or maybe to spite himself, Charlie didn't. His heart murmur kept him out of the service, at home with Gladdy and the business. We weren't in touch, but Lola wrote to me every month, and I answered. When our father died, I sent flowers. Our mother got sick. Lola, the two years after she graduated high school, took care of her alone. I sent money to support them, but I wasn't going back, not even for the funeral. A few days after, the house burned. People said Lola had thrown a lit match onto the newspapers by the stove, that the house burned so hot she must have poured kerosene from one room to another. She turned up at Charlie's lunch counter with her suitcase while the sirens were still blaring. Nonie's left her husband, she told Charlie, and she could take him to me. He asked about the fire and she said it was the only way to burn up the smell of the sickbed, all the beds. Charlie knew he'd better get her out of town while everyone was occupied. Back then, Gladdy actually worked in the restaurant. For once, Charlie told her he had to go. He put Lola in the car and drove, pulling over to sleep when he had to. Lowman's was a city block, an Atlanta landmark in those days, easy to find, and the restaurant was a third of the first floor. There Charlie was, sitting at a table by the window, where he could see his car and Lola in it.

I'd been a duty-bound insurance executive's wife, answering expectations and reading *Collier's* in bed afterward, but I was only twenty-four. Being in the same room as Charlie after so long was like opening a furnace door. I'll never forget his face and his dark eyes as I walked over to him in my waitress uniform and red chiffon apron. We didn't know it, but except for the apron and a few major interruptions, we were looking at the rest of our lives. He pulled me against him and held me and we looked into the street at Lola looking back at us, her face framed in the window of Charlie's black car. She knew she'd accomplished something I never could: him standing there. You don't need to worry, I told Charlie. She's got what she wanted and she's not going anywhere.

My shift ended an hour later and I took them to my apartment. Lola fell asleep on the sofa before I could even get a meal cooked. Charlie and I locked the bedroom against her, but we needn't have bothered. She slept for three days. Charlie drove me to my Lowman's shifts and looked for a job, but it was Lola who found him work, as a bouncer at Onslow's, a club that took her on as a cigarette girl and backup singer. She had sheet music in her suitcase, and a beaded dress like the ones she'd seen in magazines. The Irish mob was big business, and so were the Italians and their gin joints. Billy Onslow was snug with both, and he owned establishments in Atlanta and Louisville. He was a big deal then, a bruiser musician in a sharkskin coat, pulling strings. I later found he dealt in interstate liquor transport and high-class call girls, but at the time I thought, fine, he can play piano for Lola. Soon enough his headliner was hospitalized after her hoodlum boyfriend broke her jaw, and Lola stepped in. She stopped singing backup and rehearsed afternoons like a regular career girl. She loved Atlanta, she bought clothes, she wanted Charlie and me to move to a bigger apartment with her, and I was thinking it over. I'd finish a dinner shift at Lowman's and get to the club by ten, sitting there in a cream silk sheath dress and pearls while Charlie worked the door. Billy Onslow would come by and sit with me before Lola's set, always very polite, courtly, like he was making sure the staff knew I was his guest and men knew not to approach me. He was almost thirty years older than Lola, but very different from my middle-aged ex-husband—Billy Onslow had certainly never sold insurance. I tried to give the impression I was watching over Lola. He'd listen, but one night he looked at me dead on. "I don't usually meddle with the talent," he told me, "but let's not kid ourselves about your sister."

Just then there was some commotion—you could say Onslow's catered to a flamboyant clientele—and he got up and left. He could have meant any number of things, I told myself. That he was her lover, or had been. Or he was her lover and she had other lovers. Or worse, she was dabbling in entertainments the musicians enjoyed, coke or goofballs or junk. Onslow overlooked recreational use, Charlie had told me, he could hardly prevent it and was known to indulge himself, but he wouldn't employ anyone who was strung out. Maybe he'd just meant no one could watch over Lola, that the whole idea was ridiculous, that I was ridiculous, a Lowman's waitress in pearls. Yes, that was it. I was ridiculous.

It was 1941. We'd been living together six months, Lola in her makeshift room, Charlie and me in ours, coming and going together or separately, the little family Lola had finally made. We never referred to Winfield or Gladdy or the restaurant, we were together, and I suddenly wondered why Charlie had never mentioned getting married. Why I'd never mentioned it, why it had never even occurred to me. Why Lola slept so soundly on that couch behind the French screen she'd set up, the closet in the one bedroom overflowing with her dresses and lingerie. She'd bought me a big new bottle of my perfume with her first paycheck because she'd used so much of it. We sat at the same vanity at different times of day, combing our hair, putting on makeup, touching a crystal stopper from the same perfume bottle to our throats and ears and shoulders. Charlie smelled of both of us. So did the sheets of the bed. Here at the club there was a bed in Lola's dressing room, and a chiffonier and a little sink. Charlie and she shared the same hours, like it was part of Charlie's job, while at home she was just the little sister.

I sat at the bar, seeing Lola's younger face in the dark bedroom of our house she'd burned down in Winfield, her eyes as close as the edge of the bed, Charlie actually inside me as we worked our way to the swooning novena we'd perfected. Good, I'd thought then, watch us, I won't stop, I won't let you take this from me. I'd closed my eyes against her then, just as I'd closed them now. It was midnight in Atlanta. Billy Onslow stood leaning against the wall on the opposite side of the big room, watching me. I knew he was in it with me, with us. He'd always deferred to me, shown me courtesies: he thought I was respectable and hardworking. He thought the same of himself, strange as that seems, despite his discreet alcoholism and other habits. He'd delivered his news on purpose, to pull me in with him and to change the lay of the cards. Billy was a master at reading everyone's hand before they could. He knew exactly what I was realizing and how fast it would fall into place, and he waited for me to look at him. I did, and he moved toward me. His wet hazel eyes shone like glass. My dress felt hot against my thighs, and every pearl in the necklace I'd

saved so long to buy burned on my neck like a match head. He
could feel me in his hands already. He was the one man who ever
turned full force from Lola to me, who rejected her when he could
have had her. Later, even after I'd left him, he took care of Lola
when I couldn't.

That was a long time ago, when I wore that dress and those
pearls.

Billy lived above the club. I went upstairs with him that night.
I remember those hours, in rooms full of velvet furniture and
racks of the showy costumes his dancers wore, file cabinets and
piles of papers, and his bed that was big enough for four people.
He was knowledgeable, Billy was, he could be gentle, and he used
my feelings to surprise both of us. I didn't sleep, and the next day,
while Lola was at rehearsal, I went back to the apartment and told
Charlie to get out. I can't explain my state of mind. Charlie had
been mine from the time I was a child myself. I thought he'd cho-
sen me, was restored to me, but Lola had lit the fire that brought
him, and she'd seduced or confused him into staying. He was dev-
astated that I knew what he'd done and couldn't stop doing, but it
was only my knowing that allowed him to end it. I didn't tell him
to leave town. He exiled himself, drove back to Winfield and his
whole favored-son routine without even saying good-bye to Lola.

When I take stock now, I think to myself, I have Charlie and
Elise and Nick. I couldn't have cared for these children without
their help. It took time to come back to Charlie, but I love him
still after thirty years, and I like having my own house, separate
from his drama with Gladdy. I really seldom think of Lola now.
Except for the questions Lark used to ask and stopped asking, it's
over and done, it's finished. Like Elise says, there's Lark and there's
Termite. These children have got nothing to do with Lola, except
they came through her to get to me. The one has stood on her
own two feet since she was barely up to my elbow, and the other is
happy with a piece of dry-cleaner bag a yard long and a few inches
across.

Termite

He sees through the blue and it goes away, he sees through the blue and it goes away again. He breathes, blowing just high. The blue moves but not too much, the blue moves and stays blue and moves. He can see into the sky where there are no shapes. The shapes that move around him are big, colliding and joining and going apart. They're the warm feel of what he hears and smells next to him, of those who hold and move and touch and lift him, saying these curls get so tangled, wipe off his hands, Lark, there's Termite. He sings back to keep them away or draw them near. That's all he'll say, he won't tell and tell. Lark bends over him and her hair falls along his neck and shoulders, her hair moves and breathes over his back and chest in a dark curtain that falls and falls. Her hair smells of flowers that have dried, like the handful of rose petals he grasped until they were soft and damp. Lark names the flowers and he says the sounds but the sounds are not the flowers. The flower is the shape so close he sees it still enough to look, blue like that, long and tall, each flared tongue with its own dark eye. Then the shape moves and the flower is too close or too far. The shape becomes its colors but he feels Lark touch it to his face and lips like a weightless velvet scrap. The flower moves and blurs and smears, he looks away to stop it disappearing. Pictures that touch him move and change, they lift and turn, stutter their edges and blur into one another. Their colors fall apart and are never still long enough for him to see, but the pictures inside him hold still. Their gray shades are sharp and clear and let him see, flat as the pages of books Lark holds near his eyes. The books are colors that run and shine but the pictures inside him stay and never blur. They might say one color or two, bright colors that shine in the gray like jewels. He sees them when the sounds of the train or the pounding of rain flies all around him. The pictures move, revealed as though a curtain slowly lifts, moving as Lark's hair might move, parting and falling away until the picture is still and complete. The pictures tell their story that repeats and repeats again and stays inside him until it ends. He sees them without trying. It's how Lark sees everything, everywhere they go. She couldn't walk and run so fast and be so sure through his moving colors, his dark that blurs. But she can't hear what he hears. He listens hard to tell. She never knows what's coming but he can't say and say.

Lark gives him the glass moon man that smells of soap. Inside the hole behind the face there's a trapped sweet smell no one can wash. Lark's fingers are long and smooth. They come and go.

Lark says feel your soft blue shirt want to wear this? She says hold the crayon it's green as grass is green. She says listen to the radio even if it's not so loud as you like. She says eat your toast while it's hot and she gives him toast, thick and warm and buttery in his hand with the blue jam on the knife like the farmer's wife. The knife comes and goes across the plates. The table holds the pouring and crashing and banging while Nonie walks hard and fast in and out of the kitchen in her white shoes. Her legs swish every step and he can feel her stepping room to room to room. No matter where she is he can hear and he puts his head on the table to hear the sound alone through the wood without all the other sounds. But she picks him up, one strong arm around his chest and the other bent for the seat under him she calls his throne. They move fast, thudding across the floor out the door onto the ground where the sound goes hollow and deep.

The porch door bangs.

Sudden morning air floats low to the ground amid the small houses like fragrant evaporating mist, a cool bath of dew and shadow and damp honeysuckle scent. He gasps and hears the sharp grass under them move its fibrous roots. Lark has brought his chair but he leans far back in Nonie's arms to look and look into the dense white sky. Heat will climb down in wisps and drifts, losing itself in pieces until it falls in gathered folds, pressing and pressing to hold the river still. Far up the heat turns and moves like a big animal trying to rouse. All the while he can hear Elise's car roll its big wheels closer until it turns roaring into the alley but Nonie puts him in his chair. She brushes his hair back with her two broad hands while the car throbs in the narrow tracks of the alley, crushing gravel to rattles and slides and bleating loud. He calls and calls and he wants to go but Nonie goes. Under the motor sound he hears the car take her weight, a sigh before the door slams. The car roars away down the stones onto the smooth pavement and goes until it's gone. There's a shape in the air where the car was. He feels the shape hold still before it begins to end. Slowly the air comes back. The grass begins small sounds. *The ground under the wheels goes hard and soft. Lark pulls him to the trains in the wagon and the rail yard is silent. Each stopped train is a deep still weight. Water trickles in the ditch where the dogs drink. They snap their jaws in the heat and Lark throws stones to make them run. They skim their shadows across weeds and broken pavement, loping the slant to the tipple where they slink and watch. Lark gives him his ribbon to hold. She knows which train will clank and rumble, jerking back before it smashes loud. He blows on the ribbon, moving the blue, and the train begins to move. Lark is quick and strong and she pulls the wagon fast, running beside the roar that clacks and smashes and races smooth. A dark rush spreads and moves and holds them, rattling inside them and tunneling deep, leaving and roaring, pushing them back and back. The boxcars go faster and begin to flash, moving their heavy shapes. The closed doors glint and the open ones are moving holes, dark in the rattling noise. Lark runs closer, harder, and the roar begins to make the shape, long and deep like the roll of the river, shaking round and wide. The picture inside him opens in gray shades, closer and sharper until each still line and curve has its own pale sound and the lines and shapes can turn and move. He lets go of the blue to tell and say and the train takes and takes it, whistling loud, bleating and disappearing into the trees. The train shrieks and the narrow bitter smoke is a scar that whispers and falls, pouring away across the railroad bridge, over the river and on.*

Lark stops running and sits on the ground. She leans against the wagon and her breath moves the wooden slats. He listens until she's quiet. The hot rails hum and each cinder thrown into the wagon is a small rock spark. The little rocks are warm.

Termite, Lark says. I'll fix the radio. Don't worry.

Here's your ribbon, Lark says.

She wraps the blue around his wrist. He moves it to his face, just above his eyes, but he doesn't look.

Mow the grass, Lark says. Big storm they talk about.

He waits. Soon she'll go.

She says, don't think you're going to sit out here in the rain with lightning flashing all around you.

He holds still, listening. Far down the alley where the gravel meets the street, he hears the orange cat paw forward on its ragged paws. Away down the alley across from Tuccis' house the ragged orange cat is stepping careful, dragging its belly along the stones under the lilacs. The cat waits then for Lark to go. The cat waits low and long where no one sees and the growl in its belly thrums deeper. The cat knows Lark will throw a stick or a handful of gravel that lands like stinging rain.

Termite, Lark says.

She puts her face close to his, her eyes against his eyes. Lark's brown eyes are stirred like the river when the river is milky with rain. She knows he can see if she's very close but he doesn't look now, he doesn't try, he doesn't want her to stay.

She says, you ring the bell if you want anything.

He wants to hear the train. Far off the train's bell sound is long and wide and dark as the shade under the railroad bridge. The bridge goes over the river and the trains pour over top. He wants to feel the roar. *Lark and the Tuccis take him through the rail yard on the way to the river, between the Polish boys and the ditch. The*

*boys have got a snarling something in the ditch with their sticks and
Lark says they're worse than the dogs, cornering one thing or another,
beating and hitting until a dog sounds like a cat and a farmer's wife
with a carving knife. Joey and Solly fight the boys and Zeke stays in
the wagon. Lark is never scared. Joey and Solly roll in the dirt
punching and grunting with the Polish boys from Lumber Street and
Zeke throws stones behind.*

Zeke, hold Termite tight. Here's a faster ride.

*And they're riding faster into the cool where the arched tunnel
walls are furry. The leaves move up and down the rock and the ivy is
shadows on the curve above. No sky it's a stone sky Termite that's why
it's gray. Beside them the river is the only sound until Joey and Solly
burst out yelling from the bushes.*

*So you've got a bloody lip no call to yell like a banshee. Look Ter-
mite, a scrape like a star on his chest. Solly, wash off in the water and
cover that up with your shirt. If Noreen sees it she'll know you've been
fighting. You cold, Termite? Look, we'll make a fire on the dirt where
no weeds can catch. Zeke, no more telling about fires or fights and
you can have marshmallows. We only need some sticks for Joey to
sharpen, he loves his knife so much.*

Termite, look how the fire leaps up, see how warm?

*Doesn't matter if it rains the river is full of rain. We could ride the
river all the way through Winfield past Parkersburg to Sophia and
Shady Spring, past Pulaski and Mount Airy. We could ride the train
to Charleston straight through to Charlotte and Jacksonville, clear to
Florida, Termite, to the ocean. Like our seashells I show you, like
that water sound inside them, all spread out for miles, bigger than a
country, bigger than the air you watch through your ribbons.* Nonie
cuts ribbons from the blue plastic bags that cover her uniforms
three at a time. Sometimes her uniforms hang in Elise's car in the
sun and the blue is warm. Nonie works at Charlie's and she
doesn't go to the river. She says the rail yard is near deserted now
and no place for them to be. But there are no boys anymore at the
rail yard, no sounds in the ditch, only empty trains passing south
and sometimes a man in a boxcar throwing bottles out. Not at

you Termite, tramps ride the trains and sometimes they clean house. Lark takes him close to the empty boxcars on the overgrown sidings and lets him touch the hard broad sides of the cars from the wagon. Blocks of silence shift behind the huge doors, trapped inside, too big to turn or rest. The sides of the metal cars are grainy with rust and warm with banked heat even in the morning. Termite feels their low steel drone in his fingertips, a drunken stir like hundreds of stunned insects warmed and beginning to move. But the cars don't move; they're hot and cold and day and night and he stays still to hear them. Lark says there were coal cars, long flatbed cars filled at the tipple no one uses anymore, now the mines have closed. The wooden boxcars breathe, she says. They carried animals and have skinny windows too high for cattle and pigs to see out. Loud wind poured through, cooling chickens in cages so small the hens couldn't move and so they went to sleep. That was a long time ago. Now the boxcars only wait or move empty to bigger towns. The freights pour through without stopping and Lark moves him far back to watch. Once a bottle thrown from a train smashed at his feet, brief as bells in the roar. A mean drunk, Lark said, not like most of them, old men riding and drinking. They don't bother us, Lark says. It's the trains that are fierce, rumbling their rattling music to shake the ground, crossing the river and leaving the town, leaving and leaving. At night the long low whistles sound like windy cries, moist with dew and darkness. Nonie doesn't know, she doesn't hear. She comes home and takes off her shoes and says she'd give anything. *At the special school the teacher tells him to hold still. She holds his hands tight shut and says to nod his head to the music. The farmer in the dell. She puts the straps around him in the chair with wheels, across his front and his chest.*

    There. You're nice and safe and sitting as straight as you can.

    The Victrola scratches out the song and the song comes to the end. There that's once.

    She starts it again. It's Lark's song not her song. He moves his wrist to sound the bell on his chair but there's no bell and this is not his chair. The bus will come a long time after lunch to take him home. He likes the bus and its big noise even if he's the only one the driver carries up the steps. The driver belts him into his seat and he can lean his head on the window. Footsteps pound heavy while the other kids climb on and the voices go high and low. The driver starts the engine and says Quiet, quiet now, while the special bus gets quiet. The long low growl of the bus can start then, and the thrum and shaking. The whole floor trembles like an animal under its skin and the sound is warm and deep, pouring into him through the vibrating frame of his seat and the silver rim of the window. The bus stops at railroad crossings and shudders, swings the big doors open on their giant hinges. There's a whoosh and flap like metal wings slapping out, then in. He sits still to feel it all at once, breathing when the bus breathes. The bus is a long hard shape like the tunnel under the railroad bridge, but the bus is from the school. The bus goes to the school and comes from the school where the woman holds on to his hands.

Did you listen close that time? Now we're going to clap.

She reaches for him and he pulls away. The lights on the ceiling are tubes that flicker when he blinks. She grabs his hands hard and pulls his face to hers. She smells hard and clean but there's another smell, small and curled and crumbling in her mouth where her words come out.

I'm here in front of you, see? Look at me. People? I need an aide. You, please assist. Stand behind him and keep his head stationary. Both hands. Gentle but firm.

The music goes again and the hands beside his eyes are fat and damp, his head held fast in the cleft of a pillowy white chest. He can't move and his breath gets fast and hard. He reaches, trying to go, his fingers going fast. The teacher holds his arms and jerks them once twice three times and smashes his hands together. The sound stings and cuts and she grasps him hard, counting. His fingers race and his heart pounds and he hears the dull alarmed thud of a heartbeat in the back of his head. A sound keens out of him, a sound to push her back, and he goes into the sound. Then there are cold cloths on his head and his stinging wrists and his chair is pushed to the window. The needle of the Victrola bumps and bumps in air.

Stronger than he looks. Let him sit quiet if he will. Let him sit.

The smashed air swirls all around him and the straps of the chair let him lean forward just enough to touch the window with his forehead. Colors and shapes surface through the pocked glass. The yellow form of the bus sits like a loaf-shaped blob on pulsing blacktop. The black tilts toward him in a sidelong square and the hot tar surface seethes in the heat, whining deep in his head like an insect he hears through a pin. He breathes Lark's name inside himself where only she can hear and the hard black shape lies down. Now he stays still and waits for the bus to move.

Termite, Lark says.

I'm going back in, Lark says.

The ragged cat drags its belly across where the grass is short and the stones are sharp, under the lilacs that have no flowers. The flower smell is gone and the white falls off the trees. Seeds, Lark says, little seeds with parachutes to fly them, Termite, all in your hair, and she runs her fingers through his hair, saying how long and how pretty. He wants the grass long and strong, sounding whispers when it moves, but the mower cuts it. The mower cuts and cuts like a yowling knife. He hears the mower cutting and smells the grass pouring out all over the ground, the green stain so sharp and wet it spills and spills. The mower cuts everything away and Nick Tucci follows the mower, cutting and cutting while the orange cat growls low to move its soft parts across the chipped sharp stones. Deep under the lilacs where no one sees, the orange cat waits for the roar to stop.

North Chungchong Province, South Korea

JULY 26, 1950

Corporal Robert Leavitt
24th Infantry Division

You'll be safe here. Leavitt turns toward the tunnel and thinks the words the instant he hears the planes, but he's at the edge of the crowd with the boy in one clinched arm when the sky opens up. He's shouting to run for the tunnels in English and faultless Korean, to run for the cover of the railroad bridges, but no one hears over the *ack-ack* of multiple fusillade raining down on them. There are three planes or four, American F-80 jets whose swooping first pass cuts down straight rows of women and old men with kids in their arms. The strafing has them in a death grid as precise as a checkerboard, and the column of hundreds scatters. His men, lined up single file to the left of the Koreans, have the best chance; most run away from the tracks, but some sprint for the trench of the creek bed on the other side. Refugees hemmed in by the press of the crowd die first; they die on the tracks and the gravel, they die in the creek. Others crouch against the sloping banks in shallow water until the planes pull off to circle for another pass. The unencumbered, most of them men, run for the fields and distant foothills. Those with children, and the women—nearly all the women have children, one or two or three, and some a babe in arms—follow him, racing for the cover of the double railway bridge just ahead. The children are screaming. Leavitt is running with them. He's thrown down his rifle and he's holding the girl, lifting her off her feet; he has her in one arm and the boy in the other; she grips the old woman against her, dragging her; Leavitt is carrying them all. They make the cover of the tunnel as the planes open up again, flying a final pass before they lift away. Standing with his back to the tunnel entrance, shielding them from the crowd surging in all around them, he sets the girl on her feet and looks her in the face. She's not injured; none of them are. They're safe; he can leave them here. In the din of wailing and uproar, they're silent. More and more refugees pour in behind them, shoving and screaming, bleeding. The girl looks at him, motionless, her stunned eyes flaring.

"You'll be safe here," Leavitt tells her in Korean, "stay low, move in deeper." He gestures to the girl, the sister. She had to be the sister, her pelvis no wider than Leavitt's two hands. He gives her the boy and pushes them after the old woman, but she stands there, frozen. Instinctively, he shields her with his stance and repeats the order. He has to get back to his men, see who's left, find Tompkins and the radio. Command is disorganized and communication faulty; directly engaged forces may interpret the strafing as evidence there are infiltrators among the refugees. Leavitt knows it was another bloody mistake born of inept confusion and he's furious, he's turning away to find Tompkins and radio command, he's about to turn away.

When he's hit he falls to his knees like a man in awe, doesn't feel himself take the girl with him, pitching forward to cover her with his body. She throws the child from her as she goes down; Leavitt sees the boy fly from them in slow, pillowed suspension but feels only the disjunct lurching of his own body as the bullets make impact. Flames rip into his legs and hips like staccato blades and explode in one burst. They've shot him from behind, the stupid fools, his own men or the jumpy troops dug in farther back, fanned out in their trenches at two-hundred-yard intervals. Spooked by noise, panicked, reading the ricochet of their own rifle fire off the scarred concrete walls of the tunnels, they've shot the hell out of him, the fucking idiots, the babies. Tompkins has the radio. Fucking Tompkins, revved up full tilt twenty-four hours a day like the war is a barroom brawl and now where is he? *Cease firing! This is not enemy! Repeat. This is not enemy!* The words bleed through like interference, hurled fast and hard through his head in Tompkins' angry voice. There's shouting, screaming, crescendos of wailing, a wall of sound.

Abruptly, a shutter falls. Sounds diminish and recede. What and why does it matter. Like an invited guest, he pulls deep inside, poured through himself like water. Colors flash past as though he really sees them, but these colors can't be real, they're too vivid and pulsing, turning in and out of one another like cells dividing. He hurtles through them, pummeled by his own heart. He's dreaming but he's intensely awake. If death is this brilliant slide, this high, fine music felt as pure vibration, this plunging float in wind and silence, it's not so bad. They were so afraid and enraged, all the armies of boys and men: if the brass could only bottle this and give the troops a taste, they'd have a lot of heroes. He moves forward, glimpsing his jumbled past amid jagged vestiges of the present, all of it intermingled as though equally important and alive. Nothing is peripheral; it's sensual, simultaneous. His chest floods with warmth and he sees his mother on the floor of the grocery in Philly, her eyes blank and still before he shut them. He's touching his mother's face but he sees the Korean girl looking at him, waiting for him in the crowd on the tracks. The sightless boy on her back tilts his head, listening to the sky. *Mother may I, mother me.* Words he said to Lola when she tried to pull rank, be the older woman who advised and directed, who liked him to ask how to touch her. He already knew and was touching her. Her eyes as she watched him, blue, bright with tears. The dark, nearly black eyes of the Korean girl, drawing him into the crowd to give him the boy. The images distort, detach from meaning like puzzle pieces with heightened colors. The colors loosen, coalesce into glowing brilliance, pull him into shards of light that are fine as rain. He's flying in bright silence. The light grows whiter and hotter, unbearably hot.

Then, like a parcel dumped off a truck, he's in the tunnel, cold and sweating. The heat and light are in his head and the pain shifts, yawns, opens wide and tugs at him like a mouth. There are scattered bursts of fire. American forces are shooting sporadically to keep everyone inside, keep them from fleeing or retrieving the injured, as though the refugees are an enemy force trying to regroup. The troops are panicked or confused and there's no command. Leavitt holds still; the pain is a firewall threatening to break. He must be spine shot; that's why he's torn up but can't feel the depth of the pain unless he tries to move. He reaches down, relieved he has sensation in his hands, feels the drenched, slippery fabric of his trousers. It's as though he's touching wet sandbags. He feels for his service revolver and touches his empty holster. Frantically, he feels for the hard snub nose of the gun and finds it under his dead thigh; he has it in his fingers when the pain breaks through.

He thinks he screams, but it's the women screaming, and the children. He's back outside with the boy and the sky is full of noise, throttling up, homing in on them. There are four planes, he's certain now, he sees them clearly. Red tracers of fire shoot down in arcs, crackling electrically like comic-book images as he strides powerfully into the tunnel with the Korean girl and her brother in his arms. He knows this isn't happening; he's only enduring it to revise it; he's inside an altered version of what happened, inside his own wavering memory. *You'll be safe here, stay low, move in deeper.* The words echo back to him as he receives the girl's searing gaze. He gives her the boy and urges them forward, deeper in. The arched stone mouth of the railway tunnel seems to open endlessly beyond them and he gestures again to the girl, the sister, his arm opening out: Go in here, stay low, near the tunnel walls. Had he said that? It was true. Safer near the walls if there was errant fire. The scene repeats in his head: he gives her the boy, pushes them in after the old woman. He can't get past the final image, when he urges them inside. He brought them here to leave them; he was wrong. He has to get out now and take them with him. He'd fallen forward; someone has moved him. He's on his back, like an insect too awkward to move. He hears the girl speaking, whispering in a rush. She's near him, telling him to be still, to wait, but she's wrong. They have to get out now. The pain throbs. Out: the word beats in his pulse. He's got to convince the girl to help him. He needs to think, but he can't hold on or hold still. He feels himself sliding, falling.

Lola's embrace receives him. The feel of her rises around him, dark and wide like a river they're moving in. It's a familiar fantasy, especially at night: he pretends he's with her. He doesn't have to pretend now. The tunnel disappears and he forgets he's injured, forgets how urgently he needs to survive, to be conscious, how little time there is. It's night now, he tells Lola, whispering. He's touching her, he's made it back, and then it's a sex dream, swirling into the instant she was pregnant, opening like a vortex that pulls them both all the way into her. It's warm here, safe. She knew, she'd told him, immediately. Pregnant felt like nothing else. Not tired exactly, not sick or nervous, but edgy, distinct. Focused tight, in sync, like when you've hit a phrase in a song just right and it lays itself out through your throat, moving from you across the lights into faces you can't see in the dark, faces whose eyes you feel play across you. Like a unit on alert, he'd said, and she laughed. Yeah, that was it. Ready, waiting. Perfect? he'd asked. Perfect didn't matter, wasn't that kind of question. Inevitable? Evidently, she told him, fucking college boy. The hell, he said. Course you will, she assured him, after the service, the GI Bill will send you, and I will. That so? he'd teased. She turns away from him in utter silence as though he's asked the wrong question; she disappears into a quiet that stills all sound.

He waits, willing her back to him, his breathing shallow, and when he feels her move under him again, against him, her belly is huge and tight. The bed is in a meadow but there are shade trees above them, and filtered sun; the trees have grown up to protect and conceal them. They're naked and fragrant like just-bathed children and she lies back to show him how big she is, how ready to give birth, moving his hands along the hard distended mound of her pregnancy. He can feel the baby move, see a globular shift of head or butt under her tight skin, hard against her dappled belly. A yellow pitcher of summer flowers, lilac and delphinium, turns slowly at the foot of the bed as though eddied on a current. The blue of the flowers drips onto the grass and he understands the meadow is afloat. The hardwood chest of Lola's Lenox silver service is beside them, suspended in the water despite its weight. The girls at Onslow's had chipped in to give them a wedding present worthy of a hopeful debutante: a silver-plate service for eight. Lola reaches over carefully with one hand, opens the chest to show him the spoons and knives in their lined trays, the serving pieces in their velvet sleeves. They'd given her a set of perfumes too, small stoppered novelty bottles in a box illustrated with a diagram of the solar system. The little porcelain bottles drift by now, one by one, each bearing a planetary color and an aspect of a face: pink Venus, pale Neptune, jolly yellow moon. Lola doesn't care, she lets them go. She tells him it was so hard to reach him and they don't have long. The bed is beginning to move. She lies back and he curves himself into her, holds her as he feels the baby, helpless to turn or move, push from inside her. Water rises over the grass, and the trees dip their leafy branches, pulsing; they're sighing, groaning, working. He puts his hands on Lola. These are contractions. She's in labor and she cries out, and the piercing sound cuts them apart.

He's alone. It was his cry, his voice. His revolver is in his hand. He clutches it tightly but knows he blacked out. Time has passed. Hours. He sees the inverted face of the girl over him, and the face of the boy on her back. She's waited until dusk and now she's touching him, moving him, pulling him deeper into the tunnel. The boy clasps her neck from behind with his locked arms, nearly flattened against her as she crouches over Leavitt. Her hands are in Leavitt's armpits, and her long black hair has come unbound and swings against his throat, enclosing their faces like a moving curtain, dragging the ground. He sees her through it and her eyes are wide with terror. She's panting with exertion. He's dead weight.

No, he says, *anyo*, and then more loudly, *Animnida*. She drags him slowly, barely able to move him. The boy's white shirt, he thinks. Take off the kid's white shirt and rip it into a flag. Find something to tie it to and get to the tunnel opening at first light. If an American soldier is seen with a flag of surrender, they'll cease firing and send someone for him. Whoever's alive will get out, but not unless it happens soon. He tightens his grip on his revolver, shoves it into the waistband of his fatigues, under his shirt.

He tries to think clearly. Tompkins was farther to the rear when the planes opened up. He wouldn't have run for the tunnels, there wasn't time; he might have run for the trench shelter of the creek bed and crouched there, shouting into the radio. He must have survived the strafing; Leavitt heard him transmit a cease-fire order, *This is not enemy*, heard him yelling over the scream of the attack, but it made no sense. If there was such an order, the planes ignored it and returned for another pass. They were firing again, strafing survivors of the first hit as refugees poured into the tunnel behind Leavitt. Tompkins was too far down the line to see Leavitt go into the crowd for the girl, see him enter the tunnel, but the tunnel was there and the refugees were inside. Only Tompkins might think Leavitt could be with them, could have helped someone to shelter and been shot to hell when troops emptied their automatics on fleeing civilians. Scared kids with weaponry do evil things, but if Tompkins is alive and conscious, he'll be looking for Leavitt. The girl pulls him slowly, crouched low. He tries to quiet his breathing, calm his mind so that he can talk to her.

He loses track. Sees the refugees moving beside him before the strafing. He feels Lola near him. He doesn't want her here as the onslaught unfolds and tries to imagine them in another place and time, in a future, but they slip backward, into their own embrace. Before the baby, before the war, they made their way into her body under the slow turn of her bedroom ceiling fan like they would never get anywhere else.

In the endless battle of the retreat, he'd told himself Lola was his protection. He'd reconstructed this time and that one, walking

with her, cooking in her tiny kitchen, lying in bed. The sound of
their breathing ticked off time, speeding or slowing a wash of
arousal he was often too tired to feel and watched inside himself
like a story. He holds on to the story now and wakes up inside it,
her thigh flung across him on the bed, smoke of her cigarette
ascending over them. It's amazing how real it seems: the comfort
he feels, the happiness. Her sketches taped on the walls are drawings of him. Line of his shoulder, torso, loins. Back of his head.
His hand on a bottle of beer, the dark glass beaded with cold from
the walk-in freezer downstairs. Never his face. He was too beautiful to draw, she said, for her anyway, the next girl he found would
draw his face. She mostly drew shapes, pieces of things or struc-
tures, as though she never looked at anything full on. The same
images repeatedly, like she was trying to get them right. Chiseled
stones of a wall or curved arch, the mortar between the stones.
Tracks crossing in a rail yard. Small town signage: MURPHY'S FIVE
AND TEN CENT STORE. Leavitt hears typewriters, dozens of typewriters. Their keys clack faster and faster like staccato artillery
ratcheting toward explosion.

The drawings and the walls dissolve. He sees the Korean girl
looking at him through the moving crowd of refugees, through
the dust and whining heat and the sound of syncopated footfalls
on the tracks, fixing him in her mind. She knows all of it, sees the
disjunct images of his thoughts move around and through him,
and dismisses them. Her gaze bores through him in the blazing
instant of hesitation he felt before he moved toward her. He's
standing in front of her again on the gravel between the tracks,
and she gives him the boy. The child is in his arms. Time bursts
and floods over him, warm and viscous as blood, but pearly in
color, clear, smelling of wet ruined grass. He hears Lola, her
throaty voice anonymous, continuous, bovine: the powerful low-
ing of an animal. She's in labor and she's alone, calling for him.

The sound and realization force him into consciousness and
vanish in the same instant. He sees only the girl, looking down at
him through her dark hair. Her face is very close. She flicks her

gaze away, watchful, frightened, intent. There must be two hundred, three hundred refugees, crowded together in the tunnel; bodies are everywhere, still, supine, hiding, dying. She's dragging him between them carefully, silently. He sees the boy's birdlike face at her shoulder, turned to the side as though he's listening. His milky eyes have a blue cast in the dim light and he peers unceasingly backward, toward the tunnel entrance. Wait, Leavitt says in Korean. The girl stiffens, purses her lips to signal silence. Leavitt has to talk to her, make her understand. The NKPA are close, or the planes wouldn't have strafed an anonymous white column of refugees; if American troops think infiltrators are among the survivors, they won't let the Koreans out while the battle is engaged. They'll be trapped here and most of the injured will die. If the retreat continues and the North Koreans move through, they'll kill any survivors they discover. Making sure he's seen alive now is their only chance.

Sewojuseyo, he tells the girl, stop here. Tries to dig his feet in but can't move them. *Jungmoonuro kayo!*, he orders her. Go to the entrance.

She looks at him blankly, her dark eyes glancing past him, back toward the opening of the tunnel, the direction of fire. She's working hard to keep them from shooting him again; she thinks he's out of his head.

He needs to speak more formally, not bark orders she might interpret as confused delirium. Make it clear he knows he's here, with her. *Mianhamnida*, he says. *Jamkkanman kidariseyo.* He's apologizing for an impolite action. He's asking her to wait a moment.

Ne, she finally whispers, yes. *Ne, ne,* she repeats, humoring him in turn.

In Korean, "yes" is *ne* and sounds like "no," and there it was. He feels them all falling forward into the tunnel and tries to calm his rushing breath. Yes, let's wait. The American planes are impolite, the invading North Koreans are impolite, the war is impolite, and dying like this is most exceptionally impolite. He can't laugh, he can't seem out of his head.

Naeryojuseyo, he says, stupidly. Please let me off here.

It's the phrase soldiers were taught to say to bus drivers in Seoul.

Slowly, she drags him. He tries to dig in his elbows, stop her progress with his arms and shoulders, and the pain shoots through him with such heat that his vision goes white. He screams, and she stops. He feels her crouch near, put the boy to the other side of him, hears her tell the boy to stay down, not to move.

Shhhh, she whispers, *joyong*. Please. Quiet. Her hands trace Leavitt's face, touch his temples. She parts her thin fingers over his mouth. To let him breathe but stop him yelling.

He wants to tell her that he needs to yell, in English, at the entrance, where the soldiers with their guns trained on the tunnel can hear him, but she's doing as he instructed. Just before his own men shot him, he said to stay low, move in deeper. Not to die, like the others on the tracks, in the ditch and the stream.

Jamkkanman kidaryeyo, he whispers. Wait a moment.

But there's no putting it off. Death is everywhere here, constant, unremarkable. Leavitt can feel it with them in the tunnel, moving in the air around them, beyond them, in the forests and shrines and temples, silent among the strange pines and their vast, stepped boughs. Chung Chong Buk-Do: landlocked, most rural province of Korea; the giant yews and sandalwood trees here smell of spice, and Rose of Sharon grows tangled along the paths and dirt roads. Walking point, Tompkins said this was shaman country. No white man here. Two thousand years before any annunciation claptrap, a bear gave birth to Tangun, the human king. Spirit posts stand where the paths divide, to dispel evil and guide the souls of the dead. Rural people believe that violent death or death afar requires the soul to journey home, and so the most modest, isolated villages are rebuilt again and again, even if the walls are straw and mud. The living leave hints for the dead. Ghosts are not feared. There are no ghosts. The most common form of Korean greeting is a question: *Are you at peace?* The soldiers, Leavitt thinks, the invaders and foreign protectors, become the ghosts, flying through time, across oceans, nothing to guide them but intent and need.

The girl lies beside him, one arm across him to touch the boy, waiting.

Leavitt looks at her. The last daylight filters into the tunnel with the green smell of trees and earth. *Kilul irosumnida*, he tells her. I'm lost.

Anyo, she says in Korean, no. A little way more.

He thinks about giving her the revolver. He can't concentrate, protect them. The colors he saw, the plunge and vibration, the speed and floating, the thinking and then seeing, are maybe only the brain flashing as it shuts down. He focuses on the girl. He can feel her near him, the hard slim line of her body tense with energy. He looks into her face. Her lashes are short and thick, the whites of her eyes very white, her black irises in the almond shapes of her lids so perfect they look jewel-like. Her gaze darts and shines. She thinks she can move them, keep them alive until they can get out.

She seems to pause then, looks at him intently. Almost formally, she moves to hold herself just above him, and bows her head to him.

Sugo hashiyssumnida, she whispers.

There are many ways to say thank you in Korean, depending on the originator of action and the quality of gesture. There are ways to say thank you when someone has helped you beyond any expectation.

She thinks he saved them. It's why she won't leave him.

And she reaches across him to touch the boy, to indicate that her action includes him. Gently, she turns the boy's head so that his gaze falls unseeing on Leavitt's face. The uneven blue of his pupils is impenetrable, depthless and cloudy, but the blue seems quietly, deeply lit. The blue never wavers. What does he see behind it. Shadows. Sounds. Leavitt doesn't ask but the boy inclines his head as though to answer.

Ihae hamnida, Leavitt says. I understand.

The light darkens around them. Beyond the tunnel, the guns

start up. Random pops of automatic weapons fire, warning shots. Troops are shooting past the entrances, keeping everyone inside. Quickly, the girl pulls the boy soundlessly onto her back. She leans over Leavitt, her eyes locked on his, and begins to pull him, drag him deeper in. Behind her, he sees the inverted curve of the tunnel, glinting as though some reflection or trick of light moves across it.

Lark

I decorate the cake in three pale colors, and the light in the fridge makes each one glow. Icing sets up just right in the cold. After supper Nonie tells me to take the plastic stacking chairs out of the shed where they stay clean and I put them beside Termite's chair. I have a little round plastic table I put there too, for the drinks. Nick has mowed the alley. He takes off his work shirt and washes like always at our outside spigot.

"Cocktail hour at last," he says. He puts the shirt back on and his wet skin soaks it through in spots, then he combs his thick dark hair straight back with his hands. Water drips onto his collar in rivulets.

"Take a load off, Nick. You want some ice tea?" Nonie comes outside in her housedress. She takes off her apron and folds it in pieces, smaller and smaller, like her own flag, her own little ceremony.

"Jesus, is that all you're serving tonight?" Nick Tucci says. "I work like a dog on the pasture here and you give me some tea?"

It's a joke. The second husband cured Nonie of ever having liquor in her house. Nick knows the story. "I made a cake," I tell him. "A birthday cake. I'll get it in just a minute."

"Another birthday? That's the second one this month. Lucky fellow." He puts the flat of his palm on Termite's head. "How you doing, Junior?"

Termite never answers Nick Tucci, he just gets quiet and holds still, like he thinks Nick is part of the mower or he carries the sound of the mower inside him. Maybe the sound is in Nick's hand, like a vibration, and Termite hears it. Maybe the vibration is there.

"Junior ought to take up for me," Nick Tucci says. "We men got to stick together."

Nick won't call Termite by his name. He says that's the name of an insect, a bug, not a kid, a boy, but he's the one who never waits for Termite to talk back. He fixed Termite's chair, though. We had this upholstered chair with arms Termite liked to sit in like a nest, and Nick turned it over one day so the bottom showed all strange and naked. He took off the flimsy wooden stumps it had for legs and screwed on silver wheels he said were strong enough for carts that move pianos and refrigerators. He said they were sure strong enough for this dinky kid. Nonie says Nick is handy. Charlie, now, he can't fix a sink or a lamp cord. Nonie does all that at the restaurant, but Nick helps her here. Nick fastened a handle onto the back of Termite's chair so we could steer it, and he put a wooden ramp stapled with stair treads leading out the back door, over the stoop and the one step.

Termite was smaller then; he was so small when he started liking that chair that his feet didn't reach to the end of the seat cushion. His legs were always curved, but we used to keep them out in front of him. It was later that he whined and made noises until we tucked them under him, like he didn't want to see them anymore after he knew what they were.

Nick sits down in his own chair now, and Nonie sits just opposite, and he fixes her with a look. "Noreen," he says, "I'm forty-four years old."

Nonie pours us three glasses of tea. "You're a spring chicken," she tells Nick. "Good God, you can't complain until you're fifty, and if you're a man, you can't complain then."

"I got this passel of wild teenagers running around. They got three junkers between them now and I never know where they are."

"Who says you need to know? You ran around plenty, Nick. You might not remember, but everyone else does."

"Yeah," he says, "I'm still running. All day I feed the wrapper, and every night that cold beer gets colder."

I think about Nick and the wrapper, how he stands between the belts and lifts the bales from one to the other. The plant makes business forms, and the wrapper is the big machine that thuds a few thousand pages into a batch, wraps and seals them in plastic for shipping. Bale in and bale out, Nick Tucci says, his calling in life.

"I could near dive into that beer," he goes on, "I get too thirsty to live."

"You don't want to get that thirsty," Nonie says.

Termite says exactly what she does, without the words, and he starts moving.

"What is it he wants," Nonie says. "Lark, get him a plastic glass and his straw, and get him that little doo-dad he likes. I swear, he's crazy about that thing."

"I'll get the cake too," I tell them.

While I'm in the kitchen I can see them through the window, and I can hear them. They keep talking like I can't, like they think they sent me to another country.

"What are you going to do about her, Noreen," Nick Tucci says.

"What do you mean? She's finished her first year down at Barker Secretarial. That will give her something, a lot more than her diploma from that high school Zeke doesn't show up to half the time. She's got some financial assistance, for the good grades she always had. Barker girls can even be legal secretaries, if they go all three years. The last year is work-study. Maybe she can get a job with one of the lawyers in town."

"She's a woman now, Noreen, and she doesn't even have a bedroom with a door. She just going to sit here for three years, taking care of Junior in the days, and typing at night?"

"What would you like her to do, Nick," I hear Nonie say. "Run around with one of your boys, maybe?"

I'm looking for Termite's doo-dad, the little pitcher he likes. Where has that old thing got to. It's small, fits in my palm. Pale yellow porcelain, easy to lose in a sinkful of dishes. He doesn't like me to wash it or take it from him, but he holds it so often I want it to be clean. The fat moon face on the front is winking and smiling, ridged and bumpy. Maybe that's why Termite likes the feel of it.

"Jesus, Noreen," Nick says. "Someone, sometime, is gonna drive up here by the alley and open the door for her to jump in. Don't you know that?"

I have to move all the dishes before I find the pitcher; it's so small it falls through the skinny rubber rungs of the drainer to underneath. I've got it in my hand, washing and drying the face. I can hear them outside, I can hear them perfectly well.

"Uh-huh," I hear Nonie answer. "And you think she's just going to ride off and leave Termite sitting here." There's a beat of quiet. "You remember Lola, and I do," Nonie says, "but Lark is nothing like her."

Nick doesn't say anything then, and Termite doesn't say anything either. It's no wonder I think he understands some of what people say. I hear the bell on his chair. He presses it with his wrist, just a small, glancing sound, once, and twice, and three times.

Be right there, I tell him, but I say it in my head. I catch myself doing that, like I think he can hear me. Here's his plastic cup and straw, and the handle of the moon pitcher fits around my smallest finger, like a ring. I put the silver-plate pie server in my pocket, the one I found last week in the basement, in the boxes Nonie keeps down there.

The tray with the rim around it is good for carrying things. Plates slide and don't fall off, but the edge is low enough that the cake still looks pretty, sitting in the middle with dishes and spoons beside. People ought to see something pretty moving toward them. That way they get time to want what they really can have. I like coming out the door with something on a tray. Nonie looks over, and Nick does. Termite turns too, like he can feel them looking, and then Nick is up and comes to hold the door. He winks at me, pleased and jaunty. For a minute I see how he looks like his boys, young in his eyes like them, and how his boys might look when they're older, if they broaden out like Nick. I guess it takes a man built like Nick to run the wrapper. There's a lever a man swings, timed just so, and Nick fixes the wrapper too, keeps it running. It's as big as a couple of cars parked side to side. Nick says it makes a noise like a jet engine pausing to yell *Wham!* every thirty seconds. A man has to be big to throw that lever and stand in that noise, move the bales on time like he's part of the machine. Nick's boys are all long and thin and they move fluid as dogs. They have taut ropes of muscle in their necks, like they're always tense or ready, and swells of hard crescent under their nipples. Come spring, Joey and Solly and Zeke work on their cars in Nick's yard. They go without their shirts and their pants ride low on their hips. You can see the perfect run of their spines as they bend over, lean and white, lost to the chest in their engines. They were always hard and skinny, even when they were little kids. I can't see Nick's boys ever being big and broad as Nick, like a wrestler, moving so heavy, like he moves now, coming toward me. I can feel his footfalls on the stone walk through my bare feet. Then he's here, making a mock bow before he reaches to take the tray. I'm taller than Nonie now, and Nick's dark eyes are level with mine. His forearms are furred with dark, curly hair. I look away when Nick gets too close. He's like a blur at the limit my eyes can see.

"Lark, you're too much," he says.

"It's just a cake," I say.

"Yes, it's a cake," Nonie says. She shakes her head at Nick.

"But look at it, Noreen. Little white garlands in the icing, and the garlands are braided. How does she do that?" He nods over at Termite. "You were here, Junior. How does she do it?"

"An icing bag with special attachments," I say. "Gourmet baking set. I got it for *my* birthday."

"My point exactly," Nick says. "For your birthday you want some fancy cooking gadget. My thugs want new carburetors, so they can drive even faster and end up in the pokey in the next county, and their old man can come bail them out." He's in front of me carrying the tray and I follow the bulk of his back. "Joey's latest thought is to join some special forces unit in the marines. Driving delivery for the plant's not good enough, he wants to see the world. Zeke can't pass tenth grade but he's got him a car put together so he can drive away from the courthouse with his learner's permit, soon as he turns sixteen. And Saul. Graduated high school, and now he wants a motorcycle."

"He want you to buy it?" Nonie asks.

Saul is the middle one, the one most like a wolf, with his green eyes and his thick fair hair, and that dark skin, like Nick's. Solly has been in school with me since first grade over on Lumber Street. They put him back a grade though, for skipping school so much when he was nine or ten. He ended up a grade behind me, even though he's a year older. Their mother left before school even happened, when Zeke was barely walking. Nick Tucci bought the groceries and Nonie took care of those boys. She fed us all supper at night, then sent us over to Nick's when he pulled in from work. She used his car to go off to Charlie's for the dinner shift, then closed up and got home around eleven, carried me down the alley from Nick's house to my own bed. She says I never stirred, but I remember the leaves on the trees moving, blowing above me at night. There used to be trees along the alley, a long time ago. After Termite came, Elise stayed with him and me at night, after Nick's kids went home. Nonie would go to work and Solly would come back over. Guess you think we're better than TV over here, Elise would tell him, better than Jack Benny. If we weren't doing homework she'd have us "helping out," running the sweeper, folding laundry, entertaining Termite. Elise brought over a clock radio she got with S&H green stamps, and she taught us dance steps or card games. Solly played rummy with her while I read to Termite, or Elise brought what she wanted to hear. *Gone with the Wind. Little Dorrit. Ladies' Home Journal* magazine: "Can This Marriage Be Saved?" Elise said I was better than the radio, better than *Playhouse 90.*

When I was eleven Elise started running the Coffee-Stop across from Charlie's. She sold cigarettes, magazines, sodas, hot dogs, and worked long hours. After that I took care of Termite myself. He was little. I could do it as well as anyone. Solly still came by. I know Solly like I know the shelves in my room, and the turn of the walls. There's always been a wild quiet about Solly. It stays in the air near him like a scent.

"Solly doesn't need me to buy him anything," Nick says now. We've reached our little enclave and he puts the cake on the round table. "He's been pumping gas and fixing cars down at the Texaco all year. Somebody pulled in with this thing on a flatbed and now Solly thinks he's got to have it."

"Well, he doesn't," Nonie says. "He lives with you and you're his father and you can tell him he can't have it."

"Sure," Nick says, "and I'll see his back real quick. The kid got through high school not half trying. I want him to work, save money, maybe go to college next year."

"His grades were good," I say, "Solly's smart. He should go to college. Couldn't he play football somewhere?"

"You tell him." Nick turns and looks at me. "I'm serious."

"That's not her job," Nonie answers him. Then, "She's the one should be going to college."

There's no college near enough, though. Nowhere I could take classes at night. "Sit down, Nick." I'm moving the plates, handing out napkins. I put Termite's moon pitcher into his palm. He holds it in his lap, rubs the flat of his wrist across its grimace of a face that's all wrinkles and bulging cheeks, like no face, even a porcelain face, is too small to wink or sigh. Termite moves his wrist across and across the bumpy surface like he didn't have hold of it just this morning. I have the cake server, a shiny wedge shape with a carved handle and serrated edge. It has its own velvety envelope to keep off tarnish; there's just a shadow of dark along the blade. I touch that shadow with my thumb. If these are my mother's things, why are they here? I always thought of her walking, moving, some landscape streaming away behind her. Now that I've actually taken something from her secrets, I think of a green lawn holding her, or a coastline where she disappeared, even an alleyway where it happened. A dark bitter alley, cinders and trash. No. Make it an alley like ours, grass, white gravel, summer dusk. I see Nonie recognize the cake server in my hand, but she doesn't say anything. "I'll cut the cake," I tell them, "if everyone will kindly take a seat."

Termite gives me his little half smile and starts talking. *Take a seat. Take a seat.*

"He sounds like a bird sometimes," Nick says.

Take a seat is what I say to him when we're in the basement, cooling off, sitting on the old couch that has its springs out right through to the cold cement floor. It's the couch Charlie used for years in the office of the restaurant, a narrow room behind the kitchen where Nonie does the accounts and bills. It's a big couch, long and broad. This summer I realized the use they must have put it to, nights when I was a child and slept at Nick's, with Solly curled up next to me. This summer, too, I started looking through Nonie's boxes. Pretending is a lie I'm tired of telling her. Down there with Termite one of the hot afternoons, I saw how the boxes were stacked, balanced and squared, like they'd been there a long time. Termite sits on the broken couch and I put a breadboard across his knees so he can use the big crayons he likes. Once I get him started, he moves his arms up and down, back and forth, long arcs in one color across an unfolded newspaper, while I draw in my notebook. He doesn't look at what he makes, but I watch his colors get darker. Most of the time, I draw him. Standing in space. No chair, no alley. One day I turned the radio loud the way Termite likes it. "Heartbreak Hotel" was on and I looked over at the boxes. *Well since your baby left you. You've got a tale to tell.* The boxes had always been in that corner, sometimes covered with other stuff. They were big and they were all the same size, like from a moving company, a solid dusty wall stacked four across and three deep, solid and hard to rock, taped shut and never opened, addressed to Nonie in somebody's handwriting. I wiped off the dust and saw they were stamped BEKINS VAN LINES, Miami, Florida. I decided to go slowly. I know the stuff in the box I've gone through was never Nonie's. A set of silver plate in its own velvet-lined box, each piece marked LENOX in tiny script on the back, like a code. Porcelain dishes, service for eight, in a gold-edged flowery pattern, packed with cardboard, neat and professional. No pictures though, no documents, no papers to tell me more than I already know.

"Kind of musical," Nick is saying. "A bird making its own sense."

"Or not," Nonie says.

"Termite can imitate almost anything," I say. "Things just sound more like music in his version. Sounds instead of words."

Nonie leans forward to help Termite with his spoon. He can hold things bigger than spoons—his pitcher, fat crayons, toast, or candy bars. He holds his strips of blue because we wrap them around his wrist. Sometimes he uses a wooden serving spoon with a thick handle. Regular spoons and forks are too thin and hard. We know exactly how to feed him. Touch, touch, each side of his mouth, neat and fast. Nonie's looking at him. "You never make things up, though, do you, Termite," she says.

"No," I say, "he doesn't."

It's a fact. Termite can only tell the truth. I know she means she wishes, she wishes, he could say something more than the sound of what he's just heard. I pretend he thinks more, backward and forward for miles.

"Good cake," Nick says. "And this cold tea is mighty nice, evening like this. The air is goddamn still, heavy as lead. That storm coming in. Tomorrow, they say. Rain all week. Maybe it'll clean up the river a little. I don't like such a brown muck of a river."

"Lord, Nick." Nonie laughs. "That river was always brown."

"Not so, Noreen. The river was cleaner years ago. You could see into it. In the dark it was olive green. I remember."

"In the days it was—" She goes on at him, making fun now.

"Sapphire," I chime in. "It was sapphire. Bright, stone blue."

Nick Tucci gives me a look, then he nods. "Knocked your eyes out," he says. "Standing there under the railroad bridge, watching the water. Oh, that blue river."

We're laughing, and Termite hunches his shoulders, throws his head back to look up into the plum-colored sky, like the river is up there somewhere. *That blue river.* He says it in high and low sounds, and the sky over us could be a river, bruised and deep as it looks. I reach over and tilt his chin down. His head is heavy, and his neck muscles are not so strong. He throws his head back again, right away.

"He's got his opinions, has Junior," says Nick Tucci. "You tell them, Junior."

"Leave him be, Lark." Nonie's eyes get wet when she laughs hard. "He's taking a sounding. My God, that sky does look like it could fall. Should be a full moon tonight, but we won't see anything behind clouds like those."

I can see Termite's nostrils move, a vibration so slight, like the gills of a fish moving when it breathes, and I hear him smell the air like he's drinking it. I wonder does he see the clouds at all, does he feel the color instead, or does he think the word "river" is like a sky, so he looks up. Why would he think that. Because it's true. He could think the sky is like a river that doesn't stop. Nonie would say he just reacts to us, our laughing, our shouting, whatever. She'd say I give him things to know. Then I remember the candles. "Not much of a birthday, is it, Termite. I forgot about candles."

"You don't need candles every time, Lark, as many birthdays as you make him." Nonie feels the pockets of the apron she took off. They're all blue aprons she wears at work.

"I kind of promised him," I say. "Too late now." But Termite tilts his head back down, gives me his sideways look.

"Not too late. We have most of a cake here, and a few leftover candles. Somebody celebrated at the restaurant today, with a piece of Charlie's lemon pie." Nonie has a partly crushed box of those little skinny candles they give away free at bakeries.

"Pie is all wrong with candles," Nick Tucci says. There are only three candles, but he's leaning forward, putting them on the cake. "Should be nine, right? Each one of these counts for three years, Junior, so the flames gotta be extra high." He lights them with his cigarette lighter, then he stands and picks up the plate and holds it just in front of Termite. Nonie and I get up and stand with Nick, so close our faces touch. We let the candles burn, then we blow, really slow, with Termite. The little flames flutter perfectly and go out just right, all at once.

"Excellent," Nick Tucci says. "A slow-motion blowout."

"Now, Nick," Nonie says, "I'll bet those boys of yours wouldn't mind some of this cake. Between the motorcycles and secret soldier stuff, they could use Lark's divinity icing. Like a prayer in spun sugar. You're such a cook, Lark. If only someone would buy you a restaurant." She shrugs for Nick's benefit. "Lark's cakes are what Charlie would be coming up with if he really did know anything about baking, or pastry—"

"Charlie is just a short-order cook," Nick says in a serious tone. "He should forget the pies and cakes." Nick doesn't much like Charlie. I think he harbors a brotherly resentment.

Nonie cuts him off. "Charlie has no choice. Lark is not working for Charlie, and I'm not baking for the restaurant in addition to everything else." She checks her watch, the wristwatch Charlie gave her a year ago, on their "anniversary." It has a platinum band and a square little face with diamonds on either side. Once it was Charlie's grandmother's. He spent a lot to have the works inside replaced and to buy a flexible platinum band. Platinum is more dear than gold, Nonie says. The watch is waterproof, and she almost never takes it off. Those little diamonds catch the light like the ring he never gave her. Gladdy was angry that Charlie was so extravagant. She stayed away from the restaurant nearly a week. An unexpected benefit, Nonie said. "Time to stack the café," she says now. She puts her hand at the back of Termite's neck, smooths his curls. "I need to cut his hair soon. These curls get so tangled."

We're cleaning up. Nonie starts with the dishes. Nick Tucci is putting away the chairs. Termite holds the moon pitcher right up to his mouth, making sounds into its open lip. Someone might think he's talking, but he's saying his version of the plates stacked against one another, the plastic chairs scraping, our footsteps, the wheels of his own chair turning as I push it inside.

I lean down close to him and whisper, in the powdery smell of his hair, "Your birthday, Termite, every day."

Every day, he says back to me, *every day, every day.*

Nick Tucci has gone home with the cake. Nonie is doing the dishes, and Termite sits beside her in his chair, holding the radio. She makes him keep the volume lower than it's been all day and she puts the tall plastic glasses on the sideboard to drain. He looks sideways into the ridges just at eye level, like they're little fun-house mirrors he can see into. I'm making his bath. When I was nine and ten I used to wear my bathing suit and get in the tub to hold him, and Nonie would soap him and take him out. We were bathing him and she told me his head was heavy for him to hold up because there was water around his brain. He'd get stronger. The exercises would help. Like when we made a pretty sound with a bell or music box and he turned toward it, I let him turn his head against my palm, turning to hear until I played the sound again. The water in his head never got in the way of his listening. Where did the water come from, I wanted to know. She couldn't tell me.

Nonie keeps a framed picture of herself and my mother on our kitchen wall, near the clock. The circular fan on the windowsill turns its grilled face back and forth, back and forth, and the frame stirs a little on its wire hanger, settles, stirs. The chrome of the fan shows a curved reflection of the stacked plastic glasses on the shelf above, and the arms and hands of the girls in the picture. The girls are playing dress-up and my mother always got to be the bride. Because she was youngest, Nonie says, she took unfair advantage. My mother's name is Lola. We seldom talk about her and we almost never say her name. To think her name feels like breaking the rules, but they were Lola and Noreen, those sisters. They're both swathed in filmy white that was probably window curtains, and my mother wears a crocheted jacket they must have thought looked lacy. She's maybe eight or nine in her crown of braided flowers and weeds, long stalks of delphinium that are already falling apart, but she looks eerily grown up in the lipstick. It's way too dark for a bride. She stands there like she knows it, guarded or defiant, the shapes of her coltish legs dark in the sheer fabric, but she clasps her hands uncertainly and looks up into the camera. She's of two minds. The picture is the only reason I forgive her at all. If she were pulling a face or acting cocky, I think I might hate her. Nonie has an arm around her. Nonie's much taller, being four years older, so she's the boy, with a penciled mustache and her long hair plaited back.

Their father was a Jehovah's Witness preacher and they weren't allowed to cut their hair or drink cola or celebrate holidays. I don't know who allowed them to dress up or what cola has to do with a religion. My mother's hair was wavy and red and such an eyeful they made her keep it in braids. The day after my grandfather's funeral she cut it to a Rita Hayworth swoop. Their mother was too sick to stop Lola making up for lost time, Nonie says. Nonie was in what she calls her respectable phase then, having left Charlie when he wouldn't marry her. She'd gone off to Atlanta and met her first husband. He was quite a bit older, a widower with an insurance business. Insurance, like there's any such thing, Nonie will say when she refers to him, but she spent a few years a safe, kept woman down there where it was nearly always warm. She says she was shameless then. She'd never had anything, then she got it all. One day she walked off. But she left things, not kids. Lola finished high school in Winfield after their mother died, then went to live with Nonie. That didn't last long. The second husband was in the restaurant business, ran a supper club. Troubled men are trouble: that's all she'll say about him. Couple of years. Then she came back here to Charlie. I asked her once if Charlie was troubled. Heavens no, she said, Charlie's not addicted to anything but hard work and Catholic guilt.

Nonie says she wants me to be able to take care of myself. No cleaning up other people's dishes, doing anyone else's work. She says we have Termite, and we have to take care of him too. When a woman wants things she can't get for herself, Nonie says, a man can smell it. She says never let a man inside you unless you want him around forever, because you can't get rid of him after that, no matter how many times he leaves you or you leave him. Nonie was telling me that before I even knew what it meant: inside you. When I was younger I would see a heart scrawled on a sidewalk, on a bathroom stall, on the wall near the pay phone at the Coffee-Stop where Elise works, and I would think: inside you. Like it was feelings, romance, Elise's cheap mystery novels with women on the covers. No, Nonie said, it's when a man puts his body into your body. Then he's inside you, and your body remembers, each time, every man, even if you try to forget. You came back to Charlie, I said. Is that why? He's inside you? Now you get it, Nonie said. But why him, I said, and not someone else, another one? Because I was so young then, Nonie said, when we started, and there were so many times. You've got to be careful when you're young.

She got me thinking about Solly, all those times when we were little kids, then not so little. He'd be all over me but I wouldn't let him inside. I was already too full of Nonie's words.

How many times, I wonder, Nonie and Charlie. I lean over the tub to turn off the water. Heat rises up at me like some thought of them, young and warm when she was in high school and he was a little older, on the riverbank where kids went, or in the field by Polish Town. Or in Gladdy's house downtown where Gladdy and Charlie lived even then, where Charlie lives alone now part of every winter while Gladdy bakes in the Florida sun. Nonie's own childhood house, where she lived with my mother, burned down. There was always a wide slash across the ground until the Texaco expanded and built over top the scar. Nonie and Charlie are together here now, I suppose, when no one is home. That's not often since Termite has stopped going to school. They could go to Gladdy's, I guess, the months Gladdy is gone. Nonie says Gladdy went south a long time ago, before she ever got on a plane. That little beach house in Coral Gables is the only thing Charlie Fitzgibbon will ever own, Nonie tells me, until his mother lets go of it all. Gladdy only put it in his name to save on taxes. There sits Charlie waiting, and Nonie says his mother may even outlive him. Charlie and his heart pills. That leaky heart is his, at least, something Charlie owns.

I don't think my mother ever owned anything. I think she got pulled apart. Too many people owned a piece of her. Winfield did, still does. The whole town knows more about her than I will ever remember. I knew her once. I must have, though Nonie doesn't say so. I didn't come here till I was three. And Termite did, for a year, maybe in Florida where the boxes came from, when she must have been finding out more and more how much he needed. Men had hold of her. My father, whoever he was, and then Termite's, the one Nonie calls a baby, the one who died in Korea. I asked Nonie a while ago, what if he hadn't died. Would he be taking care of Termite if Lola couldn't? Don't know, Nonie said, but you're here, taking care of Termite for him.

And Nonie is here too.

Termite and I don't look anything alike. Even if Termite were normal, I don't think we would. He's so blond, so fair, with those blue eyes. My hair and my eyes are dark, even if my skin isn't.

Didn't matter. Kids at school called me Guinea and Dago, like they did the Tucci boys. Joey taught us all how to beat kids up. Maybe that's why no one called Termite names. Plenty would have, but he was always with us if we weren't in school. The sand-lot kids that hung out at the rail yard were afraid of Joey, then Solly. The Tuccis were ready to fight. And they were always strong, even before they grew up. Summers we kids took care of ourselves. Down by the river, under the railroad bridge. Joey would swing us around in circles by our armpits, real fast, held still himself by centrifugal force, and he'd swing Termite too. Termite loved it. I was never afraid Joey would hurt him. He'd hear Joey's voice and throw his head back, look all the way up, eyes cast to the right, like that's where Joey always was. Joey would say, "Jesus! That boy is ready for a ride."

Termite was so pale you could see the blue veins through his skin, and his light hair grew in soft curls you could comb with your fingers. From the beginning, I confused him with an angel, a good part of me that didn't speak and wouldn't talk in plain language. A part of me I carried around, tried to take care of, couldn't understand in normal ways. It's funny. The only thing Termite and I have alike is our birthmarks—brown marks near our navels the shape of tiny shoes. Similar, Nonie would say, not alike, and it's a shoe if you see it that way. Once I outlined them in ballpoint pen to show her, the boot shape, and the heel. It's true mine is larger. Why not, Nonie said, you do the walking. He's lucky you're a girl with strong legs.

I get that from Nonie. I might be skinny like my mother, but I'm strong like Nonie. I'm like an adopted child, related to Nonie twice, through adoption and blood. I don't have any trouble lift-ing Termite. He's so slight and he doesn't seem to get heavier. He gets longer, too long to be carried in my arms, up against my shoulder anymore, like a baby. This year I carry him on my back, with his arms crossed around my neck. Down the stairs to the basement, up to the attic when it's not too hot or cold, out the back door to the wagon in the yard. The wagon's deep enough to hold the back and seat of a padded office chair, bolted in for Termite, with straps attached to help him stay upright, room for his legs to splay out or fold under him the way he likes. The chair back stands up above the wagon sides enough that he can see just fine and rest his head. We go to the river, down to see the trains, sometimes to Charlie's for lunch. Late afternoons we might meet Nonie to walk home with her after her shift. But now if I take him anywhere else—to a store, to the doctor's, to a movie—he has to ride in the wheelchair. He complains so, it's not worth it. Nonie says he didn't hate that chair until after he started at the school. Finally she put it in the closet, so he doesn't have to see it. Home should feel safe, she says. Let Social Services threaten us all they want. Getting used to the chair again will have to wait. But I miss the movies. In the summer, when he was small, we used to pay our quarters and go every other day. We'd leave the wagon outside under the marquee and Termite sat on my lap. Sometimes all the Tucci boys came, but mostly Solly. He liked the westerns. Solly would say whole scenes to us later, acting out parts, and he could do John Wayne's rolling walk. The dialogue went into his head and stayed there. Seems a million years ago.

"You finished running the bath, Lark?" Nonie is rinsing the supper plates. "If you could just bathe him," she says. "I'll put him to bed. I know you want to practice."

She's talking about typing practice. I don't much want to tell her about Stamble. Stumble, shamble. I have to, though. "Nonie, someone came by from Social Services today."

"Who came by?"

I hear the edginess in her voice. "Not the same woman as before. A man. He was real polite, you can tell he's new. He asked for you and he said he lives near here."

"What do I care where he lives? The Social Services people are all the same."

"He said we needed a smaller wheelchair for Termite, child-sized. He's strange-looking. White hair and lashes and no eyebrows to speak of. And he was wearing a suit and a hat, all covered up in the heat, like he was afraid of the sun. His skin is pale, like the inside of a rabbit's ear, and his eyes are so light."

"Sounds like Mrs. Gaston, down at the Mercantile. Older lady, or looks older. You know her. Wears the thick glasses? She's an albino. There's one or two around town. Albinos always have bad eyes, and usually bad hearts. They don't normally live to be old."

Mercantile. I remember. The short little woman who sells ribbon in the sewing section. Thin white hair pulled back in a bun, and her skin pale as a root, like she's been dug up from underground. Yes. Like Stamble.

"You're telling me our new social worker is an albino?" Nonie shakes her head. "Social Services must have assigned us a new caseworker without telling us. Typical. First thing they do is show up without calling, just to see if we're torturing Termite. Like he'd rather live at that school, farmed out the way some of those poor kids are. And a lot of them not as disabled as Termite."

"So-called disabled," I say. "I'm not going to talk about him that way."

"Well now, Lark." She looks at me dead-on. Arches her brows in that way that shows up the star-flared lines around her eyes, the shadows beneath them. She turns back to the dishes. "How do you want to talk about him then?" she asks me.

"They're not as well off," I say, "not as well off as Termite."

"They're sure not," Nonie says. She's pulling the stopper out of the sink, drying her hands on her apron. "Our prince here gets bubbles in his bath, and radio control, and birthdays every time he turns around. Am I right, Termite? And he'll get school at home too, if that's what we have to say he gets." She sighs then and leans near him, cups his face in her hands. "What'll we teach you first? How about local politics, how federal money pours into that school while they all stand with their mitts out, and those kids sitting there, waiting to get their faces wiped off after lunch."

"I can teach him the same things at home," I tell Nonie. "I have some of the same materials, and I can make more. They can't make us send him, can they?"

"We'd have to say I teach him, because you're not an adult. Homeschooling is not usual around here, but some parents do it. Look at all the religious nuts in this county. We've got the Temperance Methodists, the Irish Catholics like Charlie and Gladdy, the Italian Catholics like Nick, and still plenty of Jehovah's Witnesses, like your grandparents were, but it's mostly the Pentecostals and Nazarenes that school at home. No one bothers them. It's just that Termite's handicapped, like the word or not. He's past school age now and he has to go, to the special school or at home, but they'll say we don't have the training. As though we haven't taken care of him all this time."

I know they want to test him more, see what's wrong with him. What they can do about him. They all think they have to do something. It's never all right for him to be what he is. Nonie said the doctors in Cleveland wanted to look in his head when he was a baby, see what parts of his brain didn't work, what did, like that wouldn't hurt. And they would have, except they decided it wouldn't do any good.

Termite can hold his head up now, except when he's tired. From the time I was a kid I thought his head was heavy because there was so much in it he couldn't tell or say. That everything had stayed in him, whether he recognized the pictures or not. That he'd kept all the words I couldn't call up, our mother's words and words about her. Words from before we were born, what I heard until I was three and forgot. Words about what house what road or street who was there how she looked and talked and why she sent us away. It's hard taking care of Termite but she kept him for a year, she tried. Why did she try or stop trying. And I was a normal kid she didn't keep, except I'm not normal, because I don't remember her. I've got my own big blank but no one can see it in the shape of my head, in how I speak or don't speak or don't move. It's like by the time he was born there was too much to know. It filled his head too full, then wiped it blank. If I said this to Nonie, she'd say I like my own stories. These are birth defects, she'd tell me. No one knows why or what. Nothing your mother did caused them. We're here and we move on from here, and isn't that bath-water run yet? You need time to practice typing. Didn't Charlie bring you the typewriter from the restaurant so you could prac-tice? Well then.

"Lark, are you in a dream? That tub must be full." Nonie opens the bathroom door and takes a look. "He'll like this." She looks down at the frothy bath. "But you're going to have to drain some out before you put him in. It's way too deep."

Put him in, Termite says after her, but she's right; the tub is too full and the bubbles stand up above the porcelain rim. The smell of the bath is in the kitchen now, soap and warmth, and I carry Termite into the little bathroom. I get his clothes off while I let the water drain lower. "Way too high," I tell him, and he says the sounds back like he agrees. But I know he doesn't. He likes the bubbles all heaped up, he can smell them, and when I put him in he reaches straight into them, and puts his face just where they start.

Nonie smiles, shakes her head. "Give a yell when he's ready and I'll put him to bed," she tells me.

Sometimes I feel so tired all of a sudden. I've got all the windows open and the chimes hung from the kitchen ceiling are moving and tinkling in the air. There's a breeze almost, but the air is hot. Termite is clean and powdered and his hair is tousled up in a pale blur. I steer his chair toward the living room and see Nonie on the couch. She's put her legs up waiting for us and fallen asleep with her shoes off. Her toes are covered in those black half-circle feet of her support stockings, and her mouth is barely open. If we get closer we'll hear the tiny whistle of her breath, like she's an old lady. I don't want to, so I turn Termite back around, into the kitchen. He nods. He likes this time of night before bed and I face his chair the way he likes, near the window, so he's close to the turning pieces of the chimes. I glued pieces of red and green and silver foil to one side of each metal strip—the thing still makes noise that is sharp, then muted, but now he loves being near it. That's why I think he might see colors, or maybe what's shiny.

I go into the bathroom to wash, turn the bathroom light out, stand by the sink. The bathroom door is almost shut, but I can see the back of Termite's chair. He settles into a cat sound, a kind of purr that's jagged and melodious. I pull my dress off and stand on Termite's damp towel. Wind my hair up in an elastic, put the stopper in, run the cool water almost to the top of the sink. I wash with my hands, let the water run down my legs in tracks. Close my eyes and wash between my breasts, around them and under them, between my legs. It's sexual sometimes. It is now but I don't make a sound, I can be so quiet. I have to do it most nights or I can't sleep. Usually I want to go to bed with it done so I can close my eyes and not think. It can be over in a minute. Sometimes I think I could stand in a crowded room and do it without even touching myself. I think about where that room might be and who might be in that crowd. Strangers, most of them, except for two or three. There's no controlling who I might think about— Solly and Joey, or Nick Tucci, even Charlie, or other men I barely know. But they don't look at me the way men mostly do. In my thoughts, they're more like women, or they're men who know what women know. They know it all and they look inside me, straight into where I'm getting to. I get to that place and fall through it. Then I open my eyes and I'm here, and tonight the whole of the alley and all the backyards past the frame of the window look sleepy, turned inside out. Gray and pretty, fuzzy with dusk. Not like Winfield at all, not like anywhere.

I open the bathroom door wide and see Termite in his chair, turned away from me toward the chimes, sitting very still. His white blond curls and fair skin and pale blue pajamas glow in the dim kitchen. There's no air, not a breath, but the chimes move in their tiny circle like a dream, like they're in thrall to a magnet or a thought. The kitchen window holds a space layers deep above the stony shine of the alley. Lights have come on in the houses, people move in the lit-up spaces. The Tuccis' frame two-story is nearly dark, and I hear Joey's car before I see it, hear the slice and slide of gravel. Solly's driving, with no headlights. He slams into their side yard, jerks to a halt. I see him get out and pull his shirt off and lean against the car door, and whatever I just pulled down or shredded in myself begins to come together again. I see Solly go around and help Joey out. They're drunk, or Joey is, which is pretty normal for Joey but not so usual for Saul, and I see Joey fall over, then Solly gets him up and walks and drags him into the house. They leave the doors of the convertible open. Joey's little love car, Nick Tucci calls it, and it looks abandoned, like a puzzle thrown apart, white and topless and opened up. I want to walk over there naked and shut those doors, feel the air on my skin, make them see me when they're too drunk to do anything about it. Doing it is like a reflex with them, must be. Finding someone to get into. There are girls who can't resist watching them need it so much.

So much, I think I hear Termite say, and I look at him to see. But he's only crooning to himself, satisfied because it's dark and the air is soft and motionless, and he has the sound of the chimes and the colors are shining. I hang my dress on the hook by the kitchen sink and pull my nightgown on. *Day is done.* We sang that song at the camp I went to before Termite came. The only time I went away, before or since, I was Termite's age, the age he is now. I try to remember myself and it's like struggling in a sack, like those kittens Nick Tucci sent Solly to the river with, the one time I told him to bring some home from the rail yard. We think of Termite as someone who's two or three, we take care of him like that. I get really scared when I think there might be a part of him that's as old as he really is, a part of him that knows more and more, like anyone else does. *Gone the sun*, sang the little girls in rounds. But Nonie was wrong, the moon is out bright as a plate. I see black clouds sail across it fast, like mountains across an orb.

Nonie

There's choice but no choice. Kids deal with what is, and take one shape or another.

Whatever I had, Lola wanted. First she wanted to be bigger, tougher, stronger, like me. I was four years older, the one she looked up to. Our mother always seemed more a child than we were, quiet, all her edges turned down the way Dad liked them. Lola wanted to read my Bible instead of hers, my bigger, heavier schoolbooks, but she only pretended to read, her eyes skimming the shapes of the words so she could turn the page at the right time. She'd sing the hymns I hated until I hated them more, and our father let me stop singing and just play the piano for Lola. She performed, even then; she could only see herself in the way people looked back at her. I cooked the food and Lola served it. She lit stubs of candles and lay flowers alongside the plates, all in the service of the Lord. I did the work and she carried off the sleight of hand, drew Dad's gaze away from me, away from our mother. Dad worked maintenance for the city after he left the mines, but Lola would shine his shoes as though he was preaching all day at the Temple instead of emptying trash and waxing floors. Later he did preach, and she'd sit up front with me nights, working her fingertips deeper under my thigh. She'd gaze at him, nodding and mouthing the right phrases, and move her fingers under me, tickling and poking me to prove what a good show she put on.

Dad was convinced she was a kind of prodigy, that she had the spirit in her. He said he didn't need to treat her like a child. He'd shut them up in his room and make her read Revelations to him while he prayed. My mother and I were forbidden entrance, but he told us we could stand at the closed door and listen to Lola speak the Holy Word. I saw them once, through the window from outside, when he'd left the curtain open. She sat on the bed stock-still, reading from the small white Bible our mother had carried at her wedding, while he knelt before her and clasped her knees to his chest, his head bowed on her bare legs. She was young enough that her skirt came just to his forehead. Her voice never faltered.

Years later, when we could talk about it, she swore that she kept him from carrying through. Now I know what it cost her. For a while he even rented her out as a douser to farmers trying to find water. He'd drive her through the county all day on a Saturday, and she'd walk across fields with a forked willow dousing rod, the men trailing her. Once she showed me with a yardstick, in our room, how she went into a trance and held the rod so it seemed to jerk and move of its own accord. She struck it lucky a few times, then began to miss, and got out of it by telling Dad the work gave her powerful headaches, that she couldn't be clear when the men who paid them money weren't favored by the Lord. She was ten years old at the time. Amen, she'd say at Temple. Even then, her mouth was like a flower with damp petals. Her white skin and that red hair. Our father made her wear a hat or a scarf to Temple: our mother's hats, her frayed scarves. Lola tied them on tight and covered her hair completely, like it was her idea. She'd get swept away, locked into this passion or that, even if it was Dad's borrowed passion, temporary, and ridiculed when we were alone in the bedroom we shared. It was our mother who scared Lola, sitting and looking out windows, sitting in the pew at Temple, so silent she only moved her lips for prayers.

Giving a person like Lola the looks she had was like giving a baby two fistfuls of dynamite. She realized little by little, and learned early to mirror back what people wanted to see. Our father thought she was his little Witness serving at Kingdom Hall, while she hid her cosmetics and borrowed heels at school. She'd sew clothes in home ec that she never brought home. People hate girls that beautiful, but she had a way about her. She'd steal inside, up close, she couldn't help herself. Even when I knew she was doing it, when she did it to me, it felt good. She could seduce me like she did anyone else, but the terrible thing was, with me it was real. She wanted my approval desperately, like part of her was always that motherless child, but she maintained her self-respect by competing with me, being unpredictable. I let her win, even encouraged her, when it served my purpose. I was the older sister but I let her protect me: our father was fixed on her. She managed him instinctively, played to his delusions, for years. She performed and adapted. I had rules and plans. I guarded my plans and was careful. Lola learned to offer herself up, to me or anyone: her smiles, her glances, a hymn, walking into a room, like she was sharing a peach. She made it look easy, and it was, but sometimes, with me, she was frantic, and she could go from one to the other fast. I held her then until she stopped shaking, but I was angry at the guilt I felt when she seemed vulnerable. She scared me the way our mother scared her, but for different reasons. Lola was impossible to control, and taking care of her was my job.

It wasn't hard at first. When she was a little kid, she said she wanted to marry me and no one else. She'd brush my hair at night, lay out my tenth-grade outfits, fuss over me. Little by little she took over chores I'd been assigned, cleaning and dusting, laundry. At eleven, she was taller than me. I was fifteen, but she filled out my clothes better than I did. Soon enough she noticed my new interests and wanted to smoke cigarettes, wear my sweaters, walk by the river with boys who had no idea how old she was. I paid her not to with lipsticks and cheap perfume she couldn't wear at home. By then I worked after school, clerking at Murphy's Five & Ten. Lola envied my grown-up life and drew my picture in that notebook of hers, page after page, my face from one angle and another, recognizable but changed, a reflection of a reflection. The rest was sketches of tables and walls, our bedroom window, the kitchen sink, like she was studying meaningless objects in secret.

She kept her notebook hidden. She knew something about those drawings she didn't want anyone else to understand. When I started seeing Charlie Fitzgibbon on the sly, an older boy already out of school and working in his father's restaurant, she lied for me. I was working at Murphy's, she'd say, or staying late at school. Two or three times a week, we'd pretend to go to sleep and she'd help me out of our bedroom window, then wait for me to come home.

Charlie and I would meet in the meadow by Polish Town when the grass was high enough to hide us, or by the river in the shelter of the railroad tunnel. I'd decided long before that Dad's religious wrangling and hellfire were lies. Charlie had been raised with his own version of the same. Whatever we did was wrong, equally sinful and private, so there were no boundaries. It was dark and we'd find a place to lie down. Now and then we'd catch glimpses of other teenagers, or see a Polish Town prostitute conducting her quick business, but we took our time. I'd come back home after midnight, warm and wet, smelling of the river if I'd washed, smelling of him if I hadn't. Lola would be sitting up, awake as though she'd never slept, waiting for my tap on the window. We kept a washbasin and pitcher of water on our nightstand, not so unusual in the '30s. Indoor plumbing was still a recent addition in a lot of Winfield neighborhoods. Lola would move the basin to the board floor and help me off with my clothes, like she was nursing me after an accident. I'd wash with that cold water and a piece of laundry soap. Later she'd creep out of her narrow bed into mine. What does he do, she'd ask me, how does it feel. Show me. Pretend. I turned my back to her, but I let her stay, and tangle her legs in mine.

Dad began going away on weekends, preaching over near Bellington. Finally he got his own congregation there and spent most of his time living over the storefront they rented as a Temple. They didn't pay him much but I was working enough, even in high school, to cover the expenses he didn't. It was a relief to have him gone. I was the adult in the house. Our mother grew even more silent, and never stirred after dusk. Late at night, I'd let Charlie into my room if it was raining or bitter cold, into my bed. Lola would go sit in the kitchen in the dark. She'd be gone when we started but sitting there near us when we finished. After, if we fell asleep for a few minutes, she'd be in bed with us, right next to me.

Maybe it's why she never stayed any amount of time with a man I didn't find first. Oh, I'm sure there were others I never knew about. There were years I wasn't in touch with Lola, for obvious reasons. But as long as she was near me, she borrowed my men. She never intended to keep them. Lola never kept anything. She knew better.

Back when Lola was a child men watched on the street, she was sure I'd marry Charlie and the three of us would live together. Never my plan, but she thought she was standing right between us. She thinks we're her parents, Charlie joked. She was fascinated that he went to confession and told the priest what he did with me, then prayed I wouldn't get pregnant. I didn't pray. I knew Gladdy looked down on me with a vengeance, that in her mind a pregnancy would always be the only scandalous, inarguable reason for Charlie to marry so beneath himself. We'd started when I was sixteen. You can have a baby, Lola would tell me, and I'll take care of it. She was quite dutiful, Lola was, as a young girl. She featured we'd go away like a little family and live beside the ocean somewhere warm. We could watch waves instead of a river that got brown and swollen and floated all manner of things that fell into it from Polish Town.

Lola found herself an ocean, but she didn't stay. Sometimes even now, I wake up in the dark and think of her, waiting for my tap on the glass. I can still hear the river and that sound, that tapping, like a message or a question I can't answer. The smell of earth and perfume comes up at me, like she's left her scent along the ground and in the air.

Termite

Lark smells like the soap smell on her hands. She puts one bowl and another in his arms tight against him so the bowls don't move. Down the alley the ragged orange cat crawls low under Tuccis' house. The cat drags its flattened legs under the porch steps and squeezes through webs and rotting leaves, over hard black beetles hiding from the light and the small scattered bones of harvested creatures. Mice bones and bird bones, bones of voles and flat-nosed moles, and rabbits too small to hop. The cat lies still on the cool dirt, safe in its litter of bones and scrap that smells of humid mold. Lark's soap smell is like white flowers. She stands behind him so the bowl stays tight and she holds the bottle of color in his hand. Two drops Lark says, pink instead of red. She tells him how the batter folds pastel pale, and he can feel the heat outside, wavering over the grass and the alley. The heat glints on stones and gravel and presses hard to cut. Too hot to be out, Lark says. Plants droop and the grass sighs like something squeezed, but the clean almond air of the soup in the bowl lifts in the weighted heat. Lark pushes his chair away because the oven racks slide out hot, but the fan blurring side to side blows the sweet smell in circles. He sits by the window and hears the faint roots of the grass in the berm of the alley, long veiny threads that reach deep in the ground to drink where no one sees. He holds the radio to say with sounds.

The doorbell is like an alarm that no one rings. He knows it's going to ring and it rings loud. It catches like a chime that chokes and starts and then it blares again.

Who can that be, Lark says.

The orange cat lifts its ragged head. The scars on its face shine yellow in the dark under Tuccis' porch.

Lark pushes his chair to the living room. The couch where Nonie lies at night and rests her feet is empty. The piano is empty. The chairs are empty and the low table where Elise and Solly played cards is empty. The house is only for Lark and him and the sweet smell of the cake, but the doorbell rings again. There's a glow through the window in the door. When he looks from the side he can feel it on his face, faintly cool. The heat from the open oven is like a shelf falling out and slamming, but the glow behind the door is quiet. Lark doesn't always know but now she knows. She opens the door and keeps it nearly shut. She talks through the space between. Murmurs and sounds. A man talking. Not a heavy man like Nick Tucci and Charlie.

I take a secretarial course, Lark says.

The man steps closer, air that moves in a shape. The glow falls through the door onto Termite's face and shoulders, a cool pale beam that's found him.

I was hoping I could speak, the man says. Voices are swirling in his voice and the voices move when he moves. He's more than himself. Lark doesn't hear, she doesn't see. Termite sees him, a shape glowing through the door that Lark keeps nearly closed. The shape shines like a light.

This is your brother in home care don't you find it.

The man's words come and go and echo with voices. The voices layer one over another and another, and they see inside, into every corner, into the boxes alone in the basement, into Lark's room and his room, inside the wall Nick Tucci broke to make a bigger door between, into the attic with its pull-down stairs.

What's his real name.

The voices know every name. The voices touch each plant in Nonie's garden and move along the clotheslines and into the shed and between the stacking chairs Lark puts here and here. Voices whisper up and down the alley, over the dry grass and hot white stones, around this house and that, careful and fast like a wind that rushes and knows.

Someone's birthday if you need anything.

Lark shuts the door. They stay still, waiting for the man to leave. Termite feels him standing on the sidewalk in front of the house. Finally the man turns and goes. His footsteps sound going away and the voices rush after him, breathing small sounds. The glow and the cool air move away, trailing him like shadows no one sees. There's a shadow of a taste in the warm room, and the humid air darkens with a sweet tinge. Lark says oh no. She pulls the cake from the oven. Not so you'd taste, she says. *Wild mint grows by the tunnel wall where the sun can reach. Solly bites the leaves with his teeth, presses them wet in his hands. Here, he says. Taste them Termite, on your tongue. Salt and sweet and bitter green, and that's her you taste on my fingers, even through the clothes she won't take off.*

Louder he says, train's gone now Termite. I know you want it back but now it's gone. Hold on to me, I'll take you in the water. You love the water.

The water comes up high. Solly breathes and swims them fast. The sky wavers and the river smells of iron where the train bled into its shadow and poured into the water. Lark sings the song about the bread upon the waters but Solly moves in the bright shallows where Lark can't see. What can I do about her, he whispers, keeps whispering, what can I do. But the water doesn't answer, the water is still. Nick Tucci's hand on Termite's head is warm and heavy and dark as the space under his house where the ragged orange cat waits for nightfall. At night the orange cat hunts and the lilacs stir and Nonie rolls her stockings down before she puts her feet up on the couch. Now the orange cat peers through the broken lattice that covers the underside of Tuccis' porch and Lark puts the chairs just so around the plastic table. The alley bleeds its green smell where the mower cut and the ragged orange cat waits to crawl long and low where the alley is open and wet. Nick Tucci drinks his ice tea. He says he's too thirsty to live and the sounds in his throat drain down and down into the wet dark inside him. He drinks loud and fast and Termite says and moves until Nonie sends Lark into the house. Nick Tucci puts his big hands flat on the table, but the darkness inside him follows Lark, steps close behind her everywhere she steps. Nick Tucci smells like Zeke's tears smelled when Zeke cried in the wagon and put his wet face on Termite's face.

One of your boys maybe.

Open the door for her to jump in.

He rings his bell once and Lark answers. She has the glass moon man in her hand and the cold across her face when she bends to get the cake.

Then she's standing in the doorway from the kitchen. Nick Tucci gets up and moves toward her, dark as the stones in the tunnel. He steps hard across the ground, moving heavy and deep as the rolling water in the river. If he could press against Lark he would hold on tight. *Don't you make him cry more now. Joey stop teasing Zeke because he cries and Termite doesn't. I told you Termite doesn't cry. When he was a baby we could never tell what was wrong except by how he moved. Zeke you don't have to cry. A dead thing is scary but now I covered it up. The dogs got her, that's all. Look, she left her kittens before they even opened their eyes. Joey do you have to be mean. Solly take these kittens home for Zeke. Take your shirt off Solly and we'll wrap them up and keep them warm. There. The little things. Hear them crying? All little ones cry don't they Termite. Except you never needed to cry.* The cake in his mouth is three tastes he can taste. Lark says the names of the tastes are in the colors, one drop and two drops, and she moves the knife fast, icing each layer, turning them round and round so the cakes turn too like soft sweet wheels. Then she puts one cake on top of another, turning it careful like a special prize. The alley pools its sharp green smell and glows its quiet stones. Cars plow through the heat with their tires ticking, sticky on the hot roads. Everyone waits for evening when the air gets bluer and the hot air lets go slow. Every grass yard makes a different sound, higher and lower, up and down the alley. There are sounds in every house.

Nonie sits between Nick Tucci and Lark. Nick says about the

river being brown and green and they're laughing and he says and says.

Oh that blue river.

He looks up to say. Their laughter chimes all around while the sky goes up and up. High up the rain is holding still before it falls. It's going to fall and fall, roaring like the ocean sound in Lark's seashells that she holds for him to hear. Oceans have waves like a pulse, Lark says, and she puts his fingers on her wrist to feel the tiny beat. The sound in her skin surges but the sound in the shells only circles, coming and going in one curled space. His birthday comes and goes and Lark makes every birthday. Nonie has the candles. The cake comes close and holds still and he sees. The lights jump and the black thread on fire inside each flame is burning small and big, standing and falling, and then the lights go out. He can make every sound and he makes the sounds. *Lark wears her swimsuit to make his bath. Nonie tells her when to turn the taps, how much hot and cold, how high, but Lark pours the bubbles and the white froth smells of soap. Nonie crouches by the hard lip of the tub and the small groan of her legs sounds when she moves. Lark sits in the bath to hold him and she moves his arms and calls it swimming but Nonie says hold still. Keep him still Lark, he doesn't know not to breathe if the water's over his face.* Lark's shape in the kitchen is taller and thinner than Nonie's shape. Nick Tucci has gone home and Lark leans over Termite and Nonie stands by the sink. Nonie soaps the dishes and Lark runs his bath. *The bubbles leave a sweet skim and Lark's legs in the bath are long thin shapes. She says her legs are his legs and they're taller than the giant in his book. The giant lives in the sky above the beanstalk and sings sounds to the Englishman. Lark says that was a bad giant.*

We're not smelling blood like him. We smell an evening in Paris. Nonie, why is it Paris?

Because Paris has the Eiffel Tower, like that picture on the bottle.

But why do they have a tower? You said Paris collaborated.

Not all of Paris, Lark. I told you, the Resistance were heroes and they fought all during the war.

Fighting when I was born, Nonie.

That's right. You were the best thing that happened in 1942. But you were three when you came to Winfield and the fighting was nearly over. You rinse him off now and I'll get the towels.

Fighting like Solly and Joey, Lark says when Nonie's gone. Tough messy fighters, Lark says, yelling a curse to scare the Polish boys.

Termite doesn't tell or say. Nonie comes back in her white slip that she wears under her uniform at Charlie's. She's a broad shape in her white straps, the turn of her head the same and her shoulder soft where Termite leans his head. He's in Nonie's arms that are wide and clean and smell of the cucumbers she slices thin and puts across her eyes. She puts him on the floor on the towels that are a hard bed and dries his hair, rubbing with a cloth. Her voice comes and goes. She says Lark is eleven years old and mother to that whole crew.

Don't you get tired of all those boys? Don't you ever want a frilly dress and a tea party?

Lark won't say or tell.

All right, what a face. You cloud up like a thunderstorm. I guess it's better you're like you are, fast enough to keep up with them and fight them off if you have to.

Lark says she can fight anybody and Nonie lifts the towel away. Her fingers touch across his eyes and he lies still in moving air. The bathroom window is open and the morning glory vine turns and twines, reaching in, breathing its own smell.

You may not be fighting them yet Lark, but you will soon if you have any sense. You'd best remember, boys' hands wander.

The air is soft all over him.

But not this boy's hands, Nonie says.

She holds his wrists and pulls him up so his hips rest on the floor. She swings him gently and the air slips under him, cool and quiet. Do it careful, like this, makes his muscles stronger. He'll hold his head up to listen if you sing something he wants to hear.

Lark sings the rhyme about the monkey and weasel but it's the vine he wants to hear, the sound of the leaves alive like ears uncurled and furled, the flowers opened wide and the tiniest buds like soft pricked points. The smell from the dishes and the bath are two smells like different flowers. Lark bends to turn the water in the bath with one long arm and then she lets it pour. He holds the radio. The hard round knob against his wrist talks to the tubes inside. Nonie makes the dishes slide and clank.

Lark, are you in a dream? It's way too deep.

They can't make us send him can they?

Don't have the training. Take care of him all this time.

He can smell the soap and the rain. The rain comes closer and the wind is in the morning glory vines, swaying them like a skirt. Water pounds and clatters into the bathtub and pours from the kitchen spigot and the night smell settles warm against the house, close against it like one animal against another. The vine has gone blind and closed its flowers but he hears it stirred and lifted in the dark, pushed against the window screen and sucked and pushed. He plays the radio to let it whoosh and roar. Nonie says he thinks that buzz and noise are music. Lark, will you take that thing away from him. Well it's his music Lark says, but she takes the radio. She turns the chimes fast on their string so they unwind slow and slower and make their lights. Drain out some of that water, Nonie says. *Cats hide in the weeds by the river, scared of the rail yard, scared of the dogs and the ditch. The dirt is dark and soft under the railroad bridge. Termite's feet reach almost to the end of the wagon and Lark reads him the book about giants in the sky. She pours tea into Termite's cup and says Solly don't let that cat in here. That cat has a ragged lip, old ragged cat that follows us everywhere. Solly takes off his shirt and cuts it sharp as a rope against the stone walls in the echo. Fe fi fo fum, I smell the blood. Solly's shape walks up and down and Termite helps to say until Lark says that's enough, the cat's run off. Then it's quiet. Just the heat like a buzz on the water. Solly says they're going in the river after the train comes, the river is warm as a bath.*

Lark, no one can see us in the tunnel, Termite sure won't tell. I made a bed of weeds see how soft.

We have to go to Charlie's for lunch.

So go later. She doesn't know when you come and go or who you're with.

She knows.

She doesn't know. I don't come around anymore when she's there. Anyway what have we done.

The river turns and turns. The train begins to whisper in the stones. He begins to say and say.

Lark, give him your sandals to hold, before the train comes. I'll do what you say. Everything you say. You want to. You want to every day, as much as me.

He hears them. Breathing is a bath between them, deep as the river and moving.

Wear your clothes then. I know what you look like, just not all at once. I'll be still, so still. Here's the train, do it now. Give him your shoes.

Lark's sandals are warm and soft, the leather shaped to her feet worn slick and the straps thick enough to hold tight. The ground is moving and the stone of the tunnel hums itself full before the train is on them. The train roars louder and louder until the river in front of him goes dark. The brushy island in the middle of the water disappears like a sunken lump, he can't see the blurred shape anymore or hear the sticks that swak and drag by the river's muddy edge. The train goes bright inside him, shakes into him and through him so hard he opens his mouth to breathe. The tunnel is empty and full at once, so empty he spins down and down. The wagon turns quick as a powerful limb and he rides it deeper and deeper. There's a picture inside the roar, a tunnel inside the tunnel. He's been here before and he looks deeper each time and he sees. There are sleepers everywhere, bodies crowded together. The bodies are always here, so many of them in the tunnel when the train roars across above, bodies spilled and still, barely stirring. The train pulls and lifts and shows them and lets them move. They know he sees them but they cannot say or see. No sounds, just the roar, lifting them with their eyes still closed, turning them over like the pages of a book. One shape stands and turns toward him, a man's shape opening his glowing hands as though to be sure he can. The soft light goes stark bright like a white fire and the pounding starts, pounding and pounding until the train pours off, gone away where none of them can reach.

Termite? Train's gone. Lark says you hear me.

You hear me? Breathe now, Termite. Train's gone for today. Let go of Lark's sandals and we'll go swimming. Boys can go naked. I've got you just fine now, see? I know you want the train back but it's gone.

We're in the water, Termite. You're swimming. Lark, he's smiling. Any boy likes the river. Hold to my neck Termite. See how good the water feels? Don't tell Nonie or my dad I took you in the river though. Our secret. The flowers are secrets, each one like a soft taut moth whose petal wings open and fold. Lark touches her face to his eyes and opens his hands to take away the petals. Lark says each rose is a knot that comes apart, pink petals and red, and these yellow ones are farewells. She says the glories have eyes, inside behind their stamens, eyes that twist shut in the dark, blue like your eyes, Termite, but not so full of light. Colors pulled from the flowers smell of one thing torn from another. They're pieces and scraps that ache. He holds them in his hands and holds them until they're damp and dark.

They let him sit alone after his bath while Nonie sleeps. Lark fills the bathroom sink and leaves the door open a narrow space. She takes her bath standing up but she doesn't know, she doesn't see. She washes with the cloth and moves the wet soap smell that's in his hair and powdered on his neck. The high ratchety sound the crickets make is louder and softer and louder. They're under the house Lark says, and in the grass, and they know to sing when the dew wakes them.

Nonie doesn't wake up and Lark's eyes are closed. He can feel the pour of the cool water and the wet squeezed cloth. Lark doesn't see but the ragged orange cat peers through the dark and starts its sounds, rumbling the steady hum it makes when it sits near him in the alley, watching and never touching. It even stands, padding softly foot to foot, smelling him before it drops and crouches and rumbles more loud low noise. The orange cat purrs like an engine and never scatters stones like the cars that cut the alley, smoking and throwing dust and tearing up the ground. Now the orange cat stops its sounds and moves, silent in the empty alley, into the yards and flower beds where moles tunnel and field mice burrow. The ragged orange cat creeps slowly before it runs in its crouching hop and pounces. There's never a screech like the owls make in the trees. There's a muffled flying in the cat's closed mouth, like the flop of a moth against a window screen or the urged skitter of a mouse in a box. The orange cat holds the flying, moaning in its throat, and runs for the hole under Tuccis' porch. It crawls in deeper, squeezing small. There's a tearing and then a silence. Solly's car squeals into the alley, shrieking and roaring and lurching hard to stop, but the ragged orange cat only pulls its torn prey closer, deeper into its low scraped hole. The doors of the car open and don't shut. The car stays waiting and the orange cat breathes. Lark stands by the kitchen window. She's a pale shape glowing and turning, curving smooth as the face of the moon man she lets him hold and says hangs in the sky at night. She says a moon is like a planet with no people or weather, so big that its holes and mountains look like a face from far away. She stands near him. He tells her to stay without saying, and the bruised night inside the house is the same as the bruise in the alley and the bruise in the sky. He looks and looks toward the open window and the frame of the window holds still. He can't see the moon but he feels its wash of lighter air falling over them, safe in the bald black of the dark.

North Chungchong Province, South Korea

Corporal Robert Leavitt

24th Infantry Division

He can hear the pain, shifting and moving, a big animal some-where close. He knows he's hurt bad and he holds still, looking hard into the perfect white. The pain presses at him, pushing, sliding near and veering away, and he drifts, half conscious, wait-ing for it to find him. There are banks of cloud, vast, featureless, soft. He sees a shape below him, a curve in space, a mountainous line against a sea: the Taebaek Range, rocky and broken, running like a north-south spine along the Sea of Japan. They're the same barren, unforgiving mountains that rose above Taejon and over-hung the lowlands he crossed and tracked and hated during the retreat. Now they shine, banked with clouds and spread out like some dinosaur's blasted ivory skeleton. Beautiful country, he thinks, so hot and so cold, and knows he's in a dream. It's winter in the mountains and the clouds are snow, drifted and deep, hor-rendously white, yet he feels no cold. He feels nothing but sees the moon set along the jagged peaks, a pale bulge round as an orange until it settles farther down, snug against the foothills. He hears a cry then and the land shifts, settles, and lengthens. Like a woman, he thinks, like Lola, turning away from him in sleep. He wants to trace the long smooth line of her body, run his fingers from ankle to thigh to hip. The rounded globe of her belly, seemingly within reach, glows like a moon he can touch. His legs are senseless but he can move his arms, his empty hands. He reaches for her but she's far away. He sees her far below him, gowned as though for a ceremony, flat on her back in a white room, the hard plane of a steel table under her and her knees pulled up under sheets. The baby isn't born and she's bleeding. It's her pain he hears, deepening, closing in. A burnished pewter light wavers as he tries to approach. The pearled edges of the tableau darken, flickering every time he tries to move.

He opens his eyes. The movement of light is tracer fire crossing against the stones above him. He's on his back in the grit of the tunnel and he feels a subtle thrum in the ground. He thinks it's the approach of tanks or heavy artillery until he remembers the stream on the other side of the tunnel wall. The tunnel exaggerates sound, displaces echo, vibration. There are indistinct voices, whispers. It's dark and the Korean girl has got them midway in, against the side of the tunnel where the dirt of the road meets the inner wall. Leavitt hears scattered artillery reports. Soldiers dug in just beyond the front and rear of the tunnel are firing sporadically. He lies still; if he doesn't move the pain locates just beside him, and he can think. He feels the girl behind him; she's taken the boy from her back and put him on the ground between them. Now she pulls Leavitt onto his side, into the curve of the wall, and presses the boy down, behind him. Leavitt feels for the butt of his revolver against his belly, under his shirt. The gun is gone. Carefully, blindly, he feels for the revolver near him, on the ground in front of him. He has it in his hand, pulled close, when he hears the girl talking to the old woman. She's in front of them, kneeling upright. The girl is telling her to lie down, stay flat on the ground, but the old woman moves close to Leavitt and looks into his face. She's frail, smaller than the girl, her lined face almost simian. Her small eyes are black in their raisined folds. He hears her curse him under her breath, like a whisper or chant, and then she spits on him.

There's a rush of Korean words from the girl as she wipes the spittle from Leavitt's face. Crouched behind him, near the wall with the boy, she touches him with careful, flattened palms, his eyes, the line of his jaw, his cheeks that are stubbled with a week's beard, as though to put him back together, repair the insult. Her hands are warm and dry, slim and weightless as a child's, but her touch is deliberate. Maybe she isn't a child. He remembers the shadow shape of Tompkins and his girl on the paper wall of the brothel in Seoul; the girl suspended in Tompkins' arms was probably no older than this one. It was always that girl. Tompkins let her choose which others they took upstairs with them, a means of supporting her status, winning her favor. The youngest girls called him *hyoung neem*, older brother, and formed an audience of sorts; they exclaimed like little kids as Tompkins held his girl aloft over the bed, turning her balanced on the soles of his feet as she extended her arms and legs, a performer poised in midair. Tompkins and his girl were beautiful then, siblings playing at circus games.

Leavitt hears the words, *halmoni, yogi*. The Korean girl is whispering urgently to the old woman, who sits motionless, inches away, staring at the ground. She ignores the girl and croons a kind of dirge. She might be crazy, or the war has driven her crazy; she might be a shaman, a practitioner of what the country people called Tonghak, the Heavenly Way. Superstition and magic. The elderly rural people still believe in *mudang* priestesses, *jangsung* spirit posts, *japsang* protection. Leavitt hears words, phrases. He's a murderer, she says, a demon, he's not alive. She spits into the dirt, then prostrates herself over her own offering as though before a temple deity. She believes he's a murderous spirit wandering among the dead.

The old woman is mistaken, Leavitt thinks ruefully. If he were a spirit he would fly from here, lifted like a mist, and take these children with him. Tompkins is looking for him, if Tompkins is alive. He's still certain he heard or sensed Tompkins' voice on the radio. *This is not enemy*: a phantom transmission. You must listen to me, Leavitt tells the girl in careful Korean. He can see, in the dark, the shapes of bodies lying where they fell, villagers wounded in the strafing who made it to the tunnel and died, or survivors killed by sporadic fire. The Koreans still alive are terrified, silent, huddled near the tunnel walls or lying flat on the ground, unmoving. The nervous American troops seem undirected, pinned down, or shooting at whim; the fire may get worse.

Leavitt wants to tell the girl to get him to the tunnel entrance at first light. He wants to keep his eyes open, focused, but he's shutting down, losing track, his consciousness manufacturing images as though to compensate for his entrapment, his injuries. The images are vivid and acute, a sensory expansion or avoidance. It doesn't feel aimless; it feels like information, direction cut adrift from space or time. He senses Tompkins' restless, impatient energy raging near him, searching. Tompkins considered himself equally menaced by North Korean troops and American command; command kept your ass in a sling, Tompkins said, while the Communists shot at it. Leavitt knows he can't depend on Tompkins to find them. Their panicked platoon may have taken casualties and scattered after the second strafing, left the wounded. Tompkins might be hurt or dying.

His attention blurs, and then sharpens: he sees Tompkins looking at him intently, peering at him as though into an enclosed space, through a window. Then they're together in open air, moving effortlessly through a densely green Korean landscape. It's a sunny day. The sound of the war roars past like a train they forgot to board, but they don't acknowledge it. They're in a country grove where it's shady and quiet. They stop under the trees, near the red wooden posts of a *hongsal-mun,* a royal grave site. Two *haet'ae* statues guard the decorative latticework of the open gates. The *haet'ae*, fierce fire-breathing creatures that resemble lions, are massive, waist high, settled back on their haunches like big dogs. The features of their faces move and they turn their stone heads as Leavitt and Tompkins approach. Tompkins touches one of the statues and takes a round red object from its mouth; he shows it to Leavitt, a small *kwusul* disk with a flame decoration. Leavitt looks past him to see Tompkins' girl, and the other girls from Seoul; they're all with him, there beyond the graves, moving

across the grass in a gently swirling *salpuri*, a traditional improvised dance still performed in rural hamlets. Tompkins looks at
him and smiles; shakes his head as though to comment on Leavitt's illusion. Then the picture changes and they're alone, standing
in the dark near a simple *myo* shrine that marks a commoner's
grave. Tompkins' dark eyes are somber. His face is leaner, narrow
and gaunt, his high cheekbones nearly Asiatic. He gives the
kwusul to Leavitt, closed hand to closed hand, and says it's from
the mouth of the dragon: *the flaring jewel of Buddhist truth*. The
kwusul, compact as a small flat stone, is surprisingly heavy. Tompkins is speaking, but Leavitt can't make out the words. There's
something more. Something about the gun. He's saying to holster
the gun.

Leavitt hears the old woman. He's in the tunnel and the old
woman is mumbling in cadence, chanting or praying. The girl has
pulled Leavitt onto his side with his back against her, and he can
reach the empty holster strapped to his thigh. He moves his hand
to the gun in the folds of his clothes and grips it carefully, forces it
securely into the holster. His arms are heavy and it's hard to move.
He knows he's passing out intermittently, but he has to keep
track. He considers giving the revolver to the girl, but he reasons
she'll know to take it if she needs it. The old woman, her face in
the dirt, doesn't move and continues to chant. He feels the girl
next to him, by the tunnel wall. He has to convince her. You must
do exactly as I say, he tells her in Korean. She doesn't respond.
Ihae hashimnikka? he asks her. Do you understand? *Ne*, she whispers, yes. Get me to the entrance of the tunnel, he says carefully,
taking care to translate correctly. If they see an American soldier
alive, they'll send someone. I can tell them: no infiltrators, only
villagers. The girl doesn't answer, or he can't hear her. It's hard to
speak. Has he spoken? He's not sure. There's more gunfire. He
hears the *thug* of a dropped body near them, and stifled cries. He
feels the girl behind him, pulling the boy lower between them.
She's a smart girl, a good girl. They need to shield the child and
they need to rest, so that she can pull Leavitt to the front of the

tunnel. He can feel the curve of the boy against him, warm, nearly weightless. Quiet, breathing.

Gently, the girl puts something, a thickness of folded cloth, under Leavitt's head. The boy's face is against the back of Leavitt's neck. Your shy skin, his mother used to say, touching his neck at the base of his hairline. Leavitt hears her calling him. It's evening, when he was so young he didn't work in the store; he's seven or eight years old and she's calling him in from the street. If they see I'm alive, he tells her in Korean, they'll come for me. That's good, Bobby, she says. She's kneeling in front of him, combing his hair with a wet comb. He sees her young face, the face he saw as a child. This is not enemy, he says. She smooths his hair and her hands are wet. Drink, she says in Korean. Lie still. He hears his mother talking to the old woman. It's his mother's voice, softly entreating, then it's the girl's. He sees the old woman kneeling near him in the dark. She's taken the gun from his holster and holds it in her palm as though inspecting it. Leavitt wonders calmly if she's going to shoot him. The revolver looks big in her small hand. Take the gun from her, he tells the girl in Korean, give me the gun. Before he can calibrate the old woman's intentions or try to move, she puts the gun to her head and shoots. Leavitt feels warm blood spray his face and the gun's report echoes through the arched space like thunder. The sound rolls under him like concussion, and he knows the troops dug in beyond the tunnel will think the refugees have weapons. Immediately, a volley of fire pours through the tunnel from the rear. An answering volley from troops guarding the entrance ricochets against the walls. The girl screams and pulls him against her, low and tight to the wall, out of the line of fire by inches. He loses consciousness in a roar of enveloping sound.

The hard mouth of the canteen tastes sharp and metallic against his teeth. He's in a blank shell, and he wonders if the gunshot was a hallucination. The girl has turned his head up to give him water, but there isn't much left. He understands she's rationed it, kept it hidden from the other survivors, who are moaning for water, for help. He doesn't hear the old woman, doesn't see her. If it happened, her body might be gone, moved with the other dead to one of the tunnel entrances. Piled corpses are the only barrier to American fire. Dangerous now to move at all, to stand or be seen, to leave the tunnel wall. The light is gone. Shadows in the tunnel have lengthened. Leavitt sees the old woman's body near them, small, motionless, covered with the same cloth the girl had folded as a pillow. The cloth covers the old woman head to foot, but Leavitt imagines he can still see her face and her bright fierce eyes through the fabric. The girl is holding the canteen to his mouth, but Leavitt forgets to drink. Water tracks down his face and the girl's hand moves to catch the liquid, touch it to his lips with her finger. He can smell blood. She would know not to waste water; she's wiped his face with her bloody clothes. Moments have passed, not hours. The troops outside are waiting for orders, and the orders will come. Daybreak, Leavitt thinks. Command will be forced to act, squeezed by the invasion from the north, their own lack of troops, the need to move.

Who was she, he whispers in Korean. My mother's aunt, the girl answers. It's as though he's crossed beyond his own limitations of language; the Korean words come to him, and he understands her without effort. She wanted to stay in the village, the girl says, but the house was burning. He sees the burning house and knows which one it was. Am I speaking, he asks, do you hear me? *Ne, ne.* Yes. Do you have the gun, he asks. She nods. You keep it, he says. He knows he can't hold the gun now, can't lift it. She tries again with the canteen. He swallows twice, carefully, and she turns his head back, returns him like an infant to his darkness.

He sees his mother lying on the cracked green linoleum of the store in Philly, her eyes open and still. He remembers that he shut her eyes and straightened her head, then stood and left immediately. Now he stays. He rests his palm on her forehead, just at the curve of her skull, and lets himself see how fast she's finally fled, how she's letting him go in the precise moment her freedom begins. He goes upstairs this time as though granted permission and packs the same clothes and schoolbooks, takes his trumpet and a folder of sheet music. As before, he doesn't call anyone, but the dark panic he felt that day, the inability to leave, is gone. She wants him to go, he understands that she's directing him: his release is the only ceremony she requires. Eventually the old man will come home and find the last evidence of his broken promises, his estrangement. It's a moment she's arranged and neatly escaped. *Bobby? Go ahead, practice. Sounds nice.* The vague heaviness he took on as a child, as a young man who couldn't save her, is distinct; she lifts it from him, this *kwusul* he's carried in his chest for years like a red ember. Her loneliness, her aloneness but for him and the thousand details she managed daily, was her own jewel that flared in the dark. You're like me, she would say to him when they were alone. And you're like me, he tells her now. Listen, this is for you. He plays her favorite, the same euphonious solo rendition of "My Funny Valentine" that became a standard at Onslow's Club between Lola's sets, a pure melody he could play in his exacting, pitch-perfect sleep. Sometimes it was like sleep, like an exalted dream, standing there onstage in the white light of the spot. The smoke of countless cigarettes furled wavery and blue, ascending in the air around him. He must have played the song for his mother hundreds of times, late at night to block out the sound of the street. He was thirteen, fourteen. Stay out all night when you're a man, she'd tell him, you be in this house by eleven, and he nearly always was, in time to stand in her doorway before she lay down in her darkened room. She'd be up at five to take deliveries for the store and she didn't stop all day. The old man was out most nights with cronies or women and slept on the twin bed they kept in the living room in lieu of a couch. It was just Bobby and his mother in the apartment, neon signs on the street flashing altered pastels through the windows and across the floor. He played the notes in time with those hues of light, a Braille that fell across his mother as she closed her eyes. He worked to perfect each note because it was all he could give her, and he tested himself anew each time he played the song. The familiar chords pushed everything away, and his use of the tune as a solo refrain between sets at Onslow's was like a return to ritual. The fluid notes said what language could never phrase; he played them over the world that was his mother's grave. Lola said she couldn't listen while she was backstage, changing one dress for another, hair, eyes, lipstick; the song distracted her so, made her want to lie down in it. When he told her it was his mother's song, she looked at him a long moment and smiled. *Of course it was, and you're the whole world mended.*

He hears the slow swing of the song's wordless phrases now and sees himself standing in the spot, playing alone onstage, eyes closed, but he's on the dance floor with Lola. Her hands are laced easily behind his head, moving on his neck as they dance close in the crowded club. Sometimes they danced to the jukebox, but now they're in this strange split moment, hearing him play a song that only he plays exactly this way. They're together and she's got that languorous satisfied smile and wet-eyed look she wore in the wake of making love, a look that always seemed unbearably sad to him. He has to go now; there's no more time. He knows she loves this song, the serious, funny words like a question and answer game, a riddle for mended hearts. *Is your figure less than Greek?* He's kissing her because this is the last time, ever . . . *laughable, unphotographable.* They could go into Onslow's office and lock the door, but the Korean girl is watching them through the phrases of the song, holding the sightless boy in her arms, pressed on all sides by the crowd pouring into the tunnel. He looks at the boy, and looks at him, and Lola sees him too, through her own labored breathing. She cries out sharply, as though it's she who must reach the boy, save him. She often cried out as though in pain when they made love, until Bobby moved her past her first sharp arousal. It was like moving through a steep and narrow passage, like following her up flights of narrow stairwell at the club that first night, with only shadows and colors showing in the dark. He knows her body as he knows his own and he listens with his muscles and his nerves, with his pounding heart, pacing himself, moving with her and holding back, opening, opening into her. When he's inside her nothing seems haphazard or happenstance; it's all inevitable, terrible, beautiful. He touches her hard high belly then and feels the baby pushing, pushing to get out of her. The tense bands of muscle in her pelvis are like iron. Leavitt wants to hold her but she screams in anguish, falling away from him. She can't follow him; she stays, her breathing strained and loud. He knows she won't come with him; she's staying with the boy.

July 27

Winfield, West Virginia

Lark

He starts moving the colors as soon as I give him the crayons, edging a perfect curve on the newsprint. Over and over, fast, then slow, like there's one arc he can trace. He leans forward, starts and doesn't stop, both hands. He presses darker and darker, like he's been waiting to cover the words and the white, like he knows all his drawings are one picture I keep interrupting. I bring him to the basement on hot days. No matter how hot it is outside, it's cool here. I can feel him listening while I walk back up the basement stairs to shut the kitchen door. He knows I'll come back with my pencils and sketchbook, and he sits so still that I can hear what he hears. The give of the stairs, like an easing. My footsteps across the broken basement floor to the storm-cellar stairs, five stone slabs that open out into the yard. Even with the lilac bushes on one side, heat and light pour through like syrup. I remember when the storm doors were wooden. Now they're steel, so heavy I have to shut them one at a time, pull them down from inside like I'm shutting us into a cave. Termite hears the storm doors pound into place when I let them fall.

I give him his big crayons. At first I taught him colors. He knows one color from another, like he smells or hears some difference, even if he can't see. I tried to teach him shapes. I held his hands and traced shapes on the newsprint, like we were in school, but he would go rigid and tense, sink into himself. He wanted to move his arms, make the one shape he draws deeper and deeper.

Now he knows I'll let him. I start to draw and I don't think about him. I don't think about the boxes piled against the wall or what's inside them, or myself or anyone. I look at Termite and I draw, shading closer and closer to what I really see. I draw the way he moves, sitting so straight, focused so sharp and true there's nothing else. He reminds me there's a clear space inside the chores and the weather, inside cooking and cleaning up and taking him downtown or to the river, inside the books in my room and Winfield and the alley, and typing words on machines at Miss Barker's. It's quiet in that space.

In the quiet, I can hear.

"Termite," I tell him, "I know you want the radio. We'll listen later."

His arm moves, coloring.

I'll take him to Charlie's for lunch, even though it's so hot we'll be alone on the bumpy sidewalks and the street leading downtown.

"Termite," I say. "It's too hot to sit by the alley."

I draw his arm as a blur, an opening. The rest is outside. The stones and grass. Kanawha Hill and Main Street, unrolling past Nonie and the Formica counter at the restaurant. The field by Polish Town, so lush it lulls whatever moves in the tall grass. I sink shadings and shadow into the thick paper in my notebook. Everything else stops.

We get to the restaurant when the lunch rush is well over and the counter is empty. I never bring Termite until later, when his chair is always free. Charlie has one stool at the counter that's actually a child-sized barber's chair, with a leatherette-upholstered back and arms and a metal footrest. He got it years ago for Termite, from a barbershop that closed down and gave away its equipment. It's the same height and distance from the counter as all the other stools, bolted into the floor like the rest, with a foot pedal that doesn't work anymore. That chair is the first seat people take if they're alone and thin enough to fit into it. It's cushioned and comfy, ladies like it, and I've seen kids fight over it. I bring the wagon in through the wide restaurant door and park it in the space between the counter and the wall, where it's not in anyone's way. Nonie wipes down tables, resupplies condiments. Then she'll start on the supper special. Charlie's already doing prep. I hear him in the back, chopping on the broad butcher block beside the sink. I hear Gladdy running on at him.

"There's just no sense in it." Her reedy voice carries over any other sound. "The city's hiking taxes. You've got to lower expenses, not raise them. Why use country sausage when you could use hamburger?"

If Gladdy finds out what they're making up in bulk, she always gets after them to use cheaper ingredients. She gets after Charlie for hiring hard-luck cases as dishwashers or extra waitresses, even if they're excellent workers, like this place is in danger of falling off the social register. She would have been after him long ago to fire Nonie, except she knows she couldn't get the same amount of work out of anyone else. Gladdy, if she's not in Florida, is here every day for lunch, and she comes just in the middle of the rush, sashays in and sits at her own little table. She's exercising her rights as owner and checking up on everyone when it's busiest. Then she hangs around until customers clear out so she can harangue Charlie. Funny how she's always by herself. Meaning it's no wonder. Nonie refuses to wait on her. Gladdy orders the special, like she's testing it. She won't address the help, but half the time she'll send a note back to Charlie—"needs salt" or "too rich." She never orders dessert, due to her diabetes, but she'll send a note about a dessert she observes—"whipped cream unnec. on berry pie." Nonie keeps all of Gladys' notes in a drawer; she calls them Charlie's fan mail. In twenty years, Nonie says, not a compliment. The food is actually pretty good at Charlie's. Not fancy, but good, and the portions are big. Charlie says he's got just the kind of place he wants: no liquor license, no problems. Good food, reasonable costs, dependable clientele. The tables are full every meal, but it's slow enough between rushes that they get the prep and cooking and cleanup done. He closes at nine without fail, wraps up the supper special in a neat package, and takes it home. Nonie refers to this as Gladdy's dog bag. And well worth the trouble, Charlie will say, keeps Gladdy out of the restaurant but once a day. A wonder that woman can make her own breakfast, Nonie will say, and a miracle she does.

I put Termite in his barber-chair stool and sit beside him. I order the tuna-salad plate and the kids' mac and cheese for Termite. He loves it and it's easy for him, he likes to feed himself at Charlie's. Nonie's got the napkin holders lined up on the counter, and a box of napkins bound a hundred to a bunch, so I start filling the holders.

Gladdy's holding forth. Now she's standing in the kitchen doorway and glances out and sees us. Knows she's got an audience. "The kids' mac and cheese you make with American cheese and your homemade sauce is good enough for any grown-up. Inexpensive to make and perfectly good. Just put some parsley on top. That should be your special." She picks up her pocketbook, like she's got a schedule to keep, but there's always one more thing. "What about this storm they say's coming? Did you patch the roof where it was leaking, out there by the back door?"

"I did," Charlie says. "No need to worry." Out of sight, by the sink, he's chop chop chopping.

"You'd best stay here the night if we get the storm they're expecting," Gladdy calls over to him. "Keep an eye out. Insurance is so slow to pay if there's damage."

There's a clatter of pans from the back. Charlie sleeps here once or twice a week when Gladdy's in town, storm or no storm. The pullout couch in the office makes into a single bed. Elise jokes that Nonie can balance Charlie and the restaurant accounts in the same two hours, in a room the size of a freight elevator.

Now Gladdy ventures out among us, having finished her confidential chat with Charlie, and Charlie is right behind her with a bowl of the pureed soup he makes for Termite. "We have storms in Florida certainly," Gladdy says, "but not the winters, the ice." The idea of the storm reminds her of her second home, and the sacrifice she makes to be here with us more than half the year. "I know my place is here, but the sun is there."

"Sure is," Elise says. "Come January, maybe we'll all come down and visit."

"It's a tiny place, but the porch gets the sun." Gladdy sighs and goes on. "I've got all I can do to save the airfare by November, but it's worth it to stay through the worst months of ice. At least Charlie can run things here without worrying about me falling on these icy sidewalks."

"You're a trouper," Elise remarks.

"Gladdy," I ask her, "is Coral Gables near Miami?"

"Surely," says Gladdy. "I fly into Miami and take a bus right from the airport. Some would take a taxi a distance of thirty miles, especially at my age, but it's not a way I'd spend money." She sniffs. "I don't tarry in Miami. Miami has a bad class of people."

I decide to ask. "Did you know my mother, Gladdy?" Nonie shoots me a glance before the words are out of my mouth.

Gladdy doesn't hesitate. "Well, no, not really. Not to speak to." She looks into space. "I mean, I knew *of* her. Everyone in Winfield knows of everyone else."

I'm thinking about the boxes in Nonie's basement, the moving company logo. No street address. Just *Miami, Florida*, like that's all anyone in Florida would need to know to call up Bekins Van Lines. We have a moment of silence and Gladdy stands there, smoothing her dress, one of those jersey old-lady dresses with buttons down the front and a patent-leather belt. Today it's navy with white polka dots. On her way in the door, she'll have hung her broad-brim white hat on the coatrack. As a resident of the Deep South, she's always thinking about her skin. Which is funny, Nonie says, because Gladdy was as wrinkled as an old prune before she ever started going to Florida. She's a thin little thing, all bones and hardness. "Parsimonious" is the word to describe her. I don't picture my mother, I can't see her, but I feel her as a warmth, all curves and movement, just the opposite of Gladdy.

I stand beside Termite and help him hold his bowl of soup while Charlie grates cheese over top. I like the restaurant after the rush. Despite Gladdy, it's cozy, like something has just happened and now it's over and everyone's relieved, and the air is full of warm smells and the dishwasher is making its steady *whoosh* in the back. It's a watery undercurrent sound Termite likes. Usually there are two or three customers at the tables, but today it's just Elise, taking her lunch late. She often does, and refers to her presence as a visit. She'll have the chicken noodle soup Charlie is famous for, three packets of crackers, and then two cigarettes while she talks to Nonie. She takes her full manager's hour and sits at a table in the front, where she can see across the street into the window of the Coffee-Stop and make sure the girl she left in charge stays at the cash register. I like how Elise's lipstick leaves a little pink smudge on the tips of her Camels, even after she's had the soup. Elise has her own lunch rush over at the Coffee-Stop—workmen buy doughnuts and the hot dogs she cooks in one of those electric contraptions that rolls the wieners around on a slotted tray until they look sunburned. Elise gets a charge out of Gladdy. I think she's secretly pleased when she meets up with her at the restaurant, which is the only place anyone ever meets up with Gladdy. Gladdy walks the ten or so blocks back and forth from her house at the east end of Main Street for exercise. Other than that, she doesn't even go to church. A person would feel sorry for Gladdy if she wasn't so hard to feel sorry for.

Now she sails toward the door. She's on her way home, holding her pocketbook up to her chest like a shield, but she isn't quite finished. She stops just opposite Termite and me, and says, over the lunch counter between us, "I suppose you look related, but then again who could tell."

"Tell what?" I ask her.

"What he'd look like, if whatever happened to him hadn't happened."

Termite's eating his soup, vegetables and meat ground up so fine he can swallow it, using the fat round spoon Charlie saves for him. I'm putting napkins in the holders lined up in front of me, and I don't even look at her. "Nothing happened to him," I say. "He was born just as he is. And he can hear every word you say."

"Of course he can." The pocketbook snaps open. "But he can't tell what I mean. That's all right, though. None of the rest of you ever seem to know what I mean either."

Charlie's standing in the kitchen doorway. "Are you still here, Mother? Thought you were going home."

He has a harsh tone in his voice, but Gladdy's got to have her say. She nods her head, very deliberate, unfolds the hankie she's taken out of the purse. "It just seems he'd be better off where people trained to do it could take care of him."

"I take care of him." I turn full toward her, between Termite and her, to keep her eyes off him.

"Well, you're used to him. That's training of a kind." She blows her nose. "Commendable, I always say, I tell everyone. How generous my son is to work around your needs. No matter what it costs us, it's commendable."

"Actually," Elise says, "the more it costs, the more commendable it is, wouldn't you say, Gladdy?"

Gladdy ignores her and looks at me. "I don't know how you'll manage when he's a man as big as Charlie."

Elise says, "When he's as big as Charlie he'll be running this joint and you won't be allowed in it."

"I wouldn't know why not." Gladdy shuts her purse, the hankie balled up in her hand. She touches the hankie to her brow as though she's wounded. "I've never been unkind, though I get no thanks for it. Be that as it may, he's in here most days, isn't he? I don't object."

Elise raises her penciled brows. "Aren't you objecting right now?"

"We all have to make a living, partly for his sake," Gladdy says. "Most customers are used to him, I suppose."

I suppose, I suppose, I suppose, Termite chimes in and keeps chiming, louder and louder as Gladdy moves toward the door. She nods to herself as though considering, doffs her hankie over her shoulder like a wave good-bye. Then she's gone.

Charlie's walking toward us, chuckling and wiping his hands off on his cook's apron. "You're a sly one, Champ. I definitely want you in my corner. I believe I'll make you a vanilla milkshake with chocolate syrup, blended smooth just the way you like it."

Termite is quiet, listening, his ear tilted up at Charlie. He gives his sideways look and a corner of his mouth turns up in that quizzical movement that might be a smile.

Nonie reaches out and tousles Termite's hair. "A milkshake sounds fine," she says, "but not until he's had that mac and cheese."

Later, when Nonie gets home, I could ask her: What about *that?* How can you say he doesn't know what goes on? And she'll look at me and shake her head. Lark, she'll say, what about the other ninety-nine times out of a hundred, when he sounds off strictly according to his own rhyme and reason?

She doesn't understand. That's the point: he's got a rhyme and reason. We only see the surface, like when you look at a river and all you see is a reflection of the sky.

Elise has gone back to the Coffee-Stop and the dishwasher is still running. Charlie says the storm will hit late this afternoon. The river is already high, though Main Street seldom floods. Our part of town, the water gets high every big rain. Nonie calls them grass floods because the water just covers the grass a few inches. She never moves a thing and brags her basement is tight except for where the floor slants. She says that's water come up from underground where the cement's cracked, not leaking in the walls or new storm doors. Gladdy's basement floods two or three feet, any big storm. Nonie says it could be fixed, but Gladdy is too tight to spend the money. High water is a feature of river towns. When we were kids we watched the grass floods from Nonie's back stoop or Tuccis' porch. An inch or two of standing water on the alley and the yards looked magical. We made little boats from silver foil and set them moving. Sometimes they floated all the way up the alley and disappeared. When the water had gone down we'd find them two or three streets over, smashed and still glittery.

Nonie clears our lunch plates and pours the last of Termite's milkshake into a paper cup. Charlie has taken Termite to the restroom. He says Termite is old enough to use the Men's, and when he's at Charlie's that's what he'll do. I don't think Termite cares, but he likes it when Charlie picks him up and carries him off with such matter-of-fact certainty. I see Termite in Charlie's arms and think of Nick Tucci last night, reaching to take the tray from me with the evening and the alley soft behind him.

"Charlie and Nick Tucci remind me of each other sometimes," I tell Nonie. "Both dark haired and brawny, with furry arms."

Nonie laughs. "You make them sound like bears."

"They could be brothers," I say.

She shakes her head. "They're totally different. One's a hot-headed Italian, tough as nails and built like a fireplug, and the other is a six-foot, fifty-plus Irishman, afraid of his mother and balding. All they've got in common is that they grew up Catholic, they work dawn to dusk, longer in Charlie's case, and they love you kids."

"And they love you," I say.

"I suppose," she says, like it's just dawned on her. Then she adds, "For all the good it does me."

I don't know what good it does, but they really do love her, more, I think, than men love their wives. "They love us because they love you so much," I tell her. It's true. Nick looks up to Nonie, like she's an older sister he adores, and Charlie depends on her for half of everything, even putting up with Gladdy. "It's like Nick and Charlie are family who don't talk to one another. You make them family."

Nonie smiles. "Don't let's tell them."

Termite's exiting the Men's, slung in Charlie's arms, crooning sounds. *Tell them tell them tell them.* He hears words, even soft ones, through walls. I don't know how. It isn't possible.

Charlie puts Termite in the wagon. "The man's in his cockpit," Charlie says, like Termite's piloting a Spitfire, wedged in tight in his cushioned seat, the sides of the wagon shoulder high. "You get on home now," Charlie tells me.

"Charlie, it's not going to rain for hours. We'll pick some wildflowers, go by the rail yard."

Rail yard rail yard rail yard. I'm pulling the wagon out the door and Termite makes his sounds, like we're bidding everyone a civilized good-bye.

"I'll be home by dark," Nonie says. "You be there too."

"Absolutely," I say. "You know how he feels about the river in the dark."

I'm joking, because Termite loves the river anytime, but I don't hear Nonie's answer. Main Street receives us with its usual afternoon sounds. Cars going by, the traffic light's whir as it changes. I wave at Elise in the window of the Coffee-Stop and give Termite the rest of his milkshake in its paper cup. "Better drink it before it melts," I tell him, and fix the straw so he's got the end in his mouth. People who don't know Termite get nervous around him. They look away, but everyone who does know him wants to give him something. The fact is, once they know he's not the emergency he might appear to be, they find an excuse to be near him. He doesn't demand anything or communicate in the usual ways, but he somehow includes them in the way he pays attention, in his stillness. It's how people feel when they look at water big enough to calm them, a pond or a lake or a river. Or the ocean, of course. The first time I put my ear to a conch shell, it was as though I could finally hear the sound Termite lives in.

He's one reason I think about Florida. Taking Termite to the ocean has always seemed to me like taking one full space to another. The ocean is the biggest sound I could ever show him, bigger than rivers or trains. The other reason is the address on my mother's boxes. Taking him to Florida would be like taking him to her. Even if she isn't there, she must have been there once. Maybe with him, or even with me. And Florida is warm. In winter, Termite hardly gets out. He loves the feel and sound of snow, but I can't leave him in it long. Nonie says we have to be careful of his lungs, of his breathing. She worries about pneumonia, even though Termite's never had it. When he has a cold, you can hear him from across the room, a ragged purring sound. Nonie gets worried. She coats his chest and throat with Vicks VapoRub and fits a paper bag onto the spout of a boiling teakettle, and makes him sit with his head in the steam. She'll stand right with him and rub his back in slow circles, tell him to breathe, breathe, as though that's not exactly what he's doing.

People think Termite is delicate, but none of us kids ever thought so. I do what he needs, but I don't worry about him. People could tease or neglect him, but I don't let them. I don't worry about germs or accidents or about him getting worse. The worst happened before he was even born, and he's still here. In my book, he's strong, strong as me or Nonie.

Your book is a strange book, Nonie would say.

The rail yard is quiet today. Something is different. There are almost no cars on the sidings. Just one engine sitting on the main track, with four boxcars linked behind it. Engines don't usually stop in Winfield at all. They only idle and back up and slam forward to link onto cars stored here for pickup and transfer. This engine is dead stopped, like it's been sitting here awhile. Then I see the engineer, standing to the side, and another man in the cab.

"Termite," I say softly. "There's an engine on the track, and an engineer."

The engineer doesn't see us. He's looking at a pocket watch on a chain, just like the White Rabbit in *Alice in Wonderland*, but his uniform is dark, with piping down his jacket and cuffs and across his hat. The dark bill of the hat shades his face. He purses his lips as though the watch face is a serious matter.

I walk right up to him, pulling the wagon. Termite knows tramps ride the trains, but not that men drive them. I want him to hear this engineer talk, hear him climb into the engine, drive it away. "Excuse me," I say, "why is the yard so empty?"

He looks at me, distracted. "Got some weather coming through, apparently. Everything's shuttled south, out of the way. Not much stored at this siding now anyway."

"I've never seen it this empty," I say.

"Oh, this siding is slated for termination," he says. "Not worth it to the railroad to repair the lines, especially on that bridge." He nods in the direction of the river and the stone railroad bridge we glimpse through the trees. "Inside of three months, there won't be a thing through here anymore, weather or no weather."

"My brother won't like that," I say, but Termite is silent. The engineer is facing away from us and doesn't seem to notice Termite in the wagon. "When do you expect to pull out today?" It's a sensible question, but the engineer doesn't answer. I start to wonder if he's a mirage, if it's not true this train is stopped here, not true there won't be any more trains. I make my voice a little more insistent. "Where do these cars go?" I ask. "I mean, where's the end of the line?"

Line, line, line, Termite says, each tone slow and pure and clear. The engineer registers mild surprise and looks behind me at Termite. He nods acknowledgment, man to man, like there's nothing unusual about a boy in a deep wagon, eyes hard to the side and head tilted, fingers up and moving. He touches the watch in his pocket and turns toward the boxcars beside us. "These cars? The Long Islands switch off at Beckley and run east. The Chessies, now, they move straight south to Augusta, Georgia, and on to Jacksonville."

"You mean Florida?"

"Surely. They're loaded out of Fort Lauderdale and Miami.

Cheaper to run them straight down there empty. Three, four days, depending." He looks over at Termite. "To answer your question, Miami's end of the line for the Chessies."

The other engineer calls down to him then, from the cab. Our business is concluded. I nod and step away as he touches his cap to me and climbs up into the cab. I feel foolish, asking about Florida; if you're in Georgia going south you'd hardly change direction to go to any other Jacksonville. I'm walking away and Termite doesn't protest. I've changed my mind. I don't want him to feel this train pull away.

It's not far to the tunnel under the railroad bridge. We cover the distance fast, out of the rail yard into the cover of the woods, onto the broad dirt path through the trees. The path was a road once. Before the rail line, Nonie says, when freight moved by boat on the river. They widened an Indian trail that was already here, and horses hauled flatbeds of supplies and trade to a town we wouldn't recognize now. A settlement, not a town, small and rough and new. There was someone like me in that place, and someone like Termite. There have always been people like us. And the river has been here too, for hundreds of years, for a thousand or tens of thousands. If I stood just here, I wonder how far back I would have to look to see the lines of the river change. The island is different. It's temporary, a little hill in the river. Some say it's earth layered year after year over a shelf on the river bottom. Others say it started as coal slag, mine refuse dumped illegally off the bridge at night. Companies skirting regulations before the deep mines shut down. Either way, the island is beautiful now. It gets green, then barren and snowy, like any other landscape, and buds out in the spring, though it's no bigger than a city block. Sumac seedlings rooted by the water turn bright red in the autumn. The top of the island is naked grass, a green cone the scrub trees and bigger brush haven't colonized.

"Termite? We'll just stay a little while, before the storm."

He hums at me in response, a quiet, tonal code that stops and starts. We move out of the cool of the tunnel onto the dark earth

by the river. I pull the wagon up next to me and sit. I'm just beside
Termite, our shoulders even. I don't have to tell him we're facing
the water. He tilts his head to the side, and his eyes, like he's sensing the river twice.

The light is changing fast. The sky has gone mauve, and the
colors on the island look bathed in yellow. The grass top of the
little hill glows like a lit stage. That's when I see the deer. They
walk straight up into the light from the other side, three dark
forms that move higher until they gain the summit and turn to
scent the air. I see the shapes of their legs and long necks, their
flanks. The top of the island is no bigger round than an exercise
circle where you might walk horses, and the deer move across it,
raising and lowering their heads as though to smell or hear what's
wrong. One, a young buck, has two-point antlers. They're lit from
behind, black as silhouettes. The sky has lowered and gone
greener, and the air stirs as though charged. Suddenly one of the
deer, the male, plunges down the side of the island as though pur-
sued and leaps into the water. It swims powerfully toward us, legs
pumping under the surface, head straining forward. Termite is
silent, completely still, his eyes closed as though to listen harder. I
don't move or breathe. The deer is gaining, gaining, more than
halfway across, when it suddenly turns and begins swimming just
as forcefully back. I stand up then, cold to the tips of my fingers,
as though an icy core of me has blinked awake. The deer moves
away from us, pumping hard to gain the island again, as though
sensing there's no point coming here, to this shore, to the shelter
of the tunnel or the high cover of the field. It won't help.

"A deer was swimming the river," I tell Termite. "It must have
smelled us. They smell people from a long way off." I don't know
how though. There's not a breath of air to carry a scent.

Termite has clenched his fingers. I realize I'm holding the handle of the wagon just as tight. Now he opens his hands as though
to stop my voice, blows with his breath, a long sigh, but there's no
plastic ribbon, no blue to move.

I see the swimming deer clamber out of the water and crash

frantically up the slope. There are three shapes again, but they stop moving. They're still, looking downriver at what's coming. The sky pulses dark blue behind them, veiled with cloud like a swaddled fist. One long jag of lightning opens through it and disappears. I don't hear the train at first, then it blares its whistle, halfway across the bridge. The engineer can't have seen us; maybe he's signaling someone, somewhere. Such a short train ends before it starts. It disappears before I've even turned around and hauled the wagon up the slope. Then I bend down to Termite and put my eyes near his, our foreheads touching, where I know he can see me. "Everything is fine, Termite. We'll go now, before the storm."

The storm. He says it once, and I pull him away through the tunnel, under the railroad bridge. The tunnel is dark as dusk inside, and humming. I didn't use to hear it but I've learned to. It's more a vibration than a sound, like a remnant the trains leave in the stones. The tunnel used to seem so vast to me, like a cave all us kids could live in, big because of the weight and fit of the stones, and the volume of space it seemed to hold above our heads. Now I see how fast a woman pulling a wagon moves through it toward home, into the vacant lot between the tracks and Polish Town.

The lot is choked with weeds and flowers in summer, flowing waist high to the cracked pavement of Lumber Street and the leaning second-story porches of Polish Town. Nonie says Polish Town field was full of victory gardens during the war, neat and cultivated and fertilized, but the whole town was different then. The town has gone down, emptied out, but the soil of the field is still black and rich and dense. The weeds and wildflowers mix with lavender and dill and come back every year, tangled and fragrant. The field gets so high that the city mows the lot every August, to keep things from happening in the tall grass. Boys fight or drink here at night, fireflies blinking all around them in the dark, and lovers lie down where they can't be seen. Mothers in Polish Town won't let their girls near the field, but every summer there are some girls who don't listen. Boys from all over Winfield come here to find them. The churchgoing Polish girls sit on their

porches. Sometimes a boy from Dago Hill or even Country Club
Road will court them and speak with their mothers and take them
out of Polish Town. They're mostly blond girls and their mothers
are heavy, and they look at the field together and wait. The Queen
Anne's lace is shoulder high, white among purple joe-pye weed
and bright pink echinacea.

I want to pick flowers for Termite, a huge bunch to pile in the
wagon, but I move fast through the tall grass. The blades part like
a crowd. Termite moves his hands to feel them like a sharp sea
across his fingers, and the wagon cuts a narrow swath. Most days
the field is full of sounds. Bees and insects on the tall stalks buzz
and click. The dragonflies and jumping hoppers do a kamikaze
zing and flirl through our hair, past our ears. Not today. There's
silence. Everything alive is huddled at the roots of the plants, or
burrowed into the earth a few protective inches.

Thunder sounds high up as we walk into the alley beside the
Tuccis' house. It's continual thunder, rumbling like muffled barrage, and a wind has picked up out of nowhere. Right away I see
Stamble on Nonie's front porch, waiting. He doesn't see me. He
probably can't, if his eyes are as weak as Nonie says. He stands still
in his dark suit, looking out at the street. He's taken off his suit
coat and hat and stands there in his shirtsleeves, cuffs buttoned
tight and proper. He's thin, so thin. His white shirt hangs off the
sharp bones of his shoulders, and his sleeves blow back tight
around his skinny arms. There's no sun, I guess that's why he
doesn't need the hat. His pale white hair is long, almost like a
woman's, long enough to blow and swirl back from his face and
the steel frames of his glasses.

I tell Termite someone is here from Social Services. I see that
Stamble glows a little in the strange light, and I do, and Termite
does. My white blouse, Termite's T-shirt. The afternoon has
closed down, gone purple, coaxed and sucked dark by the storm.
Pale things look bright. Even the pale gray insulbrick shingles on
Nonie's house look bright, like the house is floating on a patch of

black grass. Rain has started, but it's a strange rain, blows of needling spray that stop and start.

"Ah, there you are," Stamble says, as though expecting us. "I've brought you something."

Then I see the wheelchair beside him. It's smaller, child-sized, the wheels thinner and higher than the ones on the chair we keep in the closet. The seat is a square cushion, like on a chair you might take to a beach. On the seat there's a sheaf of wildflowers, long stemmed, bushy with grass blades, fresh enough they haven't wilted. They seem to be the flowers I didn't pick, and I feel so strange seeing them that I don't say anything about the chair.

He leans down near Termite. "You remember me, Termite. That's your name? My name is Robert, Robert Stamble."

He puts the flowers in the wagon with Termite, like a gift, then touches the metal handles that come up behind the back of the chair, pushes a lever underneath with his foot. The chair folds up, the seat collapsed, and he pushes it with those handles to show it still rolls on its wheels, all skinny and compact.

"It's different from any wheelchair I've seen," I tell him.

He looks pleased. He's different too. I wonder about him at Social Services, working in that warren of eight or nine desks in the main room. The gaggle of women I know by sight must disburse when he approaches a klatch of them at the water fountain. They consider Nonie uncooperative and difficult, Termite a terrible shame, and me a poor unfortunate. Maybe Stamble was assigned our case because no one else wanted it; he was new and had to take what they gave him. Stamble is strange, with his pale pink look and pressed suit and air of having appeared out of nowhere. Maybe he makes them uncomfortable, and they assigned him to us so they'd have an excuse to fire him or transfer him when he failed. Then again, maybe he's not so incompetent. He's brought us this wheelchair without Nonie signing a form or a voucher or writing up a request. We didn't even make a request.

Rain is whipping down fast, then hesitating. We can see it stop and start just beyond the metal awning of Nonie's narrow front porch, and the wind gusts harder, moving the flowers in Termite's lap.

Stamble leans down next to him, between him and the wind like a shield. "Would you like to try sitting in the chair?"

Termite sits real still. Clearly a no. I could answer the question for him, but I don't. Stamble seems comfortable enough with the silence, and he stays still too, his face near Termite's, like he's waiting, listening for another kind of answer. Stamble's white blond hair is only a shade or two lighter than Termite's, and his light eyes would seem as startling if they weren't so pale and weak and narrow set. It's almost as though Stamble and Termite are related versions of something, but Stamble walks around in the world and Termite doesn't. Stamble's invisible to people except as an oddity, like Termite, but he's not so set apart that people don't expect things of him. He has a job and a suit, but he stands and moves in his own peculiar, leaning-away stance. He keeps a distance. Like he's careful, not used to himself. He's got nothing to help him out but that suit, and the hat that covers his pale hair and shades his face. No holler-back protector like Nonie, no radio knob to fiddle with, no blue plastic ribbon to blow and blow. Everything is gone from Stamble, you can tell by looking. He's passing through, he's visiting.

"Where's your family?" I ask him. "Where you from?"

"Not from around here," he says. He stays crouched down next to Termite and touches Termite's head with his pale hand. "That wind is going to get stronger," he tells Termite. "It's going to blow all this heavy air to smithereens." He says it like he's thinking the way Termite thinks, that any storm is a good thing because he loves hearing them.

I've got a radar about anyone who might hurt Termite, make fun of him, take advantage. I'm realizing my first feeling about Stamble had to do with Social Services, and the surprise of him appearing so suddenly with that briefcase. They all have briefcases. But he's not like them. He really is strange. I wonder if people know how strange.

"Looks like that storm they've been talking about is here," I say.

"I've got to be going," Stamble says. "You two had better get inside." He stands up now, away from Termite, and grasps the briefcase he's left sitting by the door.

"Don't I need to sign anything, about the wheelchair?"

"Not at all. See if he likes it first. See if he'll use it."

Now the rain has turned hard and solid and steady, like a watery curtain falling straight from the edge of the porch roof. "You want me to lend you an umbrella?" I ask him.

"No need," Stamble says. He steps off into the rain as I'm opening the front door, pushing the folded wheelchair in front of me, pulling Termite and the wagon behind. I look for him, walking away, but the rain is so dense I can't even see the street. It's as though Stamble has disappeared.

"You've got your storm," I tell Termite.

He doesn't say anything. He's listening to rain on the roof, pouring off the gutters, running in little rivers, while I dry him off with a towel. We didn't really get wet, but everything feels damp, cool, and the smell of the rain has filled the house. I put Termite in his soft upholstered chair and shut the windows except for a couple of inches, so the sound of the rain comes through, then I open a newspaper in a corner of the living room and steer the wagon onto it. The wheels are wet and dirty and I've got to clean up the tracks across the wooden floor. The wheelchair sits in the middle of the room, folded up, and I move the coffee table to one side so there's more space. I like the rain, the sound and the way the pouring water turns the air a pale gray evening color. Thunder cracks and rolls and repeats. It's raining hard and we're closed into the sound.

I open up the wheelchair, flip the latch underneath to lock the seat steady, then I sit. It has cushioned straps that fit over the shoulders, and a waist strap, and a seat back thick as a pillow. It might work for Termite. It moves so easily, and turns and reverses. The wheels make a light ticking sound on the smooth floor. Termite wouldn't use his hands on the wheels, though. He'd have to be pushed, at first, anyway. He'd still need help.

He's turned his head. He hears the chair now, like it's a sound timing the rain. I'm thinking I could ride him on my lap and he could rest his wrists on mine, feel how to steer and turn something lighter, quicker. Today I just want him to listen. I push his big chair into the middle of the room on its clunky refrigerator wheels and sit back down in the wheelchair. Then I close my eyes and try to feel the circle around him, the space cleared of furniture. I move up and back and around, reverse, turn backward and forward. I bump into the table and the piano, but only at first. The tick of the wheels gets faster and smoother, and when I'm just near Termite I can hear him, distinct from the pour of the rain, making his own sound in the back of his throat. I know he's turning his head, listening, keeping track of me and the sound of the chair. He's like the second hand of a windup clock ticking so smooth it blurs into another sound.

That's how Nonie finds us when she comes home, drenched just running from Elise's car to the back door. She turns on a lamp in the softly dark room and sees us, Termite in his chair, me in mine.

"Well, I never," she says.

I don't say anything for a minute. I have to get used to her, standing there stolid and wet, when the room felt so closed and pure before. "Stamble brought this wheelchair by," I tell her. "It's smaller, easier to use."

"I didn't ask Social Services for any wheelchair."

"We're just trying it out."

"Who's trying it out?" She shakes her head at me. "I suppose you can use it if he won't, if it entertains you so. But I can't imagine Social Services will allow us two wheelchairs. They'll have to come back here and get the other one. Right now I'd like you to heat up the chili I brought from the restaurant. Tomorrow, with the Flood-Relief people coming in, we'll sell a lot of chili—it offsets the damp." She steps out of her wet shoes and nudges them with her foot, onto the newspaper I unfolded in the corner. Her white waitress shoes sit empty near the wagon like they belong there. She gives me a wry smile. "They say half the town will flood, but they've been wrong before."

I stay still. I want to get out of the wheelchair, fold it up and tuck it away, but not in front of her. It's like Stamble convinced me the chair is secret. It has the feeling of him all over it, and his whispery sound I'm just starting to hear. But Nonie doesn't look at me. She's standing, quiet, looking at Termite. "What do you think, Termite? Are they wrong?"

Termite doesn't answer, doesn't say. He turns his head away, tilts his head up, listening, like the answer is in the air, and anyone should be able to hear it.

Nonie

I come into the kitchen soaking wet, the sky thundering and rain sheeting in drifts, pounding like it has its own weight. The blue glass barometer Lark hung on the wall is cracked to pieces at the top—too cheap to register the pressure. The blue water has leaked out and stained the cardboard frame, and the light inside the house is stained too, lit up and olive green. The storm has squeezed daylight to a thin shine, and there's Termite in his chair in the living room, with Lark turning circles in a wheelchair I've never seen before. It's like she's performing just for him and he's listening, with that look he gets. It slays me. So much was taken from that child before he was even born, yet he always seems to want exactly what he has. He's himself, so intent and fixed, when Lola was never still.

Lola always got what she wanted, until she lost all she had.

She wept, about me, she said, not Charlie. She was calm, as though I was the one who didn't understand. *I wanted to be with you both and he was the only way I could.* Then she stood back and accused me, like she had a right. *You left me for so many years! And you wanted him, you needed him to stay.* Yes, I answered, and he was a chore you undertook for my sake. Did you think I'd never find out? She said he would have left us. Then you should have let him, I told her. *You would have sent me with him.* I didn't disagree. You have a job, I told her. You're making a living as well as I am, and you can't live here anymore.

I didn't see her for days. She stayed at the club, and Billy and I packed her things. Like a father, Billy threw away her battered suitcase and bought her new ones, to hold her new clothes and shoes and the satin sheets she'd bought for the bed. Then he asked me to marry him. He said it was time I had a man worthy of me. He paid some boys to move Lola's things into his rooms above the club, and he moved in with me. We got married at City Hall the next week, and Lola stood up with us. Charlie was gone, but there were three of us again. She went right on, smiling, somber; it was as though she had a more appropriate set of parents and she assumed her place, rehearsing in the afternoons, singing at night, sleeping all morning, while I quit my job and managed the books at the club. I kept Billy's hours, though I didn't indulge in his habits. He concealed most of them at first, the drinking, the cocaine, his occasional heroin use, but he couldn't conceal his cooked books and the way he actually made his money.

As for Lola, I think now that she wanted Charlie with us as much as I did, for different reasons, but she was certain he'd leave after a few weeks if he wasn't so mesmerized and aroused and at fault that he couldn't go home. Maybe she was right. He'd told Gladdy his address was a rooming house, that he worked as a chef at a restaurant. He wasn't inside a church the whole time he was in Atlanta. Later he told me he confessed to an Atlanta priest before driving nonstop to Winfield. Gladdy allowed he was ill when he got home and put him to bed like an invalid. He went back to work and stopped thinking anything at all, he said, until he got the phone call from me three months later. Lola was pregnant with his child. We were family again, or still, despite everything. Lola wanted the baby. She said she'd intended the pregnancy, though she didn't want to marry Charlie or anyone else. *This is Charlie's baby, and yours, the only way the two of you will ever have a child. Someday you'll understand, you'll forgive me.* I told her I wasn't interested in babies. I wanted to leave, get away from her; now I couldn't. I had to stay until she'd given birth and I knew they were safe.

Things were falling apart for Billy Onslow in Atlanta. He had a smaller place in Louisville, where his family practically owned the county. He was going back to run the club in Kentucky, and if he liquidated fast enough he'd stay ahead of any charges in Georgia. He was going to dry out, he said, run a low-profile operation. We all moved to Louisville, and Billy and I were at the hospital when Lark was born. Billy handed out cigars. He really did see Lola as a daughter by then; his business would support her and she would sing in his club, but he vetted any suitors and made it clear she wasn't for sale, like certain of his other employees. Their choice, he said, his protection and business guidance for a clear percentage.

It was a world Lola could live in. Billy was kind to her and his operation was classy enough, she saw herself as a legitimate performer in a stable situation. But she didn't kid herself, as Billy might say. The baby couldn't grow up here, she said, or in any life she could provide. She sensed I was going back to Winfield before I even told Billy. *No one needs to know. Say she's your child, with Billy; you're married, after all. Or she's your divorced sister's child. Just let me keep her with me while she's so small she won't remember me.* Maybe she couldn't raise a child, she said, but she could take care of a baby. The other girls loved Lark, she'd have plenty of help. *Then I'll send her to you. Billy will bring her, and I'll help you, every month. I won't ask to see her, ever. Don't tell her anything. I*

don't want her knowing any of it. She's yours. I didn't believe her.
That baby is your responsibility, I told her, I had all I could do to
take care of myself. If she didn't think she could raise a child, I
said, she shouldn't have had one, especially with Charlie.

I resolved things with Billy. Despite his various enterprises, he
was more honest than the politicians and cops who profited from
his hard work. He dealt with a lot of people, and I never knew a
soul who said he'd abused them. I couldn't settle in his life,
though; I couldn't stay. We went to Reno for a weekend divorce. I
didn't ask for a settlement, but he declared he was going to win me
one and show me a good time. He didn't clear as much as he'd
hoped, but in those days the five thousand dollars he won at
blackjack was plenty for a down payment on a little house in
Winfield. Charlie wanted me to buy in a better part of town and
help me with the payments, but I wasn't owning a house with
Charlie. This is my place, I told him, not yours. In fact, he
couldn't afford to help me. They were about to lose the restaurant;
even Gladdy admitted as much. I arranged to borrow enough
from Billy Onslow to help us turn the business around. Lola
wrote to me, sent photographs of the baby. I never answered. Lark
was almost three when Billy Onslow showed up with her. I had to
take her, Billy said, Lola wasn't doing well. Everyone in the place
was only getting more attached to the baby. Lola had to finish this
and pull herself back together. Yes, I said, well.

Lark had a grave little face, and Charlie's Black Irish looks, his
dark hair and liquid brown eyes. Lola's sculpted features weren't
much in evidence yet, and that was lucky. To me, Lark looked like
Charlie. He and I were together again, after an initial few months
of his sad, hopeful courting as we worked to save the restaurant.
He said Lola got into bed with him one morning after I left for
work and he wakened making love to her. It was confused and
crazy, part of a dynamic between Lola and me we both knew Lola
had wanted all along. When he left, though, it was clear he'd lost
me, not Lola. I wouldn't marry him, ever, I told him. I wouldn't
live with Gladdy or even be related to her, but we were together.

Now here was this child. Maybe life hadn't cheated us out of so much after all. At the time, I didn't really care what Lola suffered, giving Lark up. I told myself Lola had created her own suffering. I put away all I knew: the child on the bed with our father at her feet, the skinny girl waiting alone in a dark kitchen, the teenager left in an empty house with a mother who didn't speak.

I told Billy he could bring in Lark's things, clothes and toys and a half-size bed he set up in my spare room. Then he hugged me, said he missed me, and left. Lark had never called anyone Mama, but she certainly knew Lola's name. She said it like a constant happy question at first, but I'd busy her with something, and little by little, she forgot. My name was not so different from Lola's, to a toddler.

I took two weeks off work to spend every minute with Lark, and then Elise came over while I did the supper shift at the restaurant. She'd put Lark to bed and read romance novels till I got home. It was manageable, and the Tucci kids were right across the alley. Nick's wife was still with him. She was a drifty, sweet girl, and those little boys hung all over her like satisfied puppies. Lark joined them. By the time she was four, I took her to work with me; she napped in the office and played in one of the booths, and Charlie adored her. Gladdy was so angry she "retired," but town gossip settled any scandal on Lola. I said Lola's marriage hadn't worked out and the father wasn't involved; I really didn't know anything about him and it didn't matter. Lark was my niece and I was her legal guardian, she'd take my name, the adoption was in process. Gladdy was getting older; she stopped by the restaurant every day but mostly left it to us.

Those years when the war was ending and Lark was a child were good years, and light and bright compared with the struggle when Termite came. That was hard, all of it. He seemed the damaged mystery of everything I'd never finished with Lola, and the sadness of all that had gone wrong for her. In '49 she wrote to tell me she'd married that young soldier, and signed the letter with her married name. She was pregnant; they were going to buy a little house when he got back from overseas, maybe in Florida, by the ocean. She promised never to try to take Lark from me, said she only wanted to see her, to be her auntie, and she hoped we'd come and visit after they were set up in a cottage with a yard and a palm tree. A palm tree! It turned out there was one, a scrawny spiny thing with spiky fronds, and the picket fence she wanted, not that she probably cared anymore. She had a long difficult labor and a damaged baby, and then got news her young husband was dead in Korea. I asked Charlie to help her buy that little house in Coral Gables, and he mortgaged the restaurant to buy it free and clear. Gladdy was livid. She only agreed to sign if the cottage was in Charlie's name and the restaurant in hers.

Billy and some of the Louisville girls helped Lola move. Billy helped her with expenses, and one or another of the girls stayed with her the first weeks. She wouldn't let Charlie or me near her. She said she could manage. I decided to respect her wishes, give her time to get on her feet, and then I tried not to think about her. I didn't hear from her again until Billy Onslow called to tell me what had happened, what she'd done, and then Termite was here. A soldier who'd known his father brought him in Billy Onslow's car—all according to Lola's instructions. They were a whole crew—the soldier, a big man with a terrible limp, his young Korean war bride, and a nurse Billy had hired to care for the baby in the backseat of his big black Packard. The nurse turned around and left with them, of course. The Florida cottage became Gladdy's "retirement bungalow"—another reason I can't stand to think of the place.

Once Termite was my responsibility, I went day by day. It was only Lark's pleasure in him that began to change how I felt. They have such privacy between them. I'm here to protect them until Lark can manage it herself. And she will, as well as I ever have.

You think anyone at that school would tell me what happened, why Termite got afraid to go there? I went with him one day, but I couldn't see what scared him, and he couldn't tell anyone. He can't do puzzles or draw or learn letters. He won't hold a pencil, only those thick round crayons Lark puts in his hands. He can listen to music and repeat sounds at home. Social Services likes to threaten, exercise authority. They said he was past school age and he would have to go; they'd initiate an Aid to Dependent Children investigation if I didn't send him. The county could intervene, petition for a special-needs placement. It's in the boy's best interests to be stimulated, they said, as though he suffers for attention, for people to care and do for him. Lark's had him all over town nearly every day in that wagon since he was a baby. She took him everywhere. Summers they'd go off with the Tucci kids and I wouldn't see him until lunchtime at Charlie's, and I never worried a minute. Lark fed him, she kept cold drinks in a thermos, she found bathrooms, she kept him propped right, pillows all around him, she talked and jabbered at him. It might seem a twelve-year-old couldn't take care of a kid like him, but she watched me and she knew how and she never seemed to get tired of it. Winters after school she'd sit right down with him like she'd missed him all day. Elise helped us the first couple of years, but by the time Lark was twelve, it was her. I worked evenings at the restaurant and Charlie helped me financially. I'd have Termite bathed and their dinner ready and then I'd go to work. How else could I pay the bills?

Elise will say even now how maybe nothing happened at the school and Termite just doesn't want to leave the nest. Maybe he needs a push, she'll say. Never mind about you, Noreen, but doesn't Lark need a life? You can have a break if he's in school. Don't you need a break? So what if they don't teach him anything, as long as they take care of him. He might be Lark's doll now, but he'll grow up someday and be a mighty big doll. Finally Charlie tells her he's heard enough. Lunch hour's over, time Elise got back to the Coffee-Stop. Without Charlie even saying so I know he's thinking what are the chances Termite will ever grow up, and that's what he thinks I ought to be telling Lark. I should tell her Termite's on loan. High interest loan, Charlie would add, very high. Aid to Dependent Children, some aid. Like how special that special school was. Made him scared of his own shadow, not that anyone could ever tell him what a shadow is. Lark is the dark and the light and the shades between, and the names for those are not what he considers. And what did she ever consider? He was her mother's and that was all it took.

Termite

In the basement the cold comes up from the hard cracked floor, up from the broken places where dust layers and the cracked concrete flakes and pebbles. The cold sits on the floor and breathes, one low shadow that folds and settles and stirs like smoke when Lark turns and walks and moves. Lark doesn't know, she doesn't see. She closes the storm-cellar doors that open wide as flat steel tongues under the dark green lilac leaves. The heavy doors clang shut and heat falls across them like an animal that can't get up. The ragged orange cat lies in the cool of the railroad tunnel, on the concrete of the buckled road the railroad made and left to break and crack. Lark says men from the scrap yard hauled away big pieces they smashed loose with axes, so long ago that moss and straggled weeds grow in the empty places. The orange cat sleeps on a tilt of slab but its notched torn ears stay tense and turn to hear. Rats by the river scuttle and thump. The orange cat slits its black-rimmed eyes at every sound and Lark shuts the kitchen door at the top of the basement stairs. Her feet step down each wooden step. The basement windows throw their light across in slender pools that move.

Termite, Lark says, I know you want the radio.

We'll listen later, she says.

The kitchen is shut away. Above them the spigot ticks its drip and the refrigerator hums and stops. The fan turns its metal face to no one, clicking side to side. The basement couch is deep and broken and he sinks into cushions and cold. Lark puts the wide breadboard across his legs and gives him newspaper to color. Here's a sheet with no pictures you make the picture Termite, and she holds his wrist to show him where. The crayons are cool and poured and silky slick and Lark says to start with the green. Small, see Termite? You don't have to color so big, but he says until she lets go of his wrists and gives him colors in each hand. He knows she'll stand by the workbench with her notebook and her thin pencil that whispers and never stops. He can move then, both hands to make the shape, mixing the colors dark, moving his arms to color deep. He presses hard and the colors get deeper and rounder, he makes them darker and harder until the space inside them is deep enough. Lark is finished and she stops his wrists and holds his paper up, close to his face. He smells the deep smooth waxen colors and the dark. He knows he made the shape.

See? Lark says. Always a blur in your picture, here, like a man or an animal standing.

She tells him the blur is there because the board is gouged underneath and makes the color go on lighter in just one place. She hangs his picture on the line with clothespins. In summer they hang the wash outside and the basement clothesline is empty except for his sheets of newspaper, open to show each shape.

Here are last week's pictures, Lark says. Here's yesterday, here's today.

Black rainbows Termite, all the colors at once.

He feels his pictures stay. He smells their dark gloss and hears them move on the line, their paper edges curling small, pulled in by the shape. Lark doesn't see, she doesn't hear, but the orange cat hears the dogs, yelping and crashing through Polish Town field. The dogs are running a rabbit they smell veering from its nest, weaving away from a burrow so deep and hidden the dogs smell endless tracks in the flowering weeds.

Lark says he can hold his ribbon. He can be outside but not by the alley. He has to sit here by the kitchen stoop where there's shade. She says the sun is boiling and the storm that's coming has sucked up all the air. He tells and says to be near the alley but he sits in his chair and the alley is across the grass. The white stones in the alley are still and their long tracks lead to the rail yard and the tunnel and the river folding its shape. Deep inside his pictures, a shape stands up and listens.

Lark says, I'll turn the radio loud and put it in the window.

She gives him his ribbon and she goes. The kitchen door slams and he hears her put the radio against the metal smear of the window screen.

He says until she lifts the screen while the radio buzzes loud. It whines and then it talks. Top ten hits. Number one song for the Platters. Water pours in the sink while the faucet sputters. Lark moves the hot sponge on the dishes and steam comes up behind the radio. She's told him that whirl and thrill that opens songs is an orchestra, men playing horns before the voices sing *asked me how I knew.* He moves the blue and moves it and hears Lark singing *true is true.* She's told him replied means yes and denied means no. Cannot be denied means always yes. No in songs is yes and smoke gets in your eyes. He feels her standing at the sink with the heat around her face. *Nonie holds him on one hip and flares the paper bag over the steaming spout of the kettle. Nonie melts salve in the kettle. The kettle was screaming but now it only pours wet smoke. Nonie says steam will help him breathe, here Termite, with your face just at the edge. Deep now. Breathe in. The brown paper of the grocery bag smells of wilted boxes but the steam gets in his eyes and he breathes the warm white smoke. There now, Nonie says. Breathe, breathe.* Lark says steam is wet smoke that doesn't sting but there's no smoke. He sees through the blue into the sky and there are no clouds. The sky goes away, whiter and whiter. Termite moves the blue and moves it and the radio rolls its sound like a blue swell through the alley. Flies smash and fumble through the open window. They bump and move inside the music. When Nonie gets home she'll hang a curl of gluey paper from the ceiling and say screens are to keep flies out, why do they lift that screen.

Lark says they have to go to Charlie's now. She takes his strip of blue and rolls and folds it and says they're going. Rush at the restaurant is over, Charlie will be wanting to see them. Heat shimmers along the alley. Bars of light are pouring in a yellow sheen all the way to the tracks at the rail yard. He wants to go there, but Lark puts him in the wagon. She pulls him up the alley to the paved road. The wheels tick on the concrete sidewalk and go silent on the tarred street. The tar is hot and the surface breathes small bubbles that bloom and break. Water beetles trundle from the gutters. They stick in the tar, upended in their hard shells. Sometimes Lark turns them over with a stick and skitters them back to the dark, to the wet insides of the grates along the curb. The beetles are long and fat as thumbs. Termite hears one move its legs in smooth wild blurring clicks. Lark stops to look but she won't let him touch. Termite hears it minutely lifted, swarmed by ants. The ants keen fast, piling into an edge that wants to pump and push. Lark knows to go.

They go one way, up the hill into town, past Gladdy's house and Murphy's Five & Ten, past Dairy Joy and the Coffee-Stop. Elise sits in her chair at the Coffee-Stop or she sits in her chair at Charlie's. She tucks her feet behind the wooden rungs and turns her hips and props her arms on the table. She sits warm and curled like a cat that's safe and sucks her cigarettes. She takes care of Nonie and Lark and her hair is a dark orange blur. Red highlights she says, and paints her eyes in thin hard lines. He sees them when she puts her face close. *Elise stays in the kitchen and Solly puts him in his chair. He's small and Elise says he's excused. These other kids can work when she babysits. Solly, make yourself useful and move the furniture while Lark vacuums. Then you kids get the laundry off the line. It's near dark and dew will be wetting those sheets.*

The vacuum roars in and out, working its billowy bag, blaring muffled wind and wrenching the rug taut. The whirling in the bag is like bees packed tight. The machine sucks air through its long neck and Lark holds the cord in one hand like a hard rat tail that whips and smacks. She pushes and pulls and the noise howls louder. Dust flies in clouds, stirred and rising. Solly pushes Termite's chair, following Lark each way she turns. She can't hear them in the roar and Termite rides the cutting buzz that rattles in the floor. He smells and hears each shape in the clamor until the vacuum dies and the fat black bag goes small.

Stop it, Solly. He shouldn't breathe this dust.

The dust hangs, drifting, settling back, hiding, covering. Solly says laundry is girl's work but he holds Termite and follows Lark through the kitchen into the yard. The screen door slams and Solly's chest is smooth and moist and streaked with dust. He holds Termite on the curve of his hip, against his low jeans and the slim ridge of his leather belt. The clotheslines run in front of the laurel hedge and fill with colors, each with a sound for the deep hedge to murmur back. Lark hangs sheets over two lines so there's a narrow space between. Solly stands in the space and turns Termite in slow circles until they're dizzy. They lie back along the hedge inside the twisted white and the laurel leaves under them go back and back. The dark leaves hold the dark, rustling all night, awake.

Lark snaps pins off closer and closer along the line, throwing them in her apron pockets and filling the basket with clothes. She's pulling the sheet from under them and Termite says until she stops. Solly pulls her close and she leans against them with the weight of the basket in her arms. The heavy apron slips to her knees and the leaves move, taking them in deeper. Solly moves his hand and holds her. Shhhh, he says, listen. Termite hears the street grate shift as Lark pulls him past in the wagon. The ragged orange cat lies in the shade of the curb, flattened on a trickle of water running into the gutter. The grate is slimed to its depths with leaves and black decay. The cat slits its eyes at the wagon going away and splays its haunches on the bars of the metal grate. Water is runneling deep, down where Solly threw pebbles and Joey fished for coins with a magnet on a string. Termite wants to stay but he's in the wagon going away. They're moving past Gladdy's house, under the trees that shade the sidewalk. Today the trees are still, their heavy limbs flung wide. The orange cat stirs on the cool grate by the curb. There's a blur of small prone motion in the middle of the street and the cat slides in a fluid crouch to stand over the beetle. The ants ripple unevenly and the beetle moves. The ragged orange cat noses close to touch the smell, a dark tinge like a little hole.

Gladdy's not home, Lark says, or she'd be watching us from the window.

Gladdy only has Charlie, Lark says. That's why she's afraid, like a dog that snarls and bites. She's afraid of ice and storms and heat and anyone Charlie likes.

But you don't have to be afraid, Termite. Main Street won't hurt you.

Cars move in blurs past Lark's shoulders and hips and her white form pulling the wagon. The curved metal eyes of the stoplights never shut and the air in the colors changes in long coned beams. Sounds shout and wobble. Main Street is never a long smooth stream like the roar the trains pour in the rail yard.

Termite, you like big noises and small sounds, but regular noises won't hurt you.

You can't always be quiet. You can't always be at the river or sitting in your chair.

The striped cloth awnings of the stores hang limp and the asphalt glitters. Far behind them now, the tar street near the alley hums. The orange cat shifts foot to foot, bats at the beetle and bats it. The cat flings the beetle small and large, back and forth, across to the concrete curb. The ants scatter or struggle, caught in the tar in their own piled wedge. The orange cat tongues the beetle like a stiffened jewel, mouths it softly, and carries it away. *Elise stands nodding her head to the music. Lark I'll teach you the Lindy. Solly you're taller than Nick and half his weight. And this one! Are you twelve yet honey? You remind me of someone lately. You kids will never be prettier. Throw that laundry on the bed. I've got the big bands station on the radio, loud as Termite likes it.*

Elise taps her stocking foot and Lark walks forward and back with Solly. Faster, Lark, smoother. Relax, it's dancing. Lark, run at

Solly and jump, split your legs tight to his waist. Solly, you catch her, both arms. Then swing her, full body left, then right. Now step, turn, and back to the swing. Yes! That was dancing twenty years ago. People knew how to dance and they didn't wear any pedal pusher trousers.

Then it's night. Solly and Lark put him in the middle on Lark's bed and rock him slow and slower until they say he's asleep. Now they breathe.

Elise stands in the doorway, against the light.

Look at you three, like a pile of cats. Solly, you get up and go home.

Nonie says the restaurant may be home to Charlie but she's not moving into it with him. She meets him late to go over the books in the office. Charlie says she does his figuring and he does most of her cooking. He makes sauces for Termite, ground fish or meat with crushed nuts and cream and basil, and soups with every vegetable boys won't eat. He stirs in soft sharp cheese he grates while Termite watches.

Hold the bowl, Champ. This Parmesan came in just now on the refrigerator truck. Have a little of this. Get your vegetables and beef. Painless.

Termite sits high and tight against the lunch counter in his chair. He holds his bowl in his arms and Lark leans near to help. The counter murmurs sounds and the bitter ashtrays smell of circled ash even after Nonie washes them. Gladdy walks and talks. Her shoes tick small and fast.

He'd be better off where people trained to do it just no sense.

Termite feels her hands flutter, moving to open and shut and close and fasten. She flutters and nudges, blind against a screen.

Used to him training of a kind I don't object.

I tell everyone, she says. How generous my son is. Work around your needs for his sake I suppose.

Suppose suppose suppose.

He says loud and tells. He feels her urge and push, turning her small square purse to blur and cover. Then she goes. Her sounds

are small dark flares going away. The bell over the door shakes to
say she's gone.

Well, Champ, Charlie says.

Charlie picks him up. He says an excursion after a big lunch is
the thing and he takes him to the Men's and puts him on the seat.
Termite's skin is cool where the air moves. Charlie shows him to
move his wrist and aim down while he makes the clattering
sound. Men got to aim, Charlie says, and holds Termite up to
wash his hands. Termite holds on hard to the soft slick soap but
Charlie pulls it away. Charlie stands warm and broad behind him
and puts his cool wet hand on Termite's neck, holding water with
his big fingers.

There, Champ, cool you off. Now you'll want to touch that
dishwasher.

The big machine sloshes, shuddering the floor. It rumbles on
its feet, tinkling small chimes where the glasses touch. Termite
feels it rattle plates in the hot spray and the pounding. His hands
are up to let his fingers play every sound but the dishwasher stops
with a lurch and clicks and wheezes once. Cycle's over, Charlie
says. He's in Charlie's arms and they're through the kitchen and
past the office, into the dining room.

Charlie puts him in the wagon between sounds and talk and
then Lark is pulling them away, out the door.

Lark walks fast. He can hear the river but he wants the train.
The rails in the empty rail yard curve and cross and the steel lines
gleam but the train is tunneling deep. He feels it rumble in the
shade of the woods, moving faster than the black furled smoke it
pours. *Clouds are scudding across the sun, blocking the light and
showing it, sounding air and changing. The trees are blowing without their leaves. Solly says Lark is finally a teenager. Tell her, Termite.
Teenagers have boyfriends and Nonie doesn't have to find out. Nonie
made the birthday cake and Lark's new skirt is from Lowman's in
Atlanta. Box pleats, pink and brown. See? Touch, Termite. Wool. A
nice weight in a cold spring.*

Leaves on the ground fly up, twisted like torn scraps. The new

grass is pale and the bright forsythia dips and slashes. Solly pulls the
wagon through the woods. They're going to the tunnel, he don't stand
talking in the wind. Remember that movie, Termite? Sure as the
turn on the earth. Last summer, every day for a week. You liked the
rifles. The river is moving and the green mound of the island is
still. Sounds roar and pound and open in the stones of the tunnel.
The tunnel hums the pounding sound that slides into the river.

Termite, Lark says. We'll stay a little while before the storm.

Lark says the island draws lightning like a steel pole, standing
bare in the water between two shores. It's why they stay in the
tunnel in summer thunderstorms, hearing the double blur of the
river and the rain. He can feel the air go tight before thunder
cracks, he can smell the burn. He smells it now above the clouds.
They're piled one on another, bruised and bunched. Lark smells
of her dark hair and the lemony close scent of her mouth. She
touches her fingers to her lips and rubs at his skin, near his mouth
and nose, and he smells the taste of a kiss. A kiss is small on his
forehead or his face, but the island stands up in the water like a
dense, pushed kiss the river could swallow. The river shifts in
silted layers, stirring the dark and dropping it. *Wind cuts the water*
in white pieces. Solly's on his knees beside the wagon, holding Lark in
the cool of the tunnel, his face against her legs. Lark says to let go.

You're bleeding, aren't you, Lark. I can tell when. Does it hurt?

The river is clattering, running fast and rushing.

Solly says he knows. The elastic belt with the metal clasps and
thick napkins. Two on heavy days. Joey's girlfriend keeps all that stuff
at the house.

Lark, I can make the pain stop. Let me.

Termite wants the roar and blur. He says until they turn the
wagon to where the water flashes white. Lark puts her skirt on him
like a blanket. Wool, to keep you warmer Termite. Blanket head,
Solly says. Now you can see the river. Lark wears her sweater and
jacket and knee socks. Her long pale legs, her shoes.

We're here at the river, Lark. Lie on my coat. Let me touch you.

Your hand will be bloody.

Fill my hand. There. Shhh. You see? Lie back.

The river is rattling loud and wind stirs the trees one way. Naked slivers of the smallest branches move, far up in the tops of the trees. Lark is breathing and Solly says inside her sounds. Give me your hands. See how warm and wet you are. Touch me, like that. The river is flat and turns, sparkling before it smashes the stones of the railroad bridge and rushes against the island. Clouds move and the light goes bright and soft and bright.

Solly, it's the last time, last time, last time.

Solly stands in the water to his hips, looking at her and looking. The river moves fast around him.

You never let me, Lark. Don't let anyone else.

Wind edges the water. Lights in the water turn and dive, little fish that bend. The lights go down, sliding and stabbing deep. Termite wants to be inside the river. He wants to stay but Lark goes. Lark sits close beside him and the river holds the island, pressing on every side. The island is round and the river makes the shape. He turns his head to listen. Deer stand up from the flattened weeds of the island and walk into the open. He feels them move, three forms lit dark against the sun, slashing dandelion with their teeth and tearing the ruffled grass, raising and lowering their heads. Then they're still, smelling the air.

They're waiting for the roar. He closes his eyes and the river opens inside him. The river and the tunnel darken around him and he feels the river roll, deep and thick, folding like drenched fabric. The deer dips its antlered head and plunges, ripping the water, tearing it in sheets, moving toward them in a shape that churns, huffing like wind in a box. The roiling water is thick and dense and the deer's chest heaves. He feels the animal thrash in the deepening pull, froth in its teeth, and he tells the deer no, tries to tell, and he breathes. He wants to go, ride the stab and thrust of the deer's legs, the thrash of animal limbs against the weight. The roar of the water is a train pouring through the dark and the picture inside him opens wide. He sees inside the roar to where the bodies are sleeping and waiting to move. So many bodies, tangled in one another, barely stirred. They want to move, lifted, turning, but they can't speak or see. One shape stands and opens its shining hands and the roaring light goes white. The pounding starts, pounding and pounding until the picture blurs and stops.

It's all right, Termite, a deer was in the river.

You're tired, Lark says. We'll go now.

The field is tall as Lark's shoulders when she turns and moves. He sits quiet in the wagon and the grass is all around him. She tells him the locusts are still because rain is coming, but he wants to hear their rapid clatter. Not today, Lark says, they've moved to the woods, to the big trees with cracks and holes deep enough to hide them. The ragged orange cat hides too, nosing the beetle and biting small, deep in its stone cleft, high in the wall of the railroad tunnel. The wagon crushes a path and the grass parts sharp around him. He hears the field growing, surging like an engine, flung erect in the heat, and he opens his hands to touch the slow hot buzz that runs to every root. But Lark walks fast against the push of the grass. The field ends and the grass stops. The white stones in the alley make their rolling whisper.

Clouds are blowing apart. Soon they'll fall. Lark pulls the wagon to Nonie's low front porch. They never go this way, on the sidewalk to the street. Someone stands there, blowing like a flag.

Termite, Lark says. Mr. Stamble is here from Social Services.

A cool pale light has found him. The light bends over him.

You remember me, Termite. That's your name? My name's Robert.

Voices rush and tumble behind Stamble's voice, flying and gathering. The voices are in the stones of the alley and in the street by Nonie's house, moving along the slanted broken walk by the front stoop. Voices gather in the rusted pleats of the metal awning over the front door. All the spaces are thick with sounds.

Stamble puts flowers in the wagon. He piles their smells on a pour of grasses so thick and sharp Lark says no one can pull them up. Don't pull at them Termite, they'll cut you. A round stem breaks but blades have threads like cloth. The grasses and their white roots lie quiet under the flowers. Colors too deep to see, thick with dust and nectar.

Stamble moves above him, unfolds a ticking of wheels Lark says she's never seen. The rain begins, pouring, spitting hard. Blowing away and stammering back.

You see would you like to try.

Termite feels Stamble's white hair blow and hears the wind whip his clothes. Stamble knows about the roar and the field. He knows the river turns and slides and tunnels deep and he knows about the trains. He comes close, his face by Termite's face. He's a blur of pale hair and rippling white sleeves, lit with the light inside the roar. He opens like a moon, round and soft with voices that could push and move, but Stamble holds them still. He stands with the wind behind him and he opens his hands. He touches Termite's head and his hands leave a shine where they touch.

The wind is going to get stronger, he says.

Smithereens. All this heavy air.

Stamble knows the blue can pour and break. Termite hears it burst in Nonie's kitchen, a tiny shattering and drip of blue. The lowering sky is too full to move. Banks of cloud high up are rolling, darkening. Stamble speaks without talking. *You'll be safe here,* he says. *I'm going now. I'll be back for you.* Then he's gone. The rain begins, thundering in sheets, swallowing voices and sounds. Lark pulls Termite inside. The rain is drumming, pounding and pounding. He knows his pictures hang in the dim light of the basement, curling their paper edges. Deep inside his pictures, the man and the animal stand up and hear the shapes.

North Chungchong Province, South Korea

Corporal Robert Leavitt
24th Infantry Division

He's conscious, alert, as though no time has passed. He covers vast distances and then he's here. He can't feel his legs or hips or loins, yet there's intense physical sensation in his thoughts, his delusions, a sense of movement in space and time. He knows the girl won't take him to the entrance of the tunnel. She doesn't believe the Americans would come for him. They're shooting at any sound or movement, and she won't risk being injured or killed, leaving the boy alone.

She's left him alone though, left him with Leavitt. It must be after midnight. Leavitt sees the boy sitting near him, hunched in his odd posture as though keeping watch, listening. Leavitt is left in the care of a blind child, left to care for the child if she doesn't come back. He sees the boy's hands hovering over him, his fingers open and parted, faintly moving. Leavitt tries to speak to him, but he only makes a sound, an exhalation. The boy turns his head as though to hear more intently, moves to touch his wrist to Leavitt's face. It's as though he reads sound with touch, as though his fingers are too sensitive to bear contact and he discerns sensation with the underside of his wrist. He holds himself carefully, expressionless but for the careful tilt of his head. His face is smoothly flawless and distinctly heart shaped, his forehead unusually high and broad. His straight black hair is chopped short in so many lengths it looks feathered, wispy. He sits, insectlike, his thin legs drawn up. He seems to stare at Leavitt with eyes that never move or waver, and the startling pale blue splash in his black irises is the last image Leavitt sees as his vision quietly fades, a light turned down to nothing.

The dark is low and painless, and Leavitt peers into it, fighting a low flutter of panic. He feels the boy with him, deeply near him. It's as though he's waiting for Leavitt to hear, just as before when the planes were approaching, but now he doesn't seem alarmed. Leavitt can't move, he's only here, drifting behind his eyes. He tries to listen intently, sense fragments of information as the boy might sense or apprehend them. He thinks of the old woman, the *mudang* priestess wrapped in her cloth. Shamanism was country superstition, a practice of the rural poor. He wonders if the boy was shunned in the village, or if the old woman's status protected him. He's calm, intensely present. What was their word for a male witch. *Paksu.* Male shaman. Called by the spirits through heredity, or after hardship, deathly wounds, illness. Survival was transformation. Not so strange, when survival itself was miraculous. They communed with the other world in trance states, delivered messages, directions.

Leavitt listens for the boy, senses him move closer. He hears, then, the flow of cool air high above them, moving along the pocked ceiling of the tunnel, thirty or forty feet up. The air they breathe is dense with smell and fear, but the air along the curved stones above them is clear and buoyant and fast. Leavitt hears it moving as though windblown, scudding along like water. He closes his eyes, opens them, discerns no visual difference, but feels the boy shift his crouching stance. He touches Leavitt's face and moves away, stays near, waiting. Leavitt can't see, but he feels the displaced air move and separate, thick and viscous as honey disturbed with a spoon. He hears patterns of sound, dappled and distinct. It's the sound of the stream, murmuring in the ground under them, to the other side of the dense wall. The water sighs and rattles and crosses the road at the far end of the tunnel. The boy is no *paksu*, but he has a blind, hyperalert focus and awareness. The boy only waits, as though Leavitt will know what he knows, hear what he hears, inside the inability to move or do. To be nothing that way, Leavitt thinks, this way, to be held and carried, placed or taken, a bright awareness moved here or there like a fire in a cup. Or had the boy moved and walked in his hamlet, dependent on familiarity, never far from the girl, until the flight and confusion of the war. The bombing, the sounds of approach and skirmish, of invasion, the smell of smoke. Leavitt and his men striding through, gesturing with their rifles, shouting.

Leavitt tries to slow his breathing. He closes his eyes to let the dark go black, and listens. Slowly, sounds deepen and layer. They're dimensional, spatial. He begins to hear what the boy hears, the sound the boy wants him to hear. He hears the girl, her quiet breathing, her effort and silence, as though he's in her head. He hears her pulling herself forward with her arms, low and careful, toward the stream at the rear of the tunnel. Smells the dirt of the tunnel, the damp of the moss near her face. He's behind her eyes, moving with her, creeping forward flush with the wall. The soldiers answer any skitter of stones, any involuntary cry or motion, with artillery rounds, one group shooting in response to the other. The girl waits, moves, waits, crawling, flat to the ground, Leavitt's empty canteen strapped to her back. Her torn clothes are stained with blood, brackish dark red patterns pressed into her as she lay against Leavitt, moved him, moved the old woman and wrapped her body. The girl pauses, listens. Even her undergarment is stained black orange. There's a smell to the water when she reaches it, and patterns of tree limbs, leaves, eddying movement. The arch of the tunnel opening above her is reflected in the moonlit surface, and the inverted image shimmers, a black curve, anonymous but specific. He doesn't know why the image is so familiar, why he knows this shape of curves and shadows. It's as though he was on his way here, or it's the same curving image everyone sees as the brain shuts down, the same apprehension of space curving into the unseen. Yet he's awake, aware.

He hears, in the dark, the sound of the girl pulling off her bunched shirt, feels her throw it into the water by one long sleeve. It's as though he's beside her with the stream in sight. Quietly, she lies prone, one pale arm extended beyond the mouth of the tunnel. The white she wore when he first saw her would have attracted attention, but the stained cloth is dark now, filthy and discolored. She drags the shirt back over the ground. He hears her bury her face in the wet cloth, drink the squeezed water. She throws the shirt back repeatedly to soak it, draws it toward her soundlessly, wrings the water into the canteen. Finally she holds the wet cloth in her arms and turns to come back to them, moving against such resistance, such terrible drag, close to the tunnel wall.

She's speaking to him, whispering. She wants him to drink. Her long black hair smells of the stream and falls across his throat. Somewhere, Leavitt thinks, no matter the confusion, command is deciding on a plan of action. Squeezed by the speed of the invasion, endangered by their own lack of troops, the need to support the retreat, the Americans will move at daybreak. Only some massive reversal, a melee in which the Koreans in the tunnel are overlooked, can stop what is coming. Leavitt feels it approach, a weight and dense opacity, a pressure in the air, a storm of vibration coming closer. The girl wets her hand and touches his throat, his mouth. It's a cloudless night. He can't see the moonlight but he can feel it, shining off the pale wall of the tunnel.

July 28

Winfield, West Virginia

Lark

Rain falling across the alley and the backyards looks green as grass against washed brush and soaked trees. You see through it like it might rain forever, and you forget how hard it's pouring until you stand out in it. Nonie said the rain drummed all night, and she went to work early in case they have any water to mop up at the restaurant. The backyard looks thick and spongy. Dimpled water stands in the tracks of the alley, and I'm staring out the screen door, feeling the rush of breath falling water makes. Termite likes the sound and he likes it if I shut the back door, open it, shut it again, like I'm changing the weather in the room. I shut the door and think about the water coming up, how it's moving up the slant in the basement floor. I butter the toast, and when I turn to open the door again Solly is there, up close in a dull black slicker, water running off his face in the billed hood.

"Lark, you OK?" He's nearly shouting in the sluice of the water. "My dad said to drop off these water jugs. He said to fill them while the tap still works, in case the power goes off."

I move to let him in and the hood falls back off his wet hair. I realize I haven't seen him close since before I left school, since I'd pass him in the halls and he'd look at me, some girl or other trailing after him. It got around that we were cousins, to explain the looks between us and the growing up together, our houses like two shambling arms of the same building, except Solly's is bigger.

Cousins because people think of Nonie and Nick Tucci as weirdly related, both alone with kids living off the alley, like we're all a tribe down here, not quite across the tracks but almost. And we've got these missing persons, like old mysteries.

"You want some toast?" I ask Solly.

He looks at the hot bread in my hands, and then he's at the sink with the plastic jugs. "No thanks," he says.

He steps out of his boots and I see the shine of blond whiskers along his jaw, on his cheeks that look hollowed out. He's got such long bones, Solly does, and a bruisy mouth, like his lips are a little swollen. Most people wouldn't say he's handsome. His face is too mismatched, the square chin and straight nose, the deep-set eyes. He stands there dripping on the linoleum by the shelves of cans and bottles, filling the plastic jugs and capping them, and a steam nearly rises off him. The rain is cool and warm at once. "Seems strange to put water by with so much of it pouring down," I tell him.

"Yeah, well, if you end up on the roof you could catch it in your hands and drink it. May not come to that, but the river is rising fast. They don't expect the crest until tonight. Lumber Street will flood for sure and they've closed the bridge. Nonie go to work today?"

"Sure. She and Charlie? You kidding? They'd go to work unless the town closed down."

"It just might. Lark, the Armory is open. They've got food, cots, a generator. I could take you and Termite there now, just in case. No need for boats."

"He'd like a boat ride." I smile, but Solly doesn't. I fold Termite's toast in a four-square and put it in his hand. That way he can hold it himself. "Solly, you know the Armory will scare him, all those people, all that noise. We need to stay here unless we really have to leave. Even if Nonie can't get home tonight, I can manage."

"How will you manage?"

"We have a bed in the attic, and room for groceries and blankets and water. I've stacked up some of the furniture down here. Maybe you can help me get some things upstairs. The rest will have to fend for itself." I'm standing behind Termite's chair, and I look over at Solly. It feels hard to walk over near him, cross a few squares of linoleum flooring, but I do. We stand at the kitchen window, inches apart, nearest the pour of the rain. "If it gets bad enough, you'll come and get us."

"Yeah," he says, "I will." He's not going to argue. He looks at me with that mix of hard and soft in his eyes, and he won't look away.

I open the refrigerator and reach into it like there's something I need. "We'll be fine," I say.

There's a silence, like he's waiting for me. "All right, Lark."

Termite is still. I can feel him, tuned in to us, to the spaces between our words, and I rattle the loose metal shelf in the fridge, shift jars and milk bottles, before I shut the big door.

Solly is moving the water jugs, lining them up beside the wall. "You've got plenty of bottled water now, anyway," he says. Then he moves past me and crouches by Termite's chair. "Hey Termite," he says, "you like rain? It's raining. No wagon today." He puts his hand on Termite's shoulder. "That wagon would fill up and float," he says softly, then he looks up at me. "He used to talk to me. He doesn't answer me anymore. I know he knows me."

"Of course he does. Just not so used to you as he was."

"Yeah. That wagon. I see you pulling him in it, up the alley. He still likes it. A couple more years though, he won't even fit. He still like the radio? Termite, I know a station you might like. Jazz, with voices but no words." Solly pulls the radio toward Termite across the kitchen table, but Termite looks away. And I know he won't eat. It's too different that Solly's here. I'll have to make him food later.

"He'll listen another time," I tell Solly. "It's just, he's listening to the rain. Like he thinks he can hear when the sound of it is going to change."

"Change? He's a weatherman now? Maybe he could stop it

raining. Someday it'll stop. Things do stop." Solly stands. "You need me to go to the store for you? Anything like that?"

"We've got plenty of food from the restaurant. But there's water coming up in the basement. I wonder if you could help me move some boxes. I don't want to ask Nonie, and I can't lift them by myself."

"Lights working down there?"

"By the workbench. But I'll get a flashlight."

I get into the drawer for the flashlight and I feel Termite start to nod and rock in his chair, like he does if there's a new hum of energy, anything strung out.

"Yeah, Termite, it's me." Solly touches Termite's back, a man's touch, quiet and still, and Termite stops.

I turn away from them and start down the basement steps. "Termite is all right up there," I call back. "He'll let me know if he gets bored." I hear Solly on the stairs behind me in his boots and I feel a shudder inside, like he's come back and we're both much smaller, together all day like we used to be. I pull the chain over the workbench and the light goes on over words we carved in the wood, our names, a little family of stick figures, and the requisite bad words, *s*-words and *f*-words. We wrote prayer words too. We wrote "Jesus." Angled into a corner, small, like a flower almost, is Joey's faint drawing of a cock.

Solly runs his hand over the scarred wood, over Joey's little hieroglyph. "Joey," he says. "Always such a father figure, wasn't he."

I shine the light where the dark is darker, and I hear the slip of water. I see it's higher than it was two hours ago. "There are eight boxes," I tell Solly. "Big ones, stacked up."

"She used to have a bedspread over these," Solly says.

"How do you know?"

"I remember a big shape in the corner, and the cloth of the spread was red checks. Don't you remember? We bounced balls against it. We climbed on it." He looks at me, unsmiling. "What is it with you? Holes in your head?"

"I never paid much attention, I guess. But there's no cloth now, and I've been home with Termite, and I noticed the boxes, the return addresses. Florida. I opened one, and I think they came from my mother. I can't imagine why else Noreen would be keeping them."

"You ask her?"

"I'm not ready to ask. I want to go through them."

"For clues."

"Maybe."

Now he smiles. "Don't you ever think our mothers might be drifting around a swimming pool together on one of those blow-up floats, sipping cool drinks under palm trees?"

"They didn't know one another, did they?"

"No, they didn't, but it doesn't seem like that, does it? My dad, he knew them both, and they both left, and left their kids. Remember that next time Nick gives you the eye."

"You think it was all about Nick?" I smile, to show him it's a joke.

"No. He's just another link between them. But doesn't it seem sometimes like they were sisters under the skin, or maybe even the same person?" He pulls the slicker hood off, unzips the front of the jacket. "After she was gone awhile, I started pretending that. It made you and me more the same."

He looks at me so hard I step back. But he's already grabbed me, without ever moving. It's because of the room. Now I remember the red-checked cloth, with lawn chairs leaning up against it, and a couple of old cot mattresses thrown over the top. Nonie kept the storm-cellar doors open in the summer, and we came in and out that way, under the branches of bushy lilacs that hung over both sides. They're gone now. "You think you need me to help you with those boxes?" I ask him. "They're pretty heavy."

"I think I can manage, Lark," he says, with an edge. "You want them in the attic?"

"It's the only second floor we've got."

"Don't worry. The water won't get that high unless most of the town floods. Which might not be a bad idea. We could all float away."

I hear the bell on Termite's chair. He rings it once. "He wants something. I'll go up."

"Yeah, go on up with him." Solly pulls off the slicker and he's wearing a flannel shirt with the arms cut out. His arms are tight. For so many years, even though he was a year older, he was my size. I'm always surprised at how tall he is, muscular and lean, like I turned around and he changed. He does all the sports with the dumb jocks and he gets what the dumb jocks get—the blond girls with their flipped hair and a job at the gas station the summer after graduation. I suppose now he pretends he's like those girls, with their sweater sets and college funds, like he lives in that sec- ondhand convertible of Joey's that he keeps so clean, driving girls here and there. Probably a good plan. Even if their Mommies and Daddies figure it's high school stuff. They'll ship their girls off now, get them away from Saul Tucci. Solly is not what they want.

"You going off to school, Solly?" I can't help asking him.

"Like the rest of the sheep? Go play some football fifty miles from here? Nah, I don't think so. There was one letter I answered—Fort Lauderdale. Lure of the sea. My own palm tree." He rakes his fingers through his wet hair and I see the darkish roots at his hairline. One of those girls bleached his hair like hers, playing at twosies. My twin. He looks straight across at me. "Shot in the dark. We're only a double A team. Wasn't like I had endless offers."

Solly in Florida, I think. Solly in Florida.

"Don't know about that one yet," he says. "I haven't told Nick about it, or anyone."

"Well. Let me know, when you hear."

"Yeah?"

I want to get away from him. "Sorry it's so close down here. Gets hot, with the windows shut against the rain." I turn and start up the stairs and he stands there like he's watching me walk out of a story. For a weird moment I think I hear his heart beating, but it's my own head pounding, a thud I only notice when I get up the steps and back into the kitchen. Things stop, Solly said. I think about living here on and on, and he wouldn't. I think about going away myself, living a whole different life, like I could exist on a different planet and this life wouldn't know about me, and I wouldn't know about it. I sit down in a kitchen chair close beside Termite and I see his toast on the table where he dropped it. "You hungry yet?" I ask him, but my voice has a dead, automatic sound, and he puts his arms across my knees. He smells of the baby powder Nonie and I still dust across his shoulders after baths. I realize I'm never going to leave him, not in this life. He's so quiet, listening. His open hands in my lap barely move, so faintly, like his thin fingers touch a current of air I'm too thick and gross to feel. The undersides of his fingers are white as alabaster, unlined between the knuckles, like he's always just born. There's a faint pink blush under his skin. When he has a fever, his skin gets dappled.

We hear Solly coming up the stairs with the boxes. I feel him look in at us. He turns in the little hallway, walks into Termite's room and on into the attic, up the pull-down steps in Termite's ceiling. Termite hears Solly in his room. He likes the attic steps, the creak they make pulling down, how they sound under someone's weight. It's like the air in the attic falls down those stairs in moted streaks cast through the dormer window above. Termite can smell it and feel it, but he doesn't stir now.

"I want you to have a real breakfast," I tell him. "I'll make you and Solly something." He lets me talk.

I peel some peaches and start the toast again. All the time I'm cooking the eggs, Termite touches one wrist to the radio, but he leans away when I move to turn it on. I get the food on the plates and I hear Solly, up and down the basement steps. Then he's in the kitchen.

"I lined up the boxes along the wall by the attic window," he says. "You'll have enough light to sift through the evidence. May as well leave them up there. Safer. Nonie's basement takes in water, any big rain."

"Thanks, Solly. I made you some food." I'm washing the cast-iron skillet in the sink and Solly comes over near me and puts his hands on me, up under my hair, on my neck, just for a second, as though to move me aside. He's taken his shirt off and tied it around his waist, and he leans in to splash his face in the stream of water.

"Those boxes were dirty," he says. "I kept wondering why. Like mud splashed up on them. Then I realized the backs were covered with crumbled hornets' nests. Old ones. Muddy dust." He unties the shirt and wipes his face with it. Then he sits down by Termite, puts the spoon in Termite's hand, starts helping him. The water is running, but I can hear Solly talking. "We used to go down by the rail yard, Lark and me and you, or down under the railroad bridge by the river, and we'd take bottles of soda pop and those cans of ravioli Joey heated up for Tucci dinners when the old man wasn't home. I'd feed you and we'd wait for trains. Bet you don't know that. Bet you don't know that anymore."

By the time I'm finished cleaning up, Termite has eaten and Solly's plate is just sitting there. Solly is tuning the radio.

"Joey used to listen to this station. Jazz piano, and someone singing scat vocals. That's sounds, no real words. Termite might like it. If he wants to listen." Solly's talking to me, but looking at Termite. He wipes Termite's mouth with his fingers, touches his face. I see Termite lean so slightly, rest his jaw on Solly's palm, and stay quiet. Like he's reading something he remembers. Someone he lost.

I never even thought, all this time. Termite lost Solly too. He just didn't know why.

I see Solly realize. His face changes and he puts his hands flat on the table, like someone's punched him and he needs a moment. It's something else between us, all we've done and all we didn't know. He looks over at me, but he keeps his voice smooth.

"Joey's down at Camp Lejeune, getting an education. Left last month. You knew he was going down there, didn't you, Lark?"

I nod. Termite turns his head to listen, hear our voices, but we're not talking. The radio is playing low, like whispering. I move to turn it up.

Solly stops me. "Here, let me. Listen to these voices, Termite. They sing the way you talk. No words." He stands and moves the radio across the table to Termite, turns the volume louder. Piano, horns, voices trilling low and high, bebop and fluttering, then sliding long. Wail of a sax. The voices solo, join, move apart, rippling like instruments. Termite leans forward and touches the knobs, both wrists, turns the volume steadily, slowly, all the way up. Then he rests his head on the box itself, one ear pressed tight. Turns away from us, into the sound.

"He likes it." I look at Solly. We're by ourselves now.

Solly signals he can't hear me and moves us back from the table, out of the kitchen. "Anybody would," he says, "like it."

"You better go, Solly."

"I was going to. As soon as I finished with the boxes. But I kept thinking about what was in them. I never saw a picture of your mother except this one that you keep in the kitchen, her as a kid with Nonie. When she looks like you. I get you confused with her." He steps close, so that we can hear each other over the music. "Then when I can't picture your mother, I get to not quite picturing mine."

I don't answer. We're in the living room now. I want him to go.

"We used to get in bed with my mother."

"You told me that. I don't remember her."

"You were three. I was four. It must have been soon after you came here. Probably with those boxes."

"I don't know when the boxes came. Maybe they came with Termite." I look past Solly, out the living room window into the rain. But he keeps talking.

"She'd have Zeke asleep in the crib beside us and we'd get in bed with her and she'd let us nurse what was left. She was in your mouth and she was in my mouth. It kept us quiet and it calmed her down. We'd fall asleep, and she would."

"How could you remember that?"

"Because I know I crawled over her to get to you. That's where I slept, next to you."

I look at him. Then I can't look away.

"Do something to me," Solly says.

"You've got girls to do that."

"I want you to. Do what you used to do."

"Not anymore. That was a long time ago."

"I'm like your brother, even if I'm not. I'm like Termite except I can talk to you. I can touch you back. I remember things." He's so close I feel the words on my face. I can see Termite in the kitchen, holding the radio now, ear to the speaker in front, eyes closed. I look at Solly. He's so familiar, like he's me, he's mine, like he's my child, but he's a stranger, the cold, hot look he gets, like any of them. If I let him do what he wants I'll get that look too, the look that cancels everything. It's like a pit I could fall into. I need to keep out of it.

"Let me," he says.

Solly could talk me into things because in my mind he still wore the face he used to have, behind the older face I saw. I forgot and I thought doing things with him was like doing things to myself. I got my period early and he was drawn to me then. I was eleven and kept myself so clean, but it was like he could tell. He would come and tease me and talk at me. It wasn't just looking. He would try to get me to want to be touched, he would show me things. I liked it, thinking about it, liked watching his body work, how he delivered himself into it so quickly, so easily, what he could do to me, how my not letting him do what he wanted just extended everything, how he'd find some other way to get around what I wouldn't let him do. He'd hold on to my wrists and mouth, the backs of my legs, I'd be blue on that soft skin behind my knees. He'd get to me, talking without words, with sounds. I'd have that achy, crampy feeling in my belly and he'd say he knew it hurt, he'd pull me across him and stroke the bones of my hips, those socket bones the belly sinks between, until the pain turned syrupy. I lay there feeling him harden under me and I thought about his hands, about bleeding into them. He wanted me to, he said. And other things. Lots of things.

He's looking at me and his eyes are tawny and gold, flecked with green. His lashes look wet. "Lark," he says.

I shake my head. "Solly, it's not true."

"What's not?"

"We don't have the same mother. You know we don't. But it's like you said: Nick knew them both. And Nick says things, about my mother." I'm looking at Solly like he can tell me. "Suppose it's Nick. Suppose Nick is my father, and he's a reason your mother left, and mine did."

"No," Solly says. I can feel the tension in his shoulders and chest, his clenched hands, even though he's not touching me. "If that were true, and he looks at you the way he does sometimes, I'd want to kill him."

"If we're related by blood—"

"We're not, Lark." He closes his eyes, opens them. "But if we were, it wouldn't matter. What they did, any of them, doesn't matter."

"It matters what we did, Solly, why we wanted to."

We must have stopped when I was thirteen or so, when we weren't kids anymore. There was that one time, the last time. I told him so. After that I stayed away from him. Then he got angry and stayed away from me. Or not away, but we were never alone anymore, or trying to be. I'd left him, so he left me. He had this one and that one. I'm sure he got to a lot of them. He was too young, but that's how he was; I guess it's how I was, but only with him. It was like we ruined each other. I'd see him and I'd look away, but I always knew if he was in a room, or across a street or in a hallway at school, or tackling sandbags at a football practice,

outside some classroom window. I'd sense him lunging and hitting, pounding at all the anonymous smeared bodies in their pads
and helmets.

"Lark," he says.

He puts his finger in the center of my chest like a hard little
point, and moves it down like he's writing a line on me. It's the
storm, I think, the storm has closed us off here, the rain has
drowned everything out. I can hear the rain, pouring behind Termite's music. The voices are chiming, high, sharp sounds against
the rolling, the long low slide of the music.

"Don't put your hands on me, or your mouth," I tell him.

He knows this game. It's an old game. He opens his mouth
slightly and breathes, like he's filled with some horrible relief. I
feel like something has got us, just swallowed us.

"OK." He mouths the word like he can't talk or even whisper.
Just the shape of a sound on his lips and he clinches his teeth.
Now that he knows I'll do it I can see the feeling come on him full
blown, into his eyes, into his breathing and the tawny flush of his
face.

"Don't touch me with your hands," I tell him, but he doesn't
have to. Just the force of him moving toward me backs us into my
room and against the wall. I can see the flecks of dirt across his
chest. A gleam of blond hairs and sweat fills the space my eyes can
see and his nipples are hard and tiny. It's so long since I've been
this close to the smell and feel of him. He flattens his palms on
either side of the wall at my head and keeps his hands still to
promise he will. I put my mouth on him, and the brown nub of
his nipple fits between my teeth like a little stone. I pull on the
other and touch and roll it under my fingers, and the sounds he
makes seem to start inside me. There's a measure of time we have
before he can't hear me or listen to me anymore. He reaches down
to pull the laundry basket, piled with all the clothes and sheets I
haven't folded, over behind us, and his face moves down my chest
and belly, along the bone of my hip, and he nudges me back onto
the basket. He arches over me and I get my shirt off and push my

forehead hard against him through his jeans, then I put my hand inside the button and feel for the zipper, pull his pants down, close my eyes. I feel him hard and silken in my mouth, and in my hands, and against my face and in my hair. He's pushing and pushing at me, all over me, not fast, on and on. I hold him at the hollow of my neck and then I raise my arms all along the line of his torso. The blunt head of him moves its tear of wet across my ribs and my breasts and finds the hollow under my arm, and that's how he comes, and on my neck and my chest, with me holding him so I feel the pulsing as it moves through him.

"Do that to me," he says, "do that to me, Lark." He sinks to his knees and lies across me and we slide down on the towels and T-shirts and sheets that have spilled. It's easy now, like no time has gone by without this, and I put my hand on the cleft of his buttocks and touch the secret fur, push my finger just inside, like I own his body, like he would own mine if he ever got inside me. If he got inside me I would never get away.

I told Solly I wouldn't leave. We wouldn't need to leave, I said, we never had. Once, years ago, water got knee deep in the basement and rose in the yard to the kitchen door, and we stayed right here. We'll see, Solly said. I packed food, rain slickers, boots. Solly helped me empty the bureaus, gather the winter coats, strip the beds and linen closet, pile everything in the attic. He got Termite's fat upholstered chair up those narrow pull-down stairs, tilting and turning it on his shoulders. We brought up jugs of water, my transistor radio, flashlights, candles and oil lamps, even Nonie's safe-deposit box. He'd signed on to help Civil Defense evacuate and they were opening shelters as well as the Armory, some of the churches. They were saying the water could rise fast, especially near the river. Before he left, he grabbed me hard by the shoulders to make sure I was paying attention. "When the water gets to the back stoop," he said, "get into the attic. Don't wait, and stay there

all night, even if the house doesn't flood." I told him we liked the
attic, we'd camp out. "If it's bad," he told me, "I'll be back for you
in a boat, and we won't be taking anything out that attic window
but you and Termite. You be ready."

I'm in the kitchen, making peanut-butter-and-jelly sandwiches
on the Wonder bread Termite likes, when the power cuts off. In
the silence, the storm is louder. It's afternoon, but the light in the
house is pearl gray. There's a sound to the rain, a rush and pressure, and I can't see through it to tell how high the water in the
alley is rising. The roads between here and downtown will flood.
Nonie won't get home tonight, but I'll manage. I've got cans of
baked beans and Vienna sausage up there, jugs of water, cheese,
the cold chicken from the restaurant.

I have Termite sitting where I can watch him, propped with
pillows on the living room couch. The windows are open a crack
so he can hear the rain. He's got his hands up but his fingers are
nearly motionless, like the air is so heavy he can't move them. I'm
putting the sandwiches in a plastic bag, and I see him sit up
straight and go still. He can't do that, and he doesn't. It's not like
he's scared: he's waiting, expectant, and what's coming is now. I
turn to the window, and suddenly, like a magic trick, the rain
deepens and darkens. The wind changes direction and crashes a
wall of rain flat against the house like a breaking wave. Wind hurls
the rain and sucks it back, and just for an instant I see the surface
of the flood. The water is murky, moving like a shallow lake.
There's no alley, no yards, and the little fence between the houses
is gone. It's like we're on a boat in a bowl someone is squeezing.
The water is coming up so fast that I can see it rise. Termite hears
it coming.

"We're going upstairs, Termite." I'm across the room, slamming windows shut as I pass. They bang like gunshots and I pick
Termite up, not too fast, but quickly, water pooling at my feet.
The flood is in the house, almost warm, like a summer puddle
deep enough to splash through, and we're up the stairs.

It's nearly dark in the attic, with the glimmer of the one win-

dow under the eaves. Solly put Termite's chair there, turned to the
rectangular view, but I don't look. I put Termite in his chair with
the bag of sandwiches in his lap and the flashlight in his hands. It's
a long metal flashlight with some weight to it, like mechanics use,
and he likes it. He holds on to it tight and I turn it on, aimed at
the stairs. "I'm getting a few more things," I tell him. "You'll see
me there, coming and going."

I don't hear him answer because I'm moving down the steep
ladder stairs in the dim light. I'm thinking about what's irreplace-
able. What we'll need if everything is gone.

I grab an empty bureau drawer in my room and throw in my
notebooks, my pencils, the drawings from my wall, drooping off
their tape in the damp. The skirts and blouses, nylons and under-
wear, the one good cardigan and pair of heels Miss Barker says an
executive secretary might need, are already upstairs. I don't care
about anything else. The seashells in their trays on my desk can
float away, back to water, and the postcard Main Streets tacked to
my walls can pull apart. It's not my room anymore, it hasn't been
for a while. The novelty pitchers I collected can fill, sink their
doll-sized dream scenes and souvenir words. I've got to find Termite's moon-faced favorite, though, his moon-man doodad, and
here it is, centered on his table like some miniature royal orna-
ment. Maybe Solly put it there when he stripped the bed—Solly
would remember it, he would know. If the phone worked, I could
call Nonie. She'd tell me to get the first-aid kit from under the
sink, the jewelry box with her pearls, the salt box with the wooden
lid where she keeps household cash. I fill the drawer, splashing
room to room, shove it across the floor at the top of the attic steps,
and remember what Stamble said: smithereens. I need to get the
wheelchair he gave us. My boots feel clammy when I pull them
onto my bare feet, but I remember floods are poison, full of what's
burst and broken. That's why Termite can't stay here. Maybe we
can't be here anymore and something came to say so.

Downstairs the sound of the rain is calmer, steady, like the
flood has come in and hushed the storm. It's quiet and strange.

Water stands evenly in every room, a foot deep up the legs of chairs, opaque and still as a mirror. I open the door to the deep closet where we keep the wheelchairs, both of them now. A piece of the vacuum cleaner floats out around my ankles. Then a hat and some gloves. I leave the heavy old chair where it is and pull the new one out by the handles. It's folded up and the flood is only midway up the wheels. It pulls through the water like a ship or a toy, and I push it up the attic steps on its big thin wheels. It glints like a creature and *tick ticks* across the attic floor in the thin space left—an aisle that leads to the window. I move it over near Termite's chair and set it just opposite, angled toward the window like his. Then I open it, lock the seat in place with the levers on the wheels. "I'll sit here," I tell him. "We'll have supper and watch the rain."

He doesn't say anything and I wonder if he's scared. The beam of the flashlight pours past us to the space above the steps. I leave it lie and lean over Termite, press my face to the attic window. It's not day or night. The water moves like a shallow river between the houses, level with the sills of first-floor windows. I see an old wooden doghouse float by, bobbing its peaked board roof, dragging a length of thick rope with a collar still attached. Something about the boxy shape and floating rope reminds me of Termite's wagon. I should have thought, should have got it up the stairs, had Solly help me. I know we're leaving here, I can feel it. Maybe we'll stay with Elise in her little house until we know where to go, but he's got to have his chair, and the wagon, big and heavy as it is. They're all he knows about where he is.

"I guess you'd like to have your wagon up here, wouldn't you, Termite. I think I'll go and get it."

Think I'll go, think I'll go, he says, quiet, like he's not convinced.

"You take your moon man," I tell him, "and give me the flashlight."

I move his hands, each finger, until he closes his palms around the little moon-faced pitcher, and I stand at the top of the attic steps, play the beam of the flashlight down across the water. The flood has made the third step and looks black in the light, scary, like oil or paint. I switch the flashlight off, and move closer. There's nothing to do but step in. Water fills my boots and rises midthigh. The flood has come in all at once, cool now, the color of coffee with milk. I'm standing in Termite's room. His bed, a metal cot with fold-up legs, turns just slightly, floating like a raft. The thick plastic mattress is still dry and the water bears it along like a special platform. I move through to the living room, where I left the wagon. The door to the basement stands open, moving with the flood. I think about the basement underwater: the empty space where the boxes sat, the workbench, Termite's newsprint drawings disintegrating on the clothesline. I tell myself the house has a granite foundation: it will hold, even if it fills. Nothing else matters: the water will decide. The marooned piano in the living room has shifted to the left, water stirring almost to the keyboard, and the piano bench is upside down. Sheet music circles on the water, silent, open pages, weighted and wet. I train the beam of the flashlight over the words. "Meet Me in St. Louis" drifts by, and "My Funny Valentine."

Termite's wagon is partway onto the back of the couch. The metal handle sticks up like a long neck with a skinny head, gleaming its wedge-shaped face. The wagon is tilted out of the water, but it will fill if I try to pull it away, and I'll never get it up the steps. My boots are like weights, but I get in position to balance the wagon and give the couch a shove. It moves, like a sodden, heavy boat, and nearly lurches backward, but I hold it steady and push. There are no doors in my path. I can float the couch through the archway into my room, through Termite's room to the attic stairs, then angle it and pull the wagon off, up the last five or six steps. Nick Tucci made the arches wide. I think about him plastering those arches when Termite was two or three: Nick made space for the flood, for the brown muck of a river he said he doesn't like. I know Nick was in high school with my mother. He's the only one who ever mentions her to me, like she's a secret we share, but we don't. You remember her mother, Nonie told him, when she thought I couldn't hear.

I was a child and Nick would throw me over his shoulder like he did his sons, hold me in his lap, teach me fingerplays and silly songs. I'd beg him to take me to work with him, night shift at the plant, and sometimes he did—Nonie must have needed a baby-sitter. He'd find me a soft chair to sit in by the wall, put earplugs in my ears, and tell me not to move. I could feel the wrapper slamming bales so hard the big room jumped, and it was like Nick made the sound. The pounding lulled me to sleep. He broke walls with a sledgehammer the summer he made a room for Termite. We kids cheered while Nonie took Termite into the yard, not to breathe the dust. Solly and I smeared each other with chalky powder, ran in and out of the gaping holes Nick smoothed and shaped. Nick used to call me his girl but I got older and he stopped. You remind me of someone, he started saying. Lark is nothing like her, Nonie told him, and I tried hard not to be. I could pour myself into Termite and it was never enough, he needed me all the time. But I was like my mother with Solly, all along. We were children, doing those things, and I remember thinking about Nick. Like those nights at the plant, sitting in the near dark with my ears stopped up. I could feel the wham of the wrapper pounding through the floor into my feet, through the seat of the chair into my hips. I thought about Nick, pressed hard against a wall with a woman whose face I couldn't see, like I knew what had happened to him with someone else.

The rain has lessened. The sound now is like the flowing of a stream, light and high and constant. Parts of Winfield flood worse than here—Nick will be with the men, taking people out of houses and off the tops of cars. He'll be asking Solly where the hell I am, and where's Junior? Solly will say we're fine, and we are. I'm moving the couch, edging it along the wall in the mud-colored water, but I keep slipping in the wobbly boots. Carefully, I step out of them, reach down, find them in the murk, and empty them into the flood. I feel the floor under my feet, throw the boots on the couch, balance the fat length of it along the wall, through the arch into my room. My bed is underwater. The tall headboard stands above the dark reflection of the flood, and I see something move past it. The water ripples, ripples again in a long streak, and I look away. That cat, I think, that feral alley cat that's dirty orange and sits and watches Termite, that slinks away at the rail yard. I don't want it in the attic with us. I'll pull the steps up, as soon as I manage the wagon. The steps seal tight, to hold the heat in winter. They're fitted with a plywood rectangle on the back, layered over with the same pale blue bead board as Termite's ceiling. They fit so tight you wouldn't notice them from below, except for the wooden handgrip that's broad as the steps, and the cord that dangles from it. The steps are not much wider than the wagon. I feel the couch nudge them, blind and blunt. It's getting dark. I've got the flashlight in one hand.

"I'm coming up, Termite." I move around the couch, feel my way onto the submerged lower steps. I can just reach the handle of the wagon. It pulls easily over the back of the couch, but I'm pulling dead weight at a steep angle when I move farther up the narrow opening of the attic steps. I put the flashlight on the top step and hold the wagon in place, arched up on its front wheels like some awkward reptile emerging from a pool. I pull it up one step, and two, then the couch spins away and dips into the water. The weight of the wagon lurches back and pulls me forward so fast that I'm in the water before I can brace myself. I hear the wagon thud to a lower step as I fall, but the wheels lodge tight. The flood is higher, nearly to my chest, deep enough to swim through. I keep my head out of the water and remember those sandwiches in Termite's lap. If something happens, he'll have enough to eat until someone comes for him. He wouldn't, though; he wouldn't eat. I feel for the steps and pull myself all the way up, careful and quiet, not a sound or move to jostle the wagon, and the wheels stay locked.

I'm wet through and I smell of the flood, a smell of ruined fruit and dank motor oil. I angle the beam of the heavy flashlight so I can see the wagon just below me, then I sit on the attic floor, grip the ladder steps with my ankles, legs spread, and pull the wagon toward me. I'm pulling it up, locking the wheels higher step by step, and I see the water ripple below me in long glides. They're rats. I see their eyes glisten in the light, and one of them leaps onto the back of the wagon, feeling its way fast along the wooden edge toward me. I scream, feel the flashlight in my hand, and throw it hard. The rat plops back into the water, then I'm scrambling in a panic, pulling the wagon up fast in the dark. I get it just behind me and realize they'll be up the steps. I see motion in the water, grab for the rope handles of the attic ladder, pull hard to angle the steps out of the flood, midway to the ceiling. The shape hangs in the dark, too high, too high for rats to jump. I look for any movement, slam the wood hard with my fists. The wobbling scuttle rats make is so different from the streak of a mouse. I wish for that alley cat, that filthy vicious cat that eats what it catches, and I wish for a hammer or a gun. The steps will latch tight. I pull off my dress that smells of slime and rot and drop it into the water, then I look down before I close us in, count the long glides across the flooded space. There are three of them, or four. Smooth torpedo lines that shine and search, dark little bullet heads. The rats from the river and the Polish Town dump are swimming out of the flood.

Wooden houses, Nonie always says—about reckless people, risky ideas. I light the kerosene lamps anyway, and the fat, thick candles that won't fall over. Light to shine through the window, for Solly to see in case he needs to come before daybreak, putt-putting toward us in a Civil Defense motorboat. The flood is all over me, dark soil lifted from Polish Town field and drowned creatures floated from the river, so I twist up my stinking hair and wrap myself in a white bedspread like a girl stepping out of a bath. I pull the wagon over and turn it upside down, with the handle folded inside so it's level. A table for candles and oil lamps, and I set the food out, baked beans in cans and the cold chicken on wax paper, open the sandwiches on our laps. "Here's our picnic," I tell Termite. "See how nice the lights look? And we have a bed for you to sleep in. It's cooler now. The flood has taken the heat."

He turns his head toward the window, like we're discussing it.

Everything tastes better than it really could, like fairy-tale food. We're sitting in our chairs, him in his upholstered nest, me in Stamble's wheelchair, knees touching, two ladies at a tea party beside a dark window. I try to rub the dirty glass clear, but all we see is the reflection of two kerosene lamps, wide-lipped forms side by side, and a separate nimbus for each candle flame.

"I don't hear the rain," I say out loud.

Stamble's new wheelchair is thin armed and pulls up right next to the windowsill. I open the window and lean far out. The rain is a mist, a thin cloud pulled apart in patches, and the flood has reached halfway up the houses. Things are moving in the water, dark things, and the surface glimmers, tingles, with the wind pushing along behind. It's quiet, so quiet, and there are no lights. No glows or lanterns. Just a constant unblurred *shush*, like a loud wet whisper over the running of a broken pipe. The river is in the flood now, racing, rushing along over gardens and tipped-up cars and the surprised tops of trees. They're strange trees, new ones, and they trail their leaves in one direction, like they all hear the same music. The houses stand up chopped off, showing their roofs and second-story windows. The blank windows look glazed and shiny. It's a new town in a new world, an empty town for water and wind in the dark.

No one stayed. They've all left, run away, and they didn't get to see.

"It's just us," I tell Termite. "It's all ours. Come here. Listen."

I pull him carefully onto my lap, into his wheelchair, wrap him close in the bedspread with me to keep him warm. We lean out in the dark, into the air and sound. I can feel, through his skin almost, how much he likes it. Holding him, I can see into the

water the way he must hear it, in layers, colors mixing in the
black. Tomorrow the flood will be brown as diluted mud, ugly
with what it ripped and tore, but now it moves and rolls in one
dark sheen, silvered in dim moonlight through the mist. Termite
moves in my arms, leans far down, turns his head in small movements as though he's hearing sounds in the layers of the air.

"That's enough now," I tell him. I pull him back against me,
feel him nearly vibrating, tense in his limbs like an animal poised
to leap. At the school he hated, they hold kids tight when they're
excited or upset, force feeling out of them. I let him be, comb his
hair with my fingers, wait for him to rest against me. I talk, quiet,
like a story. "You need to sleep. Just sleep, with the lamps lit. I'll
be awake. Solly is bringing a boat he can steer with a motor. We'll
sit still in the boat and ride through the flood, Termite. Maybe in
the dark, and maybe when it's daylight. We'll find a place to stay
until the water goes down. The water will sink back into the river,
leave things everywhere. You'll see."

I keep talking but I don't hear what I'm saying. The boxes from
the basement are piled behind me and I begin to feel them at my
back, solid, radiating heat like stones in the sun. I know there's a
scissors in the first-aid kit, for cutting the roll of gauze bandage
sealed in paper. I'll open every box. They're mine now, ours, like
the flood drowning the alley. The basement is gone, like Nonie's
kitchen and Nonie's house. Anyone could stand up here now, in
this small space under eaves and beams, and claim us, say her
name. I say it, part of the story, but Termite is asleep against me,
his face in my throat. I carry him to the bed that's piled with
clothes and bedding, a soft nest to sink into, and lay the bedspread over him.

Now I can start. There's wind from the open window, cool
stirred air that prickles my skin. He's asleep, deep asleep the way
he gets when too much has happened. I can be naked, opening
the boxes. I don't care if they're dirty with old mud. The tape on
the boxes rips like brittle ribbon against the open scissors, and the
glow of the lamps leaps and wobbles. Here's the felt-lined wooden

chest and the Lenox silver service. Dishes, white plates with gold edges, stored professionally in cardboard sleeves. Two boxes of linens: tablecloths and napkins, pink sateen sheets, lace-edged pillow slips. Like someone's hope chest got used, washed, packed away. Four boxes, five, six. But it's just a house someone emptied in her absence, with no thought but to send what seemed worth money. No ribbons or knickknacks, no junk like people keep in drawers, like I find at Topsy Turvy, full of facts about who people were. No shoes or lingerie or everyday clothes that would say what she wore, how she really looked. One box, stored too close to the crack in the floor, is tinged pink inside: faded dye from a pile of beaded dresses, like costumes, discolored and rotten from the damp. Other boxes stayed dry. There's a dress, folded like padding under a layer of wrapped goblets, a white dress or a nightgown. Fitted in the shoulders and bust, tucked in at the waist, loose in the skirt. Proper. Saved because it's silk. I put it on, to feel how it felt to her and know it fits. And there's a robe, Japanese, with huge sleeves, red silk with dragons in blue and orange and white. I wear that too, and keep looking. No books, no records, no framed photographs, nothing personal, until I find the notebook. An artist's sketchbook, no name, but it must be hers: hardbound, not like mine, and the pages don't tear out. I start at the back, turn toward the front. Her drawings are shadows on walls, edges, shaded corners. A hand holding a bottle beaded with cold. A man's hand and wrist. His torso. No faces, nothing to recognize. But she drew the sign that hangs across Barker Secretarial: MURPHY'S FIVE AND TEN CENT STORE. And she drew the tunnel, the railroad bridge by the river. She remembered it exactly, the way the stones and mortar curve at the top.

I forget the flood. I keep looking, unpacking the boxes and repacking them, like puzzles, so I have room to spread things out. I go through cut-glass punch cups and dismantled glass lamps. No letters, no photograph albums, no bills or account statements, nothing I can use to find out where she was or what happened to her. Why her own sister won't talk about her, why no one will.

Here's a cardboard box printed with an old-fashioned illustration of the planets: FABERGÉ'S HEAVEN SCENTS. A silk-lined perfume set from a fancy drugstore. Inside, a molded velveteen inset for little porcelain bottles and stoppers, labeled with stickers I can still read: VENUS, SATURN, MARS, MORNING STAR, CASSIOPEIA, THE MOON. The bottles are all here except the last: Termite's moon man. They're all tiny pitchers with molded faces. Maybe they're better than photographs: they're empty pictures that smell of scent when I pull out the stoppers. Whatever was in them evaporated. Each cork nub is topped with a plastic star. There's a card like someone might send with flowers: *Reach for the stars!! Love from your girls.* Hearts under the exclamation marks. Who were her girls? But I know what happened. She let Termite hold the moon bottle and he liked it, he went on at her if she tried to take it away. He liked the smell when it was her smell, and the shape of the bumpy face, so small and fat: he liked her. He was hers, and I was. I was hers.

I pull the silk robe closer around me and go to the window. It's near dawn. The rain has stopped, but the fog in the damp air is heavy. Cold, clammy. The water is higher still, angry looking, windblown, and moving. Solly will be coming for us. There's one box left. Right on top, there's a folded receipt from Bekins Van Lines made out to Gladys Fitzgibbon, 40 Beech Road, Coral Gables, Florida. A secretarial error. Gladdy talks about her place on Beach Road, how she can see the ocean from her little porch, across the narrow sand road. I don't know why she'd have my mother's things, or pay to send them, but I know why so much isn't here. Gladdy threw it all away, all the personal things, the photographs and letters, all the things that told secrets or stated facts, and she paid someone to pack the rest. I wanted wedding pictures, something to say who. Lola probably wasn't married to my father, but she married Termite's. He was a soldier and he died, but none of that is here. There's only a folded American flag in a tight triangle, inside a plastic sleeve, and the hard lump under the fabric is a little gun with a curved pearl handle. It could be a toy, but it has weight and it's real. I know the army sends a flag to every soldier's grave, but they never found him and he didn't have a grave. This flag is all there is, and I put the gun back inside it. There's a trumpet in a hard, heavy case, packed with a silk handkerchief under the mouthpiece. Tucked inside is a snapshot: twenty or so enlisted men, soldiers in uniform, sitting in a bandbox emblazoned with a script marquee: THE MATCH BOX. They're not holding instruments, so no clues there. Anonymous faces. Gladdy didn't throw it away because she never bothered to open the case.

Underneath is something else, folded, big and bulky, wrapped in paper taped layer on layer, as though to waterproof the package. I have to use the scissors to get it open. It's heavy: a military jacket, a uniform jacket with brass buttons and a name tag: LEAVITT. He wore this. I unfold it to see the size of his shoulders, his arms. Strong, like he's standing here in the shape Termite might have grown into. There's a small tin box folded inside the pocket. It has a metal clasp and a key taped on the bottom. It's here because Gladdy didn't know: she didn't open the package my mother sealed and taped. My heart is hammering, but the box has only a few papers. On top is a business-sized envelope, opened, bound with a rubber band that snaps when I try to remove it. Inside, typed on onionskin paper with a bad ribbon and an *h* that jumps, a letter to Lola Leavitt from Sergeant Ervin Tompkins, postmarked April 10, 1951, Belle Glade, Florida.

```
Dear Lola. I was in Japan and Korea
with your husband, injured bad the day
he went missing. I am sorry to take so
long to find you but I was in hospital
and then rehab in the States. I had
your Louisville info and Mr. Onslow
gave me your Florida address. Somehow
your photo Bobby carried everywhere was
in my gear. I want to return it and
```

```
give you a letter he wrote you. I am in
Belle Glade. My wife and me would like
to come and see you.
```

Then his name: *Sergeant Ervin Tompkins.*

There's no phone number. But I can call information, see if he's still listed. Let him tell me what happened, tell Termite. Underneath is a flattened cigarette pack, Lucky Strikes, still cellophaned. When I turn it over, I see the photograph, small, cut to fit into the pack. I look hard and it's her, grown up, propped on pillows in a hammock, one arm behind her head. Smiling, happy. Long, light hair, not dark like mine, a hand on her stomach. On the back, her handwriting: *Seven months along.* I see now, she's pregnant. It's a photograph she sent, that he carried in the war, in Korea.

There are no other letters. Just one snapshot of Nonie and her, children, the same one Nonie kept. And four school pictures of me, small ones, paper-clipped together, inscribed on the back in Nonie's hand: my name, the year, the grade. First grade through fourth. Then I was nine. She died. Termite came here. There should be a death certificate, a funeral notice, something to say how or when. But it's not here. Our birth certificates are: two half-sheet squares just the dimensions of the box itself. Both from Central Baptist Hospital, Louisville, Kentucky. Termite's name is Robert Onslow Leavitt. July 28, 1950. On mine, my name and birthday. Her name. And my father's name, in my hands, in black and white: Charles Fitzgibbon.

At first I think it's a mistake, some confusion. He was there with Nonie, and my father wasn't. Or they didn't know who my father was, and Charlie volunteered his name. But that's not how it works. If the father is unknown, that's what it says: *unknown.* No lies. The room wavers and then swims back. I think the motor sound of the boat is a low buzzing in my ears, that I'm hearing my own name in my head, over and over. Termite is saying it too, my name as a sound, in the same loud tone. Then Solly cuts the motor on the boat, and I can hear him yelling my name.

The air is white with cloud, and the sun is a flat, bright blade at the horizon, like a slit under a door. All else is drifty, misted. The warmth in the ground rises in a fog over the cold water, stirring in slow patches over a dark, swift weight. The boat, an aluminum rowboat with an outboard motor, bobs and moves. When I look straight down from the open window, the water is five or six feet from the sill, lapping the wall of the house with the slow wash of the wake Solly has made, angling so close. Solly lifts his relieved face to me and I see Stamble sitting opposite him in the boat, very still, no glasses, no hat, no suit coat or rain gear, just his white long-sleeved shirt, dark trousers, businessmen's shoes. He could be sitting behind a desk, hiding in plain sight, his shoulders drawn in, knees drawn up. He gazes up at the window into us, his white hair blown back from his face, looking toward us with those weak blue eyes as though he senses where to find us.

Solly has the boat within a foot of the house, and he tosses a rope up to me. "Lark? You OK? Didn't you hear me calling you? The flood crested at midnight. This is as bad as it gets, but the water is fast. They wouldn't give me a boat until daybreak. Tie up to something braced so we can keep the boat stable. We'll get him in, here at my feet, then I can lift you down."

I'm wrapping the rope under and around Termite's heavy upholstered chair, through the steel bearings of the heavy wheels, knotting it twice and three times. "Give me a minute. I need to get his rain slicker."

"Yours too," Solly says. "What are you wearing?"

"Something I found." I drop the long robe and it swirls, a red trail on the floor. I'll come back here for it, for the tin box I wedge into the cushions of Termite's chair, for everything I want to save. I have Termite in my arms, but I only find one rain slicker in the tumbled room, and I pull it on him backward.

I hold him facing the window and talk low, my face on his and my mouth at his ear. "See, Termite? Here's the boat. Like Noah's Ark. Two of them, two of us. I'll lift you down first. We need to leave now, Termite. We'll ride the flood and come back when the water goes down, after the storm."

The storm. He says it once, soft. He can hear the edge in my voice. But he stiffens, arches against me, turning his head, one wrist pulled in close and curled, the other clenched on the arm of the wheelchair he wouldn't touch. He wants to stay here at the open window, in the sounds and the wind, water beneath us, a layered nest built up around us.

"He doesn't want to leave," I tell Solly. "If it won't get worse, maybe we should stay."

Solly stands in the boat, his thick hair lank and damp. "You can't stay. The water will go down now, but there won't be power, lights, anything. I'm not leaving you."

We're leaning down, out of the window, but I can't move Termite. I look at Stamble and he stands in the boat, easily, naturally, and raises one white arm toward us. His smooth white face seems almost luminous. He can't reach us, doesn't need to, but he opens his hand, indicating the way as though we're walking through a door. Termite relaxes against me and I lift him through the window, down into the cloudy air. Solly's hands touch mine under the slicker, take him from me. I feel suddenly weightless, punchy with fatigue. I don't get a sweater, shoes, anything. I only climb backward out of the window, Solly's hands on my ankles, my legs, hips, until he has me around the waist and lifts me down to him. He puts me to one side in the boat so smoothly that I never have to stand, only balance on the hard metal seat, my back to Stamble, where I can see Termite. Solly has belted a life preserver around Termite and put another under him, in the floor of the boat, so that he can lean back, his head at an angle. He's close to the flood, so close.

We're moving. The motor of the boat rumbles and the flat, overcast sunrise can't seem to lighten. The murky water is brown, thick. Solly looks at me, then switches on the floodlight at the head of the boat, peering into the fog like he's threading us through it along some narrow watery tread. His dark tan makes his gold-green eyes look lighter. He seems all that's alive in the beige, washed-out air: his hard shoulders in the black slicker, his full pink mouth, the strong lines of his face. Stubble edges his lips and throat like an animal mask. I want to slip inside him, into his limbs and long muscles. The dank wind smells of soil, and there's the sound of water rushing, moving, pouring, and the feel of turbulent current under the boat. The flood is full of sounds we can't see.

Termite listens, head erect, his hands before him, fingers moving, hearing the air.

Solly hasn't slept. He's wearing the same clothes as yesterday, a pair of hip waders pulled on over his jeans and a Red Cross shell over his shirt, under the slicker. He reaches a hand toward me, grasps my knee. He can just reach me. I nod back toward Stamble. "Where did you find him?"

"Find who?" Solly answers.

He's looking at me, his hand warm on my cold skin, and a shadow looms up beside us in the clouded air. It's as though we slam a wall in the fog, but it's a massive branch or a dead tree the flood has set rolling in the water, flung at us like a battering ram. The hull of the boat shrieks as the tree rolls under us. We're all thrown up and forward but Solly's hand keeps me in the boat. I see Stamble arch past me like a white blur, reach Termite before I can, then pitch forward past him, into the water, and disappear.

I hear myself scream and I lunge forward, holding Termite, trying to reach for Stamble. The metal edge of the boat is cold and I can't see my own arm in the water.

"We're OK, Lark," Solly says, "we're OK."

"No, he fell. He's in the water. He's down there, I saw him fall."

Solly pulls Termite against him and feels for the oar in the bottom of the boat. "No, I've got him, Lark. Look, he's right here."

The motor has cut out and he steadies us with the oar against the dark edge of the tree, turning past us now on the other side of the boat.

"Look, Solly. There, where the water is pale."

"It's mud, Lark, stirred up by that dead tree dragging its limbs."

I'm kneeling then, holding to the bow of the boat. "He was sitting right there, when you came for us."

"Lark, for Christ's sake, stay still, before you turn us over." Solly balances the oar in one hand, pushes gently, gently against the flung skeletal limbs of the tree, launches us into the sweep of the water. The tree rolls slowly in response, caught in some drag, and catches, stationary as an island. The current carries us past. "Lark, there was just me in the boat. I didn't bring anyone else. Here, take my hand. Listen to me. Everything looks strange. You've been in the attic in the dark all night, with the water rising. You haven't slept. You're seeing things."

"Where's Nonie?"

"She's in the Armory shelter, with Elise. They took Gladdy home in the car, then they couldn't get to Elise's and they couldn't get over here. Charlie stayed at the restaurant. That part of town never floods, so they're using his place to feed Civil Defense and anyone who's helping out. We have a little way to go through the high water. Keep Termite close and put this blanket around you both."

I pull Termite against me and close my eyes. The boat turns gently, turns away. I feel Solly touch me as he stows the oar, takes his place. I feel him sit, pull the choke cord of the motor once, twice, before it sputters and revs. The throb of the motor takes hold and we're moving. I feel Stamble in the immense weight of the water, holding and moving the flood with his pale hands as though he wanted and willed it: smithereens.

"Lark, look at me. You all right? Did something happen, before I got to you?"

"It was yesterday," I tell Solly.

"What was yesterday?"

"Termite's birthday. I found our birth certificates last night in the boxes. Yesterday, on his birthday."

"That's good," Solly says, "to know on his birthday. What better day to know? Like a present."

He waits for me to say more, but I don't, and he doesn't ask. He turns and cuts the motor to a low rumble and steers us slowly, into the band of light cast through the fog. The boat rocks in sudden eddies, over submersions dragging in the current, and the water pushing back. I can see the rise of Main Street in front of us, where the water stops, as though across a wide, rolling lake, and then the fog closes up.

Nonie

Charlie insisted we go home. He sent us off with instructions to stay in our houses until the storm blew out. Elise lives at the top of a hill, and Gladdy's part of town seldom floods despite her own wet basement, but I was anxious. Gladdy demanded Charlie take her home himself and wouldn't get into Elise's car. We threatened to leave her at Civil Defense, which is what Charlie calls the restaurant when Flood Relief moves in. Finally we pile her in the backseat with two cloth bags of food, bags that won't break if they get wet. Gladdy sits between them, simmering with insult.

"I should think he could spare a moment," she says. "I've given my life to him, but there's no point saying so."

"I suppose you have, Gladdy," Elise answers, "and so have certain others. I'd say you and Noreen have that in common."

"I'm sure I don't know what you're talking about." Her mouth snaps shut, but she can't resist saying exactly what she's thinking. There's a bitter warble in her voice. "How dare you speak to me so! That I should be put in such a position! You're a clerk!"

"I am indeed," Elise says. "And you're the retired owner of a greasy spoon in a shrinking town no one even drives through." She pauses, angry as I've ever seen her, but she keeps her voice deliberate and steely. "I'm sure it does get lonely for you in that big house. Charlie's not there much, after all." She pulls to the curb in front of the house with a lurch, switches off the engine and windshield wipers abruptly. The car is instantly awash in deluge. "Still, Gladdy," she says in the enclosure of the downpour, "you've got the leftovers, and Noreen to help you carry them."

We sit enveloped in the pounding of the rain. Water pummels the metallic shell of the car and cascades in falls over the windows while Gladdy flails from one side of the backseat to the other, feeling for the door handles. "Gladdy," I tell her, "stay where you are." Then I try to quiet my voice. "You may need this food, and you'll need help getting up the steps in this rain."

The big door of Elise's car swings open with a crack and I'm instantly drenched. The slap of cold and wet is almost a relief. Sheltering myself is too much effort, but Charlie's big umbrella will very nearly keep his mother dry, along with her cloth bags of food. I grip the straps of the bags in one hand, the handle of the umbrella clutched to my side, and reach into the car for Gladdy, haul her to her feet in the arc of refuge available. She's fairly shaking with rage as I steer her toward the house. I remember how hard it was snowing the Christmas before Charlie's father died, the one time Charlie brought me to a family holiday dinner, or any family dinner, for that matter. Winfield was a different town then, twenty-five years ago. Main Street was strung with lights to within a block of Gladdy's house. Her parlor and dining room were ablaze with Christmas trees and greenery and candles, the long table set with crystal, but not for me. She put on her martyr's face, made it clear she was suffering my presence. Once I got up to help her in the kitchen, but Charlie's father stood with me, put a hand on my shoulder. I should sit back down, he said, with them. Charlie and I loved each other and that was what mattered. He seemed embarrassed for Gladdy, and he was dead by spring.

"How dare you!" Gladdy is muttering. "How dare any of you!"

"Gladdy," I say, "if you don't want to be spoken to, don't speak."

She's fumbling with the keys, but I have to put the bags down and help her, lay the umbrella to the side. Wind blows the rain in crazy sideways sheets. We nearly fall into the house and Gladdy sails on into the kitchen, leaving me to follow her with the heavy satchels. By now I'm simply weary. I don't know how Charlie stands her, stands this house. I resolve to take him in before it's too late, before his heart condition kills him and he's never lived with any other woman, none but Lola and me together, for less than a year, almost twenty years ago. Gladdy's harangued him all his life, disappointed, disapproving. She's standing at her open basement door when I get to the kitchen, peering down the steps. Then she turns and glares at me as though it's my fault her basement is filling. "The two of you!" she says, furious, nearly sputtering.

I think she means Charlie. "Yes," I say, in confirmation.

"Harpies!" she shrieks back, in apparent reference to Elise and myself.

I put the bags of food on the kitchen table. "Charlie asked us to bring you home, and we did," I say. "I'm leaving now." But she's advancing on me, shaking with anger, red in the face. I wonder if she's going to have a stroke, or disappear in a puff of smoke. No, that would be too easy.

"You know what your sister was, and you're not much else!" She's hitting me with the pointed fingers of one hand, every two words, then thudding her fists on my chest. "You! Divorced twice, godless. And they say she was a whore, a prostitute! That child might have been fathered by anyone. I'll never believe she's Charlie's child!"

I stop giving way and move toward her, force her back. Of course. She's talking about Lola and me. And Lark. Truly, especially Lark. To Gladdy, we're the world. "For God's sake, Gladdy, look at her. Don't you see him?"

"No! I don't see my son in any of you!" She's screaming now. "And that boy, that crippled, idiot boy! He should be in a home!"

"He's in a home, Gladdy, my home. And you're not good enough to stand in the same room with him, or breathe the same air!"

She's on me then, both fists, pounding at me like an angry child. "You should have gone away and stayed away! You've taken him, and the business. You want everything but you'll never get it, not legally. I've seen to it, do you hear me? The idea that he'd give everything, *anything*, to *you*—"

I try to push her away but she pulls me toward her, grabbing with both hands at my arm, my wrist. "Give it to me!" The sound of the rain pulses against the house like surf and she's got us just in front of her open basement door, the dim steps behind her. Water rising in her basement babbles like a brook, like the cascade of a busted pipe. She clasps my watch with her fingers, ripping at it, pulling with her entire weight, and the band snaps in her hands. There's a slow-motion instant in which her eyes widen, and mine do, and she falls backward hard, away from me, into the dark.

I can't see down the steps, and I can't move. The air itself seems to shift, come together seamlessly in the space she moved. I step to the sill of the basement door. The cord of the naked bulb over my head is still swinging, and I pull on the light, my fingers muffled in the damp cuff of my sweater. Gladdy lies facedown, askew across the steps, her neck at a sharp angle against the concrete basement wall, her head at the edge of a shine of water. She fell headfirst, twisting like a diver, as though to see where she was going. I can't see her face, only the back of her, in her clothes damp from the rain, and her sling-back shoes, with their little heels pointing up. She looks broken and small, used up as the scratched bottoms of her shoes. Exposed. Now the cord hangs still. I pull it, my hand mittened in my sweater, and she's in the dark.

I back up, into the table, fold my arms around myself, and breathe. One deep breath, two. I don't touch anything. The room floats in the sound of the rain and the flow of the water, a sacrament I never would have believed. How strange that Gladdy would instruct me about endings. All these years, I tried not to hear or see her. She's alone, so alone in this house, but the water will rise and ease her in. She won't lie there long. I realize I'm sobbing, choking on long, deep sobs that won't stop.

Gladdy's front door opens like a door to the rest of the world. Charlie's umbrella blows across the porch and back, skittering fast as the wind fills and turns it. I realize I can't move my wrist and step into the storm, feeling with my other hand for the wrought-iron stair rail Gladdy gripped hard every day, the way she gripped everything. Beyond six concrete steps and across the narrow sidewalk, Elise's car sits directly in front of me, vague headlights casting short glows in the pounding rain.

"What took you so long?" Elise has cracked the window to take the smoke of her cigarette, but the car is dense with tobacco scent and moisture, and the smell of the food Charlie packed. Elise takes a closer look at me. "You're crying. What's wrong? What did she say to you?"

"I hurt my wrist."

"How?" She leans across to me.

"Gladdy ripped my watch off. It broke."

"What broke? The watch? She took your watch? Well, Jesus. Let's go back in there and get it."

"Just go, Elise."

"Look at your wrist, it's all scratched. I'm not letting her get away with this. You stay here. I'll go back and get that watch."

"Elise, it doesn't matter now. I'm worried about the kids. We'll be lucky to get through before they close the roads. This is bad. The house will flood. Lark will have to get them into the attic. Go, please."

She starts the car, protesting. "That woman is unbelievable. Why are people like her alive?"

"I don't know," I say. "I don't know why anyone is alive. She's Lark's grandmother, and never enjoyed her, never cared." I see Lark, years ago, turning circles in the yard in her ballerina costume, holding Termite in her arms, and him looking back at her with his blur of a smile. "Such a loss."

"Loss for who?"

Gladdy, I want to say, but I can't speak. I don't see Gladdy, crumpled on her narrow basement steps. I see Lola, her long, slim body when I last saw her, on a hospital bed in a white silk nightgown, after Lark was born. She lay on her side on the white sheets, like an offering, the baby cradled in one arm. It wasn't an easy birth, and when she looked at me her freckles stood out in her white face. Everything was white: the room, the tightly made bed, the swaddled infant I never touched, Lola, her nightgown that was like a child's dress. She looked stunned and alight, unfocused by transformation, happiness, exhaustion. Someday you'll forgive me, she said.

Maybe I do. Surely that's why I'm still crying, quietly, the way Lola cried.

"What happened back there, Noreen?" Elise looks steadily into the rain, gripping the steering wheel. She doesn't wait for an answer and I realize she doesn't want one. "Thank God there's nobody out here but us. Do you hear me? Nobody."

"No," I say. And nobody was with Lola. Someone covered her later, picked her up, but it wasn't me. I wasn't with her when she died. I know she lay on a sidewalk by the police station, a few blocks from Onslow's club, so the reports wouldn't mention his business, and strangers made the phone calls. She'd gone to Louisville and the people she knew, got her baby that much closer to home, to me. She'd been there a week, just long enough to make sure they knew how to take care of him, and to leave the instructions she'd typed. A soldier who'd contacted her, a friend of her husband's, was to bring the baby to Winfield. She used the little derringer her husband had left with her. For her protection, he said, and that was how she used it: to protect herself from further harm.

"Can you move your wrist?" Elise asks me.

I circle my wrist with my other hand, at the bruised laceration where the watch ripped apart across my skin. The streets are a blur. Elise's big Ford keeps moving, but I can hear water under the wheels, arcs of spray flying up. We can't see buildings, trees, the sides of the road, only wavy shapes changing as we pass. Smears of color collide and separate beyond the sheeting distortion of the rain, clearing and filling, all the edges pouring off.

"It's just a sprain," I tell her.

We ease past the intersection, and suddenly we're driving through shallow water.

"I don't know, Noreen. Lumber Street will be flooded. I'll try to get across, but I don't think I can get you home."

Home. Later they brought me the gun, small, not as big as a man's hand, cleaned of any traces, and the folded flag from the military service months earlier, a service I didn't attend. I never saw that house in Florida. Only photographs. Pickets of a back-yard fence. A mailbox covered all over with glued seashells. That scrawny palm tree. Lola never lied, if anyone asked. She could only tell the truth. Even about Charlie. Everything was in plain sight, if anyone cared to look. I wanted to throw the gun in the river with her ashes, but I kept it with the flag the army sent. She had the flag in her arms that day, folded tight, encased in the same plastic someone wiped clean. "Soldier's Widow a Suicide" was how newspapers in Louisville reported it: a war story. She protected that flag. Later I put the gun inside it, tucked into the thick fabric. I hid them both in one of the boxes Gladdy sent from Florida, the only one I ever opened, to fasten them both inside. Gladdy went through the Coral Gables house, had any vestige of Lola removed by professionals. Articles of any worth, she said, came to me, and the rest went to Goodwill. I didn't care. I was Gladdy's willing partner in putting away Lola's life: no photographs, I told her, no personal effects. I wish I'd never seen the gun, never touched it. I wish it was in the river, a flicker of silver scudding along a stirred mud bottom, sidled in a current, miles and years from here.

Elise is still driving, but I feel the car eddy and shift in the rising water. It's as though we're in the river, or the river's come after us.

That soldier, a Sergeant Tompkins, came in uniform, with his Korean wife. They'd gone to see Lola in Coral Gables. They were nearly strangers to her, but she requested they bring Termite. They brought her note too, her instructions to all of us, and the urn of her ashes to scatter at the river. The note said she wanted to vanish, like he vanished. She couldn't take the baby with her, she said, he was beautiful and calm, he knew things, and he was all she had for Lark. He was Lark's baby, she said, as Lark was mine. Please, for Lark's sake, would I care for him until Lark could. At the time, I was so angry. I scattered the ashes in sight of the bridge, put my hand into them and threw them out across the water, while the soldier held the baby. His wife, so slight she seemed a child herself, held the tightly folded flag and chanted words in Korean. I was glad she did, because I had no words. Later, in my own kitchen sink, I burned Lola's instructions. For Lark's sake. Ridiculous and sad, I told myself. Lark was a nine-year-old child! Termite's age, I realize, the age he is now.

Lark's sake. Lark's sake. The words are beating in the rapid thump of Elise's wipers. And then the car stalls, and the wipers stop.

The sound of the storm comes up louder. Now it's the only sound. Through the rain, we see an orange Civil Defense pickup wavering toward us like an opening bloom.

"There," Elise says, "we're saved." She's rolling the windows down, leaning across me to open the passenger door.

"Elise, what are you doing?"

"You get out, Noreen, where they can see you. Then you reach in and help me. I'm going to need a hand."

The flood catches at the open door and pulls us deeper, and the car fills so fast that water pours into our laps.

Termite

He hears the rain open and shut, hushing and pouring and falling hard, waiting for the wind. Rain sheets the roof in long falls, silvers the windows and fills the tracks of the alley. He wants the rain louder but the windows are shut and water studs the glass in clear round drops. Each drop runs fast and slow, high thin sounds that tremble before they fall. Rain pours fast like the river would if the river could stand up. He wants to be outside in the hard pour of the rain but Lark only shuts the door and opens it, pulling the sound and pushing it. He hears the river surge, waiting with the rain, and the ragged orange cat stands on its stone crag, high up in the tunnel wall, scenting the river and watching. The dogs in the tunnel turn and snarl before they yelp and whine and burrow close. The orange cat knows to wait until they sleep, warm in their damp fur, each tongue a long red slather. The cat will climb the steep rock bank to the rail yard when water fills Polish Town field, when the woods stand still in the smattering fall of the rain. The rain will pound harder, whirling in the wind, but now there's a long smooth hush where the tallest trees are thickest. High up their layered boughs hold a flattened mesh of slick wet leaves and needles. They block the sky, bending with the weight of the water, and the deer stand sheltered, touching flanks. They lean into one another and listen.

The white stones of the alley float in the drowning grass. Termite hears them move and the grass is one clinched root. Lark doesn't know, she doesn't see. She opens the door and Solly stands

at the sink, moving all the air. His black coat shines and drips and
his long thin hands turn the faucet side to side. Solly holds the
jugs while the water pours and fills, trapped in a shape and changing sounds. Solly makes them change and sound. He says Nonie
won't get home if the water is high.

That wagon would fill up and float. I know he knows me.

Solly, all those people, all that noise.

Termite hears the water sounding low, rising in the dark slant
of the basement. Lark gives him toast and the warm square smells
of butter but then they turn and go. He hears them on the basement steps but he doesn't tell and tell. The water sliding up is the
green edge of the rain, clogged with earth, seeping through the
concrete floor in a line that moves, tasting slow and reaching.
The boxes Lark watches and touches are full of weight. Each thing
inside is wrapped and closed. Solly stands in the basement dark
and the one bulb hanging from the ceiling throws its yellow glow.
His hard black coat is on the floor and Lark steps back and away
and up the stairs. Termite hears her move each step until she sits
with him and tries to say. She smells of warm flowers like her hair
and dark like the water on the floor. The water will slide high.
Maybe he could stop it raining but he holds still and listens.

Lark makes the eggs with the yellow smell. Water on Solly's face
and the soap smell on his hands. The spoon comes and goes and
Termite hears the river in Solly's skin, moving long in Solly's arms,
wet in Solly's hair. Listen to these voices Termite, they sing the
way you talk. Solly holds the radio and finds sounds that glide and
sweep, slide bright and swerve, swing and stop and start. Termite
turns the knobs loud and louder to listen for the sounds behind.
Clicks and beeps are deep inside the wires, stops and ticks that
snap. He wants the hum of air between, the urgent pause and fall
inside the trills and crashing. *He hears snow falling on the alley
behind the restaurant, flying and covering like blurred white petals.*

Noreen, will you hold the chalice?

Father Salvatore, I never agreed to this.

Noreen, Charlie asked that I administer the sacrament—

I wouldn't let you baptize Lark. No sign of the cross will make Termite more pure than he is.

Noreen, Lark may decide to come to God, but the boy can't. God's church exists where His sacraments take place. The child is compromised. Grant him the protection of God's grace.

I don't know where God's grace was when Termite needed it, and his natural father was a Jew, if that makes any difference.

They're silent.

Charlie holds him.

Nonie, I consider him my boy, my son, the same as Lark is mine.

I won't take him from you, Charlie. Because I don't want him upset. But I won't hold the chalice or be any part of this.

There now, Charlie says. He doesn't mind.

A big hand behind Termite's head, a warm palm on his forehead tilting him back and the water running into his ears. The water in his ears fills and swells and he moves and says to hear. Lark doesn't know but Termite hears a wall of rain gather in the river and the wind, a billow of weight and cloud. He feels it slam the house and then the flood is inside, softly, the spread of a silver finger going darker as it moves and pulls. Lark is splashing toward him before they're up the stairs. He likes the attic piled high with shapes in the dark and she gives him the heavy flashlight to hold. He wants it dark but she turns the light to shine a narrow beam and says she'll come and go. She says he likes storms and this one is his and she's up and down the narrow attic ladder. The ladder folds from the ceiling of his room like an arm flung up or down and the air falls smashed around her as she moves. The boxes Solly stacked in the attic are breathing all the space. He feels the attic go darker with every sound. Lark says they can eat by the attic window and watch the water rise. She says Solly will come with a boat. You might like that Termite a ride in a boat through the water.

Lark doesn't hear. The rain is a black field, falling and pulling the wind. The ragged orange cat claws its way along the splintered tipple to a broken overhang and squeezes small. Polish Town field is deep and tossed, silent now, filled and covered. Termite hears the river roll inside the flood and tear the island loose. The island begins to slide, groaning and sucking before it turns and floats. Deer climb to the top of the mound and stand, moving on a clutch of silt and dump and roots. They kneel and roll in the softened ground, dig down to hold fast in the pouring. He feels Lark bend over him in the dark and the curve of her forehead is like the shine of a plate. Downstairs the flood holds still and the plastic mattress from his bed can move and turn, nudging the walls. The rats are soft dark lumps, scrabbling when they tilt and slide. They hold still and ride, moving their small faces. The farmer has a wife with a carving knife but Lark sings the song about the cheese and feeds him with her fingers. *It's summer and Lark says she's wearing the dress he likes, the one their mother wore that Nonie still keeps in the closet. Lark's a white blur pulling the wagon, walking the short grass between the stones with the wet of the grass on her feet. The wagon crunches across the gravel to the Tuccis' tall porch steps. Electric buzz inside the house is raging and smashing loud.* American Bandstand *won't hurt you Termite, but she calls Solly out to the porch. He yells in for Joey to turn it off, Lark's come to make them dinner. The television goes off, crackling to stop the hornet buzz that might leap up and up.*

Solly brings him inside and Nick Tucci is drinking a beer. He says he remembers that dress, she wore it with red shoes but it looks better on Lark, even barefoot. Hey Junior, he says, Lark's cooking dinner for the lugs while the old man makes do with a lunch pail on night shift. Ain't it the way. He pounds down the steps and the car door opens and slams. Solly sits still. Joey stays at the table shuffling cards, snapping and cutting the shapes. The cards stop moving when the car sounds fade. Lark is in the kitchen. Water running and refrigerator sounds. Joey and Solly at the table while Joey cuts the cards.

Joey, you see him looking at her?

Everyone looks at her, Solly. You'd have to be dead. She reminds him of someone.

Someone. Her mother, that walked off and left her kids.

And ours left us. So what. Dad's not saying why and we don't know.

I know Lark. We know each other. Nobody else raised us.

Click of the cards on the table. Joey shuffles them fast and pulls them apart in falling lines. Zeke bounces a basketball upstairs. It pound pound pounds against the wooden floor.

Dad would say goddamn it he raised you, Nonie and him. He'd say Lark is like a sister to you and don't you forget it.

Yeah? So she's like a daughter to him?

He wishes. Thinks he would have done better by her.

I'll do better.

You? Solly, you're almost fifteen. Old enough to be doing something else. You should be out with me in the car at night, screwing whatever moves, not sitting here playing house. She keeps you off her and you're welded to her. Anyone can see it. Hell, Termite sees it. You need to stay away from her.

Then they're silent. Joey puts the cards in Termite's hands and they scatter like small sharp pages.

I'll sit with him awhile, Joey says. Then I'm out of here. I got someone I'm meeting. She might like to meet you too, but fine. Go on out there.

Solly goes into the kitchen. The fan is on loud. Joey makes the cards appear like whispers at Termite's ear. He makes them stand and fall across his forearm, near Termite's face where he can see. They twirl their numbers before they fall. Then Joey says he's leaving and he's turning the TV on loud so they'll know he's going. He smooths back Termite's hair and puts his forehead close a moment, dark and rapid and blurred.

You're my boy, he says. Here's a kiss.

His mouth is on Termite's hair but there's no kiss. He turns away in two strides and the TV blasts its bright lines, blaring and talking loud, layers of shouts and words and hums between. Joey's car squeals as he backs out fast and gravel flies up in the alley. Termite begins to say until Lark picks him up and says they won't come back here anymore, she'll make him dinner at home. The cards fall on the grass and he's in his seat in the wagon. He can smell Joey's car like a cooling smoke. Lark is walking fast and she says it's no one's fault. Lark makes the candles blaze little fires. The attic is shut tight but Lark opens the window wide to let the sound come in. The rain is a cloud Termite, sit with me and see. She lifts him close and leans out to let him hear. The flood is rushing wide around the houses, churning and knotted in the tops of trees, slipping fast in white streams. He turns to hear it race and pour, one layer touching another, then Lark puts him in the bed. The bed is a nest and the candles glow in his sleep but the ragged orange cat sees the flood, working its pale shapes. The splintered wood of the tipple is fuzzy with damp, high over the town, and the flood in the dark is like a sky looking up and moving. *A dell sounds like a bell Termite but it's a valley deep with trees. The farmer takes a wife and the wife takes a child. The child takes a nurse but a nurse is for a sick child not like you. Derry-o is a dairy where the farmer milks the cows. The dog takes the cat that catches the rat so the cheese can stand alone. A song moves a story fast or slow like the river moves the water. Fast makes it funny and slow makes it sad. I'll sing it slow now listen.* He hears the boat far off, buzzing and droning like a fly caught in a glass. The yawning flood churns where no one sees, opening deep where the boat can't float or ride. The boat moves high by the house, pulling on the rope that grinds, wobbling on the water. The boat will find the river in the flood and the flood will open. The flood can turn and spin, a froth and fall like music. Stamble's cool pale light is in the air. Clouds drift on the brown murk, moving when the flood moves. The boat's blades turn in the muddy water, pushing in the pull of the flood. Termite feels the dark branch reach under them, pronged like a hand with fingers. The boat slams and screams and he wants to go but Stamble goes, flung like a white cloth, furled out and diving deep. Stamble spirals down and down in the heavy water, finding the dark and the shapes and the light in the curve.

The moving air is full of dense wet cloud. Termite hears it rain and rain the story of the train. The water and the train and the pounding are raining and pouring through. Even on a clear day, he can hear it. Now the sound is wide. He listens.

North Chungchong Province, South Korea

JULY 28, 1950

Corporal Robert Leavitt
24th Infantry Division

Mashuhyo, mashuhyo. The girl is talking in the dark. She's come back; it must be nearly dawn. Drink, she whispers. The word in her language is sibilant and hushed, like the sluice of water in the stream none of them can reach. She lies near him, pressing the dripping fabric of her shirt to his mouth. It tastes salty and black. He thinks the words or says them. No, she tells him in Korean, the water is pink. There are so many bodies in the water. She squeezes the wet cloth against his lips, his teeth, touching his tongue with the bloody water. He thinks he moves, pushing her away, but he only opens his hand. She drops her forehead onto his palm and a pulse in her temple beats like a minnow holding still.

The day before he left Louisville, he gave Lola his mother's little derringer, the pearl-handled pistol she kept out of sight beside the cash register. She'd never had to use it but she kept it loaded. The musicians and junkies took drugs that made them crazy, and the drunks and merchant seamen got mean late at night if they hadn't found women. She was always alone, closing up. The old man was always out. Bobby was out by then too, an underage teenager haunting clubs that let him sit in with bands, pick up what he could. Ma, he asked her, do you even know how to use that gun? Does it work? Sure it works, she said, it's just you have to aim for the head, or a knee if you're stopping someone running. You ever fired it? Bobby asked. How hard can it be, she said. I told the man I wanted a lady's pistol, small, no kickback, something I could put in a purse. And why would you do that, Ma, put it in a purse. I might want to take a trip, she said. He didn't worry about her at night. The grocery didn't sell liquor or even beer. It was the safest place in Philly at 10:00 p.m. Waitresses and women and cops, bus drivers going off shift. He talked her into taking the derringer upstairs with her after closing up. To keep it safe, he said, suppose someone broke in, despite the iron grates she slid across the doors and windows. They'd open the register and see the gun, more use than cash and day-old bread. Really, he wanted her to have it in case the old man showed up loaded and Bobby wasn't home yet. It was what he feared. Long ago he'd taken sides, become her partner, but when she did die, alone on the floor in quiet he could only imagine, he ceded all territory. There was no territory without her. He'd hated the store for the shabby continual way it imprisoned both of them, he'd wanted out, but he hadn't protected her, he wasn't there. Blood clot in her brain, they said, wouldn't have mattered. It mattered to him. He wouldn't let anyone move her things. When he left a few weeks later, all he took from her room was the derringer.

He'd thought he was a man at sixteen; he felt free, unencumbered, capable. He'd been with girls for years and found women, always, easily, but he stayed clear of commitments and was somehow loyal to his mother's aloneness, to her life and death, without ever thinking of her, until Lola. *Mother may I.* Lola knew, almost by instinct, who he was. Something in her was that alone. They began to tell each other why, with their bodies and words. Lying in bed, smoking cigarettes, talking for hours. The postwar army was a good job, a start, and there were no emergencies. They had their whole lives to plan.

He joked that his mother's gun was a wedding present. He wasn't worried about Lola, with her girls and Onslow close by, not worried for her *safety*, he said. Not worried, the phrase itself, was a shadow, a dark tug inside him. Every woman should have a firearm, he told Lola, for her own protection. It was your mother's, Lola said. That's why I'll keep it for you. She touched the pearl handle to her face and held the derringer on the flat of her palm, like jewelry, an object. It was just the length of her hand. Leavitt sees her hand, and the old woman's hand, holding his service revolver. The two images are startlingly clear: one picture superimposed on the other. The soft flat of a woman's hand, the guns, the angle and attitude of support the same, but the bigger gun dwarfed the old woman's small palm, and the barrel shone in the dark. Your weapon is your life. Basic had drilled the phrase into him. He heard the girl pleading. Let him stay with them. And the old woman listened to her, took her own life instead. All their lives, if she'd given the troops an excuse to say the refugees were armed. Or maybe it didn't matter, had no bearing. Command had sealed the tunnels, treated the refugees as combatants from the beginning.

He can't see the girl, the boy, but he feels them against him, as though constant physical contact is their only safety, all that's real in the dark.

He's with them and he'll stay with them.

He'll never get out. None of them will. What he sees is wobbly, unreal. What's real is inside him, not outside. He sees, he can still see, along a tunnel, stone and cracked concrete. It's Lola's picture of an arch into a tunnel, the walls curved, turning like faces he should have recognized, the arch, the stones and the wide river beside, not this place, this stream running bloody and small, feeding him, wetting his face. He hears the girl whispering against his hand, every syllable distinct, a rush and cadence of words. He's not speaking, can't speak, and she thinks he can't hear her, but he recognizes the words of a Buddhist chant having to do with journeys, purification.

There's movement outside, a groaning of wheels and heavy equipment. He hears her reach for the boy. She lies down behind Leavitt and pulls him against her, with the child between them.

Sound stops, as though by some agreement or mutual sense. Leavitt hears the click of the searchlights come on. Impossible, but he hears it. They're powerful circular searchlights on wheels, each the size of an airplane engine; the North Koreans use them in battle and now the Americans use them too. The lights are in position at either end of the tunnel and their white beams cross midway. The American units have lit the tunnel and they're going to fire until no one's moving.

He feels the girl behind him, holding the child. Leavitt feels her mouth on the back of his neck, silently forming syllables. It's now, he can feel it. His baby is born, deep inside him where the pain throbs. It's all wrong and it's true, his legs are dead and his guts are torn apart but his spine opens up like a star. He can feel Lola split apart, the baby fighting her, tearing his way. The girl's arm tightens across Leavitt. She holds the boy motionless and pulls Leavitt tighter against them, against the tunnel wall. He draws back, into her hard thin limitless chest, inside her embrace.

The bodies are lit and white in the arched space. Those still alive draw closer to one another; mothers lie down to shield their children. Light pours through them and over them like an avalanche. He can't see but he can hear acutely, in slow deliberate measure, the sound of the machine guns turning on their pivots. He hears, surrounding them on all sides, a deepening pressure, an approaching density, like the roar of a vast train so wide and heavy it can fall forever, a barrage of fire to scream over and through them so hard and long it will pull the war into nothingness with it.

When the pounding begins the white light on his face goes blue. Look inside, he tells his son, inside is where you really are. He wants to lift his baby away from this beautiful deadly world. The planes always come, he wants to say, like planets on rotation, a timed bloodletting with different excuses. Part of a long music. Don't look, only listen. His son is born. Leavitt feels him turn in the salt and the blood, squalling and screaming in the close hot wet. Stop screaming, Leavitt tells him. Never scream. They'll find you. Stay still. Listen. You can't come with me now. Breathe, breathe. Take your turn.

July 31

Winfield, West Virginia

Lark

I put Termite in the wheelchair Stamble gave us and take him with me downtown, past Barker Secretarial. Murphy's flooded but those old ceilings are high. Barker's is open, same as always, or will be, for third term in two weeks. I think about Nonie this morning, her arm in that sling, walking toward the sheriff and me along the mud path Nick Tucci dug out to the alley. Mud piled up on either side like sloggy drifts and the boarded-up kitchen windows of the house behind her. "I'm sorry about this, Noreen," the sheriff said next to me, "but there's going to be an inquest. We're going to have to hold you until we can straighten this thing out."

Gladdy Fitzgibbon had swelled up some when they pulled her out of her flooded basement, and Nonie's wristwatch was in her tight-shut hand. Otherwise, with the gash on Gladdy's head and her twisted ankle, they might have assumed she fell down those stairs when she was alone. There was no one to say she didn't— Charlie stayed at the restaurant two full days, and it was full of Civil Defense workers and volunteers. Everyone knew that Nonie and Elise took Gladdy home in the car, it was raining so hard, and Nonie would have walked her inside. Gladdy was nervous about ice and weather. She would have demanded help walking up the porch steps that were slick with water, and Nonie would have carried the bags of food Gladdy brought from Charlie's, more than usual because she knew she'd be housebound a few days.

But no one knew how long Elise waited in the car. Like a lot of people, they didn't get home the night of the flood. They couldn't drive to the river side of town because the water was too high, then it came up around the car so sudden. The car was half submerged, and the rescue squad wouldn't push it onto dry ground. They said they had enough to do. Unless Elise and Nonie wanted to climb up on the roof of that car and hope for the best, they had better get into the truck and get themselves driven to the Armory, where evacuees were spending the night.

All night Nonie was gone, her wrist sprained and scratched from where the band of the watch pulled apart. Someone holding on awful hard, like Gladdy always did.

I keep on going with Termite, left on Spring Street to Miss Barker's house. We turn up the walk to her front door. Like everybody else's, her porch is full. Rugs laid open, drying. Ruined things on the grass. Miss Barker would have saved a lot, moving whatever she could upstairs. She's very practical, Miss Barker is, never distracted. I have to put the brake on the wheelchair and leave Termite at the foot of her porch steps while I go up, ring the bell without thinking. Then I knock hard.

She opens the door looking mismatched like we all do. That red-and-black hunter's jacket must have been her father's. "Lark," she says, eyes wide like she's seen a ghost.

"Sorry to bother you, Miss Barker. But I came for my evaluation? We're going to be leaving town, Termite and me. Going to stay with my mother, down south."

She steps back on that one. "Your mother?"

"Yes. She heard about it all, and we can't stay here. The house is pretty much ruined, except for the attic. Anyway, I'll be getting a job, in an office, I hope, and the evaluation would say what I've studied so far, my speeds and all."

"Well, what about him?" She lowers her voice, looks down at Termite, sitting below us in his chair. "How can you get a job when you have to look after him?"

"My mother will help. He's her son, after all. She's looking forward to some time with him. Or I may get a job where I can bring him along. He can be quiet, if he feels safe. In small towns, you know, people might be understanding. Especially if I have good evaluations, and a letter of recommendation that, like you say, inspires confidence."

She's nodding, though I'm sure she finds the idea of taking Termite to a job site completely unprofessional, and absolutely out of the question. "Of course," she says. "I have your evaluation, and a letter of reference as well. I'd already typed them all out, and I brought all the files here before they locked the building. You were best of class. Executive ability. Remember, bigger firms, insurance, lawyers. Room for advancement. Of course the evaluation will help, and the letter will serve as a character reference." She's the same Miss Barker, with her hair uncrimped, in a man's odd camphor-smelling clothes. The cedar chest would be upstairs. Anything in there would have stayed dry.

"I'm sorry I couldn't finish the course, Miss Barker." I turn then and look back at Termite. "Just a minute," I call down to him. "Be right there, Termite." He surprises me then, starting up for all he's worth, good and loud. *Right there, right there, right there.* Pounding his wrist on the right armrest, like the bell from the old chair at home is there when it's not. Moving his head side to side.

"Let me get them for you," Miss Barker says. "I'd ask you in, but of course, there's nowhere to sit. You go stand with him, so he won't be upset. I'll bring them out to you."

She disappears into the house and I'm waiting behind Termite's chair when she comes back with a manila envelope. "There are multiple copies of the reference *and* the evaluation, and if you need more, you just let me know. You realize it's perfectly proper to apply for several positions at once." She takes my hand, shaking it like she showed us in mock interviews. Except both her small dry palms enclose mine. "How wonderful you've heard from her. That you've got somewhere to go until all this is . . . resolved."

"That's right." I know she'll tell people, discreetly, over the next few days, as they begin to ask. "Good-bye, Miss Barker."

"Now, if anyone wants a phone reference, have them call me. I'm here."

"Thanks, Miss Barker. Thanks for everything."

"Of course, dear. Of course."

She stands politely while I turn the chair around on the narrow walk, then I hear her go back inside, quick fast steps, as we move down the walk and out the gate. She always kept the gate shut, but it's gone now. The curlicues of the iron fence are clogged with brown tufts, grass and weeds that got caught.

"We're going to see Elise now, at the Coffee-Stop," I tell Termite. "The power is on along Main Street. She's probably getting ready to open." I can use her phone, I think. Then we're coming up on the phone booth at the corner of Spring and Main, and I realize it's better to call from here. Privacy. I slide the glass door open on its hinges. The glass is beige about two feet up, but when I put a dime in the slot, the dial tone comes right on. I pull Termite's chair around so he can see me. "It's working, Termite. I'm going to make a call, and you watch me, OK?"

He tilts his head to look past me.

"I'll be right out," I tell him.

I know he hears me, but he's quiet since the flood. The moving around, everything missing and changing. Things I can't help. Maybe he thinks I can't manage, and doesn't know I will. I line up some dimes on the little metal shelf in the booth, and shut the door. If someone walks by, I don't want them hearing me. I dial the number, and Social Services answers, sounding just the same, like there was never a flood or a Civil Defense motorboat in the fog.

"Winfield County Social Services?" She says it like a question.

I know this receptionist's voice. She's been there for years. "Hello? I'd like to speak with someone about Mr. Stamble, please."

"Is he a client, Miss?"

"No, he worked at Social Services. He was my social worker."

"And your name?"

I tell her my name, and Noreen's, and Termite's. I'm sure she knows who we are, but she doesn't let on. Confidentiality. I hear phones ringing on her end. Pandemonium, and I'm glad.

"Stamble, did you say? I'm almost certain there's no one by that name working here, but I'll check the personnel files."

I can hear her opening file drawers, flipping pages. "He doesn't work there now," I tell her, "but he did. A young man, thin, blond. Stamble, Robert Stamble." I need his previous address, I want to say, next of kin, some way to find out more.

"No, nothing here. I think you're confused. I can tell you there's not been anyone here by that name, not in the eight years I've been here."

"He'd only been there a few weeks. He was new."

"Oh, then definitely not. Our last caseworker hire was two years ago. We certainly could use more help, but we don't have it."

"Could I speak to your supervisor, please?" Phones ringing, and ringing.

"Miss? Let me look up your file and refer you to your assigned caseworker. Whatever the problem, she can help you. I'm sure you understand greatest need takes precedence now, but we're doing everything we can to assist Flood Relief."

"No, don't bother," I tell her. "I must have been mistaken." I don't want a referral, or anyone to take notice. I hang up fast, before she can ask if I want to leave a message. They're supposed to log calls, but she's so overwhelmed, maybe she'll forget.

Stamble never worked at Social Services. That's why there were no forms about the chair. Social Services can't flip a light switch, Nonie says, without duplicate and triplicate forms. The chair just appeared, like he did. Solid, when he wasn't. He was real in his way, but not from now, or here. And he was right, a smaller chair is easier, especially when you've got somewhere to go. We've got to take it with us, before someone asks where we got it. If they asked, what would I tell them?

Termite's listening. I look at him through the glass and turn my fingers in the round dial of the pay phone. It clicks and makes a

chiming sound, like a call to nowhere. Maybe that's where Stamble came from, and where he's gone. I don't know if they'll find
him, washed into the mounds of mud and debris and broken
buildings they've pushed aside with bulldozers. Or if he's somewhere else. *I come and go,* he said. Maybe Solly was right, and
Stamble wasn't in the boat. Maybe he didn't need to be there for
us to see him. And he didn't need to work at Social Services to
bring us a wheelchair we didn't ask for. I can feel he's gone. He
gave us what we needed, like he knew who we were, and where we
needed to go. The rest is up to me.

I look down the street and see the lights on at the Coffee-Stop,
dimly, in the bright morning. Elise will be talking to lawyers and
police on Nonie's behalf. It's better if I don't tell her anything, but
there are things she needs to tell me.

Nonie said it was amazing how fast Flood Relief got to us, that it
was what came of knowing people in high places. Charlie's command center, she called the restaurant. We stayed with Elise two
nights, but then we were back home. The yard was packed mud,
but the house had been scrubbed and nearly emptied, down to its
stained walls. Flood Relief said it was "relatively sound" but not
worth renovation. They frowned about the cleaning, a misuse of
resources: they were putting our house on the buyout list. Elise
wanted us to move in with her. She had an extra room and a pullout couch, and it would take weeks for the government to resolve
the paperwork or cut a check. We didn't have lights but the
plumbing was working, and there was plenty of bottled water.
Solly brought Termite's wagon down from the attic, and his big
upholstered chair for him to sit in. Flood Relief left us blankets
and cots and I set them up in the living room. Here was our
couch, I told Nonie. So to speak, she said. The waterlogged piano
was left, too big to move, but the top made for a shelf, and the

bench was a table. "You'd set up housekeeping in a ditch," Nonie said. "Don't be getting comfortable here."

I didn't have to tell her what I knew. She guessed at all of it, the minute I walked her up to the attic and she saw the opened boxes, the red kimono robe still on the floor. She touched Robert Leavitt's uniform jacket where I'd put it on the bed with my mother's metal box. "You saved so much, Lark," she said, and I knew she meant it. I had questions, but she looked so tired, her wrist bandaged, her arm in the sling. She wanted me to pack everything, she said, all the clothes, the bedding. Fasten up these open boxes, and any papers and documents should go into the safe at the restaurant. Someone would be moving us out. We were sitting on the bed and I saw a police car pull up on the packed mud where the alley used to be.

"That's the sheriff's car," I said. "Is Flood Relief buying the house now, already?"

Nonie leaned over me to look out the window. "No," she said, "the sheriff is here about Gladdy. They found her yesterday, before Charlie even got home, and they want to talk to me." She looks at me in the narrow space between us. "Lark, Gladdy fell down her basement steps during the flood, and she died. The police did house-to-house searches before the all clear, when evacuees were allowed to go home, and they found her in her flooded basement."

"Oh." I thought of Charlie. His mother dying alone, like mine did. Like I think she must have. "Nonie, why do they want to talk to you?"

"Because I was the last to see Gladdy, when Elise and I took her home in the storm. And because she took my watch, broke the band, actually, and she was holding it, like Gladdy would. Her body had been in the water of her basement almost two days, but the watch was still in her hand. There may be some sort of hearing." She could see I didn't understand, or couldn't believe it, and she sat beside me on the piled-full bed. "Elise knows how I hurt my wrist, but they're investigating how Gladdy fell, whether I pushed her." Nonie touched my hair, smoothed it back from my face. "Maybe Gladdy deserved pushing, but not to a death like that, and I would never have hurt her. You know now that she was your grandmother, and you have every ounce of her drive and determination, without her more irritating qualities."

We heard, through the open window, the slam of the car door, and saw the sheriff standing in the alley, wearing rubber boots that came to his knees.

"Lark," Nonie said, "you and I never had this conversation. You don't know anything but whatever the sheriff chooses to tell you. If they want to hold me, I'll stay voluntarily, because I don't want them arresting me, and the women's facility at the court-house is perfectly comfortable. Don't worry, and stay away. Don't remind people you're alone, taking care of Termite. This may take time to sort out, and if it does, the county may try to enforce pro-tective custody of both of you."

I was already thinking, trying to plan.

"You're not of age," Nonie said. "I'll look into assigning guardianship to Elise, but they may want to put Termite into care, until—"

"Will Social Services accept Elise? She isn't a family member." And she's small and skinny and getting old, I wanted to say, and works ten-hour days at the Coffee-Stop. She chain-smokes, and that's not good for Termite. "I'll think of something," I told Nonie. "I'm going out to the alley now. I don't want him coming in the house, thinking it's too bad for us to stay here."

"There's over two hundred dollars in that salt box where I keep loose cash," Nonie said. "You use it, and Charlie will get you whatever else you need."

I checked on Termite in his chair in the living room and went out, and asked the sheriff, cheerful, if he was here about the buy-out. No, he said, was my Aunt Noreen at home. He didn't say anything else until Noreen was there, and then she got in the front seat with him as though they were going to a meeting. They drove off down the alley in the cruiser. There were chains on the

tires, like for a snowstorm, but they were silent, clogged with
mud. The surface was dry enough to crack under the wheels, but
underneath the mud smelled wet and dark. I looked down the
alley after them, and that dirty orange cat that trails Termite
everywhere came right out and sat itself in front of me, like a
warning, not ten feet away. Someone would come in a car soon,
and take Termite. I looked back toward the Tuccis' house, and
Solly was walking toward me.

The Coffee-Stop has a CLOSED sign on the door, but I see Elise
inside, wiping down the narrow counter. Elise's store is the shape
of a diner. She likes to say she has an eight-person seating capacity,
every seat a window seat, but the Coffee-Stop is really just a grocery that sells hot dogs and cigarettes and coffee. I knock on the
glass and she opens the big door to let us in, leans down to make
a fuss over Termite.

"Well, look at this new chair you're riding in." She tousles his
hair. "The power's back on. You want to hear some music?" Elise
has a jukebox unit on the wall. Her favorite songs, regardless of
fashion. Now she joggles the coin drawer and takes out some
quarters, turns Termite's chair so he's in front of the little window
where the 45s slide and click. "Chet Baker," she says. "He has a
new one. Termite can listen while we talk." She knows he likes it
loud, but the song's melodic, and I can hear her under the
phrases. "You want some coffee, Lark?" She's got her ashtray and
cup at the end of the counter, and she beckons me over. "That
Chet Baker," she says, "pretty as a woman, and sounds like one."

I sit just beside her. "Elise, do you know who my father is?"

"I do know, honey, but even if Nonie had never told me, I
could hazard a guess."

"Why? Why can you guess?"

"Charlie helped Noreen raise you in that restaurant and dotes
on you completely. Even Gladdy accepted it. Charlie wouldn't

have it otherwise." She looks at me, lights her cigarette, and nods. "It's not unusual, an aunt raising her sister's children."

"Why would Charlie have a child with my mother? And why would Nonie come back here, after he did?" I'm asking, but I know, I remember. *Inside you. Be careful when you're young. Now you get it.*

"Lola"—Elise is saying and her voice trails off—"well, she had a hard time. She was too much for anyplace. And she wasn't lucky, not from the very beginning. You're not like her, honey. You're just about as pretty, but you're steady, like Charlie. There's no one steadier than Charlie, or as loyal. He stood by Gladdy all those years, a woman only a saint could love, even if he is her son. And he's stood by Noreen as well, in his way. I know you blame him for not marrying her, but truth be told, it was Noreen who wouldn't marry Charlie, after she came back to Winfield. He'd betrayed her, and his being sorry didn't change it. He talked her into coming back to him, and she helped him save that restaurant. She hasn't married him since because she's happy as she is."

"It was me," I say, "I'm the reason no one would ever say my mother's name."

Elise holds up her thin hand. "It wasn't you, Lark. From the time you got here, you were the joy in Noreen's life, and Charlie's. Noreen couldn't have children. More every day, they were grateful. Lola gave them the child they could never have had. And she told Noreen she'd intended just that—you were no accident." Elise leans forward and takes both my hands, her birdlike face intent. "I'm telling you this for your mother's sake, Lark. My mother used to say, with babies, there are no accidents. And she was right. We can plan the bad, but who can plan the good?"

She looks at me like I might answer. "I don't know, Elise."

Elise smiles, wry and quiet. "You can understand Noreen didn't appreciate Lola's intentions at the time. She stayed with her, though, until you were born, there in Louisville. Then she left the second husband, the nightclub owner, and came home." Elise leans back and lights a cigarette, looks out the window of the

Coffee-Stop. "Small towns talk. Noreen kept Lola secret for you, to protect you from the rest of the story, your mother's story. It was painful for Noreen, and it still is. She wanted you to grow up before you had to know about it. And you have." The smoke from her cigarette lifts, trails its way to the open window.

"What happened to her, Elise?"

She doesn't answer for a moment. "Sadness," she says then. "The war happened. That boy she married was killed in Korea. People forget that a soldier's death goes on for years—for a generation, really. They leave people behind. If he'd come back, they would have managed with the baby."

"Did he die before Termite was born?"

"No one knows, but Termite was born by the time they notified Lola. Afterward she moved to Coral Gables."

"Coral Gables?"

"Oh yes. That was Lola's house, where she'd planned to live with her husband. And wanted Nonie to let you come and stay with them when he got back, which Noreen was not about to do."

"But he died," I said.

"It was a confused mess over there in Korea, first weeks of the war," Elise says. "They never told Lola how or why he died, or sent a casket back." She looks over at Termite and leans a little forward, lowers her voice under the music. "And the baby, at first she only knew he wasn't normal, he didn't cry. She kept going for over a year, thinking what to do and then deciding. I can imagine her wondering about taking him with her, as much care as he needed. Deciding, for some reason, not to."

"She knew better," I say.

Elise doesn't say yes or no, just looks at me.

"And Gladdy kept the house," I say.

"It was never Gladdy's. She went down to Coral Gables to sell it for Charlie, and took such a liking to it that she told him to keep it. Her retirement home, she called it. Charlie was never there once."

"My mother," I say to Elise. "How did she do it?"

"Lark, Nonie wouldn't want me telling you."

"Nonie isn't telling me. But someone has to, Elise."

"I'll tell you," she says, "only because it would be so hard for Charlie." She stubs out the cigarette, moves her hand to dispel the smoke, but it hangs in the air. "She'd arranged everything. She locked up that little house and hired a car to drive her to Louisville, to Billy Onslow's club. He was Noreen's second husband, older, well, much older. He was like an uncle to Lola. Owned a nightclub. Lola had moved back there, where she'd lived all during the forties, where she met that soldier in the first place. She still knew most of the girls who lived there."

"Why did they live there?"

"He owned the building." She barely pauses. "Lola sang in his club for years. Oh, she had a voice. Sweet and husky, like, say, Rosemary Clooney. She never was famous like that, of course. For her it was a job, a job she liked. They thought she'd come back to sing again, where she had help with the baby. She'd been there about a week and had put him to bed. The girl she paid to watch him was on her way but hadn't arrived. It was evening, plenty of people around, before the club opened. She walked downstairs, told everyone she'd be right back, she was going outside to have a cigarette and would they check on the baby in just a minute. Smiled. Waved. Walked a few streets away and shot herself with that little derringer the soldier had left with her."

The gun in the flag. Someone packed them into the boxes.

"Lola was gone," Elise says. "What could Nonie do but take the baby? She sent you away."

"Church camp," I said.

"Yes. Now *that* was uncharacteristic. You know what she thinks of religion. It was all she could find on short notice. A veteran brought the baby, someone who'd served with the boy in Korea. He was in uniform, I remember, walked with a bad limp. That was why they let him come home, because this was in '51, the war was still on. I guess he was badly injured and spent months in a VA hospital. Then he looked for Lola, brought her a letter. The boy had asked him to give it to her personally, that kind of thing. Anyway, it was several weeks later Lola died."

"Sergeant Ervin Tompkins," I said.

"Was that his name? Came with his wife. Korean girl, war bride. Brought a nurse with them to care for the baby. Billy Onslow hired the nurse and provided the car, a big Packard."

"Is Billy Onslow still in Louisville?"

"No. Died years ago, heart attack. But he did what Lola asked. Had that baby brought here, where her family was." Elise looks over at me. "That was you."

I don't know when the music stopped, but it's quiet now. Elise looks around, like she's just noticing as well. Termite is still, holding his head to the side, turned toward the jukebox and the window that looks out on Main Street.

"Well," Elise says, tearful. "We'll get through this, and you and Termite will stay with me until we can." She sniffs and stands up, takes a breath. "Don't you worry about Noreen. The coroner's report will clear her, and so will I. They had words about that watch in the car. Gladdy grabbed it off Noreen's wrist, broke the band right in front of me. Noreen helped her anyway, carried those heavy bags of food up the steps." Elise looks past me and nods, definitive. "I wouldn't have, but Noreen did. She wasn't gone a minute. Didn't step foot in that house."

"Nonie told me about Gladdy," I say, "this morning, before the sheriff came."

"Well, of course, she would have." Elise fixes me with her near-sighted gaze. "I don't know if she told you she saved my life. Reached into that car in the flood and pulled me out. I have a fear of water, and I wasn't myself. I sprained her wrist, fighting her. I'll tell them as much, on a stack of Bibles."

The jukebox sounds a series of clicks in the quiet, finishing up.

"I've got to open the store soon, honey," Elise says. "Just wait here while I go across the street for a minute, will you? Soon as I get back, you'll go talk to your father." She's out the door.

I go over and stand with Termite. "My father," I tell him,

"Charlie is my father, and yours died in the war. He never wanted to leave you." I lean down close. "We're going to Florida, Termite, to the ocean." I feed the jukebox a few more quarters from the open drawer, push REPEAT. The street in front of us is empty and mostly shut down, but Elise's music glides along like the sound of a movie we're not watching. A horn, a tinkling piano. Couples could fill the sidewalks, dancing slow like they're moving in another world.

This morning, in the alley, I told Solly I was leaving with Termite. Quickly, tonight. Gladdy's house in Coral Gables would be empty. We'd go there, and hope they didn't find us. With the flood and the cleanup, they might look for us or they might not. If we were gone, and our own family said we were accounted for, they might just figure we weren't their problem. Charlie would give me the keys, and directions. The story I told Miss Barker would get told.

"Lark, if you're leaving, I'm coming with you." Solly was walking me back into the house, pulling me inside. The houses on the alley were empty. They were all on the buyout list, but Solly was already being careful. "The water ruined Joey's car," he said. "All I've got is the bike. I used the lift down at the garage and got it onto the second floor of the shop before the flood, but it's half apart."

"It's no good to go in a car," I said. "Cars are easy to find. We'll go on the train, in one of the boxcars, right out of the yard. No way to trace us. The Chessies go direct to Miami, and I know exactly when they run. They're shuttling cars through, moving them out. In a few days, the yard will be empty. It has to be tonight."

We were standing with Termite then, in Nonie's nearly empty living room. "I was on my way to Florida, more or less," he said. "I already told Nick I'm going to school, and gave notice at the garage." Solly knelt down to talk to Termite. "Termite, you mind if I come with you? We'll grow a garden, maybe build a patio. I'll take you to the beach. We'll look at the ocean. What do you say?"

Termite only breathed, short sighs. "He wants his ribbon," I said. "Termite, there's no time."

Solly touched Termite's hair. He left his hand there, on Termite's head and white neck. "He's never had a mother or father, and he never will. He has us." Solly pulled me close to them, put his mouth almost on mine, made his voice quiet, every word distinct. "We'll take him and we'll leave here. We'll get married as soon as you're of age. You have the birth certificates. You can prove you're his sister. Even if they find us, no one will take him."

"Solly, I'm not eighteen for seven months."

"That's not long. We'll go to Florida, lay low in Coral Gables. A good mechanic can always get a job. I'll wait on school."

"You might not have to. Lauderdale isn't far. But if you come with me, Solly, you have to do it my way. No record of where we are or how we got there. And tell no one you're with us, not Nick, not Zeke—no one. You're going to school early, that's all. Be at the rail yard by eight twenty, just after dark. If you can't get there, or you change your mind, promise me, tell no one. The cars move at eight twenty-seven. We'll have to find an empty Chessie."

He looked at me. "I'll be at the rail yard. You're not riding a boxcar to Florida alone, with him. I'll be there."

Now I see Elise coming out of the restaurant and I wonder if everything I'm planning is a dream, like this music. If I'm in a panic I can't feel, and I'm not thinking straight. Then Elise looks up and sees me through the window, and she waves at me. A little wave, like, It's all right now, come along. Just like that, I know we're going.

I won't ask you why," I tell Charlie.

"The 'why' was you," he says. "I knew the minute I saw you. All the regret began to end. For Noreen as well. And then, you are who you are. It might not have turned out that way, but it did."

"I'm sorry about Gladdy."

"There were things in her life she couldn't see, things she wasted. I tried to take care of her, without doing the same."

Once I would have told him he was wrong, but now I'm glad they kept their secrets, glad there's no gravestone or public knowledge of what happened to my mother, what she did or where she is. Not here, anyway, or where we're going. I put my hand on Charlie's.

"Things caught up with me," he says. He looks white in the face. The restaurant is empty except for us. He's so alone here without Nonie. He takes my fingers into his big palm and holds them. "I don't want you to worry about Noreen. Elise told you. She saw what happened, and Noreen will be cleared."

"You can all stop telling me not to worry. I'm not a child. We don't know what's going to happen, or how long it will take."

Termite is sitting in his wheelchair, pulled up to our table, like the three of us are a meeting Nonie and the sheriff have missed. Charlie looks at him, and nods.

It's all laid out like a hand of cards someone's holding and hasn't played yet. I smooth Termite's hair back from his face. "With all that's happened, Social Services will put Termite in one of the 'care situations' they've mentioned before. I need to leave now, while they're occupied with the mud and the mess. We can go to Florida, to Gladdy's house. No one will know us there. No one will be looking for us. I'll tell people we're going to stay with my mother. That she's contacted me. But I won't say where, and you won't either."

Charlie gets up and goes to the safe. It's under the counter, behind a shallow false shelf he calls his security system. I hear him dial the combination, open the heavy door of the deep box. "The house in Coral Gables is yours, Lark. I put it in your name years ago, after your mother died." He sits down with us and gives me an envelope. "This is a copy of the deed. It's down on paper, held for you with Noreen as trustee until you're eighteen, in case I kicked off while you were growing up. It was always yours, not

Gladdy's, not mine. I mortgaged the restaurant to buy it for your mother, but it's paid off now, free and clear. She'd made the down payment just before Termite was born, but his father wasn't coming back from Korea, and Noreen and I wanted to help her."

"We're leaving tonight," I tell him, "Termite and me."

"How?"

"We have transportation to Miami," I tell him, "and then we'll take a cab."

He looks doubtful, starts to speak.

"I won't tell you more," I say. "You'll have to trust me. We'll talk about it another time."

"I don't want you going alone," Charlie tells me.

"I'm not going alone."

He wants to ask, but he doesn't. "This is the address." He's writing it down.

"Beach Road," I say. "I know the address."

"There's a phone," he says, "and a used car Gladdy bought. The bills are paid through the restaurant, but she has a checking account in a bank there. After I get things settled, I'll put it in your name. But take this." He gives me some folded bills and the keys, on a key chain that's a plastic daisy. "Gladdy's keys, to the car and the house."

A car, I think. Solly can teach me to drive. On a sand road by the beach.

"You call us as soon as you arrive," Charlie says.

"I will," I tell him, "but not from the house."

We both stand, and he embraces me in his big arms. He has, lots of times, but it feels different now. I turn Termite's chair to go, and then I remember. "Charlie," I tell him, "I'll want you to send me my mother's things. And mine, and Termite's, whatever's in the attic at Nonie's. It's going to be Lola's house again, and ours."

.   .   .

I hear someone at the kitchen door. Solly, I think. But I look through the glass and it's Nick. I almost don't let him in, but I open the door. "You out of work early, Nick?"

"Night shift tonight," he says. "On my way. I've come from seeing Noreen."

"She told me to stay away. Charlie says—"

"Charlie," Nick says. "If it weren't for Charlie, Noreen wouldn't be in the county facility. I'd like to strangle him. Playing the big cheese. He should have taken his own mother home in the storm."

I could say Charlie is sorry now, sorry he didn't. But I don't. "Elise says Nonie will be cleared."

"Maybe," Nick says. "And how long that takes depends on how aggressive they want to be."

At least Nick will tell me the truth. I'm moving back just enough to let him into the kitchen. I don't want him coming into the living room and seeing that I'm packed to leave.

"I've talked to a lawyer," he says.

"I'm glad, Nick, but I hope she won't need one." I move as though to walk outside with him, but he takes my arm, touches my shoulder. He turns me, lightly, almost like we're dancing, so that I'm standing against the wall in the empty kitchen, and he's very near me.

"I should get back to Termite," I say.

"This isn't for him to hear," Nick says softly. His hand is warm and cushioned and I remember how strong his arms are. How I used to fall asleep on his chest. "Listen to me, Lark. It's only a matter of time until they take him, and not much time. Fighting it could take weeks, and you have no home, nowhere to live. Staying with Termite at Elise's won't satisfy them, and you can't live with Charlie, it doesn't look right. He's too involved."

I want to tell him everything, that I'm leaving and taking Termite, but I can't speak with his hands on me.

"If you were married," he says, "to someone with a home to offer you, someone older, with a good job, and a family to support and help you, the county wouldn't pursue it. They'd let you be. You're like a sister to my boys, you grew up with them. I've always loved you, Lark—"

I draw in my breath, turn, and he turns with me.

"Yes, like that," he says, "for years now, for too long."

I can't breathe, or move, with his mouth so close to my eyes. I feel the heat of him near me, how practiced his body is, how powerful.

"I wouldn't have said anything, maybe ever, but everything's changed now. In this state, you can marry at sixteen with parental consent."

"You asked Noreen if—"

"I'm not asking Noreen," he says. "I'm asking you." He touches his hands to my face, moves them, touching me, until he's laced his fingers lightly behind my head, but he doesn't pull me toward him. He's waiting for me to move, or even let him know I want to. Anything, a breath, a look. "I don't want you to pick the wrong person, or series of people. You can't. There's too much at stake. And I—" He stops speaking, tense, trembling. His dark eyes are wet, like he's holding something heavy, straining not to move.

I feel that syrupy pain coming up in me like tears I want to jam down. I want to put my fingers into the dark thick hair of Nick's chest and pull hard, hear the sound he'd make, see his eyes.

"You feel this," he says, almost like he's surprised. Then he steps away from me.

I don't let myself move after him. He stands across the little room from me, by the kitchen window, looking at me, and looking. This is how people get caught. Past his shoulder, I see that it's dusk.

"You shouldn't stay here tonight," he says.

"Termite wants to."

He shakes his head. "Keep the doors locked. This part of town is deserted. I'll check on you as I come home. I don't know where Solly is, but I can send Zeke over to stay with you."

"It's OK, Nick. We're fine." I open the kitchen door, and he walks past me, into the yard. All the dark, wet warmth spills out with him.

He turns to me, halfway to his car, his eyes lit and full. "You're my girl. I'm going to take care of you, both of you." I watch him drive away. The wrapper, that thud. He would have left his car at the plant, to save it from the water. Nick is gone. He did that just right, I think, so that it could go either way. I feel warm with relief, almost faint, as though I could lie on the floor and sleep, but it's getting late. There's not much time.

I hear Termite in the quiet, letting me know. *We're fine. We're fine. We're fine.*

You have to ride in this," I say to him. "Again. You have to."

I fasten the strap snug across him and pull down the metal footrests for his feet. He didn't want to move from his soft chair, and he doesn't want to leave it. I'll ask Charlie to send it to us somehow, bring it to us in a truck. The day has cooled off some. I pull on an old sweater of Nonie's because Termite will miss her and like the smell of it, then I tie the wagon onto Stamble's wheelchair by a length of rope. I pile in the duffel bag of clothes, the sleeping bags, jugs of water Solly filled, a laundry bag of food. If I stand just behind Termite's chair, pushing and walking, the line of the rope pulls taut beside my hip and the wagon stays in line pretty well. It's not downhill to the rail yard, it's nearly uphill, a long gradual slant. Good thing you're a strong girl, Nonie would say. Just at dark we get going. It's hard through the alley, but the street moving out of the dank flood zone gets easier. The broken pavement that leads to the rail yard is a hard surface, and we don't make much of a sound. His chair is near silent on those wheels and we've got Stamble to thank, in his nowhere, wherever he came from, wherever he went. The chair looks almost new, and I've got Termite's blanket in the pack slung over the back, his pillow, the moon pitcher, the deed Charlie gave me, the money, and the keys. In the duffel, folded in with our clothes, I brought the flag and the gun, and my mother's metal box.

All the rest is gone, gone from us, the alley and the house, and the town and the stores and the flood. Flood Relief will buy the house and tear it down. Nonie should come south, see what's left where it's never winter. Charlie can open a diner where the ocean is a flood that stays in place. The river will follow us to it, branching and turning, visible awhile, dipping away beside the tracks, retreating into woods, crossing along and under us while the train roars over it. We have to get to the rail yard in time. Find a Chessie car. To make it happen I think of the cat's face on the steel sides of the boxcars, that silhouette shape as big as we are, and I say to myself, I can manage, I can manage, in case no one is there, no one but us.

I must have said it out loud, because Termite says it too. Low, careful tones. *Manage, manage.* "Shhh," I tell him, then he's quiet, and I am. It won't do, talking to myself, it won't do in job interviews or offices, in a town where there are flowers all winter.

Closer to the yard, I can see the stray dogs loping between ruined houses, over the mud that's dried on the drowned grass. A door lies twisted off its hinges, flat as a raft across a sodden shoe. All the Polish kids are gone, the houses empty. Flood Relief is maybe a chance to do better. But Nonie said most of them will move into subsidized housing on the other side of town, no more floods, no high water, just brick apartment buildings with concrete courtyards. She says Nick will keep his house, clean the mud off the porch and kitchen linoleum, renovate with Relief funding. Zeke and Solly carried nearly everything, even the rugs, upstairs. Finally, Nick told her, a reason for sons, and if Joey had been there he'd have held back the water itself.

The water's nearly gone now, but the mark and smell of it are everywhere. The rail yard is higher than the alley houses or the river, and the steel of the tracks glows ahead of us in faint lines. No one sees us but the dogs, and they gather a house lot away, six or seven of them, furtive for now, separate from one another, like they're seeing us off. They've got to be hungry. Nothing here anymore, no trash cans to turn over, no scraps. By the time we get to the yard, they've come together behind us. They're pretty far back and they've slowed, catching some instinct drift, sizing us up. I move a little faster, but not too fast. I could back them off with a few well-aimed stones if I turned around and yelled, but I can't yell. It seems there's no one but there's always someone, and no one can hear or see or find a sign of us. I'll have to find an open car, lift everything up quickly.

The yard looks almost normal except that the ditch along the edge is full of floodwater and wider, like a little canal. The chute from the tipple's been gone for years. The double ramp up to it, the platforms they loaded from, are still there, running alongside the tracks like a roller-coaster structure no one ever finished. Tracks for the coal carts still gleam along the slant on top. They ran up a few carts at a time, emptied them into the tipple so they could load the long flatbed cars that ran north to Cleveland, east to Pittsburgh, south to Memphis, and everywhere. The lower platform's for freight, with a broad dock behind. They moved boxcars opposite to unload. Once a wide steel ramp slid across right into the cars. There was noise and motion. Men walked back and forth, heaving, hauling, but there's no freight now, and the boxcars sided here are empty. Some go by with their big doors flung open. The engines that push and pull them don't even have engineers. They run on switches, shunted and slammed from empty yard to yard until they're run down south and loaded. Winfield is just a siding, not even that, now the tracks from the northeast are torn up. No reason to fix them. The trains will stop altogether. These cars will move on schedule to be switched off down south, all the way south. We've got fifteen minutes.

There are three Chessie cars and I stop at the one with open doors. It looks clean, where I can see. Moonlight slants in at the back, like it's falling through a window. There must be slats on one side, ventilation for moving livestock. In the days we'll have to be careful, but there'll be air and a way to see out. "This one's ours, Termite."

He looks up, head back, like he's thinking it over. I start to lift him out and realize he's listening hard. The dogs. He's heard them, creeping up, and I grab a handful of gravel, throw it hard behind us in a steady arc. They back off. The floor of the boxcar is about as high off the ground as my chest. I throw in the capped water jugs and hear them roll along the floor, then I lift in the duffel bag, the laundry sack with the food. I push them in as far as I can reach, then lift Termite in beside. He tilts over onto them like a rajah on his pillows, hands up, fingers still. Speechless. Soft bars of moonlight fall across his face and his pale hair. His eyes move. He's in a darkened, shattered marble with its colors held tight, waiting inside a roar he must know is coming. He can't see me, but he hears me throw in the backpack, the sleeping bags. Boxcar camping, I'll tell him, three days and nights, maybe four.

Solly's nowhere. I don't see him, don't hear him. I'll manage. I've got to get the wagon and the wheelchair in. I can't leave anything to say we were here, where we're going, how we got there. The floor of the car is smooth, not slatted; I put in a couple of big stones, to stop the wagon wheels, keep it from rolling once I get it in. The wheelchair isn't as heavy as the wagon. I fold it, push it up sideways, and I've got it just inside when I feel the dog come up. I've got the rock in my hand when it pounces, slams into me snarling, hard and lean, turning with me against the side of the car. Nonie's thick sweater rips in its teeth as we swing round and I slam the rock into its head, slam its head so hard against the steel car I think the world thuds. But it's the train, slamming into motion. Somewhere far down the line, a shudder starts and builds. The dog drops away from me, silent in the noise, wobbling like a broken toy. I can hear its brains click, stunned or smashed, and I want it to creep away, crawl if it has to, away from here. In case it doesn't, I throw the bloody rock into the dark of the car. There's an almost human, overwhelmed groan as the train lurches sharply backward. The wagon is heaviest so I lift it at an angle, front wheels in the car, lean hard, and push. The boxcar shudders and helps take it in, pulls it up, moving. There's an instant when I realize the click I heard was time ruined, thrown off just long enough. Running, I think about my mother's little gun folded into the bottom of the duffel, about Termite, how I would have shot us both if I'd thought we could be separated. Lunging for the edge of the boxcar, I feel the hard metal edge in my hands and vault up, swing my legs up and over, scramble to fall forward rather than back.

I don't know at first. Then I feel the roll of motion under me, and how lightning fast things can go right or wrong. In just a mile or two we'll pick up speed, ride along the road before we cross the highway. Cars stop there at the crossing, the train moving just beside them. When we were kids, we used to watch each car pass to get that weird tickly feeling of moving backward. The car has got to look empty to anyone seeing it pass. After the crossing, we'll roll out of town, across the rail bridge and the river. I thought about throwing the gun into the water, but I'll take it to the ocean, let the waves float it far away. I move the wagon back into the corner, slam the rocks under the rear wheels. Later I'll find the other rock, the one I'll keep, flecked with a stain I decide is sacred. I'll wedge it under the right front wheel in the beam of the flashlight, but for now I hope the wagon will stay put. I pull Termite to the other side of the car, into the corner with the duffel and rolled-up sleeping bags soft and secure against him. He can see out from here, but he's far from the doors and no one can see him. "You can talk now," I tell him, "we're on the train. No one can hear us." But he's silent. He's scared, or maybe not. He has to hear my ragged breath. He knows what almost happened. Or he doesn't. Please, he doesn't.

I may not be able to shut the doors by myself. They're going to be heavy, rusted even, except these cars have come in here from somewhere else—nothing smells wet or damp. I'm standing to the side of the open doors. Now that we're inside, the train has

slowed, like in a dream. Like we're holding still and everything is
moving past us in blue and gray. We're still in the rail yard.

Then I see Solly. He's on the Harley, keeping pace with us. He
nods at me, like *hey*, from across a street.

He's too late. I see him across a million miles.

He rides along beside us and I don't know what he's doing,
looking over at us and back, back and forth, calculating, then he
roars on ahead, up alongside the adjacent track to the freight dock
as the train starts up the slant to the tipple, slow and steady.
Through the wide-open doors of the car I see him pull up hard at
the edge of the platform and stop, the bright light of the headlight
a stark white beam. He revs and revs the cycle, waiting. We come
up on him and he guns it, sails over space into us. The machine
hits the floor of the car and there's a bellow and whine as he pulls
the keys and jumps, falling against me. We both go down as a
boom of impact shakes the car like a cannon shot. The cycle
bounces off the back of the car and falls over smoking, confused,
spinning and roaring on its side. Then Solly's up and off me,
straddling the cycle as smoke blurs around him inside the quick-
ening rumble of the train. He looks at us over the Harley with its
big wheels still turning, and he smiles.

Nonie

There we all sat in a room at the courthouse. Elise nodded her
head at the men around the table and the stenographer taking
down the interview. We'd known them all for thirty years. Some
of them worked with Civil Defense, still were, cleaning up the
flood. Now they wore suits and looked tired. We all did, except
Elise. She wore her white pillbox hat and pearl earrings, and her

black raincoat that she didn't bother taking off, as though she hadn't time.

Gladdy was a hardworking woman, Elise told them, but demanding. They'd all remember. Was the stenographer getting this down? The stenographer was, and Elise went on. Gladdy demanded the watch as soon as I stopped the car, Elise said, and grabbed it so hard she broke the band. Noreen helped her anyway, carried those heavy bags up the steps. I wouldn't have, Elise said, but Noreen did. She set them just inside before Gladdy slammed the door in her face. Sent her back into the storm, hard as it was blowing. Elise said she thanked her stars Gladdy was satisfied to have the watch. If I'd driven off alone, Elise said, I wouldn't be here. Then she was silent, and sat up erect in her chair, as though she wasn't only speaking to them. God as my witness, she said, it was me that hurt Noreen. I sprained her wrist when she pulled me out of that car against the flow of the flood. I've a lifelong fear of water, Elise said, and I lost my head. I scratched and fought Noreen something awful. I was in a panic, the water came in so fast. Well, the men driving the truck saw how quick the car swamped, how Noreen got me out, and I clung to her even after, until we all saw she was injured. Hold Noreen if you like, Elise told them, though she saved my life and didn't hurt anyone. She went on to say, as though they didn't know, that Charlie Fitzgibbon was Gladdy's son who cared for her every whim. If he was satisfied Gladdy's fall was an accident, why wouldn't they let him get on with mourning his mother? She looked at them outraged and her tears were real.

I had no tears and that was fortunate. I'd already agreed it was all as Elise described. I told them I didn't mind staying at the county facility until the coroner's report was final. The women's quarters were more comfortable than my house, with nowhere to sleep but the attic. I suppose I was making a point. I knew Elise and Charlie would look after things, and Lark was perfectly capable. Charlie leaned forward and took my hand. He knew I didn't push his mother, but no one could prove I did or didn't, and

Elise's story had to be the only one. She'd put herself at risk. I wouldn't have let her, except that I was certain Gladdy wasn't breathing when I pulled that string over her dark basement stairs and the light fell over her. I've let Lola go too, finally, into whatever she's claimed for herself, and now Lark knows the truth. She'll find out what else she needs to know and Charlie will finally be her father.

I told Charlie to bury Gladdy with that broken watch. We didn't need it anymore. If Gladdy had needed help, I would have found it, but she didn't need us, or anything. The flood took its time and floated her free while her kitchen stayed pristine above her, dishes in the drainer and the table set. The fact that Gladdy lived in that big house, blocks and blocks from the flood plain, while Elise and I were driving into it, was simple geography. She fell because she insisted so hard on what she wanted.

The wash of the old stories is gone. We're all going somewhere else now, somewhere different from where we've been.

Termite

He hears the ragged orange cat crouch small on the beam of the tipple. The cat stays and waits and sees, watching the train pull away in shadow, leaving the mud smell of the town. The staggering dog lies down to slide into the ditch. Termite feels the water move, a ripple in the rumble of the train, in the shaking of the boxcar that throbs in every board. The boxcar clacks its iron wheels, ticking every seam, spinning steel and waiting for the roar. Solly moves the roar and the sound races, hovers, races. The train slows and climbs and Solly rides the roar, pulsing, cutting through. The roar shines a light and leaps into them before it smashes, sparking and crashing and cutting up the dark. The light comes on white and Termite sees inside it when the pounding starts, pounding and pounding while the bodies are slashed and spilled. The bodies fall still and stay and a blue air slips up from between them, from this one and that one, air that is thin and veiled and curls, smooth silvery ribbons turning to find a way out. The man who stands alone and hears the shape lies still, but a shape stands up in his shape. He opens his hands in the pale ribbon of himself and Termite can see his fingers moving, opening. He turns toward Termite and his face comes clear in the moving blue. His face blurs and clears and blurs again like a face underwater. He picks up a shape that clings to him and another shape moves beside him, crawling and then standing, a slight feminine shape that turns and moves next to him. The man looks back before he turns to walk away with them in the ribboned air of the tunnel. He looks at Termite. The ribbons all around them are veiled as smoke and move like the river moves, rippling and curling, pulled in the air. No eyes, no ears, the ribbons only move and flow. Thin silvery ribbons, moving in the tunnel. So many of them, more and more, moving toward the opening, to where the light gets big and bright. He sees his father clear against the light and his father turns and walks. His father has a boy like him and a girl like Lark, and he takes them with him, out of the tunnel. He sees his father walking between the ribbons and the ribbons make everything blue.

Louisville, Kentucky

JULY 31, 1951

Lola Leavitt

She sits by the open window, looking out. It's the same third-floor room she shared with Bobby, first night to last. Nearly empty now. She'd taken the furniture when she moved to Coral Gables with the baby. There's only the chair she sits in, their valise, a double mattress on the floor, like those last weeks when Bobby moved her mattress off the bed frame so the only sounds were theirs. Lola hears the club downstairs, prep and start-up for Onslow's Sunday night crowd. Sunday nights were slow except at Onslow's and a few other bars. Soldiers from the base poured in. Onslow would introduce her, especially those months she was obviously pregnant, as a religious experience. The church service they'd missed earlier that morning. She hears him at the piano now, through the open windows. Lola's the cat, he told soldiers, she can purr, she can scratch. You boys behave and she'll arch her back when she sings to you. Onslow is playing her songs, her repertoire, as though it makes a difference.

Now that she's here, she's calm, settled. It's the right thing. The baby's breathing is good, clear. He's strong in his way. He doesn't move much but still she's got him propped with rolled blankets, every side, so he's safe and doesn't stir. She's nursed him just now in this chair, whispering songs, and now he'll sleep the night. He sleeps more than most babies, and he's quiet, doesn't cry. In those ways, he's easy. He can hold his head up now, and his arms. He moves his fingers. He moves them fast when he's agitated, and his

skin flushes. He goes rigid if he's scared. He's silent then, but anyone caring for him knows what's wrong, begins to know. She's left
a list. He takes formula and she's brought plenty, but her milk
calms him most. It's the only thing she regrets taking from him.

She's been here a week, long enough that the girls have learned
how to care for him. In case Noreen won't take him, or not right
away. But she will. The letter, the instructions, are in the big
valise. It will all seem backward to Noreen. She'll be angry. Don't
I have enough to do, she'll rage at Charlie, but not when Lark can
hear. They'll care about him, protect him, even if they don't
understand. She can't take him, though she's decided to stop. She
thinks Bobby would forgive her. She went on as long as she could,
until she knew what to do.

She reaches for a cigarette to steady her hands. Lights up and
leans toward the open window so the air will take the smoke.

She's careful what he breathes, careful about noise. He loves
music, or he'll focus on a sound so small she barely hears it. Drip
of a faucet, night cries of those penny-sized frogs in the grass in
Coral Gables, the hush of the surf across the little road. Confusion
scares him. Doctor's visits. Strangers. So it was just her, the days
filled with taking care of him. Onslow sent them money. Charlie
wrote every month. Then the soldier came with his Korean wife
and gave her the picture Bobby prized and carried with him. The
cigarette pack, the little photo slipped inside the cellophane, still
seemed curved to the contour of Bobby's chest or the shape of his
hand. The Korean girl only nodded, smiled. Not much English,
Tompkins said. Her parents were dead, so he'd married her, and
the government let her leave. She'd worked on gaining weight
here, to look older. Still, now that he had the limp and the cane,
people thought she was his nursemaid or his daughter. Watching
them, she realized she'd been waiting, but Bobby would never be
here, on a cane, in a wheelchair, missing whatever parts of him the
war took. She had the house in the quiet town. They could have
lived simply, on disability like half the retirees in Coral Gables.
Instead she had the widow's pension, and a survivor's benefit, for

the baby. She'd make sure Nonie got it. The thought came to her then, sitting in Coral Gables with the Korean girl and Tompkins. She'd wait a month, more, so Tompkins wouldn't feel responsible. She'd make plans. She could plan now. She could look at the picture and see all that might have happened if the war hadn't. And read Bobby's letter, the one Tompkins brought her.

She smokes, closing her eyes, upright and tense in the chair. She senses the trail of the smoke, doesn't watch it. She knows it curls and weaves, blue in the late-afternoon light, moving away from her.

She left the house as it was, only paid the man who mowed the grass to pack up the carriage and high chair, send them to Winfield slow freight. They'd arrive in a week or so, about as long as it would take Onslow to contact Tompkins and his wife, fly them up to drive the car, arrange for a nurse. And take the baby to Noreen. With the valise, his clothes, blankets he was used to, her perfume bottle with the moon face he liked to hold. The girls smiled when they saw it: it was part of that novelty perfume set they'd bought for her trousseau.

She pulls her upright chair soundlessly closer to the window. She knows these rooftops, this skyline, and she leans out to look. They'd lie in bed with these windows open, the smoke of their cigarettes curling over them. Breath of their bodies, moving in the air, drawn to the open.

She smokes her cigarette. It's dark enough that fire glows in the ash. She looks now, and follows the smoke with her eyes. Air pulls the thin blue trail out the window, into the evening.

Lola's the cat.

They brought the yellow telegram to her hospital bed, days after the birth. She knew before she read it. Bobby was missing, presumed dead. She was too weak to hold the baby but she wouldn't let them bind her breasts. She made them help her feed him, prop him on pillows. She coaxed him to nurse until he did. He began to move his hands. Never his legs. His head was too big for his small, thin body. The baby has problems, they told her.

You have problems, she said. She needed rest, they said, she'd lost a lot of blood. They kept trying to take him from her but she wouldn't let them. He was going to live, she told them. No one should presume, she said. Rest, they said. No one is trying to take your baby. Is there someone we can call? No one who can hear you, she told them.

Now she knows how to sense him. Tompkins brought her the letter, but she waited until they left to read the words. *If you're reading this, it means I'm not coming back.* Just like that, it was true. It was his voice and she believed him, when before all she'd had was the folded flag. She read the words and read them until she could feel him near her. It's as though he's released now into his son's breath and smell, into the baby's eyes and hands. The baby moves his fingers every moment he's awake, slowly, carefully. The birth certificate she brought from Florida says his name, but she's never called him by a name. She sings to him while she feeds, bathes, rocks, carries him. He answers in sounds, singsong tones.

At night, on this mattress on the floor, like their bed before Bobby left, she falls asleep holding the baby. She says Bobby's name into his skin, against the cloudy pale hair, the broad forehead. Delicate blue veins are visible at his temples, just beneath the flesh. In the first weeks, she was sure he would stop breathing. Now he's a year old, almost exactly. She can see some blended distortion of them, a resemblance transformed and shattered into what he is. He's not like her or Bobby. He's what happened to Bobby. He's where Bobby went, where Bobby is. How can she reach Bobby. Maybe not touch him, but find him. Know where he is. She thinks it's all still happening, existing where she can't see. It doesn't end until she ends it.

Lola's the cat. She takes a last drag on the cigarette and stands, watches the smoke unfurl. The little derringer Bobby gave her is in her purse, with the folded flag, the telegram tucked into the front. We regret to inform you. She'll walk to the police station down the street. They'll take care of everything. She knows the baby is safe and she'll think about Bobby. She'll be on her way.

Acknowledgments

The author wishes to thank Yaddo and the MacDowell Colony for the gifts of time and space in which this book was written. Thanks to the Howard Foundation for crucial support. Thanks also to Ann Close, my generous editor at Knopf, to Lynn Nesbit, my agent and friend of many years, and to Tom Jenks, Jo Ann Beard, Mark Stockman, Ivy Goodman, Pamela Rikkers, and Jill McCorkle, who read early drafts. Thanks to artist Mary Sherman, whose long-ago gift of a drawing of Termite became his image. Thanks to traveler and author Robert Nilsen (*Moon Handbooks: South Korea*), who sent geographic details and present-day photographs of the tunnel at No Gun Ri; to Suki Kim and to Suji Kwock Kim, who advised on Korean words and phrases; to Colonel Jeffrey J. Douglass, U.S. Marine Corps Historical Division, who corresponded regarding KMAG and Task Force Smith; to the late David Halberstam, who offered advice and counsel on the Korean conflict; and to Sang-Hun Choe, Charles J. Hanley, and Martha Mendoza of the Associated Press, who broke the story of No Gun Ri.

Portions of this book appeared in slightly different form in the following publications: "Termite's Birthday, 1959" in *Granta;* "Termite, 1959" in *Southern Review;* "Nonie's Words" in nerve.com; "The Bad Thing" in *Ploughshares;* "Termite Makes the Shape" in *Murdaland;* "Language Immersion Seoul" in *Narrative Magazine;* "Solly and Lark" in *Granta 100;* "Leavitt's Dream" in *Conjunctions;* "Nonie Talks About Lola" in *Appalachian Heritage.* "Termite's Birthday, 1959" was included, with permission of *Granta* and Alfred A. Knopf, in *Love You to Pieces: Creative Writers on Raising a Child with Special Needs,* ed. Suzanne Kamata, Beacon Press, 2008.

A Note About the Author

Jayne Anne Phillips is the author of three previous novels, *MotherKind* (2000), *Shelter* (1994), and *Machine Dreams* (1984), and two widely anthologized collections of stories, *Fast Lanes* (1987) and *Black Tickets* (1979). Her works have been translated and published in French, German, Italian, Spanish, Swedish, Norwegian, Finnish, Hebrew, Greek, Danish, and Dutch. She is the recipient of a Guggenheim Fellowship, two National Endowment for the Arts Fellowships, a Bunting Fellowship from the Bunting Institute of Radcliffe College, a Howard Foundation Fellowship, a National Book Critics Circle Award nomination, and an Orange Prize nomination. She was awarded the Sue Kaufman Prize (1980) and an Academy Award in Literature (1997) by the American Academy of Arts and Letters. Her work has appeared most recently in *Harper's, Granta, The Southern Review,* and the *Norton Anthology of Contemporary Fiction.* She has taught at Harvard University, Williams College, Boston University, and Brandeis University. She is currently Professor of English and Director of the MFA program at Rutgers-Newark, the State University of New Jersey. Information, essays, and text source photographs can be viewed at www.jayneannephillips.com.

A Note on the Type

This book was set in Adobe Garamond. Designed for the Adobe Corporation by Robert Slimbach, the fonts are based on types first cut by Claude Garamond (c. 1480–1561). Garamond was a pupil of Geoffroy Tory and is believed to have followed the Venetian models, although he introduced a number of important differences, and it is to him that we owe the letter we now know as "old style." He gave to his letters a certain elegance and feeling of movement that won their creator an immediate reputation and the patronage of Francis I of France.

Composed by North Market Street Graphics,
Allentown, Pennsylvania
Designed by Anthea Lingeman